Master Thorn and the Mothers of Midnight

A Minimus Mu Adventure

Pattison Telford

eBook ISBN: 978-1-7781240-9-9
Paperback ISBN: 978-1-7781240-8-2
Hardcover ISBN: 978-1-7383288-1-9
Audiobook ISBN: 978-1-7383288-0-2

For Sarah, who may read this book too, if her schedule allows.

Acknowledgements

Thank you to my early readers: Jesse Snyder, Carissa Fawaz

Cover illustration by Audrey Jacques
Cover design by Darin Morrison-Beer

You can find out more at www.pattisontelford.com

Books by Pattison Telford

Redferne Family Series (Contemporary Fantasy)
Sky Lanterns Over Nether Ides
Shadow Over Loch Ghuil
Whispers Under Middle Ides

Minimus Mu and Friends: Adventures in the Nineteen Queendoms
Master Thorn and the Red Bean Princess
Master Thorn and the Mothers of Midnight
Sala Doon and the Demon Carrot (Forthcoming)

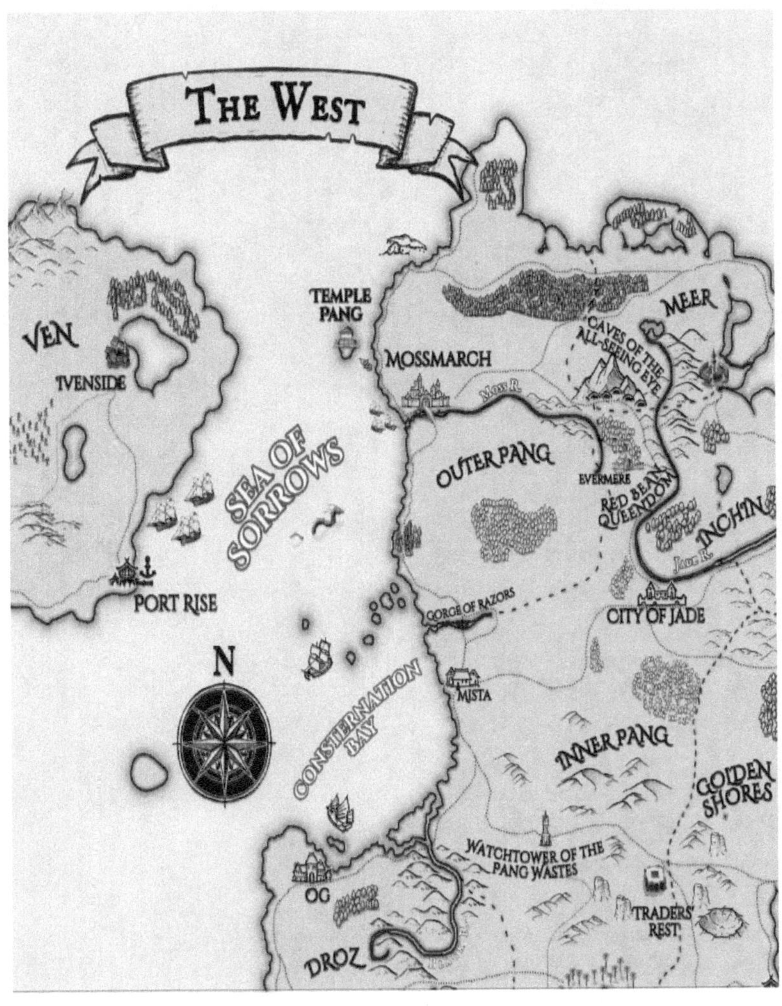
THE WEST
VEN
IVENSIDE
TEMPLE PANG
MOSSMARCH
MEER
CAVES OF THE ALL-SEEING EYE
SEA OF SORROWS
OUTER PANG
Moss R.
EVERMERE
RED BEAN QUEENDOM
INCHIN
Jade R.
PORT RISE
GORGE OF RAZORS
CITY OF JADE
N
CONSTERNATION BAY
MISTA
INNER PANG
GOLDEN SHORES
OG
WATCHTOWER OF THE PANG WASTES
TRADERS' REST
DROZ

THE NINETEEN QUEENDOMS
OCEANPLAT
OBLIVIA
VEN
TVENSIDE
SINISTERA
PORT RISE
TEMPLE PANG
MOSSMARCH
MEER
SCALISPORT
MAGNIFICENT BAY
OUTER PANG
RED BEAN QUEENDOM
INCHIN
Mou R
Todd R
SEA OF SORROWS
GORGE OF RAZORS
CITY OF JADE
TEMPA
FADING SEA
N
CONSTERNATION BAY
MISTA
INNER PANG
HORNF
YINTI
WATCHTOWER OF THE PANG WASTES
GOLDEN SHORES
OG
TRADERS REST
DROZ
SUNDI
STONK
ING
GLASSPORT
LONG JIN
DEL CARTA
FORBIDDEN SEA
PHAN TONG
SUBARIS
FROSTBITTEN SEA

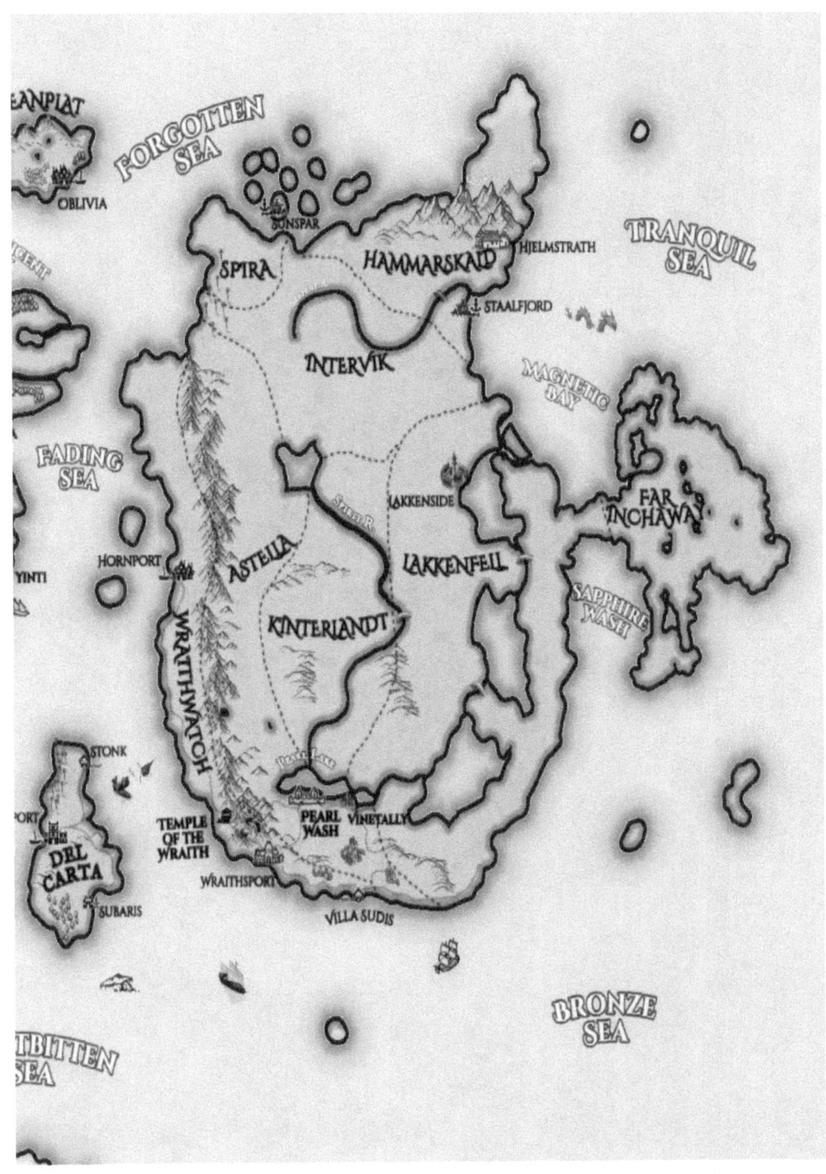
EANPLAT
FORGOTTEN SEA
OBLIVIA
TRANQUIL SEA
SPIRA
HAMMARSKAID
HJELMSTRATH
STAALFJORD
INTERVIK
MAGNETIC BAY
FADING SEA
AKKENSIDE
FAR INCHAWA
HORNPORT
YINTI
ASTELLA
LAKKENFELL
SAPPHIRE WASH
WRAITHWATCH
KINTERLANDT
STONK
TEMPLE OF THE WRAITH
PEARL WASH
VINETALLY
PORT
DEL CARTA
WRAITHSPORT
SUBARIS
VILLA SUDIS
BRONZE SEA
TBITTEN SEA

CHAPTER 1 - THE FADING SEA

A Few Months After the Trials of the All-Seeing Eye

If Minimus Mu lost his grip on the cutlery merchant's cart they called home, Master Thorn would perish. But if the soaked fingers of his other hand let the ship's tilting rail slip free, the cart would drag the orphan and his master, floundering and drowning, into a storm-wracked Fading Sea. Despite succeeding in the trial of strength not four months gone, Minimus knew that one of his arms would soon fail. A decision loomed.

The purple fabric of a hot-air balloon rippled above the pitching deck. Master Thorn climbed hand over hand up the rope attached to its basket. As he neared the safety of the balloonist's outstretched arm, he shouted a revised plan to Minimus, who strained to anchor the balloon to the deck of *Boundless*. The lashing wind tore this plan's details from Master Thorn's lips, kept from Minimus's ears by the sound of splintering timber.

The original plan had been straightforward, although not easy. Minimus would steady the rope as Master Thorn and their monkey, Jing Jing, evacuated the sinking ship. They would climb up to the waiting arms of their friend and balloonist, Ezra Longshanks. As the only passengers aboard the ship, the crew would pay them little heed amidst the pirate attack. They would need to make their own escape or risk drowning. Once the others were safely nestled in the balloon's basket, Minimus would untie it and power his way up to join his makeshift family. The rope twisted around one broad iron-shod wheel of Master Thorn's cutlery cart, which was in turn fastened to the starboard railing of the three-masted schooner, *Boundless*.

That plan splintered into tatters, much like the hull of *Boundless*, after the vicious spiked prow of the attacking pirate sloop exacted its revenge in a wind-sped broadside. Their merchant captain had dared to journey the Fading Sea from Del Carta to Wraithwatch without paying his due respects. Or coin. Pirates became hot under their tattered, frilly collars with money at stake. Whatever got the men and women of the approaching ship wagging their cutlasses and shouting insults toward the *Boundless* did not involve its passengers, but using the tethered balloon to escape the sinking ship certainly did.

This was not what Minimus envisioned for his first sea voyage. In his daydreams, it was all dozy afternoons swaying in a hammock, debating what seafood delicacies might await him for dinner. Doubtless, he'd use his recently invented runcible spork—a piece of cutlery with the bowl of a spoon, tines of a fork, and a serrated cutting edge added for completeness—at the captain's table.

But above him, in the non-dream world, Master Thorn climbed with an unexpected wiry strength that belied his slender dagger of gray beard and deep wrinkles. When the ship's rail, to which his cutlery trader's cart was lashed, broke free in a spray of spindles that flew like javelins, he managed to swing from the suddenly slack rope and held on with a single hand before recovering.

Minimus Mu shouted a wordless cry of surprise and terror as the sliding cart ushered him across the ship's deck. The musclebound boy foresaw a brutal crushing in his immediate future. He had one hand on the hot-air balloon's rope and the other on the cart's tall wheel. The cart skidded the width of the deck, and the far rail advanced at speed. An instant before the collision between cart and rail pinched him into human jelly, Minimus sprang from the slick boards, twirled around the rope, and found himself looking down on the rail as he landed atop the cart. He still held the rope.

Despite the weight of the myriad pots, pans, cutlery, and raw materials on board, the cart halted only briefly against the ship's listing rail. The pull of the balloon above edged the cart part-way up the railing until it teetered above the slate-colored waves of the Fading Sea. The boy flung his weight atop the cart, holding the rope in one hand and flattening his muscular bulk to latch his other to the ship's railing. Although he wasn't a believer in the gods of the deep, now seemed like a good time to hurl a prayer toward the waves. He must prevent the cutlery cart from creeping over the ship's edge.

Minimus glanced up, relieved to see Master Thorn continuing his scamper toward the balloon's basket and safety. But if the cart toppled into the sea, its weight would drag down the balloon as well. Minimus had learned enough of the balloonist's crazy *science* to know that much. Jing Jing shrieked and gestured at the cart and the rope, gripping Minimus's straining bicep with his prehensile tail. It seemed everyone was an amateur scientist, but the proper task of halting the cart's slip into the depths was a job for Minimus alone.

"I *know*, Jing Jing," the boy shouted. "I'll cut us free once Master Thorn is safely aboard. You and I can follow him up."

Minimus knew the more likely outcome was that the balloon would jerk away when he cut the rope, leaving him aboard the sinking ship, wishing he'd learned to swim before setting out on a sea voyage. But there was no time to dwell on such thoughts. With the cart stable for the moment, he released his grip on the rail and scouted around for a knife as everything tilted toward the roiling waters.

Jing Jing released himself from his dangling position and jumped in agitation on the cart's shifting surface, sliding drawers open, his hairy-backed hands ablur with magically assisted speed. Finding a knife on a cutlery trader's cart was simple, and soon Minimus grabbed a serrated bread knife that catapulted from a drawer that burst open as the cart tilted yet further. One hand on the rope and the other clutching the knife, a few lunges of his own toward the cart's shipward side persuaded it to slide halfway back down the railings. The commotion on board the ship barely registered. Shouting sailors, the shriek of terrorized horses—these provided little more than background noise to the boy's frantic endeavors.

Jing Jing climbed onto Minimus's shoulder as the boy hacked at the thick rope with the bread knife. As usual, the artistry and toughness of a Master Thorn blade paid off. Six or seven frantic slices reduced the rope to a wisp of fibers. Dropping the knife into the waves below, Minimus wrapped the rope once around his wrist just as it broke free from the cart. His other hand shot out to clutch a thick spoke of the cartwheel even as the balloon dragged him out and over the ship's edge. Forearms straining, Minimus Mu formed a human bond between the rope and the cart, wedged against the rail of the *Boundless*.

"*Go!*" he shouted to the monkey. A veteran rope climber, Jing Jing could have scaled its entire length in a matter of seconds, but the monkey paused a short distance from Minimus and beckoned to him with a long-fingered hand.

"I can't let go now!" Minimus screamed. "I need to hold the rope steady until Master Thorn is safe."

Jing Jing looked up the rope. A worried, begoggled face peered over the lip of the purple balloon's basket, eyebrows sending a message of deep concern to Minimus, even as the balloonist hauled Master Thorn aboard.

But in that short time, the rope slithered through the callouses of the boy's damp hand. Only his finger strength linked balloon and ship, but that would not—could not—hold more than a few moments. Minimus thrust his chin upwards, urging Jing Jing to join Master Thorn.

As his grip failed and the rope trailed away, skipping across cresting waves, the cart broke through the railing and dragged Minimus into the sea.

CHAPTER 2 - THE FADING SEA

The Next Day

The memories were almost enough to induce a state of panic in Minimus Mu. How he'd clung to the cart as it plummeted into the Fading Sea like an anvil. It was ridiculous, and definitely not part of Master Thorn's plan. But Master Thorn had been blown away in Ezra's balloon. He had seen the upturned bath bucket, filled with air and yearning to bob free from the doomed cart before finally wiggling loose. Minimus had snagged the bucket's handle as it shot toward the surface, pulling his flailing body along for the ride.

After surfacing, he had kept the bucket half submerged, conscious even in his spluttering coughing fit that if he released the air from the giant woven reed vessel, sealed with bee's wax, that it and he would sink together. He kept a crooked knee locked over the submerged handle.

Rays of sunlight peeked through torn cloud cover, lighting patches of the sea and the tableau of destruction. The *Boundless*, unbound, had split into segments in various stages of sinking. The other ship bobbed in victory, its black sails turned broadside beyond the sinking wreckage. A pair of ill-kept rowboats, tethered to the foredeck, were used by the crew of the pirate vessel to haul survivors who could swim well enough to approach their ship. Two horses flailed alongside the pirate vessel, the rope loops dangling from the yard arm, offering a chance of salvation.

Mr. Apples! Their steadfast cart horse at least had the sense to swim toward the buoyant ship instead of accompanying the boy who couldn't swim and his dodgy bucket of air. Minimus spared a moment to say a silent prayer for the horse. *May the gods of the deep favor you with safe passage and kind treatment from your new pirate masters. May you float like the fruit you are named after, your favorite meal.*

He closed his eyes and calmed his breathing, now that he'd coughed the salt water out of his system. He tried to imagine what kind of plan Master Thorn would invent in this situation. Surrendering to pirates would never be considered, so Minimus knew to keep a low profile as he bobbed on the waves. His inventory list was short: one large bath bucket, one set of clothing, and the leather-bound diary that Master Thorn had shoved inside the boy's tunic as the pirates holed the *Boundless*. Not much to work with.

His eyes popped open. Was this a recent memory he'd lost track of in his panicked entry into the sea, or something his addled mind created? He tried to remember if Jing Jing had sped up toward the balloon, because this memory was of the monkey creeping back *down* the rope just as it slipped from his cramped, burning hand. Surely, the foolish creature wouldn't have come back to his adopted brother when Master Thorn waited in the safety of the balloon above? He scanned the sea around him as he crested each salty wave, but saw nothing but flotsam in the waters nearby.

The bucket drifted. Soon, the remaining chunks of the *Boundless* slipped beneath the waves and the sails of the pirate ship glided out of sight. Only the spattering sounds of light rain striking the upturned bottom of the bucket and the sloshing of the waves remained. His ragged breathing. Nothing else.

It was late afternoon, but his exertions with the cart ushered surges of exhaustion across his body. What if he dozed off? The bucket would surely capsize, and his nonexistent swimming skills would haunt him for the few seconds before he slipped beneath the surface for the last time. Although there had been no land in sight when the pirates attacked, maybe he would drift to shore. He kicked with his free leg, giving an illusion of control over his floating journey. Must stay awake!

* * *

He tried closing one eye at a time to stave off sleep. Maybe he could let his left half sleep for a minute, then swap eyes and let his right half doze. His arms were so heavy, and the warm salty water had wrinkled every patch of visible skin. He figured he could close both eyes for a while and just focus on balancing the bucket.

An impact jarred Minimus awake, and he quickly repositioned the tilting bucket. Puffs of dusty smoke punctuated the air in a trail leading to his position, and a glossy black coal rayvn cawed directly into his ear. The four-legged bird left its signature trail of rayvn dust to mark its unobserved approach. A beak and two inscrutable obsidian eyes regarded him from atop the floating bucket.

The odd birds had shown up at key times in Minimus's life, seeming to nudge him each time in the right direction. He dreamed for a moment about Rayne, who rayvns had visited since she was a baby in the orphanage. Rayne! He regretted separating from her after the handmaiden of the Red Bean Queendom's princess had travelled with him aboard Master Thorn's cart across Inner and Outer Pang. But maybe it was for the best. He wouldn't wish his predicament on anyone he cared about with such ferocity. He returned his thoughts to the coal rayvn. Minimus could raise his voice no louder than a croak. "Do you see land, girl?"

The coal rayvn cawed again, then fluttered off, leaving another cloud of dispersing black dust in the air just above the boy. Soon, he heard the cawing again, a short distance away. He didn't bother to turn his head to see what the pesky bird was doing. It stopped its racket and switched into monkey talk. Stupid bird.

Wait! Minimus looked over his left shoulder and spotted a slab of flotsam. Atop it perched the coal rayvn and a small tan monkey, wearing an embroidered waistcoat. Jing Jing! The monkey *had* leapt from the rope in a fit of poor decision-making.

It seemed like an hour, but perhaps it was only a minute or two before Minimus kicked through the murky water and the wooden square that provided sanctuary to the monkey and coal rayvn bumped up against the floating bucket. Minimus hauled himself and then the bucket onto the bare platform. He recognized it right away: it was the roof that had covered the captain's quarters, which had nestled below the forecastle. A thick layer of cork had lined the room for soundproofing, and that same layer now gave the makeshift raft considerable buoyancy. Minimus lay on his stomach, spent, while the monkey clasped his neck in a warm hug. The coal rayvn ruffled its feathers and flew off again.

* * *

The fading glow of sunset cast an orange radiance upon the raft and its riders when the bird returned. It flapped mightily, bearing a weighty parcel in its four claws, which it placed gently aboard the floating platform.

Minimus squatted and regarded the salvaged item. "Not that I want to be critical of your gift, but there are plenty of other things from Master Thorn's cart I'd rather see. Is this the only remnant? A jar of eyeballs?"

Jing Jing mimed two eye stalks sprouting from his tufty head of hair. It had been the monkey whose quick-thinking action had brought the eyeballs into our possession. He'd plucked the four mottled blue eye stalks from the grasping, tooth-laden tentacles of the fanglimb that had attacked them at the scarlet sand beach in Outer Pang. Thinking they may prove valuable, Master Thorn had sealed them inside a jar of brine. If only he could see his adopted son and pet monkey now, the only remaining relics from his beloved traveling cutlery cart a dingy bucket and a set of pickled eyeballs.

Minimus chuckled to himself, then shook his damp head. "I have a bird cawing at me, and a monkey babbling, but nobody to answer me." He looked at the jar of eyeballs. "Since we're discussing our current predicament, I might as well include you. I'll call you Seymour."

Minimus wondered if each eye stalk should have its own name, but since they came from the same beast and he was exhausted, he couldn't come up with any extra names. Seymour would have to do.

"Okay team, let's do this. I may not be able to swim, but there's nothing that can stop the champion of the trials of the All-Seeing Eye from paddling his way to safety."

It was simple for a person with his incredible strength to separate one board from its neighbors to use as an oar. The cork made for a pleasant grip. "Wraithwatch is east, so let's paddle away from that sunset."

The coal rayvn, seeming satisfied with its salvage operation, flapped off in the heading Minimus Mu had chosen.

* * *

Thirst, hands, shoulders, sunburn. The abuses seeped into Minimus Mu's being in that order. He veered a little north during the night but had learned enough star lore from Master Thorn's educational puppet shows to guide him mostly eastward as he paddled through the night.

By dawn, his mouth cracked and burnt. His self-murmurings and occasional comments to the spread-eagled Jing Jing and Seymour grew raspier. The saltiness of the sea spray pierced the abrasions on his palms like hot daggers.

As the sun climbed overhead, his shoulders thrummed and ground with each stroke of the makeshift paddle.

By mid-afternoon, his drooping head sloped away from his blistering shoulders. Despite the warm breeze, Minimus shivered. The exposed parts of his arms were red beacons caked with white powdery rime. Still, he paddled, shifting from one side of the raft to the other to maintain its heading. His success in the trial of endurance had been easier than this, but still, he continued. If he found his way to shore, he could entertain hope that somehow he might also find Master Thorn. Beholden to the winds and unable to descend until over clear ground, perhaps the balloon would await him upon landfall.

The crashing of breaking waves made him raise his gaze. The raft approached a sand bar, beyond which glimmered a patch of calm shallows, a beach with a shady patch beneath waving palms, and the jagged peaks of snow-capped mountains beyond, lit from above by shimmering strands of wispy multicolored light.

His voice was unrecognizable to even himself as he nudged the monkey awake with a gentle paddle prod. "Jing Jing," he croaked. "Wraithwatch."

CHAPTER 3 - TEMPLE OF THE WRAITH

One Day Earlier

The controlled fire that filled the balloon with hot air and kept it hovering a respectful height above the Fading Sea gave the two men's faces an orange glow in the twilight. Ezra's balloon had abandoned the scene of the pirate attack propelled by high winds, but now moved in a moderate breeze, heading east toward the coast of Wraithwatch.

"The problem with your science," Master Thorn began, pointing a crooked finger at the balloonist, "is that it does what it pleases. Sure, this balloon allows us to fly, but it made us fly *away* from Minimus and Jing Jing. Science left us no way to return and rescue them!"

Ezra stretched the band of his goggles, raising them from his eyes to rest on the conch shell he used as a helmet. His bushy eyebrows plastered his forehead. "It's not our place to question science. Only to understand it. I know you regret losing your apprentice—and by the Gilded Shoemakers of Thun, the boy did a great service to the Red Bean Queendom—but surely it's obvious you would have perished without my balloon. His sacrifice saved you—and me!"

Master Thorn exhaled a sharp breath. "But Minimus can't swim! That overcurious monkey is doubtless now picking the pockets of every pirate on board the ship that rammed us, but there's no way my boy survived after falling into the sea. I should have made a better plan."

Ezra placed a gangly hand on Master Thorn's bony shoulder. "I know it's little consolation now, my friend, but Minimus Mu will live forever in song and verse. He's a vivid part of the trials of the All-Seeing Eye. He will endure while you and I are only dust."

Master Thorn wiped what could have been sea spray but were more likely tears from his cheeks. "Aye. And he invented a revolutionary new piece of cutlery. Once I replace the materials sunk within my cart, I'll forge all the runcible sporks my old hands can fabricate. I know he wanted to travel, so I pledge to get hands in all nineteen queendoms eating from his creation."

The two men stood in silence, peering westward as if they could pick out a lingering sign of everything they'd abandoned. When they turned once again to their direction of travel, they observed the shifting wisps of light that gave the queendom of Wraithwatch its name. Slender tendrils of icy blue and cold green shimmered above the mountain peaks that encroached upon the narrow coastal plains. It was as if scintillating vapors sought to reach the clouds but lacked the impetus and instead dispersed to nothingness before arriving.

"I've heard of the wraithsign before, but never expected it to be this dramatic," Ezra said. "We're headed directly toward the Temple of the Wraith."

Master Thorn nodded. "They worship the illuminations, don't they? Could we land this contraption at the temple?"

Ezra wrinkled his nose, as if detecting an unfamiliar scent. "I'd planned on setting down as soon as we reached land. The problem in the mountains will be finding a safe strip without hazards. We're really at the mercy of the wind. It could drag us over jagged ridges or, if it's friendlier, deposit us right above the temple grounds. We will only know once we arrive.

"But if it's unsafe to land, we could just glide over into Astella, no?" Master Thorn asked. "Personally, I've got nothing else to lose, so throwing myself at the mercy of science seems as good a path as any. Maybe a wind lemur will take mercy upon us and blow us right to the temple."

Ezra checked the supply of logs that fed the cast-iron stove. "We've enough fuel to get us over the mountains, I expect. And you're right. If my maps are correct, the city of Pearl Wash should be just beyond that ridge ahead. It's probably better to land there than on a barren beach in Wraithwatch. Let's get a closer look."

The men took turns snoozing through the night as the eerie, shifting lights grew closer. As the sun's rays broke between the mountain peaks, the curtain wall of the Temple of the Wraith became visible, and the glow became harder to detect. The balloon's path would skirt the temple, and it looked like the pair would be able to wave to the priests but must pass them by and continue into Astella. As they drew closer, the phantom, twisting lights lit the shaven-headed templars in their white robes as they went about their early morning chores. The laundry fluttering in the cool, light breeze changed from orange to blue to green as the illumination fluctuated.

"Look at that herd of golden mountain rams!" Ezra exclaimed, pointing.

Master Thorn spotted them. A cluster of forty or fifty thick-wooled rams milled along a ridge beyond the temple, the occasional thud of clashing horns indicating contests of dominance. He knew their magical power but had never witnessed it; if threatened, a ram could detonate itself in a ferocious fireball, sacrificing itself in a display that would scare off or destroy any threat to the herd. One of his customers at the Mossmarch market had once revealed a hand scorched by a startled exploding ram. According to the man, he was a good distance away when the explosion happened, suggesting it was extremely powerful. It was one of those magical spectacles one secretly wished to see, but from a safe distance.

In retrospect, Master Thorn often wondered whether contemplating an exploding ram somehow caused what happened next. As the line of rams cavorted in silhouette along the ridge, the rise of an object as large as Ezra's balloon occluded for a moment the slanting sunbeams. From behind the rim, the powerful flapping of six wings and the ear-shredding screech could mean only one thing: an abomination bird.

The golden mountain rams swiveled as one to orient on the outstretched claws and vicious curve of the abomination bird's serrated beak. The surprise attack lasted but a few seconds, but time seemed to halt as massive talons targeted two rams amidst the pack.

Multiple rams must have sacrificed themselves. The explosion's fierce heat knocked Master Thorn and Ezra to the far side of the balloon's basket. Flames raged into the sky, disrupting the wraithlight, and the nearly indestructible abomination bird careened down the mountainside back toward Astella.

Master Thorn had seen his first display of ram magic, but another, even less desirable occurrence soon confronted him and an open-mouthed Ezra. They could see the indigo morning sky through a gaping slit torn through the balloon's topmost panel.

* * *

Master Thorn could remember the frantic zig-zagging plummet as the balloon released its remaining hot air, but could never recall the impact. As the basket made its swirling descent, flinging them toward the temple, the quality of the sunlight seemed to change. Maybe the blast had jumbled his eyes so color and focus lost meaning. The next thing he knew, he was peeling himself from atop Ezra where the pair had jumbled together on the blanketed floor of the balloon's basket.

The basket rocked and bumped against the chunky granite blocks of a featureless wall. Above them, the lines tethering the balloon to the basket drew together before disappearing over the wall's crenelated peak; the fabric of the balloon draped on the wall's other side. In the sky above, a few tendrils of ram fire darted and fizzled. The wraithlight had constricted into a more concentrated and well-defined ring, spinning in place and cycling through every color in the spectrum. Its openings pointed east and west, the whole ring rotating in stationary, lethargic circles. A handful of mountain rams staggered away from the scorched central ridge.

Master Thorn offered a hand to Ezra, who patted himself down and searched for his goggles. "They're still on your conch," Master Thorn said in both a helpful and playful manner.

"Right, right," Ezra said, accepting the proffered helping hand. "Everybody okay?"

Master Thorn half-frowned. "I think a few rams are disintegrated, and that's the first time I've seen an abomination bird attack thwarted, but yeah. Tomorrow will bring me nothing more than a few bruises."

The basket inched lower, scraping along the wall. "How do you feel about rope climbing?" Master Thorn asked.

"Not great. But I'd prefer to test my skills than see what happens when a giant basket rolls down a mountainside with me inside. You go ahead—I'll douse the stove's fire before I follow."

"So much for the charity of priests," Master Thorn grumbled to himself as he hauled himself atop the wall without so much as a single person appearing above them to help. Seeing and hearing no one else atop the parapets, he lay on his stomach and dangled an outstretched arm to encourage Ezra's wheezing ascent.

Master Thorn noted that the ropes holding the balloon to its basket dangled across three crenelations. The stitched purple fabric of the deflated balloon hung defeated down the inner side of the tall temple wall. There was no leeway for the basket to drop any further unless several ropes broke. Ezra could have stayed in the basket, but Master Thorn knew his new plan, once he formulated it, would not involve them being separated. He coaxed Ezra through the final few inches of the climb and tumbled him over the parapet. Ezra lay huffing for a few moments, careless that his conch helmet had rolled a short distance away.

"The local priests are like the apprentice I had before Minimus," Master Thorn chided. "They were lolling around as we passed overhead, but now there's work to be done, they've scarpered."

Ezra rose and surveyed the inner courtyard of the temple. A collection of boxy, single-story thatched buildings lay scattered around a rudimentary church. Its spire rose to the level of the four towers, one at each corner of the curtain wall. All was made of local gray granite and reedy thatch, with most of its color drained by years of exposure to the mountain elements.

Ezra's brow furrowed as he narrowed his eyes, trying to pick out missing elements from the scene below. "Well, they took their laundry down in a hurry. They can move at pace when they want to, I guess."

Master Thorn had not noticed this detail. "Weirdos! With all the commotion, their first thought was to move a load of drying robes? Who'd miss a chance to see even the aftermath of a golden mountain ram detonation or a fallen abomination bird? They should have rushed to the walls."

The rams seemed to think the abomination bird was no longer a threat. The two splintered groups combined into a single herd along the ridge once again, and a smattering of half-hearted headbutting had resumed between a few pairs of thick-skulled males.

Master Thorn beckoned to Ezra, who wobbled as he retrieved his helmet and goggles from the floor. "Come along! Let's head to the mess hall and see what crude implements they use for cutlery in this windswept place."

They headed to a corner tower and its steps down, but Ezra paused and took a sideways squinting glance into the sky. "What's happened to the sunlight? Seems orangey, no?"

"Must be the remnants of the explosion. Come on, man, I smell porridge."

Both men held the railing as they descended, legs still full of adrenaline and its accompanying shakes. Across the courtyard with its wide irregular flagstones, the source of the smell was obvious. Only one building's chimney emitted the telltale smoke of a cooking fire.

Dark gray and black robes hung from pegs lining the entry hall. A clutch of robes lay flat on a drying rack, and Master Thorn noted their oddly curtained hoods, with fabric stretched across the facial openings. Handy when hunkered down in a storm, he thought, but impractical otherwise. Hadn't they invented scarves yet in Wraithwatch?

Tiptoeing deeper into the building, the two men crept into a high-beamed dining hall. Ezra ventured a weak-sounding greeting that echoed across the wooden tables and empty benches. "Uh, hello? Anyone here?"

A smattering of unfinished porridge bowls lay divided between the thick-beamed trestle tables, and several of the long benches lay scattered, as if an explosion outside had rudely interrupted breakfast. Had the residents rushed to safety, on hearing the explosions, somewhere deeper within the temple complex?

Master Thorn ambled to the porridge bubbling in a cavernous cast-iron pot. It hung above a modest fire within a hearth large enough to accommodate a horse. He fished two wooden bowls from among dozens balanced on on open shelf and spooned steaming dollops into them. He grabbed wooden spoons and brandished one at Ezra. "I find that once you start eating someone else's food, they miraculously appear. Ignore these diabolical spoons and have a seat, Ezra," he said. "Want a dash of cinnamon?"

They ate in silence, grateful for the food but suspicious of their circumstances. Their eyes flitted between the doorways as they shoveled sustenance into their mouths. There were no sounds other than the susurration of the wind through the courtyard. Wherever the templars had gone, they seemed to be staying put and staying quiet.

Moving and calling from kitchen to barracks, from smithy to chapel, the two men found no signs of human life. A half dozen horses raised their heads from recently filled feeding troughs as the men entered the stables, but even the guard posts flanking the portcullis blocking the entrance trail sat abandoned.

A rickety pen that backed onto the stables housed about twenty goats. Unlike the ones Ezra and Master Thorn were familiar with, these were firmly ground-bound, not hovering weightless, like every other goat they'd encountered. An inquisitive kid trotted to the fence, and raised its forelegs to drape over the waist-high fence. It eyeballed Master Thorn and voiced a plaintive bleat.

"Huh. These goats are weird," Master Thorn said. "They don't even have the magic to make them weightless. Never heard of a non-hovering goat before. I wonder what these guys have as a magical power? Must be pretty good, or they'd have their teeth out already."

"Maybe they still have the bad luck defenses," Ezra mused. "But their teeth would be worthless. How could you believe they were real money unless the teeth floated?"

That was a good point. Although goat's teeth were the primary currency across every queendom Master Thorn had visited, it would be very suspicious if the teeth weren't weightless, like their former owners. And the magical curse that would result from harming a normal goat that causes permanent misfortune might still befall anyone foolish enough to mistreat these goats. Master Thorn settled for a friendly ruffling of the tuft of coarse hair between the kid's budding horns.

"Could the priests we noticed earlier have retreated lower down the mountainside?" Ezra wondered aloud. "Should we hike out and find them?"

Master Thorn pondered the idea for a moment before answering. "Unless your science knows something I don't, we will not hoist the balloon from its position without many helping hands. The locals are bound to come back at some point. I say we settle in, fix ourselves a nice supper, and overnight here. If the temple occupants have not returned by morning, we can borrow horses and supplies and descend.

Come back and mend the balloon later. The trail down forks, so we can choose then whether to go to Astella or remain in Wraithwatch."

* * *

The wraithlight remained visible, spinning overhead in its torus throughout the day. Neither man knew if this was a normal occurrence, or if the exploding rams had altered its usual form. The pair ate sandwiches piled high with cheeses, beans, and salad from the well-stocked larder, sitting at one of the unadorned tables that dotted the courtyard.

Ezra jostled Master Thorn's arm and pointed at the main gate. He nearly choked on the mouthful he'd just taken before stammering out, "Here they come! And they don't look happy."

With the noise of the approaching rabble, Ezra's gesture was redundant. Master Thorn had already twisted in his seat at the sound of running feet, armored men shrieking battle cries, and the clatter of iron-shod hooves upon the approach to the portcullis blocking the temple gate.

These were no templar priests. It was an armed and angry jumble of mounted invaders. Most wore gold cloaks, but they dressed without the uniformity of a royal army. Both Master Thorn and Ezra stood, holding their hands out in a display meant to show they meant no harm.

At least the portcullis stands between us and a thorough trampling, Master Thorn thought. But that idea lasted only a few moments. The lead rider stood tall in his stirrups and clenched his fists as he approached the gate at pace. The deep indigo light of powerful magic blazed in rings around each of his wrists. With a flick, the rings released themselves, whirling at the portcullis.

On impact, the swirling magical projectiles blew the massive metalwork blocking the entranceway from its moorings. The portcullis flew several paces into the courtyard and spun, sparking, beyond where Ezra and Master Thorn stood with their mouths agape.

Pikes were leveled, swords were pointed at sensitive anatomical parts, and riders circled the courtyard. Magical energy writhed around each one, poised for combat.

"Where are they? The Mothers?" yelled the rider that had blown away the gate. He glared at Master Thorn.

Shaking, Master Thorn raised his empty hands even higher. It probably would have been best to answer the question, but he was unsure what it meant. Plus, most good plans involved never answering a question directly. Instead, he said, "What kind of horses are those? They let you use their magic?"

The lead rider rode closer. Master Thorn felt the beast's ragged breath rush past his cheek. "What nonsense are you babbling on about, old man? You think I've got a magical *horse?*"

Master Thorn retreated a half-step. "It's just, well, I've never seen magic flow into a person before."

The man spat. "It's not flowing into us, as you very well know. You, of all people, surrounded by these heretical hags, must see it every day. Oh, they may claim they detest magic, but they use it all the same, don't they? Now, last chance, before I let my magic flow *from me*—where are they?"

The explanations Master Thorn and Ezra gave sounded implausible, even to their own ears, as they tried to explain their balloon crash, the explosion, and the disappearance of the temple priests. It seemed impossible that every man inside could have vanished in the scant minutes between the abomination bird's attack and the two unexpected arrivals had hauling themselves to the battlements.

"I'm not sure if I can believe that tale," the lead rider snarled. "But if it is true, they weren't men you saw. It's hard to tell with their faces covered by their cloaks, but this temple is full of Mothers and Sisters, not men."

Master Thorn raised an eyebrow. "They wore only their tunics as we drifted over. And we saw their shaven heads. Everyone knows the Order of the Temple accepts only men and boys."

"You must have hit your head when you crashed, old man. There are no men in this temple, only the Mothers of Midnight. We came once again to end their campaign of anti-magical terror and all we find are two half-crazed westerners?"

CHAPTER 4 - MOSSMARCH

Three Days Later

The devious knife-thrower Sala Doon and the crafty swindler Mirko Leatherfoot reveled in the mild chaos now soaking the queendom of Outer Pang. According to Master Thorn, their kindnesses toward the orphan boy Minimus Mu had helped him tackle the five trials of the All-Seeing Eye that ultimately led to the downfall of Queen Jada of Mossmarch. As usual, they found themselves revelers in disorder of their own creation.

Most Outer Pangans were confused. Would the queen return, or would Princess Tasha of the Red Bean Queendom eventually assume the throne proper? Could a tiny Red Beaner even rule over people four times her size? And what about the market stallholders, the drovers, bargemen, and the taverns? Would tax collectors continue to make their rounds?

Sala and Mirko agreed that with confusion came opportunity. They stalked the shadows of Mossmarch and found their purses filled with more goat teeth than ever. But even though it was against their natures, they also strolled in the sunlight, mostly to accompany their friend, Rayne Sun of the Red Bean royal household, if she felt the urge to venture beyond the palace walls. It would not do to have such a slight and beautiful handmaiden wandering the streets unguarded, and Rayne persuaded Princess Tasha to let the two friends escort her during the princess's diplomatic trip across the Sea of Sorrows to Ven.

Rayne's voice called out with a tinkling quality that still made Sala smile. The two dark-clad men glanced down at her to see where she pointed. "There they are! I knew we'd find them at one tavern or another."

At the sound of her voice, two sets of cloaked shoulders turned her way from a lopsided table and a pair of rickety chairs outside the Crossed Swords, a tavern of modest ill repute. One cloak was a featureless gray, the other a flamboyant paisley.

The more colorful of the pair was Virgil Longspeaker, the poet and songster who'd accompanied Minimus Mu throughout the trials that saved the Red Bean Queendom from being overrun by Outer Pang. "Rayne, get over here! We forced the publican to organize a sensible chair for you. Come, try it out." Virgil elbowed his companion. "Dando, go grab it from behind the bar. You've seen the service—Rayne will be a spinster before anyone bothers to take our orders. And I'm a tad parched, if you take my meaning."

His companion, Apostle Dando of the Truthsayer's Guild, who had also accompanied Minimus as an official of the trials, rolled his eyes but mouthed, "Hello, my lady," as he ducked into the tavern to retrieve the special chair. He emerged a minute later bearing not just a high-seated wooden chair, but also five arch-handled ceramic tankards full of a purplish ale.

"Barkeep called this one a *child portion*," Dando said, gesturing at the smaller mug he plopped in front of the newly arrived chair. "And I took the liberty of ordering for you two fine persons, as well. The plum ale here is contagious and well worth tomorrow morning's headache. Business good, Mirko and Sala? Pull up chairs."

Virgil laughed, a heartfelt burst of mirth that started somewhere low in his well-fed belly. "My man Dando normally refers to people as fine *gentlemen*, but it seems once again his magic compulsion of truth-telling has colored his speech. You've been relegated to simply *persons*."

Mirko joined in the laughter, and Sala smiled in a typically restrained fashion. "I've been called much worse than a person. And you move with confidence, carrying all five drinks in one hand. That's quite a feat!"

Dando nodded. "Barkeeping is a skill we learn in our guild. When work opportunities are thin, there's always call for an honest bartender."

Sala offered a toast to rare skills, and the five of them clinked tankards. "Many thanks for the flagon, Dando, but if it's okay with you, we'll guzzle and dash. Business is so good that delicate negotiations down at the docks need our attention. Can we leave Rayne under your care here for an hour until we return?"

Sala had half drained his frothy drink before the minstrel or apostle could answer, and Mirko was not far behind. They took their leave and left Rayne deep in conversation with the two men who had become minor celebrities after their brush with fame during the five trials of the All-Seeing Eye.

After a further round of plum ale, which Rayne politely declined, and consideration of a further trip to the bar, Dando preached the virtues of his truth-telling. "At first, after the order had pricked me with the land urchin quill and its magic had run its course through me, I found it very taxing. I kept blurting out regrettable incidents from my past and couldn't restrain myself from uttering every passing thought aloud. I pointed out each passer-by's deformity and commented on every point of conversation I disagreed with."

Virgil interjected. "Great way to make new friends, I'll wager."

Dando chuckled. "Not exactly. But now I've settled into that comfortable space where everybody knows I cannot lie, so they ask me questions they fear others might avoid answering truthfully. 'Dando, that nobleman's son seems to fancy me; should I consider his offer and visit him on his boat?' Or, 'Dando, is that really crab meat in Benji's fritters?' Stuff that others might shy away from answering."

Rayne considered the importance of tact for a truthsayer like Dando. "But what about—?" she began, before screams from the market stalls across the courtyard drew everyone's attention.

Six figures concealed beneath black robes moved in an unhurried V across the cobbles, leaving behind a distraught stall-keeper waving her arms and shouting grief-wracked cries about her daughter. The cloaks revealed almost nothing; they skirted the cobblestones and flared sleeves edged halfway down hands, exposing only fingers. But more striking were the hoods. They not only thrust forward enough to cast deep shadows over the wearers' faces, but walls of thick fabric fronted them, leaving only a hint of chin visible and a snatch of neck and collarbones. With faces so obscured, Apostle Dando couldn't imagine how these interlopers could see.

Stallholders and patrons alike shrank back from these severe figures as they glided through the open space at the center of the improvised marketplace. No weapons flashed, but something upsetting had happened and everybody avoided confrontation. The lead figure pointed at several locations, including the table where Virgil, Dando, and Rayne sat. Wordlessly, the pack split, with three drifting toward the small throngs of local folk forming at the courtyard's periphery, and three advancing on the Crossed Swords.

Dando and Virgil sprang from their seats, chairs toppling behind them. The kilted minstrel drew a curved dagger while Dando scooped up Rayne from her elevated chair and lowered her to a position against the tavern wall. "Stay behind us, my lady," he hissed.

A girl of no more than six years old in a fading and threadbare blue dress ran barefoot across the path of the three cloaked figures, speeding toward her mother's beckoning calls. With a rapidity of movement at odds with its fluid grace, one of the shadowy interlopers veered toward the child, a pale hand extending to snatch her by the wrist. With a popping sound, the pair disappeared. A momentary sizzle of magic hung in the air before chaos erupted.

The invaders transfixed every eye in the courtyard, and their actions, although inexplicable, seethed with malicious intent.

Shouts and screams echoed as feet clattered and a merchant's stall collapsed in the surging evacuation of the square. The steely sound of a drawn sword crossed the open space from where the lone visible queen's guard had dozed a moment earlier.

With three more pops, cloaked invaders winked out of existence, each taking a child or young woman with them. Amidst the shouting, these mysterious visitors uttered not a word, shouted no warnings or intentions to the panicked locals. The remaining two advanced on the Crossed Swords.

Dando stood beside Virgil Longspeaker, pulling himself to his full, gangly height. Less well armed than his companion, he raised Virgil's lute in a two-handed grip over his right shoulder, trying to appear as threatening as possible.

The crowd scattered, leaving an open space around the two figures. The hooded ones approached at pace, still seeming unhurried, stopping just beyond dagger range. "Stand aside from the girl, or you will get hurt," one said. With only a hint of jawline visible, Dando could not tell which one spoke.

Virgil made a shallow lunge, the point of his blade aiming for the chest of one black cloak. Its owner retreated a fraction, leaving the dagger to swipe through nothing but air. With shocking speed, the second figure crouched, extended a hand, and twisted Virgil's wrist, the dagger falling useless to the stones. With a second twist, Virgil fell to one side, then to his knees, ending up on his back, cradling his hand.

Springing across Virgil's fallen body, the other assailant landed on the table beside Dando with remarkable agility. Before Dando could swing the lute, a hand gripped his throat. Surprisingly slender, he thought, before a blaze of magical energy flashed before his eyes. With no comprehension of what had happened, Apostle Dando found himself sprawled on his back, three paces from the cloaked pair who reached toward a cowering Rayne. An echoing, "I told you not to interfere with the Mothers of Midnight." throbbed in his ear. He felt oddly unable to lift his arms as magic fizzed through his system. It reminded him of the land urchin prick at the start of his truth-telling days.

With one still balancing astride the wobbling table, both shadowy attackers paused as if they had heard a bugle call inaudible to everyone else. The one closest to Rayne pulled its hand back in a blur, twisting at the torso and positioning its head at an unlikely angle. The hood's thick cloth still obscured everything but the pale jaw as three speeding daggers flew past. One bounced off the stone wall, right where their arm had snatched back. The second would have impaled the cloaked chest, but the twisting lean allowed it to glide by. The third was head-bound. It missed its target, but sliced through the thin copper chain of a necklace left in midair by the invader's swift backward lean. The chain and its pendant—a dark, metallic, eleven-pointed star—fell to the cobblestones. Grazing a cheek, the spinning blade pierced the hood's margin, pinning it to the wooden table's edge.

At the square's corner, a sprinting Sala Doon shouted after another pair of blades that tumbled in a low arc toward the Crossed Swords. "Back off now, or you'll lose an eye," he warned.

Dando watched in horror as this threat lost its sting. With a jerk, the backward-leaning intruder shimmied its head, tearing the cloak to free it from the knife that pinned it, revealing the head and face of its wearer. It was a womanly face, with a dark gray-flecked bob framing the remnants of her facial features. A web of crinkled scar tissue took the place of each eye, the sockets flattened. Both ears were also gone, rough scarred patches marring each side of her head. Sala's daggers couldn't poke out what had already burnt away.

The other invader flattened into a compressed split-stance squat to avoid the two new incoming blades before springing to Rayne's side. A sinewy arm adorned with a dark metal bangle grabbed Rayne's arm. They both winked out of existence. Her companion flicked her hood back into place, and with the twist of one wrist, she, too, disappeared.

* * *

Sala cursed, spitting, as he helped Virgil back to his feet. "How'd I let them take Rayne? That's unforgiveable! I threw the first three blades with different arcs so they'd arrive at exactly the same time. They were Master Thorn blades, too. Would've torn that thuggish man to shreds. I don't know how he avoided them. Don't normally miss from that range."

Virgil massaged his wrist. "Not entirely your fault, Sala. None of us managed to protect Rayne any better. But we'll figure out where she's gone and get her back. Although they didn't offer many clues about their identity—I can't believe they remained silent the whole time," he said. "Here, Dando, get off your ass."

Dando shook his head, both in disbelief and to clear it of the magical shock he'd had. "Didn't you hear them speaking?"

Virgil narrowed his eyes and peered at his friend. "Uh, no. Don't talk nonsense. They stayed silent."

Dando's eyes narrowed and he cocked his head to one side. "No! One of them *didn't* speak. And I *didn't* see one's face. Looked like a *man*. Wait, no—what am I saying?"

The apostle of the Truthsayers' Guild massaged his still-tingling cheek and tried again. In the tussle, something had gone haywire with his truth-telling compulsion. "I *wasn't* trying to protect Rayne, and the one in front *didn't* tell me to step back or I'd get hurt. She *didn't* call herself the Mother of Midnight. Ahh! Wait! I keep saying what I meant to say."

CHAPTER 5 - TEMPLE OF THE WRAITH

The Same Day

It took three days before the Order of Magical Preservation entertained the idea that Master Thorn and Ezra were telling a twisted version of the truth. Their leader, Skain Two-Hearts, came to question them in their locked and sparsely furnished barracks room for the seventh time after the Order's search of the temple grounds and nearby mountainside uncovered no sign of his quarry.

"So, you *really* don't work for the Mothers of Midnight?" he began. "And you think *we're* insane for not believing you when you say a sect of baldheaded priests staff the temple, but they somehow vanished because of exploding goats?"

"Golden mountain rams," Master Thorn corrected. "It's so weird you haven't heard of their magical powers. They're legendary. But normal goats? They just hover around, nibbling everything in sight, the blighters."

Skain turned to Ezra. "And you believe in this silly business about animals having magic, too? How would they even learn magic? Some wise master sheep gives them lessons when they're kids?"

Master Thorn cut off Ezra's attempt to answer and shook his head again. "Baby *goats* are kids. Baby *rams* are lambs. But no—they're *born* magical. Every land animal and bird, anyway.

Don't they have any animals in Astella?"

"Now you're pulling my leg," Skain said. "Do you know how long I had to study before I could harness my magic? I started when I was four years old." Skain looked away, his eyes losing focus. "Probably didn't study enough, to be fair."

"It's no joke," Master Thorn said. "I must admit I'd never known that Astellans could do magic. Why didn't any of your countrymen mention it when I encountered them at the markets in Outer Pang? I've only heard one person mention humans could have magical powers, and she was … well … unreliable."

This thought uncorked a rarely visited backwater of Master Thorn's memory. He cast his mind back to the days when Minimus Mu was a baby. The pang of loss resurfaced, as it had every few moments since the boy tumbled overboard from the *Boundless*. He lost track of the conversation, according Ezra and Skain's voices as much attention as a mosquito's drone. Was there a chance Minimus still lived? Maybe the pirates rescued him before he sank. Like an unbolted cartwheel, his mind spun, bouncing in every direction but making no meaningful progress. Eventually, his focus returned to the conversation.

Skain sighed. "There's no point in holding you any longer. We've pulled your so-called balloon over the wall and shuffled it into a corner of the courtyard. You're free to continue your journey, wherever that may take you. Use the horses in the stable and any provisions you can find. Avoid selecting those sporting a gold ribbon, marking them as one of ours. I'd say the other horses' owners are not returning."

Skain's squire trotted up to them, a youthful lad with a spring in his step and a face free of the misadventures and character that came with age. "Everything's ready for departure, sir. They've chosen the garrison to leave behind." The squire opened his mouth to add something more, but then glanced at Master Thorn and slapped it shut again with an audible pop.

"What is it, lad? You can say it here," Skain said, examining the boy's reluctant expression.

"Well, you know the Mothers, how they can snap themselves back here whenever they want?"

Skain nodded.

"Well, what if they could transport themselves somewhere *else*, too? Maybe the circle of wraithlight is a sign of that—we've never seen it spin like this, have we? Remember that girl that found her way back to Pearl Wash? They'd snatched her three years previous. She said they brought her here first, but then she ended up at Temple Pang."

Master Thorn perked up. "You mean the island temple just off Mossmarch? That Temple Pang?"

The boy hesitated before nodding. "Well, I own that I paid little attention to geography lessons, and I didn't know it was an island, but yes, sir. In Outer Pang. That's the other home of the Mothers."

"Maybe, lad, maybe," Skain said. "I knew I should have brought the damned Finder with us. Let's hasten back to Pearl Wash and see if she can locate the missing Mothers. Farewell, sirs, we've got a frustrated hunt to continue if we're to preserve our magic."

Skain Two-Hearts turned to leave the barracks, his squire following at his heels.

Master Thorn cleared his throat with too much drama to be natural. The man and boy turned. "One last thing. This Finder. Can she locate lost children? Like ones that went overboard during a shipwreck?"

CHAPTER 6 - WRESTLE VINE BEACH, WRAITHWATCH

The Same Week

It took the smell of simmering clam broth to raise Minimus from the beach. After staggering through the shallows, carrying Jing Jing on a sunburnt and exhausted shoulder, the shoeless hulk of a boy collapsed on the sandy beach, overjoyed to abandon the makeshift raft but too faint to move another inch. After an unfathomable time with his toes washed by occasional waves, Minimus Mu urged himself forward once again.

Ee Clot, the foreman of the wrestle vine farm, took one look at the boy who crawled to the doorless opening of the cooking hut and without another thought, helped Minimus into a shaded sitting position and plied him with broth. After that, Ee had several thoughts, primary among them that a sturdy lad like this could do the vine extraction work of at least two men. Even three. Even before Minimus awoke later that afternoon, Ee had planned the rest of his life for him. The next day or two would be his training period, after which he could harvest vines until a mishap ended his petty and meaningless life.

Ee shooed the monkey with the curious-looking jerkin away with a poker. Jing Jing sulked in a nearby beach palm, casting occasional monkey insults at the circle of primitive huts.

When Minimus's sleep-clouded eyes cracked open to the sight of a large mug of sweet-smelling water and a variety of dried fruits, he noticed Ee's face for the first time. He looked like his eyes had an ongoing disagreement. They mostly looked in opposite directions, but one would occasionally glance at its neighbor.

"Eh, boy! I saved you, I did. Gave you some broth, dragged you into the shade, got rid of that monkey that pestered you."

Minimus paused mid-gulp. "Jing Jing?" his cracking voice asked. "What'd you do to him?"

Ee pointed with half-hearted accuracy toward the tree line. Minimus relaxed his clenched shoulders. The monkey could handle himself. The fruits were tasty and included two that had flavors he could not name. A little strength returned to his muscles.

"I need to find my master. Master Thorn."

Ee chuckled, joined by a pair of loiterers who only now came into focus through Minimus's tired eyes and dehydration headache. Their smiles showed a bare minimum of tilted teeth, framed by ruddy faces that had seen too much sun and salt. "Only one master 'round here, lad, and that's me. Forget this Thorn character. You're a wrestle vine farmer now."

Nobody would dare take liberties like this with Minimus if they knew Master Thorn. But he wasn't there, was he? He wasn't even from this continent. Minimus figured he could play along, get his strength back, and a plan would come to him in time.

"You don't understand. I'm Minimus Mu, champion of the five trials of the All-Seeing Eye."

At this, Ee Clot and his two companions laughed so hard Minimus thought what teeth remained between them might shower the sand floor.

"Minimus Mu?" one spat. "I heard he has blue hair and a talking parrot."

"They say he has a peg leg," Ee added. "Come on, lad. You can invent a better story than that."

"I'm not lying," Minimus muttered, knowing these men

would never believe him.

* * *

As he staggered to the hammock near Jing Jing's tree, Minimus noticed a massive whorled shell clamped to the trunk of a tree. That's lucky, he thought. A serenity snail. The shell out-measured his head, so Minimus needed both hands to coax the snail from the bark. He stripped out of his tunic and lowered himself onto his stomach on the cool sand, shifting the snail so its damp but soothing foot spanned his sunburnt shoulders. Serenity snails, with shells harder than granite, served usually as a salve for the brain. They enjoyed human contact and worked their magic against anxiety, sleeplessness, pain, and trauma. They also had mild effects on physical issues, and as the snail rippled and repositioned itself on his back, Minimus felt the terror and trials of his voyage adrift recede. Even the sting of separation from Master Thorn diminished as he fell asleep.

The next morning, easing the serenity snail from an outstretched leg with his peaceful dreams fading, Minimus approached full strength. The boy peeled off his salt-stained tunic, rinsed it in the fresh water of the nearby whispering spring, and lay it on a hot rock. Jing Jing sprang onto the rock, making Minimus smile. The monkey embraced the still raw skin around the boy's neck, only releasing him when Minimus offered to clean the monkey's top and deposit it alongside his own.

Ee ushered Minimus once again into the Fading Sea, having deemed him well enough to begin his new duties. The task at hand would take them only waist-deep, so he waved away complaints about missing swimming skills like a pesky gnat. The boy waded into the shallows, along with the two men he'd encountered the previous day.

Wrestle vines grew underwater, where they waved in the current. When brought onto land, they would reflexively coil around whatever they encountered, and once severed from their roots, would petrify into a substance as hard as stone. Prized by architects, cart trains arrived every two weeks, bringing new frames for the harvested wrestle vines to twist around and removing the hardened shapes deposited during their earlier visits.

Ee Clot delivered the first of the only two lessons needed to become a wrestle vine harvester. "Just follow a vine until it sinks into the sand, and yank as hard as you can to uproot it. Sling it 'round your shoulders and drag it to shore. Them lot carry two at a time, but by the looks of you, three or four might seem easy. And don't worry about twining them 'round the frames. I'll handle that."

Minimus circled his shoulders, estimating the degree of sunburn pain hoisting salty and waterlogged vines might trigger. "What are those floating balls?" he asked.

"Oh yeah," Ee said. "Lobster traps. Check 'em while you're out there, and drag them ashore, too, if we've caught any."

The man shooed Minimus toward the vine field and waited thigh-deep in the low waves. Minimus couldn't be sure that Ee's gaze followed him, what with the man's wonky tracking, but he felt a pressure to follow the basic instructions without asking more questions. He saw the tendrils of a vine near his foot and walked deeper, following its length. One of his fellow workers paced beside him, following a second vine, while the other vine farmer lifted wooden-framed lobster traps to check for their dinner. When Minimus saw the vine disappear into the sand, he placed a foot on either side and turned. He kept his voice low, so the nearby farmer would hear, but the potentially stupid question wouldn't reach Ee's ears. "So, I just grab and pull, right?"

The man slicked back his spray-dampened hair and rested a palm against the pommel of a machete strapped to a thigh sheath. "Uh, yeah. Go ahead. That's it, *champion.*"

They'd eat their spiteful words when they found out the truth, Minimus told himself. He flexed both knees and grasped the vine in a two-handed grip that skimmed the sand. Unfamiliar with how deep the roots ran, he prepared for a mighty tug.

And then he was underwater. The writhing vine looped around both his ankles and snaked around one arm, pinning him.

Had Minimus Mu survived a shipwreck in the middle of the Fading Sea to drown in waist-heigh water? He tugged at the vine, attempting to wriggle free, but for all his flexing and squirming, the vine was now around his neck and the other arm.

The tension disappeared in an instant, and he lurched upright again, taking a deep, relieved breath. The other man stood an arm's length away, his unsheathed machete dripping. A few telltale vine fibers clung to the blade where he had sawed through the root to save Minimus. His toothless laugh echoed across the water.

While Minimus was submerged, Ee Clot had waded closer. He held out a sheathed machete. "Here, boy. This might just fit that massive thigh of yours. Want the second and final lesson of wrestle vine farming? Always stand on the ocean side of the root when you pull it up. They're bloody murder when they start wriggling and strangling, but for whatever reason, they don't try to take you unless you're between the root and the shore. And always carry a machete just in case one gets overactive. Here endeth the lesson. Now stop lollygagging and get to work."

Minimus felt heat throb through his sunburnt torso and only half-bit back a shout. "Why didn't you tell me that *before*? I nearly drowned!"

Ee smiled a crooked grin. "Most kids learn better by experience. My words would have run through your head like melted butter down a lobster claw."

Minimus shook his head and turned his back. Arguing wouldn't convince Ee Clot. Two or three days. That's all he'd need to get his full strength back. Then, he could set off and search for Master Thorn.

The vines lost strength after being uprooted. They still coiled themselves around waists and arms but with no real menace. Minimus looped one, then two, then three around himself and hauled them ashore. Jing Jing lay on the angled rock where Minimus had laid their clothes to dry, the fluff of his white belly fur stirring in the sea breeze as he snoozed.

As Minimus sloshed ashore, aiming for the architectural frames where Ee waited for the incoming wrestle vines, a coal rayvn landed on all four of its furry legs atop the boy's drying tunic. It pecked Jing Jing's tiny jacket before grabbing it in one clawed foot and flapping away with it.

Minimus didn't bother to call after the bird. When you only have a few shreds of clothing, no shoes, a notebook, and a bottle of eyeballs as your possessions, losing even one item feels like a big deal. But if their total value is zero, there's no way to sink lower. Jing Jing would just have to live a normal monkey life, jacketless.

* * *

The days became elastic, filled with insignificant events that raised Minimus Mu's boredom to levels he'd never before endured. He declined the offer of a hammock in the worker's huts set back from the beach, and instead slung one beneath Jing Jing's favored clump of trees, sleeping through the warm nights and waking up with the sun for yet another day of wrestle vine harvesting.

Ee Clot traded one of the wagon trains that pulled in for a new pair of oversized sandals, part of the deal for the hardened wrestle vine arches and columns that littered the beach like washed-up antiquities. Minimus accepted them but cast them beneath his hammock. What use were sandals when his only footsteps were across a beach and into the sea? He was hungry, and relished the lobster and kelp dinners, but as four days stretched into a week, even dinner became just another marcher in the parade of boredom.

Each dawn, Minimus considered how he might find Master Thorn, and by each mid-morning, he arrived at the same conclusion. There was no way he could ever find his master again. If the wrestle vine farmers were anything to go by, nobody in Wraithwatch would believe he was the real Minimus Mu, so he couldn't trade on stories of his heroic feats. He was just another hopeless orphan.

Even Jing Jing's enduring optimism eventually failed to rouse any response from Minimus. He'd brush the monkey away with a gentle nudge or a disparaging look. "You should head into the bush. Find some real friends," he'd say, closing his eyes against the monotony.

He'd even resigned himself to cracking open the boiled lobster shells with whatever rock was closest to hand, like his fellow vine farmers. Master Thorn would disown him if he discovered Minimus had fallen in with a crew of barbarians that possessed no cutlery. Not even a lobster cracker, let alone the requisite forks.

It was not until two weeks later that Minimus snapped out of his internal doldrums, when dolphins nudged the puppet theater ashore.

CHAPTER 7 - TEMPLE PANG

The Same Week

The first five days of her captivity had passed with no face appearing in the barred window set high in the door of Rayne's cell. Sun and fresh breezes tinged with the tang of salt freshened the room from a generous window set high in the thick outer wall. Sea birds called in the distance. An occasional scattering of bread crusts, nuts, and dried fruit segments would rattle through the door slot into a waiting trough inside the cell. And twice per day, at times that followed no pattern the young woman could discern, a bubbling stream from the wall spouts would fill the drinking water and rinse out the waste station.

Rayne had tried calling toward the hallway and the outdoors—both to no avail—although she was too short to look properly through either window. She'd jumped and grasped the bars across the door's window once and held on long enough to figure out she was a smidgeon too large to squeeze between them. The room seemed designed for full-sized captives but was not quite lax enough to let a Red Beaner escape.

Rayne imagined the room more like a scholar or priest's chamber than a cell. Its bed was comfortable, including pleasant cotton sheets and a feather-stuffed pillow. The crude desk looked more well-loved than dilapidated, with pens and ink well positioned precisely. A book of poetic verses had been left part-way through transcription by the room's normal occupant, whoever that might be. A cloak hung from a wooden peg bearing the silver feather of Outer Pang centered on its black back. Rayne figured wherever they'd whisked her away after the attack in Mossmarch must still be somewhere within Outer Pang's sphere of influence.

Between spells of crushing boredom, Rayne wrote gushing letters to Minimus Mu that she had no way of sending, drew unaccomplished and blotchy sketches with the quill and ink, and teased away leg stiffness by jumping onto and off the bed.

After four days, a face accompanied the day's food rations. Straight dark hair, cut to shoulder length, framed a face with skin so fair and features so delicate it would have been called beautiful if the eye sockets weren't covered with the same network of scarring Rayne had seen on her abductors. Was it ludicrous that the quizzical arched eyebrows should frame such violence? The visitor said nothing, and Rayne would find it difficult to say that an eyeless face stared at her, yet she felt the weight of its unwanted gaze for nearly a minute before the clack of woven reed shoes sounded the visitor's retreat along the hallway.

On the fifth day, the visitor uttered something to Rayne. With her burnt-away eye sockets again seeming to inspect the Red Bean handmaiden, a voice sounded in Rayne's ears. Face fully in view, she did not see the lips move. The comment came from the doorway, or maybe from somewhere within the cell. "You won't be able to learn the magic. Not like me. You're small and weak. Material for a subjugate, maybe. Not a Sister."

The voice could have been another handmaiden her own age, although it had an unusual lilt and unfamiliar accent. Rayne's head turned to scan every corner of the cell as she slid from the bed to stand upright. She directed her response to the figure at the door.

Although she clutched her hands together to hide the trembling, Rayne's unwavering voice echoed. "Small, yes. Weak, no. You show me what you want me to accomplish, and trust me, I can do it. I'm Rayne, by the way. What's your name?"

Rayne found it disconcerting to hold her gaze upon the eyeless visitor. She could hardly expect any blinking from the scarred sockets, but without eye movements, she imagined the face beyond the bars stared at her with incessant intensity.

"Catriona." Again, the lips did not move. The voice came from everywhere and nowhere. "Why are you so tiny?"

Rayne took two tentative steps, halving the distance to the door. "I'm from the Red Bean Queendom, and quite normal in size, I assure you."

The burnt face swiveled a fraction before returning to face Rayne. That movement canceled the fierceness of the eyeless stare, but it soon built up once again. "My father taught me everything about the eighteen territories. There's no queendom of that name. You need to invent a better fairytale, shorty."

Not wanting to sound accusatory, Rayne replied in kind tones. "It's compact, the Red Bean Queendom. He may have forgotten to mention it. We're right below the Caves of the All-Seeing Eye. On the Jade River, between Meer and Inner and Outer Pang. Have you heard of Evermere? The capital?"

The sneer in the disembodied voice stung Rayne, even though the face remained an expressionless mask. "Evermere is part of the Kingdom of Outer Pang. Everyone knows that. Not sure why you're pushing your lies further, you little wretch."

The face swept away from the window, footsteps echoing along the outer corridor. The voice still sounded like it came from nearby. "Training starts tomorrow. I'll decide quickly that you aren't suitable as a Sister."

* * *

Catriona's tunic rippled around her lithe frame and the cords of her sinewy-strong arms stood out, such was the force of her fist pounding the table. Rayne flinched, while the other two girls who had been abducted from the Mossmarch market screeched and jerked back in their chairs.

The facial muscles may have twitched, but the lips still did not move as Catriona's voice echoed from the stone walls of the unadorned lesson hall across the hallway from Rayne's cell. "I asked a simple question!" she thundered. "I will test you for the potential to use the magic of the Mothers, but like me, you may also maintain any existing powers. So I will ask you one last time. *Do you have any existing magic?*"

The younger girl burst into tears and the older one bit back a screech and clutched the other's hand. Rayne leaned forward. "Look, Catriona. You've frightened them, and like me, they don't understand what you are asking. How could they have magic?"

Catriona poised to pound the table again, this time attempting to reduce it to tindersticks. But as she raised her fist, she paused, cocking her head to one side, as if she'd just noticed an intricate spider web in the rafters, smelled smoke, or heard the ringing of a distant bell, inaudible to others. After a pause, she unclenched her fist and focused again on the three girls.

"Well, that was fortunate timing," she said. "Before I was— um, before I joined the Mothers—I came with my own particular skill. Now, the Mothers' power runs alongside my previous power. And you will have the privilege of seeing it in action. You two crybabies, come to the window. And you! Push a chair over, stumpy-ass, or you won't get a proper view."

Hating that the desire to look through the window outweighed her pride, Rayne scraped her chair across the floor and nestled it between Catriona and the two Mossmarch girls. The younger pair cowered as far from Catriona as possible, while still peeking outside. The wall's stone blocks were thick here; space enough on the sill for both girls to lie flat, side-by-side, if they hadn't been shrinking in fear. Beyond the window, a grassy slope gave way to the rocky sea shore. A path snaked down its length to a quay, its four jetties poking into a sheltered half-moon bay.

In the mid-morning sun, a two-masted sailing ship

approached, sails puffed out in a stiff breeze. Rayne knew at once it was Vennese. The flag of Ven, like the sails of this ship, was a horizontal strip of green sandwiched between two blue stripes. The verdant island queendom prided itself on being an oasis between sea and sky.

Catriona's voice was hushed, a contrast to her rage moments earlier. "It's not like we didn't warn them. We let everyone leave on their ships when we arrived. Told them to warn off anyone else foolish enough to approach us."

She inhaled a sharp breath, casting her senses into the nearby chambers and the exterior of the temple, performing an instinctive scan for anything that might intrude as she summoned her power. She preferred allowing her magical sight and hearing to work like before, limited to the space around her. Vague recollections of normal senses squirmed somewhere deep in her locked-away memories, reminding her of how she used to detect the brightness and colors, the echoes and quiet sounds of her local environment. But like her sisters, she could range those senses to a short distance, viewing scenes behind her, from nearby rooms, or even taking an overhead view. It was like looking through the eyes and hearing through the ears of an observer of a play; that person could watch Catriona's performance, or could peek offstage. The colors altered subtly and indescribably, with grass changing from green to a shade somewhere between blue and the scent of drifting lavender. It was confusing, but something the Mothers of Midnight had grown accustomed to. And when projecting her vision, everything shimmered, especially the silhouettes of those with magical powers. Her hearing was the same; clearly spoken words remained crisp, but sounded like they echoed along a grand hallway. Birdsong took on an extra aspect of distant waves rolling up a beach. It was best to keep those senses local, lest a sister be driven into madness.

Oddly, Catriona felt an extra pull to keep her senses local. This tiny waif who stood up to her like none of the other girls ever had both frustrated and fascinated her. Even though she'd never met anyone so tiny, she felt a kinship with Rayne's courage. The girl would make a fine Mother of Midnight, worthy of the same begrudging praise Mother Justicia occasionally handed her.

Although Catriona's tunic was sleeveless, she ran each hand up the opposite arm, as if pushing up invisible sleeves. "Move back a step, shrimpy. Just in case."

A hum drifted around the room. Catriona spread her fingers and tensed them into claws. The muscles on her forearms rose and indigo hues infused her fair skin, coursing from her hands toward her upper arms. When the dark energy reached her biceps and triceps, a torus-shaped ring of near-black energy formed at each elbow. At first, the rings were translucent, wispy, roiling chaos, but they became more substantial as the background hum reached a crescendo. It felt to Rayne like the magical rings leeched from the air a substance she'd never noticed.

The hum left the room as the rings spun along Catriona's forearms to her now-pointing hands. The left one shot toward the approaching ship a fraction before the right-hand one. They traveled with an accompanying cacophony, like a soldier's metal shield yawing on its rim on a hard stone floor. Circling on themselves as they flew, and dipping only slightly, the blazing circlets carved a path that defied the lazy speed with which they approached the sailboat.

The first magical torus struck and pierced the ship's wooden hull, passing right through without losing speed. It sizzled into the sea beyond the ship, leaving behind a charred circle and a cross-sectional core of the ship that hung in the air for a moment before dropping inside the obliterated section of hull. By the time the second circlet struck nearer the aft, the vessel was already folding in upon itself and dipping below the waterline. As the faint crack of timber reached their ears, they saw the remaining crew leap into the water, like ants abandoning a flooded anthill.

The tingle of the unknown fizzed deep inside Rayne's consciousness, the cocktail of wonderment and fear she felt bringing her to full alert. This girl brimmed with magic as powerful as any animal! Catriona expelled an exasperated breath through her nose before turning away from the scene below to face Rayne and the other two girls.

"So. Can you do anything like that?"

CHAPTER 8 - WRAITHWATCH

Four Days Later

As first light crept into the sky above Wrestle Vine Beach, it met Minimus Mu's already-open eyes. When the sun peeked above the horizon and Jing Jing yawned in a nexus of palm leaves above the low-slung hammock, Minimus still lay inside its cocoon, summoning the willpower to get up. But what was the point? Conversation with his fellow vine farmers involved him trying to explain his history and plight, and them mocking him. In Inner or Outer Pang or the Red Bean Queendom, they'd recognize him at once and either celebrate or demonize him, depending on the audience. Here he was but an exceptionally strong worker of uncertain heritage.

He drew Master Thorn's journal from his tunic's inner breast pocket. It was the one item of interest in his current world. Less journal, more sketchbook. The pages near the front held illustrations of a baby Minimus, drawn with Master Thorn's typical economy of line. There were several sketches of a powerful-looking woman, one in which she lifted a massive boulder overhead. The later pages showed Minimus as he grew, a few drawings of Jing Jing, and annotated specifications for elegant cutlery.

With eventual reluctance, he eased himself into a sitting position. The slender rope mesh of the hammock stamped diamond shapes into the flesh at the back of his legs. After a lethargic shake to expel yesterday's sand remnants from his tunic to make way for today's, Minimus rose. He spared a glance for his unworn sandals, as he did every morning, then bent double to retrieve the machete he'd let slip onto the beach the previous night. He might as well work, even though the rest of the crew would likely nurse heads fogged by fermented coconut milk for another hour or two before blinking bleary eyes in the hut doorway.

Although he'd given up on reuniting with Master Thorn, a thought came unbidden to his mind. His new job description. Master Thorn would probably call it *de-vine intervention*. He smiled a fraction inside, but felt no twitch of lips on his stony face.

As usual, he had a message for Jing Jing who descended the tree in lethargic jerks. "You should go, Jing Jing. There's nothing here for you. Nothing to steal, even, unless you want one of my sandals."

The monkey held his only remaining possession coiled in his tail's grasp. Now that the cheeky coal rayvn had pinched his jacket, he carried the jar of fanglimb eyeballs wherever he went.

Shuffle, shuffle, wade. Yank, yank, yank. Wade, shuffle. Minimus dragged the first round of vines ashore, coiling the fresh material around a waiting archway frame. With no sign of Ee Clot, Minimus didn't want to leave the vines hardening in a clump, so he did the farmer's job, too. Ee was smarter than the other vine farmers by a good margin, but still nowhere near a match for Minimus and would be a flickering candle to Master Thorn's bonfire. The boy placed Ee somewhere on the wisdom scale between Jing Jing and driftwood.

He felt his own mind edging toward driftwood state. There was nothing here inspiring enough to engage him. He turned and waded into the lapping waves of the vine crop.

It was unusual enough to make him pause and sheath the machete when three dolphins wriggled across the barely submerged patch of piled sand and entered the calmer inner waters. He'd seen dolphins cresting in the deeper water beyond the sand bar many times, but never in the shallows. Two moved in tandem, balancing a significant piece of flotsam on their snouts. A third followed close behind, towing a woven reed sac, its drawstring encircling the dolphin's body and prevented from slipping off by the proud dorsal fin.

The first two nudged their cargo ashore, urging it forward while they wriggled across the sand on their bellies. This was behavior Minimus would expect from a seal, but dolphins? The third one shimmied backwards to tease the bag's drawstring into its sharp-toothed jaws before flinging it to the beach with a violent flick of its snout.

Minimus would have returned to his work, leaving Jing Jing to investigate the newly arrived detritus, but a coal rayvn swooped low in a series of passes. It wouldn't cease until Minimus stopped swiping at it and trudged toward shore.

He saw the familiar shape on the shore as he approached, but it took several strides more before it registered. It was the puppet theater that Master Thorn would drag to the back of the cutlery cart each morning, the scene of countless educational, entertaining, and often downright bizarre puppet shows. Jing Jing was already working at loosening the tie on the reed sac, which Minimus knew would contain the felt puppets and gossamer-stringed marionettes that comprised Master Thorn's official cast of characters.

This was a sign. Of what, Minimus was unsure. The boy turned back to the sea and scanned the horizon and saw nothing beyond the dolphins leaping away into the vast expanse of rolling waves. It had to be a sign, didn't it? Could Master Thorn summon the important bits of his beloved cutlery cart from the murky depths? Minimus looked at the mountainous spine of the Wraithwatch-Astella border and saw no change there, either. Just the ring of wraithfire squirming above the jagged peaks.

* * *

Neither Master Thorn nor Ezra Longshanks were used to traveling significant distances on horseback. The animals bore their weight, yet it was the two men's backs that ached after each day's riding.

Skain Two-Hearts had led them away from the Temple of the Wraith which remained crowned in its stubborn rainbow ring, his men following a respectful few horselengths behind in a compact line. The three-day ride to Pearl Wash mostly involved the horses descending with precision along the winding path down to the Astellan plains. Ezra pointed out several times that, with the right wind, the trip would take only a couple of hours by balloon.

"Yes," Master Thorn began. "But then that infernal racket from the bellows would prevent me from telling you the story of how the Lion of Og was defeated using nothing more than a belt and a bellyful of courage."

"You've already recited that story," Ezra replied. "Twice!"

Master Thorn nodded, and a smile cracked his pursed lips. "Indeed I have. But the story is so entertaining, you must hear it at least thrice before you can appreciate its finer details. Plus, Skain here has *never* heard it. I only wish Minimus was here with us so I could show everyone the belt in question."

Master Thorn grew silent, and Ezra hoped the tale of the Lion of Og could wait for another day. But after the horses twisted their way onto the next switchback, the story began in earnest. He followed the first story with a description of the great goat assembly of Inner Pang in year eighty-nine, and a wistful tale of Master Thorn's long-lost love.

"It's funny," Master Thorn said, cocking his head in Skain Two-Hearts's direction. "She said there were several people with magic in her village. And when we traveled there, to Sorrow's Reach—which I'd never heard of, even though I'd often traversed the northern shores of Outer Pang—there was no sign that there'd ever been a settlement around that cove. I believed her, even after we couldn't find her village on the shores of the inlet she recognized on sight, but she said many things that lacked proof."

Skain gazed in appraisal at Master Thorn. "I know Sorrow's Reach. Were you able to see the island of Temple Pang from that inlet?"

"Uh … yeah," Master Thorn replied. "But there was no village there. The cart path skirted around the inlet and carried on. Maybe it's just a map-maker's error that you've both seen somewhere, although Lord of the Lilies knows where she could've laid eyes on a map."

Ezra huffed. He specialized in cartography. "Map-maker's error? I'm sure no map-maker could mistake barren coastline for a village."

Master Thorn realized he'd uttered an inadvertent snub about Ezra's chief mission, to map the nineteen queendoms from the air. He leaned over in his saddle to pat the wild-haired man on his shoulder. "I meant nothing by it, friend. There's probably another explanation."

Ezra settled into his saddle, his shoulders loosening at Master Thorn's apology. "And what happened to her? Your lady?"

"To Ma—to my love? That's a story for another day. A day when Minimus is here. I met her before Minimus came to me. He needs to hear it."

Ezra shook his head in mock surprise. "So, you'll repeat the tale about the Lion of Og three times, but you won't even tell this story once?"

Skain's powerful baritone answered. "You'd better watch it, or there might be a fourth retelling. But if a story of loss is your desire, I'll tell you why I need to eradicate the Mothers of Midnight."

Master Thorn didn't look up from his saddle pommel, but Ezra perked up at the hint of more information about the Order of Magical Preservation—or, as Master Thorn now called them, *the Omps*. "You already explained why your forces stormed the Temple of the Wraith. It's to stop the Mothers from wiping out your magical powers."

"Ahh," Skain said. "That's why *we* need to vanquish them.

I'm going to tell you why *I* lead them. I told you how the Mothers of Midnight grow their ranks—by snatching away young girls and enslaving them. Forced into indoctrinated service and mutilated. It's a joke that they view magic as a force for evil, and yet they themselves practice it constantly! Anyway, let me leave my ranting aside for a moment. The reason I rallied this force, I admit, is for one real purpose only. Revenge! They snatched my daughter from Pearl Wash three years past. She was just edging toward womanhood, and now I may never see her again. They either discarded her because she wouldn't conform, or they've manipulated her into becoming one of *them.*"

Ezra replied in solemn tones. "Myself, I'm childless, so I have only an inkling of your anguish. But how could the Mothers have dragged her away from someone with powerful magic like yours?"

"Even if I had been there in the streets when they snatched her, I probably couldn't have done anything. One of their key powers is they can transport themselves in an instant," Skain snapped his fingers, "to their temple. And if they are holding a girl's wrist, they'll also whisk her away. It's why we confront them within their own temple. But even then…"

Without looking up, Master Thorn posed a question. "If they can only flit themselves *to* the Temple of the Wraith, but not *away* from it, why weren't they within the walls when you arrived? I mean, we saw the monks, and I don't know where they disappeared to, but by your description the temple should have been swarming with these so-called Mothers of Midnight."

Skain sounded defeated when he replied. "There is another place to which they can transport themselves, it seems. Temple Pang. We dispatched a second force there, to attack at the same time. They must have met the full fury of the combined populations of Mothers. We can only wait for them to send a message, hopefully of their success. We've tried twice before, bringing our best magicians, but the Mothers always drain away our magical abilities before we can do them much harm. It's only by the grace of the Dinner God that I keep my powers after the other missions. Many were killed and almost all lost their magic. So, this time, we came with arms, not only charms. And I scouted the situation here, alone, just last week. All was ready."

"Maybe they took the bald priests, too," Master Thorn grumbled.

Skain guided his horse around a crook in the path and the other horses followed. "Look—we're on the last switchback before we hit the flat road. We can make Pearl Wash by nightfall if we're quick about it. We'll consult the Finder. Your apprentice, my daughter, the Mothers of Midnight—let's hope she can find *something.*"

* * *

The fine sandstone buildings of Pearl Wash caressed the shores of a broad but calm lake. Master Thorn noted the fine arch work, wondering at the number of artisans needed to embellish the blocky construction. As Skain led his fighting force and the two older men through its gates, the townspeople waved friendly hands, many eyes betraying unspoken questions on their lips. Skain ignored this and waved his men into a walled stable while he carried on with Master Thorn and Ezra through the laconic flow of market traffic.

The market crowd included blond-haired northerners and the darker-skinned locals of southern Astella. A pair of young men scraped their stall across the hardened earth to allow the newcomers' three horses extra room to tether alongside a stone cottage with jutting thatched eaves.

As they tied their mounts and Skain motioned to the stallholders for water to be brought to the drinking trough, the hut's door opened and a round, amber-hued face with springs of brilliant gray hair appeared. "Gracious, Skain," the woman said, vowels long and languorous. "I was expecting to see you either with a smile wider than an oxen's yoke or in a vision of death from the temple gates. Yet here you are, and neither is

65

true."

Skain shook his head with vigor, mail jangling and leather creaking. "They weren't there. Not a single one! I discovered only these two, so obviously I need a new Finding."

Master Thorn slid alongside Skain. "Excuse Master Skain's haste, m'lady. He surely meant to offer a proper introduction. I am Master Thorn, cutlery merchant of Inner Pang, and this is my travel companion, Ezra Longshanks. He's ... er ... a scientist, I guess. Or maybe a balloonist? What exactly *are* you, Ezra?"

The woman chuckled as Ezra answered. "You know full well, I'm a royal cartographer. Map-maker, if you must. Formerly for Outer Pang and now for whoever may require my maps."

"Yes, yes," Skain added, exhaling sharply. "And gentlemen, this is the Finder I told you about."

Tutting, the woman held the door open. "I'd prefer to be a person, not a thing, so you young men can call me Bonchanta. Much more pleasant."

Master Thorn gave a slight bow, acknowledging someone with good manners and flattered to be called young.

Inside the dim interior, only the lowest beams of sunlight angled below the eaves. Skain pulled a chair, smoothed from years of use, to a simple wooden table, stained from countless meals and indented with the characterful impact marks of past misadventures. He motioned Bonchanta to a more elegant chair opposite, but she bustled away into a second room.

"I know you are in a hurry, dear, but it's not a proper Finding without a preparatory mug of tea. Surely you missed my brews on the long road into the mountains, Skain? I've got vixenroot tea steeping and won't be but a moment."

Skain huffed but remained silent, sliding two similar chairs to the table and motioning for Master Thorn and Ezra to seat themselves.

Bonchanta returned with a steaming ceramic mug for each of them. The tea tray also held a squat silver jam jar. It brimmed with sugarsap, a utensil rattling on the tray alongside.

Master Thorn snatched the implement up and held it in front of his face. "My word, look at this! Masterful filagree work! If this isn't a Hammarskald sap dripper, I'm a clonkey."

Ezra interjected. "That's half-clown, half-donkey, in case you were wondering."

Bonchanta smiled at the old man's enthusiasm. "Indeed, it is. I managed to Find a Hammarskalder merchant's daughter who'd become disoriented in the forest just beyond our walls. He left this in addition to my fee as a special token of thanks."

Master Thorn felt memory strings being tugged. He, too, had sent tokens of thanks to each of the wanderers they'd met on their journeys who'd provided key advice in driving Minimus Mu's success in the trials of the All-Seeing Eye. Knife-thrower Sala Doon received the most obvious gift—a set of razor sharp and precisely balanced throwing knives, lined up in a pair of bracers. He could imagine Sala's forearms bristling with their splendor. For Mirko Leatherfoot, he had fashioned a small device that could be strapped beneath a baggy sleeve. It was a tube with an extensible grasping pincer that could perform a surreptitious theft with a simple flex of one wrist. And for the beastmaster, Vik Gaard, he'd sent a segmented feeding trough that could accommodate many of his fabulous animals in a single seating. He hoped that the Red Bean courier wagon had located Vik's traveling menagerie by now and delivered the gift. His fourth gift was back at the Temple of the Wraith. Ezra's new anchor winder, strapped to the balloon basket, had survived the crash landing without a scratch.

Bonchanta twirled the sap dripper, added a dollop of the clear, viscous liquid to her mug, and inhaled the steam, clutching the vessel in both hands. "Very well, Skain. I'm ready. Pass me your hands and think about the person you want me to search for."

Skain closed his eyes and allowed hands, calloused by continual riding and years of swordplay, to be enveloped in the Finder's pliant grip. Bonchanta closed her eyes and Skain followed her lead. She hummed quietly and her head turned occasionally, as if she was peering around the room despite her fluttering but mostly closed eyelids.

Her voice was dreamier and less forceful than it had been in normal conversation. "Weird," she said, her eyes still closed. "Those Mothers of Midnight you had me Find before, the ones you'd directly encountered—I spotted them easily. But now they're … distant. No, not distant. It's like they're only partly there. I've Found recently dead people before, and they feel faded. It's not exactly the same, but it's like I can see *through* them."

Skain's gruff voice interjected. "Mildly interesting, but not immensely helpful. Where are they, exactly?"

"Well, they're not in the Temple of the Wraith, but I guess you already knew that. They're in that other temple—what's it called?"

"Temple Pang," Skain said. He relinquished Bonchanta's hands. "Makes sense," he said. "My squire suggested they'd whisked themselves over there, to the west."

Bonchanta held out her hands, beckoning Skain to hold them once more. "Wait, child. You know you always ask me to find your daughter? I saw something just then, at the end."

Skain's hands shot forward to rest in Bonchanta's palms again. "I don't dare believe it," he said. "Find her, I beg you."

Bonchanta hummed some more, craning her neck as she peered into a corner of the room. "I can't see her directly, but *they* can. She's with them at the temple. Along with some other, smaller girls."

"Any sign of our forces? Maybe they've freed her already!"

Bonchanta shook her curls. "All seems calm. I see the Mothers, although they're wispy in my mind. It doesn't seem like they're under threat."

Skain released himself from her grip, hammering the table with a fist. "Blast! Your first Finding of her in years, and now she's a continent away and our attack there has failed. I'll find passage across the Fading Sea. I could be there in a month."

"Let's not be hasty, my friend," Bonchanta cautioned. "For once, I'm not confident of the Finding. Because they appear so *thin*, so *transparent*, maybe they've moved on somewhere else. Or possibly, they are but ghosts of the recently living. Somewhere I cannot Find. Could be an echo left behind at Temple Pang."

"I hear you, and thank you for being a friend," Skain replied. "Let me rest my road-weary bones and we can try again tomorrow. I believe Master Thorn would also like to request your help."

Master Thorn leaned in, offering his wrinkled hands. "I was in a shipwreck and lost my boy, my apprentice. Could we try to Find him, too?"

Bonchanta smiled and nodded, her eyes crinkling at the corners. "It would be my pleasure. Close your eyes and picture the lad. Use your strongest memories of him."

They clasped hands, and Bonchanta exhaled sharply through her nose. Her head swung, eyes clamped shut, like she was following the erratic path of a crazed wasp trying to find an exit from the hut. Master Thorn smiled at his pride when Minimus Mu conquered the fifth trial and saved the Red Bean Queendom. He remembered the buttery smell of the boy's sweaty scalp when the infant Minimus had perched on the cart at markets across Inner Pang.

Bonchanta dropped Master Thorn's hands as if they scalded her, and his knuckles rapped against the table. Alarmed confusion tinged her voice. "Where did *you* come from? I always start by Finding the person searching and then Finding the distant, missing one. But I can barely detect you, and I know you're here in the room with me."

Master Thorn's brow furrowed. "Inner and Outer Pang, mostly. Does your gift not work on people from the other continent?"

"No, no—it works even *better* sometimes. But you're, well, different. It's almost like you're missing. All I see is a coin flipped on a white tablecloth. I've only had trouble Finding someone whose hands I've held one other time, and for him, I Found him twice rather than not at all, which made sense once I knew he could see past, future, and other twisty paths.

He told me this would happen! You need to visit him. Yes, you must visit the Backwards Man."

CHAPTER 9 - TEMPLE PANG

Twelve Days Later

Catriona had felt taller, drawn to her full height when she blasted the intruders from their ship. Now she could have sworn she measured a smidgeon smaller, and it showed.

Splinters flew from the end of her rod as she swung it in a vicious arc to slam between Rayne's tiny feet on the floor of the training room. Spittle flew from her mouth onto the smaller girl's face as she bent double to shout only a handspan away from that delicate nose that looked like it needed rearranging.

"If you don't obey every last command, you will fail the training. If you don't show full aptitude in the sisterhood's magic, you will also fail. And gods of the mountains and the deep help me if you have existing magic that you have not informed me about, because I will tear you limb from tiny limb and blast your worthless body into the waters below if I find any deception. You will fail. I want you to fail. And I cannot believe you will do anything but fail. Do you understand?"

Rayne nodded, but did not flinch from Catriona's rage. She refused even to wipe away the spittle that sullied her face. If the taller girl had possessed eyes instead of burnt away sockets, Rayne would have held them steady in her gaze.

"Tell me what you want, what I need to do, and I'll do it," Rayne replied. This seemed like the best—maybe only—way to bide time until she could escape. Her rescuers could even now slink toward the temple's walls.

Catriona felt the fanning of an even taller flame within her. What *did* she want? It was true she wanted to lash out and drain every person she encountered of their magic, like every other woman and girl in her order. But there was something else. She craved memories. Was her early life so bad that she'd blotted out everything before the Temple of the Wraith? And the same for her sisters, who also remembered nothing before their temple existence? She wanted the surging fountain of awareness that came from her augmented sight and hearing to fade. Although she wouldn't admit it, even to herself, she wanted Rayne to look her in the eyes. Her real eyes.

An excellent alternative to fulfilling her desires was to deny others. And before her stood a toy that she could rattle and hopefully break.

She cracked the rod on the floor a second time. "You're brave enough to be a sister. I'll grant you that much," she whispered into Rayne's ear. "But this next part is going to hurt, and there's nobody here to save you except me—and that's a sorry state of affairs. On your knees, child."

Rayne obeyed, dropping silently to the flagstone floor. Although her tormentor appeared no older than her, now was not the time to take exception to being called a child.

Catriona bent lower to continue her threatening whisper. "One last time: have you any existing powers?"

Rayne shook her head. "No, sister. In the Red Bean Queendom, nobody has magic. Only the animals, like I said."

Catriona expelled a ragged breath that spoke volumes of her disdain for Rayne's answer and fished a jagged oval piece of coral from her robes. It hung from a woven strap. "Silence, then, you wretch. Listen! Mother Justicia has infused this amulet with the power to adjudge girls like you for suitability to the order. She tested me herself, back at the Temple of the Wraith, and now I will test you."

She dangled the coral before Rayne's face. "Hold out your palm, girl. When I tell you to, form a fist around the amulet.

Squeeze it as tight as you can—there will be blood. Clench your eyes shut and decide if you want to live or die. The rest is up to you and the power of the amulet."

Rayne's hand shook as she accepted the piece of coral. It was large enough that it poked beyond the sides of her hand. She closed her eyes and thought of everyone who loved her. Minimus Mu, Princess Tasha, and her parents Queen Violet and Lord Alfred of Evermere, even Master Thorn and Jing Jing.

"Not yet," whispered Catriona. "I want to watch."

Rayne felt Catriona's fingertips part her hair, sliding back to clutch her scalp at eight points while her thumbs came to rest over each eyelid.

"Now!"

Rayne did as she was told. The jagged edges of the coral scored her palm and the ooze of blood traced paths over the back of her hand and across her wrist. It hurt, but that sensation was secondary; it was what happened *inside* her body that tore a scream from Rayne's throat. Icy shards of pain coursed through the veins and arteries of her right arm, wriggling as if alive and swimming toward her heart. An icy wind blew through her chest, as if a dead sailor's hand rose from the ocean's depths to push her organs aside, questing for her very essence.

She let her agony flow through her voice, but inside she imagined Minimus in the fifth Cave of the All-Seeing Eye, the trial of endurance. He'd had to outlast his oxygen supply in the underground stream. Rayne could pretend to be Minimus for a few moments longer, allowing the poison of the coral amulet to run its course, with the side benefit of proving Catriona wrong.

Rayne tried to imagine what Minimus was doing at that very moment. Probably swinging in his hammock as the waves of the Fading Sea jostled his full belly. Jing Jing would be curled up in the crook of an arm or a leg, and Master Thorn would conduct an impromptu afternoon puppet show. A felt-clothed puppet of obscure provenance bobbed in the foreground of

Rayne's imagination. It spoke in a high-pitched voice, Master Thorn's falsetto. "And then, the Red Bean handmaiden brought the magic close to her heart, but not inside it. Much as a skilled cutlerer may smelt an inferior knife into a set of fine cutlery, she twisted the magic from a dagger into a shield."

Catriona's fingertips pressed against Rayne's eyes and scalp, pushing her backward onto the flagstones. "Ugh. I don't believe it!" Catriona spat.

Rayne lay gasping on the floor, the coral amulet cast aside and her palm bloodied. The waves of pain receded.

Catriona expelled a long, grumbling breath. "Get to your bed, now! Take a good look in the mirror and try to remember. You'll get your eyes, ears, and voice over the next three days, Sister Rayne. And say goodbye to your memories, stumpy!"

Snatching the amulet from the floor, Catriona stomped away. Mother Justicia would want the amulet and a report. Like every sister, Catriona knew not where she'd come from, but considered the Temple of the Wraith home. Why'd they have to use the lodestone to move themselves here to this accursed seaside pile?

CHAPTER 10 - MOSSMARCH

The Same Day

Virgil Longspeaker, like most of Mossmarch, had been quieter than normal. "Have ye noticed how quiet the market's been, especially since the second time those black-hooded shrews showed up and snatched more girls?"

Apostle Dando nodded, but replied, "No, I hadn't noticed."

Sala Doon sat with them, in the shadow of the Crossed Swords, nursing a pot of ale. A few of the market stalls remained shuttered, the more timid vendors doubtless cowering elsewhere lest a third incident ravage the square. "You know, Dando, I liked it better before you got de-quilled—or anti-quilled, or whatever happened when that hag grabbed you. Sometimes I still think you're telling the truth, instead of your tongue always twisting into lies. When did you say your order is sending a replacement quill to jab you again?"

Dando replied without hesitation. "They're not coming anymore." Then he stifled a cry of anguish and slapped his own face. "I mean, eighty-seven days."

He rolled his eyes and lowered his forehead to bang against the table. Virgil patted him on the back absentmindedly, replying to Sala on his behalf. "I think a week. But who knows what'll happen then? Maybe it'll neutralize the lying and he'll slope into that happy state of *occasional* liar, like you and me."

Virgil drank deeply from his ale, slapping the empty pot to

the table in the vain hope that a serving girl would emerge from the tavern with a refill. "We've got to do *something*, Sala. We can't sit sipping ale all day, every day, hoping Rayne will saunter back. Well, I guess we could. But who wants to pay a minstrel with this gloom hanging over the city? I'll be out of goat's teeth sooner than I'd like, and Princess Tasha isn't due back for a fortnight, so I can't beg any favors there."

Sala motioned for his two friends to lean closer, and he lowered his voice. "Funny you should mention doing something. Remember that eleven-pointed star? The pendant that my blade sliced from Rayne's attacker's neck? After I flogged it behind the port warehouses, I heard it found its way to the former queen's residence, and now it's enhancing the magic of every animal in Jada's menagerie. Have you noticed the birds clustering on the keep's roof? They're attracted to it. Infused with ancient magic, they say. Plus, she's away, Jada. In Ven, visiting her cousin, Queen Veronica, apparently. Well, Mirko and I—"

Virgil chuckled. "Aren't you two in enough disrepute already? Are you telling me you're going to steal the thing from Jada's keep? Or are you proposing something more legal?"

Sala looked at each of his compatriots. "Do I look like a prefect of the queen's guard? I leave figuring out what's legal to the experts. In the meantime, we could use your skills. If it's as magical as they say, I figure the artifact may hold clues to Rayne's whereabouts. Want to get off your sorry asses and meet me at sunset?"

Dando replied with enthusiasm. "I'm *definitely* not going," he said, nodding vehemently. "In the order, they would *never* teach us breaking and entering as a life skill. I'd *hate* to sharpen my skills with experts like you two."

Virgil scowled, then smiled. "Well, if an upstanding truthsayer is down to help, how could a roguish yet handsome lutist and part-time hero of the Red Bean Queendom say no?"

* * *

On the quiet side of Jada's tower, at the rendezvous point, Sala, accompanied by Mirko Leatherfoot, crept up behind Virgil so silently that the minstrel let out a muted girlish scream as the knife-thrower tugged on his kilt.

"Keep it down, ya big Jessie," whispered Mirko. "Good thing we're not close enough to alert Jada's guards."

They slunk together to a clump of anjberry bushes at the foot of the slender keep that housed the former Queen of Outer Pang. Sala selected a blade from the knives arrayed along the bracer covering his left forearm. "See this one? Master Thorn gifted it to me for providing moral guidance to Minimus before he went into the trials."

Virgil thought the term 'moral guidance' was a little strong for advice from a scoundrel like Sala but held his tongue.

"It has winged side blades that spring out on impact. Perfect for embedding the knife firmly into wood or for reducing amusement in one's enemies, depending on the situation. Here's the plan. I'm going to loop a strand of spidersilk through the handy ring in the knife's base, like this. I'll use that to hoist up a proper length of rope after I embed the blade into that window frame at the top of the keep."

Virgil craned his neck and squinted at the window, impossibly high above them near the keep's conical tower. Only a fraction of the frame was visible, inset in the thick stone of the keep's smooth walls. "You can't hit … I mean, it's high, like … are you sure? Okay, I'll shut up now."

Dando elbowed Virgil and whispered, "Yeah, Sala Doon *definitely* can't make that throw."

Virgil glanced sidelong at the robed apostle and wagged a finger at him. "Dando! You made a funny. There's a first time for everything. Maybe you can return to your order and instruct the new apostles in the fine art of comedy."

The plan was for Dando to steady the rope while Sala and Mirko climbed. He could whistle if any unexpected visitors showed up on this side of the tower. Virgil's task was to do what he did best: entertain the guards and any onlookers until the caper was complete and the two thieves plucked anjberries once more. Virgil adjusted his kilt, tuned the high string of his lute, and strode to the opposite side of the tower, heading for the main entranceway.

With furtive glances to ensure no onlookers, Sala did what Sala did best. He slung his arm back, so the tip of Master Thorn's spring-loaded dagger touched his shoulder blade, and spun it with speed, up and away. It embedded itself in the high window frame's upper beam with a satisfying clunk.

Mirko played out the spidersilk and the slender rope jerked upward, through the dagger's loop, threading until both ends of the rope rested on the ground. Sala tugged hard on the two strands, checking the dagger's grip and that the wooden frame would hold under the strain.

Sala spoke to Mirko in hushed tones. "Let me go first, since I'm lighter. Once I'm through the window, you follow. Not saying you're fat or anything, but you might want to cut down on Balaak's fried fish."

Mirko punched Sala's shoulder with a touch more force than playfulness required. "Get your bony ass up there, Doon. That way, you'll already be at the top of the tower when I'm ready to throw you off."

Dando slunk from the bushes to steady the rope, but Mirko waved him away. "I'll hold for now. Save your strength for holding while I climb. Those noodle arms don't look like they'll hold out for long."

Sala crawled through the window with practiced ease, his wiry legs springing off the keep wall so a dandruff of loosened lichens fell around the bush. Mirko relinquished the rope loop to Dando and assessed him from boots to cloak hood. He must have found at least partial satisfaction, for he threaded the rope around his legs before cinching his way up with more power but less grace than Sala.

From around the keep's curve came muted laughter, a smatter of clapping, and a few cheers before Dando heard the opening notes of "The Ballad of Minimus Mu". Virgil worked his charm on the townsfolk, but Dando expected trouble from any of the keep's guardsmen when the song reached certain sensitive verses. He returned to the bushes and listened.

At the top level of the tower, Sala greeted Mirko with a finger to his lips. He motioned for his cloaked, brooding companion to flatten himself against the inner wall of the corridor that hugged the upper keep's circumference. Hard-soled boots stomped up the stairway.

From beneath his forearm, Sala pulled a micro-blade. Light, sharp, and without a handle, this was a tool for close-range, precision work. As the footfalls grew louder, Sala thought to himself, *I wonder where they get these third-rate guardsmen? What's the point in patrolling if you alert intruders to your presence from three flights of stairs away?*

As the figure wheezed its way to the second-last of the spiral steps, Sala spotted their left hip. Perfect. Leather belt. Scabbarded sword. Mailed sleeve. With a deft flick of his wrist, the tiny blade caught a hint of moonbeam as it flashed past the window. He glanced at Mirko and mugged a silent laugh as the blade sliced the guard's belt in half and the sword clattered to the steps. From the sound, it must have cartwheeled at least ten times before reverting to a series of metallic clankings a few stories below.

The guard uttered a few unimaginative curses, turned with a huff, and plodded after his renegade blade.

Mirko knelt before the door at the opposite end of the corridor. A ring with a set of slender L-shaped shims flashed in his hand as he felt for the perfect combination to turn the lock. It was a matter of seconds before the bolt slid free. Sala stole in front of his friend, drew a dagger in silence from his thigh sheath, and depressed the thumb plate of the latch. Well-oiled, the movement made only the faintest scratching sound. Blade raised, Mirko swept the door open. That was when he nearly lost both the blade and the hand holding it.

Onrushing jaws with teeth as long as Sala's most lethal dagger snapped on nothing but air as Sala snatched back his hand. At the same time, he sprang high, adding a half-twist to his front flip, landing behind the tiger. Tiger!

He'd seen former queen Jada's collection of tigers before,

in one of the monthly exotic beast shows she conducted during her truncated reign. This was trouble of a magnitude he'd not expected. The beast's bulk, and the silver stripes that threaded between its black and amber coloring, marked it as a *reflecting* tiger. With paws the size of dinner plates and teeth that could rip the leg off a vondabeast, the reflecting tiger needed no magical powers to overcome its prey. But it had powerful defensive magic. Any attack directed its way would reflect and affect its assailant. You could easily sever your own arm by taking a sword to this stripy peril.

And it roamed unchained! How could Jada have entered the room without being torn to shreds herself? Mirko knew the answer to that. He shouted to Sala, "There's a code word, remember? The trainer could make it crouch and remain still on command. What was it?"

The reflecting tiger twisted, its sinewy body reorienting itself on Sala, who zig-zagged to the far side of the room, somersaulting over a wide bed in the process. "Eat *him*!" the blade-thrower called to the tiger. "He's got more meat on him!"

"Pineapple!" Mirko shouted. "No, wait, that wasn't it."

Sala tried to figure out a method of restraining the beast without attacking it directly. It wore a collar, but neither he nor Mirko had the strength to wrestle the creature. As the tiger advanced across the bed, Sala flicked the fringe of the white silk sheet, covering the tiger's face. By the time he'd bounded away, squeezing between a vanity unit and the wall, the tiger had thrown off that temporary distraction.

"Banana!" Mirko cried in triumph. "That was it! Banana!"

The tiger's head whipped round toward this source of shouting and pounced on Mirko.

"There were six tigers in the show, you oaf!" Sala called. "Banana only worked on one of them. What about the other five training words?"

Mirko stumbled against the door, closing it behind him and causing a secondary lock to fall into place with a thud, signaling almost certain doom for the pair. A thick black metal plate dropped into grooves in the doorframe on either side. There was now no escape route other than throwing themselves from the bedchamber's window or examining the new lock while a reflecting tiger disemboweled them. This would not end well.

The reflecting tiger's longest claw sank into Mirko's left boot as he fell, pinning it to the floor. Luckily for the thief, the claw parted his big toe and second toe, skewering neither. He shook free of the boot and ducked as another paw swiped, grazing his flying hair. He fell flat on his back on the rug-strewn floor.

Mirko scrambled away on the heels of his hands, one jerking foot booted, the other bare. The tiger's jaws opened wide.

Then they closed a fraction. Sala took two light-footed steps across the tiger's back and leapt away as the beast snapped in his direction. Mirko toppled a side table to put a token barrier between himself and the beast. Something was different. Had Sala handicapped the tiger as he sped across the thing's back?

To be precise, two things were different. Mirko noticed that Sala's trousers were drooping loose, halfway down his thighs. That was what would happen if you removed your belt and threaded it underneath a reflecting tiger's collar as you passed.

Sala rolled from the bed, spinning upright with one of Master Thorn's spring-loaded daggers in each hand. His trousers dropped to his ankles, exposing wiry calves. "Get it close to one of the wall beams," he shouted.

Although he would recite the tale later with more heroic-sounding detail, the truth of the matter was that Mirko kicked the fallen side table toward the tiger, scuttled behind a free-standing upright oval mirror with a sound akin to a small frightened puppy, and ultimately tripped backward over a heavy wooden chair. The tiger reared onto its hind legs to make the killing strike and … hung there, snarling, paws thrashing at air. A vibrating dagger pinned each end of Sala's belt to a thick wooden pillar. Looped around the reflecting tiger's collar, the creature could do nothing but stand on its hind legs and rotate from side to side, swiping in frustration. It gnashed its teeth but went slack after a few moments, sending accusatory bulgyeyed stares at the two interlopers.

Sala bunched the front of his trousers in one hand and hiked them up. "See a spare belt anywhere, my good man?" he asked.

"Not sure Jada's waist is the same size as yours, mate," Mirko replied. He half-turned from his fallen position beyond the toppled chair, massaging his buttock, before picking up something from the floor beneath himself. "Found the eleven-pointed star, though!"

The muffled sound of boots ascending stone stairs reached the room. Mirko whipped out his picks again and set to furious work on the inner lock. He had it open as quickly as Sala's annoying oversight would allow. The footsteps grew louder.

"Outta here, man," Sala whispered. They fled for the window and the rope to safety.

* * *

Below, Virgil's ballad progressed like Dando had imagined. There was laughter as the singer poked fun at the naïve truthsayer who he'd met when Minimus Mu embarked on the first trial. There were *oohs* and *aahs* as the verses describing the trials progressed. And sure enough, there was a stampede of footsteps fleeing the scene of the supposedly light entertainment as Virgil reached the acid barbs describing Queen Jada's dethroning.

It was right after the line, *With all the fuss, oh, her sour-faced puss, finally shut its foul trap, like it took a carp's slap,* that a gruff and threatening voice spelled out the end of the performance.

"Get off, ye maggot! Don't cheapen our queen with your alehouse slanders."

The insult preceded the sound of Virgil's kilted backside striking the pavement, a sound Dando recognized from many late nights as closing time arrived at the Crossed Swords.

What was less expected was the powerful hand that seized Dando's cloak at the back of the neck, hoisting him from the bushes.

"And what might you be doing here, skulking in the bushes behind her majesty's quarters, might I ask? With a rope and all, looking up the tower?"

The hand spun Dando in a slow semi-circle, his feet still dangling inches from the dirt. A thug confronted him, face half-concealed beneath a beard that would require either intense patience or a machete to untangle, and a face that looked like a failed experiment involving a gourd, two half-chewed prunes, and a single yellowed tooth.

With his other hand, the thug pulled one side of the rope loop and the rest spun from the dagger's pommel and landed in a heap beside the bush. Sala and Mirko could no longer descend that way.

But fame had its uses. "You're ... 'ang on, you're that truthsayer. Gangle, is it?"

The apostle smiled weakly. "Yeah. Gangle, that's me. Do you mind terribly putting me down now?"

"Oh, sorry, brother. Now what did youse say you were doing here, with that rope and all?"

"By the blessed power of the All-Seeing Eye," Dando said, "I hadn't even noticed the rope. I was merely gathering anjberries. Preparing a drink for one of my truth-telling sessions, you know?"

Creases of puzzlement crossed the man's deeply rutted brow. It looked like an expression he'd perfected through much repetition. "Well, I'll be. Never heard of an anjberry draught. Sounds disgusting."

Dando laughed, a quiver wrestling its last roll from his throat. "I can't recommend it, really. But it's the truth. Obviously. I have enough gathered. Time to speed home before they go ... er ... moldy."

The burly man tugged at Dando's hooded cloak, attempting to straighten it. "T'were anyone else, I'd give them a right hiding, as both a filthy liar and a burglar's lookout. Sorry to 'ave doubted you, master truthsayer."

A shadow flickered across the moon. Were Sala and Mirko floating lazily below a hovering goat? A goat could barely levitate a toddler. It couldn't lift two cloaked rogues, especially with one of them brushing away several swooping and twittering birds. Could it?

CHAPTER 11 - TEMPLE PANG

The Next Day

Rayne dreamed she was submerged in dark water and unable to close her eyelids. Every sound reached her, deadened and distant. In the inky deep, slender wriggling lampreys latched onto her exposed eyeballs, until each eye resembled a mop with fronds formed from their writhing bodies.

She awoke with a start and a gulped-back scream at the prod of Catriona's rod.

As usual, the voice spoke to her directly, without moving Catriona's lips. "I see your eyes haven't begun their transformation yet. Nor the ears. Sometimes, it takes a day or two before everything kicks off."

Rayne curled into a fetal ball, hugging her knees to her chest, and turned her back on Catriona. Instead of protecting her, this earned her a swat on the back of the arm.

"Enough feeling sorry for yourself, whelp. If you'd *failed* the test, you'd have something to gripe about. We'll take this opportunity to start your training."

Even eyeless, Rayne felt Catriona's unnatural gaze fall upon her as she rushed into the plain day clothes someone at the temple had stitched together roughly to suit her small stature. A shapeless and dull shift dress, finished with the wide-strapped sandals she'd arrived wearing. She tied a woven band around her unwashed and tangling red hair.

Wordless, Catriona spun on her heel and led Rayne through the temple to an interior courtyard. Flagstones gave way to a vegetable patch at one end, neat rows of carrot tops framing shrugging lettuce bunches. A hovering goat drifted in a lazy bob above, and a row of quizzical rock-eaters stood on their hind legs to peek above the lettuces. Their prominent teeth glowed a fiery orange as they followed the two girls' progress, an indicator of their magical ability to crush and ingest even the toughest stones for sustenance. A rough opening at the base of the wall next to the garden was doubtless where they'd chewed through the curtain wall into the courtyard.

Rayne's voice broke the silence, meeker than usual. "Can I stop it?"

She heard Catriona's voice directly inside her head this time. "Ha! Your powers, little girl? Hardly. You'll be as potent as the rest of us soon. Probably won't remember anything before today, either. Seems to work that way, the coral."

Rayne's eyes widened. "What? I won't remember Tasha or Minimus? The Red Bean Queendom will disappear for me?"

Catriona nodded. "I remember nothing before the Temple of the Wraith. I think it's the same for us all. But we don't talk about it much. You'll get used to it, maybe, in time."

From an inner pocket, Catriona exposed a shorter metallic rod, half the length of the one she typically used.

"WE CLOSE THE GATE AND OPEN THE EYES!" Catriona shouted. Rayne knew the booming call was in her head and not a *real* sound others might hear. There was no echo, and neither the goat nor the rock-eaters startled.

Despite her resolve to stand up to her captor and tormentor, Rayne took a half-step back.

"Well, repeat it, worm. It's our mantra. Our reason for existing. We close the gate and open the eyes!"

Tentative, Rayne repeated it.

"Those are just words. Now, I will show you how to put power into them," Catriona said, with less acidity than usual. With a blur of speed, she was behind Rayne, reaching around her tiny frame to hold the dark training rod in front of her face.

Her other hand clutched the handmaiden's wrist.

"You must learn how to strip a person's magic. When I show you, you will *feel* it and then repeat it. The training rod responds to our touch and flares when we try to drain its magic away. Watch this. Feel this."

Rayne felt a nudge inside her mind, as if an invisible hand prodded her to try something she'd never attempted before. A tingle ran the length of her arm, from the shoulder joint to the wrist that Catriona clasped tighter. The taller girl's lips pressed to the back of her neck and the shouted voice flowed into her again.

"WE CLOSE THE GATE AND OPEN THE EYES!"

The tingle grew to an overwhelming, almost painful, surge. The rod flickered into life, coursing with a black radiance, suggesting the opposite of light. Rayne absorbed the new skill somehow from Catriona's lips and grasp instead of from a demonstration.

The hovering goat fell to the soil of the vegetable patch with a puzzled bleat and the rock-eaters squeaked in panic as their now dull teeth dropped from their mouths to litter the earth among the lettuce leaves.

Rayne shrieked. "By the third eye, Catriona, what have you done? Those poor things won't be able to eat now!"

Catriona responded after a pause. "Huh. I hadn't noticed that before. Maybe—".

Before she could complete the thought, a stern voice interrupted. A new figure stepped from the courtyard's shadowy corner. It wore the same style of cloak as Catriona, but an inkier black. Although the cloak obscured their face, Rayne felt certain it would bear the same eyeless look and burnt-away ears. "Yes, sister. Our work here is even more important. The sinful magic of this place has spread from humanity to corrupt the animals. We must rid them, all of them, of this poison."

Catriona bowed her head. "Mother Justicia, I did not know. Many more gates to close and eyes to open."

Rayne knew in that instant that she would never use her

powers to harm an animal. It went against every doctrine and principle of the nineteen queendoms. She couldn't hold her tongue, despite the palpable power that oozed from Mother Justicia.

She pointed a finger at the black-cloaked newcomer. "You can't do this to animals. You'll ruin them all. They won't survive."

Catriona had stunning speed and agility, but Mother Justicia wasn't even a blur. With no hint of movement, the woman appeared in front of her, clutching her throat with a wrinkled but powerful hand. Only a puff of wind and billowing cloak hinted at her movement across the courtyard.

"Let's hope your transformation guides your tongue and your attitude, sister. Otherwise, your stay here, and your time in this world, will be short."

The repeated sound of a fluttering cloak was all that remained of Mother Justicia a moment later.

* * *

After her lesson, Catriona locked Rayne in her chamber. As she paced the floor or curled up on her bed, Rayne raised her fingertips to eyes and ears several times a minute, awaiting the signs of her transformation. Nothing changed throughout the day, or each time her nightmares roused her from fitful sleep.

At first light, the familiar cawing of a coal rayvn woke her. It reminded her of her early days at the orphanage, when the glossy four-legged birds would flap in and out of her window like a constant honor guard. This one fluttered to her blanket and released a shred of fabric from its front claw.

Wait. Why would a coal rayvn bring Jing Jing's fancy jacket to her? Exhausted, she checked her eyes and ears once more, then took the bit of clothing and slid it beneath her pillow. Familiar monkey-scents feathered her dreams.

By dawn, her arms disobeyed her, refusing to be victimized by the compulsive pawing at her face. A deep fatigue beset them, and Rayne's nervous energy gave way to a desire for calm. She flung herself to the bed, closed her eyes to the early morning sunshine, and counted deep breaths, letting her mind retreat to more familiar surroundings.

She imagined her compact but well-appointed room in the Red Bean Queendom. It was in the half of the palace suitable only for the small stature of Red Beaners, a coziness she missed while serving Princess Tasha in Mossmarch, a city designed for the much taller Outer Pangans. Her floral-print duvet lay crisp on the bed, with fluffy pillows peeking over its upper edge. The sound of rustling leaves drifted through the window. Fully immersed in her memories, every detail of the scene seemed as though she could reach out and touch it. Her tarnished mirror presided over the vanity, with brushes and combs arrayed just as she liked, and a few wavy strands of her own hair visible against the whitest doily. In the mirror, the reflection showed a chambermaid at work. Odd. Rayne didn't normally picture her room with anyone sweeping it.

She murmured to herself, "Who invited Alanna into my daydream?"

And her daydream reacted. Alanna's braids flicked from side to side as she scanned the room. "Rayne? Is that you? I thought you were still in Mossmarch."

This was not at all soothing, dealing with an unexpected intruder into one's relaxation routine. And yet, another voice shoehorned its way in, followed by a familiar face. It was Lord Alfred, husband of Queen Violet of Evermere and Rayne's surrogate father.

"Alanna? Who are you speaking to?" he said, leaning through the doorway.

"Oh. Nobody, I guess," she replied. "I thought I heard Rayne for a moment. Must be imagining things."

"Just a dream, I guess," Alfred said. "I hope to hear her delightful voice here soon enough, too."

Rayne shot upright, her eyes flicking open, and the scene dissolved. Something was happening, and she checked her eyes for scarring. No change.

If these were her new powers awakening, she should try to

make use of them. She sank once more into the bed, closed her eyes, and her chest rose and fell with deep breaths. This time, she pictured Minimus Mu's possible location. Somewhere near Master Thorn's traveling cart, possibly watching a makeshift puppet show. She tried to picture the cart in her mind's eye. Familiar with its many nooks, drawers, and nestling spots, she conjured up a vivid picture. Not as realistic as the vision of her room, but richly detailed, nonetheless. She imagined Minimus Mu, but somehow, he refused to come to life as a vision. He didn't fit into her imagining the same way Alanna had enlivened her earlier daydream.

Only darkness. Could her overwrought mind be playing tricks on her? She needed to relax, so she gave up on picturing the cart. A smile crossed her lips as she thought about the voices Master Thorn would use for the puppets. Outrageous falsettos and the deep voice of the Giant, which doubled as the haughty historical hero of the trials, Colwyn the Colossus of Wraithwatch.

A box framed the puppet stage, behind which Master Thorn would hide as best he could, its frayed curtains twitching as he maneuvered the puppets. Rayne imagined being in Master Thorn's position, peeking from offstage through the half-drawn stage curtains to check the audience's reaction. No show was underway, and the curtains fluttered, damp and streaked with rime, flecked with seaweed. Through the parted curtains, ocean waves broke over a sand bar and rippled ashore. A wide, calloused foot shifted, digging its heel into the sand. That was no normal foot. Its size betrayed its owner, who could only be …

Rayne spoke aloud, but softly. "Minimus?"

The foot froze. Rayne's view expanded, as if she had leaned out to the stage's lip to gawk at some spectacle beyond. She could see Minimus in his bulky entirety. His skin was even more tanned than usual, sunburnt in places, and his eyebrows knitted beneath unkempt and tufty hair.

Louder now, she said, "Minimus, it's me. Can you hear me?"

A smile, almost wider than his jaw, broke across the boy's face. Then he laughed. "Yes! Yes, Rayne. You're in the puppet theater? How did you get here?"

He threw himself across the distance to the wooden stage, lifting it and peering at its empty innards.

Rayne wanted to call out, but choked up, words turning to tears.

"What's wrong? Where are you? Jing Jing, help me find Rayne!"

Catching her breath, Rayne was able to reply a few moments later, as a jacketless Jing Jing came into view. "I'm not there with you, Min. A cult snatched me away to Temple Pang. It's some sort of magic letting me see and hear you."

"Like the thunderbird magic?" he asked.

"Sort of. But there's no animal helping me. I think it's *my magic.*"

Minimus ground sand beneath his palm, using the texture, the faint squeaking sound to reassure himself he was awake and Rayne's voice was real. "Wait. You have magic now? That's impossible. Isn't it?" Maybe if you wished for something hard enough, it could come true. Hadn't Minimus been thinking about Rayne and Master Thorn for entire days as he dragged vines ashore? Could the dolphins have granted him a wish?

With the vine farmers asleep in their hut, Minimus had time to whisper the details of his misfortunes to Rayne, and she told him the scant few details she'd discovered about her captors and captivity at Temple Pang. If he closed his eyes, Minimus could imagine they were chatting side by side, resting shaded beneath the axle of Master Thorn's cutlery cart. When Rayne whispered that someone was approaching her room and told Minimus to wait by the puppet theater as often as he could manage, it seemed like hours had passed. Or maybe only a minute.

* * *

Later that morning, Rayne peered from the puppet stage to see

Minimus waist-deep in the sea, pulling vines, too far away to call. Her powers could find no trace of Princess Tasha. She was ship-bound or at the palace in Ven, to the west of Outer Pang—places Rayne could not picture any suitable peeking point. When she found Minimus, it was like she peered out from the stage of the puppet theater. And in her chambers in the Red Bean Queendom, it was as if she observed from behind the window pane. She needed some sort of natural spying position to flex her newfound power, it seemed.

Minimus had told her about Master Thorn's escape from the pirate attack, and that he would be in the balloon with Ezra Longshanks. She pictured the purple sailcloth and the suspended basket in her mind, imagining herself peeking through the grate of the wood powered stove that filled the balloon. She felt a richer scene trying to break into focus, but its castle-like surroundings were nebulous, and she could catch no glimpse of Master Thorn himself.

* * *

At the table outside the Crossed Swords, four men were thinking about Rayne but did not know they would soon hear from her.

A gaggle of glow-geese fretted beneath the table at Sala Doon's feet. Passers-by remarked at the outrageous illumination, each goose a powerful lighthouse of a different hue. Sala smiled, glad that no one knew it was the power of the eleven-pointed star enhancing the animals' innate magic. A pair of hovering goats had floated so high above his head that they were mere specks in the autumn sky.

"We saw you below, held at the collar by some brute, and our rope was gone. With the guards clattering up the stairs, it was a choice of death by sword or plummet," Sala said, filling in Dando on their escape from the tower. "A goat was hovering near the window, so we each grabbed ahold, hoping its buoyancy might soften the impact of our inevitable fall."

Dando nodded. "But you knew the star thingy would

enhance its magic enough to hold you?"

Sala shook his head. "Nah. We *didn't* know. It was a complete surprise that the goat could hold us. It bleated in self-righteous outrage at first but then clammed up when it found it could support us both. Eventually it settled in a tree and we climbed down."

Virgil toasted the two thieves with his half-full tankard. "I've composed a short but, if I dare say so myself, highly entertaining ballad about your escapades. Saved for another time, though, because it's rather … incriminating."

Sala leaned in and lowered his voice. "I'm worried about my belt. It has my name engraved on the buckle, and we left it stuck to the pillar. If the guards have half a brain between them, they'll be calling for my head soon."

Dando smiled. "I've *not* been taking care of that. *Nobody's* heard me saying that you and Mirko were with us that entire evening in the back room of the Crossed Swords. And I've *not* been saying to anyone that will listen that somebody stole your belt only last week."

Salah sprang from his chair, scattering violently glowing geese, and hugged the apostle close. "My darling little lying truthteller! No wonder nobody's looking at me as if I'm a pile of walking reward money. Who could disbelieve the famous truthteller Dando?"

In Temple Pang, Rayne's vision of the Crossed Swords glossed from remembrance to vivid scene, and she heard Virgil speak as he pointed and shook his head at Mirko. "You're still walking around with one boot? You've got to buy another one, man. Look at your sock! It's got more holes than one of your alibis!"

Mirko laughed in return. "I'm named Leatherfoot for a reason, my brother. Boots are only a recent addition to my wardrobe."

Rayne opened her mouth to say something but didn't want to interrupt Mirko as he continued. "And hang on there. What was that word you said that started with the letter B? Bligh? Bry? Bely? I'm not familiar with it."

"Ahh, *buy*. It's like stealing, except you customarily trade something in return. Normally goat's teeth."

Dando and Sala laughed, but Rayne's voice cut short their mirth when it called from the dingy tavern window behind them. "Excuse me, boys, but shouldn't you be planning my rescue?"

CHAPTER 12 - VEN

Two Days Later

Princess Tasha of the Red Bean Queendom and interim caretaker of Outer Pang contemplated the gravity of her voyage across the Sea of Sorrows to the Queendom of Ven. Royalty mingled often; Tasha herself had enjoyed several trade delegations to queendoms near and far on the western continent. But an edge characterized this trip. In the island queendom of Ven, she would meet Queen Veronica to explore and deal with simmering rumors of an invasion.

After Outer Pang's former queen, Jada of Mossmarch, had revealed her desire to absorb the Red Bean Queendom into Outer Pang through a dubious series of legal steps, it had taken heroics to avert disaster. Tasha's mother, Queen Violet, backed by other neighboring queens, had taken the bold step to invoke the trials of the All-Seeing Eye. Her reluctant and unexpected champion, Minimus Mu, had succeeded in the trials, scuttling Queen Jada's plans. In the aftermath, with laws bending to favor the victors, a clutch of queens selected Tasha as Outer Pang's interim ruler for a period of transition. Jada's queenhood stripped, she was forced to regard her nation from the open prison of her towered chambers in the heart of Mossmarch, but with no power to rule. She was most displeased with her new, humbling situation.

Tasha had expected grumblings and resistance from the

people of her surrogate queendom. Despite Jada's harsh demeanor, most citizens cared little about the activities of a distant queen, desiring only to go about their daily lives with as little upheaval as the chaos of life allowed. A ruler like Tasha, tiny in stature and an outsider in Mossmarch, was like a Hammarskald jinkberry surfacing in a bowl of eel broth—unexpected, exotic, and an untested flavor combination. In Mossmarch, many conversations became whispers and treads became tiptoes. But the rumors of pending inter-queendom violence crept up on her like moths in a wardrobe; holes appeared in her ability to rule and demanded immediate attention.

Taking after her mother, Tasha was decisive. She not only took the murmured threats of an invasion seriously, but sailed to meet them head-on. Jada had vanished from her residence, but not without nosy sailors at the port identifying a small party hiding beneath suspiciously luxurious cloaks as they boarded a ship bound for Ven. Jada would find natural solace there; her cousin, Veronica, was queen.

As the nook in the Vennese coastline that concealed Port Rise hove into view, Tasha, grasping the rail of the *Sun Seeker's* foredeck, took confidence in her companions. A clutch of hand-picked guardswomen from the Golden Shores flanked her. She'd thought it overkill of Queen Angstaad to insist on sending a ten-strong squad of her own elite fighters, but was more than glad of their presence on this mission. And unlike the often-ceremonial troops of other queendoms, where the pacts, laws, and traditions between queendoms made war unthinkable, the fighters from Golden Shores earned their reputation for ferocity. While it was true they had little occasion to fight other armies, the constant threat of fire bears in the hills, rage boars roaming the plains, and fanglimbs ravaging the seaside produced adept and alert guardswomen. There was nothing like assaults by magic-infused predators to keep a fighting force in peak condition.

Glancing behind her, the morning sun glinted off polished breastplates and close-cropped hair, boosting Tasha's wavering confidence. It occurred to her that her companions stood poised for violence, but the goal of this mission was to avoid it. "Ladies, we're here for peace across our nations," she called. "To avoid a Ven-on-Pang confrontation, I plan to solve this with my voice, unless there remains no other choice. So stay your swords and keep open hands, awaiting only my commands."

The steely-eyed warriors nodded and stamped in unison, needing no words to express their assent.

Looking at the approaching pier, Tasha noted a cluster of upright pikes attending the open berth. Not the friendliest reception. Tasha's stomach clenched as her brow furrowed.

* * *

In the spartan, wood-framed throne room, Queen Veronica sat in serene contemplation of her visitors. Her platinum tiara melted into a crop of short, fair hair, and feathered wrinkles at the corners of her eyes gave her a look of calm consideration. The family resemblance to Jada was obvious, but Veronica was cool where Jada was ice, calculating where rage crept into her cousin's demeanor.

This serenity did not extend to her guardsmen, who hovered only a word away from snatching knives from sheaths, gazes fixed on the Golden Shores warriors. And there was nothing remotely calm about Veronica's cousin. Former queen Jada shook her silver mane in mock disbelief, over-reddened lips sneering into action. "Well, if it isn't our snooty little fairground attraction. I'm sure nobody invited you here, just as you are an uninvited guest in Outer Pang."

Tasha had seen Jada's vitriol before and was determined to hide any signs of intimidation. She met Jada's glare, and focused on keeping a neutral expression, goading Jada to lose her cool by refusing to react.

It took but a moment of tense silence. Jada laid into the princess once again. "Well, what is it? If you think you're an actual human, use your voice, you slug. My cousin and I have better things to do and important plans to contemplate. Why would we entertain the likes of an imposter like you?"

Tasha glanced at Queen Veronica. She remained unsmiling, but had edged closer to the lip of her throne. With a sweep of her hand to indicate both women, Tasha addressed them. "It is exactly those plans that bring me to your lands. I've heard from my sources that you're gathering forces. I'll have you explain your intentions. And need I mention, violation of convention will bring the other queens' intervention?"

Jada's cheeks blossomed to a color approaching that of her lips. "Shut that traitorous rhyming gob, you—" she began before she tailed into silence as Queen Veronica cleared her throat.

The queen's voice cut across the throne room, all edge but little intonation. "My ships and troops are not one iota of your concern. My actions will be perfectly legal and none of the other queendoms will dare intervene when I enact my plan."

Unbowed, Tasha pointed a finger across the room at Queen Veronica. "Until the time of transition is complete, we'll brook no landing by your fleet."

Queen Veronica smiled, but it lacked all warmth. "Tasha, no need to get hot under the *collar*. Before our fleet lands, you'll hear from our *scholar*. Why would I break the laws our queendoms have worked so hard to maintain?"

Jada laughed at her cousin's mocking rhyming. Her cackle echoed with unpleasantness.

Was there a further challenge based on the dictates of *The Binding of the Queendoms* that Tasha's mother had overlooked? The princess's mind raced, and she opened her mouth to reply twice without voicing an answer.

"You may leave now," Queen Veronica said, a musical tone in her voice expressing dismissal of a trifling matter. One of her guardsmen, nervy and overzealous, unsheathed a blade in response. With all individuality battered from them in training, his companions followed suit a moment later.

Despite Tasha's instructions to react only under her orders, the warriors of the Golden Shores closed ranks around her and their own ten swords rasped halfway from their scabbards. They crouched as one, weight on the balls of their feet, awaiting any further threatening moves. Tasha knew that if their swords slid fully free, there would be bloodshed, required and deserved. Nervy, she still felt safe.

The sudden clatter of the throne room doors opening behind the encircled guardswomen nearly spelled disaster. Fortunately, it was apparent that the newcomer was unarmed, so Tasha's whirling rearguard concluded in an instant that no surprise attack was in progress. The entering squire danced wide around the unexpected throng of warriors and scampered to the foot of the throne, where he bowed low to his queen before blurting a message.

"Your excellency, news from Temple Pang. After the evicted templars arrived here, the invaders destroyed your return ship in the harbor, just as they had warned.

Tasha felt a flush course through her body. Every encounter with Jada was a confrontation. Her manners and accompanying rhyming betrayed her at times. "You've invaded the temple? How dare you!"

Jada whirled on her. Almost unbidden, swords slid further from their scabbards. "That's neutral territory. Temple Pang might have *Pang* in the name, but the island belongs to no queendom. And besides, it's not *us* who invaded. It's someone else. A vicious outside sect. Kicked the templars out and sent them on a ship here. With a warning. We ignored it, of course. Dirty, jumped-up little interlopers. A bunch of girls and old hags, by all accounts!"

The squire had been attempting to interrupt and eventually found a lull in Jada's vitriol. "*Magic* sank the ship, your elegancy. Blasted out of the water by rings of icy fire, according to the few seamen that swam to safety and returned here on a passing trawler."

CHAPTER 13 - ASTELLA

Three Days Later

Skain Two-Hearts spared Ezra and Master Thorn only enough interest to see them supplied for their trip to eastern Astella and find them a room above the Seven Stars tavern, where they wanted currency other than goat's teeth. He could do nothing but obsess over the Finder's glimpse of the daughter the Mothers of Midnight had stolen from him, and he prepared for an overseas trip to Temple Pang.

The road to the Backwards Man was pleasant. Skain's squire's hand-drawn map ushered them along the lake shore due east. He'd mentioned that two days' ride would bring them to a signpost topped with an eagle statue. The road south from there would find a turnip farm nestled in the rolling hills marked by a gate stained red with the juice of beetleberries. Although Ezra complained about the length of several of Master Thorn's more epic stories, he was glad of the chatter and warm companionship. Master Thorn pined for the tools and materials lost to the depths of the Fading Sea in his merchant cart, but Ezra found it odd that the first step in rebuilding his livelihood would be constructing a puppet theater. Each morning as they arose, Master Thorn mentioned what tale his puppets would have re-enacted, and guessed at the reaction Minimus Mu might have provided.

Although their aging frames griped each morning against the thin camp rolls and their extended time in the saddle, the days passed without rain. Pleasant breezes rolled across the lake, and the dried foods Skain packed were delicious. The spices of Astella offered more earthy tones than the fiery tang of the Inner Pangan diet Master Thorn normally followed. The pair rode across hump-backed bridges that carried the road across the many streams and rivers flowing into Pearl Lake. They passed a village on the lakeshore, razed by fire, its only remaining feature a partially melted metal sculpture of a fish held by a bird of prey.

Midmorning on the third day, the two gray-haired men reined in their trotting horses at a roughly hewn, rustic arch. Stained a fading red and framing a footpath that led through a turnip patch toward a log cabin, it matched the description of the farm they sought. A young farmhand, handsome with a well-trimmed beard and penetrating brown eyes, lifted his head from his basket of uprooted turnips.

Master Thorn dismounted and called to the young man. "Ho there! We seek the farm of the Backwards Man. Have we arrived? And if so, might we visit your master? Skain Two-Hearts pointed us in his direction."

The well-tanned man placed his basket gently on the earth, rose, and strolled over, clapping dirt from his calloused hands. He did not reply until he reached the archway, a slight smile crossing his lips as he approached.

"Skain, eh? If memory serves me, he's still a well-respected hunter of the Mothers of Midnight, right? Pitied as a boy, I recall, but not moved beyond fame yet? But never mind that. Master Thorn and Ezra Longshanks—most pleasant to meet you. I'd forgotten it was today that you'd arrive. And I wish they wouldn't call me the Backwards Man." He sighed. "Makes me sound like a simpleton. And technically, I should be called the Backwards and Forwards Man, since I live in both directions. But I already know you are polite enough to call me Berentz from now on."

Master Thorn and Ezra glanced at each other. This man matched neither's mental image of the seer that Bonchanta had mentioned. She hadn't described him in physical terms, telling them only that he possessed uncanny knowledge of the future. Was it wrong to assume only old men and women were wise? Master Thorn mused to himself. A woman whose power surpassed any person Master Thorn had ever met regarded this young man as the wisest of Astellans, despite him having seen only about twenty-five summers.

"Uh, you can close your mouths now," the Backwards Man said. Master Thorn felt the mortified flush of ill manners color his neck and cheeks, and Ezra stammered out a barely intelligible reply. Berentz told them to tether their horses at the arch and beckoned them to follow him along the path.

"It's quite boring, you know," Berentz called over his shoulder as they wound their way behind him. "I know everything that's going to happen to me. I lived backward first, and now forward. There are no surprises, and it sure helps with the turnip crops, knowing the upcoming weather. Although I must admit, I still look forward to tomorrow morning's puppet show. For three months, I've been trading for materials and sewing the puppets from memory. Took a good few tips on their construction from your bondsman. I met him in the springtime, and he's one of the things I need to warn you about."

This stranger had sewn Master Thorn a set of replacement puppets? And what was a *bondsman*? Some messenger from the future? So many questions fizzed within Master Thorn's mind that he was frozen into an unexpected silence, jaws working but no words emerging.

Ezra's natural curiosity kicked in as Berentz pulled crude chairs into the dappled shade of a weeping willow that grew to a tremendous height beside his home. "You mean you can see—or shall I say, have *experienced*—the future, and yet you live a simple life here in the Astellan countryside? That power is absolutely incredible. Shouldn't you be advising queens or running a business empire?"

Berentz screwed up his face and shook his head rapidly. "Nah, it's not like that. I can see the entirety of *my* future. A future that includes little other than farming and occasional interesting visits from wanderers like yourselves. I visited Pearl Wash just the once, but I'm due to remain here until I drop dead in the lettuce patch thirty years hence. Well, I assume I die. The first thing I remember from my backwards life was excruciating chest pain as I lay face-first in the dirt. But maybe I'll experience my first genuine surprise after that, eh?"

"Isn't it confusing, living in both directions?" Master Thorn asked.

"It's not at all confusing. More like the opposite. When I was a child, everyone thought I was a weird genius. I could talk as soon as I got my lips and tongue practiced enough to make sounds—*that* surprised my mother, let me tell you. And I already knew so much. Well, as much as a lifetime on a turnip farm in the rump of Astella can teach you. So no, not confusing in the slightest, for me. But hold your questions for a moment. I'll bring you some cold water from the well. And the puppets, too, Master Thorn. You're going to tell me how you lost your original set, and how much you love the ones I've created."

After sipping from a canteen for three days, the texture of the wooden cup containing frigid well water annoyed Master Thorn less than he expected. Cooling a parched throat was more important than a proper porcelain or baked clay vessel.

"But you know what *is* weird?" Berentz began. "Most of what I'm about to tell you *I learned by talking to you.* I know what we're going to discuss, and where you'll head when we finish. I just piece together a few facts from travelers I've encountered and help you along your way. Or maybe lead you astray—I never will hear which.

"For example, I already know that you don't understand what a coin is. You're going to tell me that where you are from, you use some kind of magical floating goat's teeth instead. But look here. This is a coin. We use it as money, because our goats don't float, or have magical powers to defend themselves. One side depicts the Astellan queen. Well, the previous queen. Flip the copper piece, and find an etching of a peacock, our national bird."

Both Ezra and Master Thorn struggled to grasp the concept. "Wait. How can this pass as currency? Can't you just produce as much of it as you want? Can't *anyone* make these coins?"

Berentz pursed his lips. "I think your money makes more sense. It's hard to fake a tooth that's not subject to gravity. But let's ignore any lessons on coins. I only need to use it as an example. Look here—when holding the coin in my palm, how you notice only the queen's head? Imagine it's the entire world. It includes me, Astella, Wraithwatch, even all the people in Outer Pang, where you'll tell me this afternoon you departed from on your current journey.

"Everyone looking at the queen's head thinks it's *everything*. A coin with a portrait. But the coin has another side, the peacock. You just can't see it, unless you flip the coin. That's called the coin's *obverse* face. And that, my non-magical friends, is where *you* are from. You moved onto my side of the coin. That explosion at the Temple of the Wraith pushed you across to the other face."

Master Thorn's first thought was obvious to Ezra. "So, that means my boy Minimus, if he survived the shipwreck, isn't even in this world? I'll definitely never see him again?" His gray hair swept over the hands that covered his face. He tried his best to disbelieve Berentz, but so many of his other statements rang true.

Berentz peeled Master Thorn's hands from his face and held them as he peered into eyes welling with tears. "There are still two ways to find Minimus, and I have a feeling you will see him again. The first thing you should know, which I heard from a man of science like Ezra, is that each person possesses a bond with someone strikingly alike on the coin's other side. So, there's a Minimus Mu here, on this side. You apparently have a strong affinity for him, so it's possible that if you search here, you can find him. He won't be *your* Minimus, but it might ease your aching heart to meet and befriend *our* Minimus Mu.

The second and even likelier way was retold to me next month by a roving minstrel. It's a story about three people passing through a ring of light above the Temple of the Wraith in a floating basket. They rose into the air, blown by the wind, and drifted through the ring before disappearing. If I had to guess, it was—or rather, will be—you two. And did you bring along somebody else? The minstrel mentioned that the two foreigners met someone familiar at the Pearl Wash market."

An impossibly wide smile broke across Ezra's face. "So, we can use the balloon to recross to our own side? That's brilliant! I wonder how the science works that moves us between worlds? And who's the third person? Only the two of us were dragged through the exploding wraithlight."

Berentz released Master Thorn's hands and glanced between the two travelers. "Be careful inferring things from what I tell you. Here on my farm, I only see through other people's tales. So, I don't know if it's *you two* and a third person who fly through the ring of light. All I know is the story of what will happen. Three people. And it's important that you avoid meeting the *other yous* that exist on this side. I heard—well, will hear—another story. About a meeting of two girls, one from each side. The seer that will tell me this, she said they had an inspiritive bond, that they were two sides of the same person, thrust into the same world. One acted like an anchor on the other when the chance to move between the worlds arrived."

He locked eyes with Master Thorn. "Don't let the other *you* anchor you, my friend. He passed by here not a month gone."

CHAPTER 14 - WRAITHWATCH

The Next Day

The puppet theater became Minimus Mu's most prized possession. Not that it had much competition—only a sketchbook, sweat-stained clothing, a machete, nearly new sandals, and a jar of eyeballs. But it was his only possession that allowed Rayne to communicate with him in her unusual new way.

He had promised he would make his way back to Temple Pang and rescue her. The words came from his heart, but his head nagged about how difficult it would be. With no goat's teeth and a reputation that nobody in Wraithwatch would believe, he must find his escape from the wrestle vine farm, obtain passage across the Fading Sea, and navigate the western continent. Only then could he stage a rescue. He hung his head in his hands. Good thing Jing Jing's eternal optimism needled him into action. He couldn't create a plan with Master Thorn's level of detail, so he settled on a simple plan with only two steps. The plan was so small, Master Thorn would have called it *shrimple*.

Step one was to leave the sea-farm and Ee Clot behind, taking passage on the caravan that would trade for the wrestle vine architectural pieces the next day. Step two was *everything else*.

After an afternoon session harvesting vines and a rushed lobster dinner, Minimus snuggled Jing Jing into the hammock and waited by the puppet theater for Rayne to make contact. Nearly snoozing, her disembodied voice brought him to full alertness. Jing Jing could hear it, too. His head swiveled like a church owl, looking for its source.

They talked in low voices deep into the night. The wrestle vine farmers swilled fermented drinks in the hut, caring little what Minimus got up to each evening. Rayne said that her captors locked her alone in her room, waiting for the overdue transformation whose effects frightened her, but had not yet begun. Rayne wept at the thought that when Minimus saw her, she would be eyeless with burnt away ears.

"Seeing you again is what matters, not *what* I see," the boy said.

* * *

Because of his strength, Ee Clot kept Minimus ashore on the mornings the trade caravans arrived. Today was no different, other than the fact that Minimus had secretly carried the puppet theater to a flat rock beside the roadway that skirted the beach. Jing Jing kept near him whenever he was ashore, so the monkey needed no encouragement to remain at hand.

The caravan master, Roland of Wraithsport, supervised the loading of his wagons. He had a bird-like face with a pointy nose but a friendly expression, like he'd enjoyed a comfortable life and wished others could, too. He'd chatted with Minimus during his previous visits, so the boy ambled over to him as the loading neared completion.

"Sir. Hello, sir. I'd like to help you *unload* the wagons at the other end, in Wraithsport. I don't need any food, and I'll stay silent the whole way. No trouble."

Roland spent a moment peering into Minimus's eyes before answering. "I half believe that, boy. You seem like you'd be no trouble yourself, but I find it hard to believe you'll last a day and a half with no food. Look at the size of you! You'd give

Colwyn the Colossus a good run in a wrestling match if he were alive today, I'd wager."

"So, I can go?" Minimus asked.

"That's a bit more complicated. Even if you're not trouble, I expect Mister Clot there might get agitated if you up and leave without his permission. What do you think he'd say if I asked him?"

Minimus looked at where his boots would be if he owned any, but found only sandals. "In fairness, I already had a master. Master Thorn. He'd want me to travel with you, so does it matter what Ee has to say? I can just hop onto one of the covered wagons, and he'd not even know you took me."

Roland considered this, then nodded. His shoulder-length curls bobbed beneath the hood that kept the climbing sun at bay. "I know how to handle Clot. What's your name, boy? I'll have a word while you gather your belongings."

"I only have that thing on the rock there, nothing else," Minimus said. "Oh, and my friend the monkey will follow, too, I expect. Ee Clot doesn't know my name, really. But you can tell him it's ... um ... Sang of Seven Rocks."

Minimus peeked through a moth hole in the covered wagon. Jing Jing, at his side, clutched the jar of fanglimb eyeballs. There was much waving and a little shouting as Roland had words with Ee Clot. Eventually, a wrapped package changed hands, and Ee calmed down.

The wagons rolled out, horses panting as the road rose away from the beach. Ee stood on the sand's margin and glared at the last wagon where Minimus squatted.

"I really am Minimus Mu," he called back. "You'll realize it someday."

* * *

Although most people would have found riding above the rear axle of a laden wagon uncomfortable—each rut and stone the wheel bumped over jarred the vehicle—Minimus found it a welcome change from the swaying hammock where he'd grown bored. The boy snoozed on and off through the noon heat, sipping regularly from a water canteen that Roland insisted he keep at hand. Jing Jing held the jar of eyeballs close, protecting it from harm. When the wagon train stopped for the waggoneers to lunch, Minimus hung back, trying to be true to his word, despite his mouth watering at the smell of heating grimble peas and lemon rice.

Partway through the afternoon, as the caravan rumbled along a narrow path cut into the face of the lower mountains, Jing Jing became excited, pushing his jar into Minimus's face.

"Yeah, yeah. Eyeballs. I've seen them before, Jing Jing. And come to think of it, they've seen me, back at Scarlet Sands before you pulled them off the fanglimb."

Jing Jing jumped up and down twice, then pointed a furry finger at the jar. Minimus peered closer, then closer again. Normally, the eyeballs drifted in a random jumble in the briny liquid. But not now. Every eyeball strained at the end of its severed eyestalk, and they all pointed in the same direction: toward the front of the caravan, slightly left, and a fraction upward.

The attack descended from that direction.

The first sign of unusual activity was the rumbling, then the rushing sound of a rockslide. Pebbles, rocks, shale, and boulders coursed down ahead of the lead horses, making every driver shudder to a stop. Their mounts snorted and stamped nervously.

The next sign of trouble was a group of six black-hooded figures racing down the hillside, dividing so they would reach the caravan at evenly spread points. Instead of the jerky hops from rock to boulder that typical brigands would need, these interlopers flowed across the rocky landscape like water. Although he'd never seen them before, the cloaks' hoods matched Rayne's descriptions of the Mothers of Midnight. Minimus envisioned the scarred eye sockets secreted beneath. He jumped from the rearmost wagon, thudding to the roadway in his sandals.

A chorus of girlish voices boomed in attempted unison.

"WE CLOSE THE GATE AND OPEN THE EYES!" They repeated it twice before they reached the caravan, approaching with an agility and speed that hardly seemed human. As they leapt, crouching, onto the roadway, one shouted, "Take their magic, my sisters!"

Minimus heard swords rasp from scabbards out of sight ahead. The waggoneers must be preparing to fight. The twang of bowstrings accompanied the sound of arrows splitting the air. Two of the cloaked attackers twisted back and away, balancing precariously before returning to their squatting positions. Arrows rattled off the rock face behind them, none striking their evasive targets.

"Focus, and *now*!" the voice boomed. "WE CLOSE THE GATE AND OPEN THE EYES!"

A sizzle of magic pulsed between the six figures, then broke over the caravan like a wave.

The nearest cloaked figure leapt, clearing a whole wagon-length in a single bound, before skidding to a stop to face Minimus. Her lips did not move, but a question reached Minimus, nonetheless. "Twenty men and *no magic* between you? And the horses—how'd they get magical powers?"

It wouldn't surprise Minimus to see some of them tearing free from their harnesses now, using their magic to leap incredible distances, with all the commotion. Jing Jing, too, had powers beyond any human. His hands and feet could move at blinding speed. Right now, the defensive power proved useless.

Minimus had seen no man or beast move with the speed of Jing Jing's hands, but with these attackers, the monkey had met his match. Jing Jing sprang through a slit in the wagon's arched skin at the Mother of Midnight in a blur, hands and feet aglow. Without turning her head to look at him, the cloaked figure reacted with equal speed, spinning a quarter turn while leaning back. The monkey should have grabbed her near the hood's clasp, but instead, she whisked him aside with a blurred one-armed swat. Jing Jing, deflected, rolled to a stop at the foot of the rising mountain wall, screeching in annoyance.

With the speedy-handed monkey at her back and Minimus Mu advancing with a scorched campfire kettle in one hand, the hooded figure looked at neither, head bowed. She balanced on the balls of her feet, clearly ready to move. She leaned only a fraction to the left as another arrow hissed past her head, missing by a finger's breadth. Along the caravan's length, the rush of curved swords cutting through air mixed with the thump of feet hitting the roadway. The armed men of the caravan re-mobilized to face the sudden threat.

Minimus shouted, the echoes from the mountainside surprising even himself with their volume. One step, two, then he swung the kettle. This was not his first fight, and a surprising number had involved armaments found in a typical kitchen, a hallmark of defending a cutlerer's cart. Some of his weapons had borne actual hallmarks—he recalled stabbing the buttocks of a thieving street urchin with a two-tined silver shrimp fork.

But this time, his blow failed to find a cheek, chest, or knee to assault. Instead, his swing threw him off-balance as the kettle whizzed beneath the feet of the high-springing Mother of Midnight. Jing Jing scuttled across the rocky roadway, snatching at their attacker's leg—also unsuccessful. He leapt through the slit into the wagon while Minimus recovered and squinted into the sun at the cloaked woman balancing atop the curved strut supporting the wagon's arched cover. Minimus stood clutching the now-lidless kettle. Above, the girl tilted her head as if listening to a bird's screech from on high.

Minimus could see the other five cloaked figures along the length of the caravan. Several weaved to avoid flying arrows and scything sword attacks, moving with unnatural speed. In near unison, the six raised their left arms to the sky, exposing metallic cuff bracelets. With a subtle rotation of each wrist, they evaporated with a faint pop.

Well, not all disappeared, because not all wore bracelets. The one above Jing Jing swiveled her wrist twice, then once more, cocking her head in puzzlement at her failure to leave with her comrades.

Jing Jing covered his mouth with one furry hand and held

up his newfound bracelet in the other, as if stifling a laugh. He snatched a paring knife from the floor of the wagon and gestured toward the fabric of the wagon's roof. His impressive eyebrows raised above his scalp in a silent query to Minimus, who nodded in return and readied the kettle.

Minimus whirled the kettle once overhead as Jing Jing, inside the wagon, leapt up, slicing through the fabric at the cloaked woman's feet. The rip opened wide beneath her weight, and she spun into a tumble as she fell through. The flying kettle caught her in the back of the head as she dropped. After a moment contemplating her unmoving body, Jing Jing made a rapid looting pass, using his magically enhanced hands and feet to speed him through his thieving ritual that included turned-out pockets, a full frisking of the cloak for sewn-in treasures, and an examination of the usual jewelry-adorning locations.

Minimus noted that in the jarful of Seymour, every eye was glued on the unconscious body of the Mother of Midnight. He grabbed the jar and turned it around, then upside down. The eyeballs remained fixated on the body. "Got one back here!" he called to the sword-wielding caravanners searching for their vanished attackers.

In the attack's aftermath, relieved voices of camaraderie fluttered across the caravan workers. Minimus explained how he had captured the lone remaining attacker, who now lay bound, with her robe removed and her scarred eyes and ears visible to her curious captors.

"They did something to the horses' magic," Roland said. "One tried to jump a fallen rock to get away and could barely leave the ground. It's like that sizzling spell completely drained their hooves. How'd your monkey avoid its effects, Sang of Seven Rocks?"

Minimus was momentarily confused at hearing the name of his friend from Outer Pang, but then remembered he'd given it as his alias. "Um, good question. Because he was inside the wagon? The magic couldn't penetrate the fabric?"

Roland raised a skeptical eyebrow. "And where'd their

magic come from? Did they have some kind of small animal hidden up their sleeves?"

Before considering the implications, Minimus said, "I heard they are called the Mothers of Midnight. And they all have magical powers. No animals. Their *own* magic. A bunch of them are holed up at Temple Pang."

"*Temple Pang?*" Roland blurted. "How'd you get news from Outer Pang while working at the wrestle-vine farm? I swear Ee Clot doesn't even know what year it is, let alone expound on international affairs."

Minimus shrugged and glanced at the puppet theater stowed to one side of the trailing wagon. "Just a rumor." Spotting something to divert the conversation, he pointed to the front of the caravan. "Guess I'd better get to rolling those boulders off the road. Your men can deal with the smaller rocks …"

CHAPTER 15 - ASTELLA

Three Days Later

The purpose in Master Thorn and Ezra's minds translated to their horses. The return trip to Pearl Wash possessed an urgency their outbound trip had lacked. They cantered over bridges and past the burnt-out village, Master Thorn's new puppet theater bumping at his horse's flank.

As they approached Pearl Wash, Ezra spoke to Master Thorn, fearful he'd want to bypass it in his rush to get the balloon airborne. "We first need to find Skain Two-Hearts and repeat the Backwards Man's story that he'll speak to his lost daughter at the Temple of the Wraith. I hope he hasn't left for the west yet."

Master Thorn glanced across. "If he's headed there in the future, why should *we* tell him? If the Backwards Man has seen the future, we shouldn't need to help it approach, should we?"

Ezra was silent. That made sense. More sense, even, than a man who lived in both directions through time.

"But it's market day," Master Thorn said. He patted his vest, feeling for a familiar contour in an inner pocket. "I'd like to find an engraver. Add a monograph to the one runcible spork remaining. I could carve 'MM' into it myself if I had any tools left. It'll be a nice present when we find Minimus."

The pair approached the town gate just as Skain was leaving. His squire followed, also mounted, but no other fighters accompanied them. When they described their visit with the Backwards Man and his foretelling of Skain finally speaking to his daughter again, Skain reconsidered his original plan and circled his horse to return to town.

"Maybe the men are wiser than I, refusing to sail across the Fading Sea to Temple Pang. They're under the queen's command, not mine, so I can't force them to follow. And it makes sense that my daughter will return to the Temple of the Wraith, too. That's where we think they took her originally." Skain reined in his horse and searched Master Thorn's face. "Did he say anything else? Like what would happen? Will the Mothers prevail against our next attack?"

"No. He was purposely vague about that, come to think of it. He did say you were pitied as a child, and that you'd move beyond fame. Not sure if that meant you'd retire or blaze into legend."

"Pitied?" Skain spat. "It was charity, not pity. I lost my family, my home, and Pearl Wash took me in and made me one of its own."

There was a silence that Master Thorn's politeness left unbroken. Ezra spoke as Skain's squire negotiated his mount into a half-turn. "Will you depart for the temple soon? Master Thorn and I must urgently return to the balloon, as you can imagine. We will ride into the mountains this afternoon."

They settled it with a nod and a brief plan. Skain would return with more men in an hour. They'd rendezvous outside the gates.

The steady-handed local blacksmith made short work of Master Thorn's engraving. In return, Master Thorn regaled the sweat-bathed man with an extended version of the tale of the Lion of Og. Ezra forced himself to ignore the thread of the story, but wondered whether a lion of that size might have foot problems, with such a giant mass pressed onto minimal surface area.

While the cutlerer bowed and thanked the blacksmith for his fine work, Ezra heard a shouted question Master Thorn had surely been asked before. The stall holder that backed onto the blacksmith's, out of Ezra's current line of sight, attracted a chattering audience. One wag in the crowd called the question to its proprietor, "Lazarus—your eyebrows! Do you ever need to pluck them?"

Its speaker still unseen, the reply reached Ezra, uncannily familiar in both words and inflection. "Occasionally. But only if they threaten to intertwine with my ear or nose hairs". The crowd laughed in glee, and the voice continued to regale them with a slightly gravelly edge. Ezra had heard his friend use the same line on one of the deckhands aboard the *Boundless* the day before it sank.

He edged beyond the blacksmith's overheated tent to investigate the other stall. A signboard covered in fanciful figures slouched beside the arc of onlookers. Its words prompted a chill to run across Ezra's cheeks. It read, *Lazarus Thorn's Surpassingly Excellent Theater of Puppetry.*

Turning to Master Thorn's retreating and still bowed figure, Ezra gripped him by the elbow. "You can't go in this direction," he hissed. "It's *him.* Your double, or inspiritive bondsman, or whatever the Backwards Man called him. If you meet him, he'll pin you here in the obverse."

Behind them, the puppet show burst into action. A falsetto sliced across the throng, saying, "In year two, Wraithwatch felt they could claim the whole of the mountains, encroaching on Astella. Their hero, Calvin the Colossus ..."

Master Thorn whispered to Ezra. "They have a *Calvin* the Colossus? We have *Colwyn.* He does a nice narrator voice, though, I'll give him that. Does he look like me? And does he have his own Minimus?"

"Hang on, I'll look. But don't move, you hear?"

Master Thorn nodded. "I'd give a thousand sightings of my double for one glimpse of Minimus Mu. My plan is to remain here while you peek, and then we'll leave the square via the other exit. No chance of me seeing this Lazarus Thorn character, even if he has some imposter Minimus helping him. And you know what I'm like with plans. I always follow them, and they always work."

If Minimus Mu had been there to hear that statement, he would have snorted. It sounded like a harmless plan, but Minimus had seen too many other sweet plans turn sour and too many changes of Master Thorn's heart to take its sanctity for granted.

Then Master Thorn saw her.

Her!

The woman he had never dared hope to see again. And the plan not only went out the window, but fluttered into a passing stream and washed into a distant, unknown ocean.

Ezra nodded violently at Master Thorn and mimed a long skinny beard and bushy eyebrows as he pointed at the unseen puppet stage. But Master Thorn ignored that. Beyond Ezra, a tall figure parted the arc of the crowd. She stood a head taller than anyone else in the square, and her shoulders were as broad as Master Thorn was wiry. Her brown hair fell below her shoulders, and the V of her brows above her smoldering eyes was at odds with the smile forming on her full lips.

"Thorn?" she boomed, silencing the crowd and the puppeteer. "Is that *you*?"

Master Thorn opened his mouth to call to her but realized she was looking not at him but at the man on stage. This was the wrong kind of reunion. The woman he thought about every day edged across the crowded square to a man he'd never seen but knew did not deserve her. He ran forward.

Ezra tried to ensnare him, shouting, "Don't look at him. You can't meet him!" But Master Thorn slipped beneath his outstretched arm and sprang into the crowd, arms flailing.

"Maxima, I'm here! Over here! That's not the Thorn you're looking for. It's me!"

The woman stopped wading through the crowd and turned to Master Thorn, an eyebrow arched. She glanced at the stage and then back again. She changed direction and pushed her way toward him, the crowd parting.

On stage, the puppet master Lazarus Thorn used his best showman's voice. "I wish I could say it's part of the show for my twin brother to appear and interrupt us, but this is as unexpected for me as it is for you good people."

Master Thorn and the tall woman met mid-crowd. His arms tried to encircle her, but he rose only to her chest, and his arms were not remotely long enough to do the job. "Maxima, Maxima! I finally understand where you went, and why you didn't come back."

With the ease of a child hoisting a doll, the woman lifted Master Thorn so they were face to face. She kissed him full on the lips and then hugged him close. His fingers laced through her hair as he kissed her again.

"Sorry I got so mad," she whispered. "I'll try not to do it again."

Mighty forearms and triceps flexing, Maxima Li hoisted Master Thorn overhead, laughing. She could have lifted four Master Thorns. "I *finally* found him. I'll never let him go again." Maxima spun in a slow circle, showing off her trophy to the crowd.

Ezra shouted from the throng's edge, "Master Thorn, don't look at the stage!"

But it was too late. Master Thorn locked eyes with Lazarus Thorn as he cajoled the crowd, saying, "Looks like there's two of me here—any more and you'd call it a Thornucopia. Let's have a cheer for this amazing reunion, everyone!"

Then Lazarus stopped dead, unable to wrest his gaze from his double. The crowd fell silent, too. A faint crackling, like static electricity discharging from a woolen sock, accompanied a distortion above the crowd like the super-heated air above the blacksmith's forge. The barely visible disturbance ran along a jagged path from Master Thorn to Lazarus Thorn. The crowd held their breath, unsure what to expect.

Ezra could think only of an anchor, planting Master Thorn in this obverse world. Master Thorn had fabricated a fancy anchor for Ezra's balloon, and now he'd made one for himself. Ezra figured his friend was thinking the same thing, that his double had conspired against any possible reunion with Minimus Mu. Master Thorn flapped his arms at the square's exit, urging his long-lost love in that direction. "Run, Maxima, run!"

CHAPTER 16 - TEMPLE PANG

The Same Day

The morning light lent a crispness to the foliage outside. The whispering breeze, even the inelegant call of a seven-toed fly-eater, each pleased Rayne in its own way. She'd greeted another day with eyes and ears intact, and the Mothers of Midnight had left her alone, aside from bringing tastier-than-expected meals. She didn't notice when a cheerful tune blossomed in her heart and moved to her lips. But Catriona certainly did. Her voice reverberated throughout Rayne's locked chambers even though her footfalls marked her as only just entering the far end of the outer corridor.

"Would you *stop* that infernal singing? I can tell your transformation has *still* not kicked in, and I swear you're giving Mother Justicia a headache three floors above."

Rayne paused, only now hearing the trailing notes of her own voice. She halted not because Catriona commanded her, but because her focus on the visitor pushed her cheerful, daydreaming self into a closet and slammed its door shut.

"Good morning to you, too, dear sister," she called. Rayne addressed the barred window cut into her chamber door but knew it mattered little where she aimed. Catriona somehow picked up all sounds despite her scarred ears. Rayne could now imagine that quirk. Her own eyes and ears worked across unimaginable distances, letting her communicate with her dearest friends. She had even practiced enough that she could communicate with Minimus or her friends at the Crossed Swords without moving her lips or making a sound here in the temple if she focused enough. Was this Catriona's unusual way of interpreting the world? Could she be sympathizing with her captor and primary tormentor?

There was no immediate response to Rayne's greeting, but Rayne both dreaded the approach of Catriona's booted steps and looked forward to interaction—any interaction—to push the monotony aside. She tried again. "How'd you know my eyes and ears haven't yet sealed over? Can you see inside my room from way down the hall? Will I do that soon, too?"

The window framed Catriona's uncowled head. Disconcertingly, she faced not into the room but further along the outer corridor. Her lips remained their usual flat line as she spoke.

"You're a slow learner, shortshanks. It'll happen. One more day. I've come to ensure you've been practicing our mantra. You'll need it to help with our magic-draining mission."

Rayne sounded cheerful, but an inner voice wished it could scream objections. "Oh, you mean that *We close the gate and open the eyes* business? Yeah, I memorized that in the courtyard."

Rayne followed that up with, "You remember it? That time when you removed the magic from the animals in the garden, stealing their natural protections and leaving them with a death sentence?"

Rayne half-expected the door to fly open and for Catriona to swing her wooden rod around judiciously in the name of insubordination and crimes against the sisterhood. Instead, the girl stomped back along the hallway, leaving Rayne in silence once again.

* * *

High above, in the minaret of Temple Pang, Catriona knelt before Mother Justicia. Five of her fellow sisters bowed alongside her. The noise of their breathing contaminated the absolute silence they desired while awaiting a sign from Mother Justicia, but their nervousness jaundiced any attempt at calm. The older woman continued to pace, her slippers scuffing the carpet.

Catriona remained confused about their order's current situation. Attacks happened often at the Temple of the Wraith, but Mother Justicia seemed forewarned of each incursion. Repelling the forces had required little effort. It was as if throngs of magic-wielders had trooped to the temple gates for the purpose of magic removal, saving the Mothers of Midnight from the bother of seeking them out. But the recent temple inhabitants had been both successful and oddly inadequate. Peaceful monks? Really?

In Wraithwatch, the shifting lights overhead had suddenly coalesced into a more substantial spinning ring, and in an instant, men had appeared out of nowhere to overrun the temple. Shaven-headed, fanatical-looking men. And not just them, but their possessions had appeared, too. Brown cloaks had materialized on the hooks, replacing every sister's clothing. A blanket of infernal magic must have caused the abrupt change. Yet the monks had no magic. Catriona, in the dining hall, had watched as the furniture morphed, the cooking apparatus became unfamiliar, and everything but the building's structure took on a new look. It was as if a painter had glanced at the temple and, in an overzealous set of imaginative strokes, transformed everything except the resident sisters.

The interlopers had hardly acted like invaders, though. Ladles had dropped in the kitchen and the scattering of monks in the dining hall had stared at Catriona, open-mouthed. Whoever possessed enough magic to transform the temple and transfer in dozens of people had selected the wrong set of foot soldiers. It was as though someone had sent the monks by accident, not with any plan to eradicate the Mothers of Midnight.

Their intentions notwithstanding, Mother Justicia had been spooked by the jarring arrival. Within moments, Catriona and every other sister in Wraithwatch had rematerialized in the armory. Dozens of them were whisked from their sundry locations to the lodestone, which writhed under Mother Justicia's touch. Catriona had been subject to the stone's magic several times, and each disorienting flit left her nauseous and weak. Her bracelet had pulsed on her wrist in reaction to the stone. She'd never witnessed Mother Justicia summon the entire sisterhood before. Panic was the only explanation.

Despite the confusion, the older woman had acted with decisiveness. She instructed several squads of sisters to leave the temple on reconnaissance missions to scout the surrounding region for any further signs of attack. The rest, including Catriona, would travel with the lodestone to its other terminus at Temple Pang to seek refuge with the other enclave of their order. That trip's jolt had felt unlike anything she could remember. Arriving in this very minaret, Catriona had collapsed to the floor alongside scores of her sisters, filling the room shoulder to shoulder. She'd felt like a giant had shaken every joint loose, and her nose had brimmed with the scent of burning flesh.

With no time to recover, Mother Justicia had spurred the depleted sisters into action. Monks had overrun Temple Pang, too, and with no sign of their fellow sisters, it fell to Catriona and her scarred companions to flush out the local templars using their uncanny speed, whatever striking objects came to hand, and vicious intentions. Soon, they'd herded the templars to the docks, assessed them as lacking all signs of magic, and sent them seaward to Ven on their own ship.

Was this someone's idea of a grim joke? Somehow jumping an entire order of non-magical monks into Temple Pang to taunt the Mothers of Midnight? Catriona could find no logical explanation.

Mother Justicia stopped pacing. The room sank into a silence none of the sisters' enhanced hearing wanted to experience. A sharp voice entered their heads while they remained bowed.

"What do you mean you *lost* Sister Mariana? Was her

bracelet discharged?"

Whispering wasn't possible using the *directed voice,* but the reply was as meek as speaking with internal communication allowed. The girl to Catriona's left said, "She didn't have her bracelet. It was taken from her during the fighting."

The voiceless language of the Mothers of Midnight expressed rage easily. Mother Justicia wielded it like a scythe. "Taken? Who could move fast enough to wrestle it from her?"

The silence left the anger untampered. With the gust of air that accompanied Mother Justicia's rapid repositioning, Catriona did not need her magical vision to know that the woman's head hovered nose-to-nose with the neighboring girl.

That was enough to prompt an answer. "It was taken—stolen, really—by a monkey. It moved with magic, Mother."

Another girl further along the line chimed in. "I know it sounds like we're making it up, Mother, but it's true. None of the people in the caravan had magic, but we drained the horses, which was unsettling. Made me feel sick, in truth. And we somehow couldn't reach the monkey's magic. Something blocked us. He was so fast. Faster than us, almost."

The next silence was pure agony for the five other sisters. Catriona was glad to be exempt from Mother Justicia's current wrath, but waited for attention to turn her way. She was still unsure why she'd been summoned.

After a few moments that passed like hours, Mother Justicia stepped back. "I've noticed magic leaking into animals ever since the monks appeared here and in Wraithwatch. I've no idea how they accomplished it. You lot are dismissed! Leave your bracelets to charge on the lodestone, then find yourselves chambers. I will endeavor to locate Sister Mariana."

Five clinks, bracelets striking the lodestone, preceded the sounds of five pairs of feet moving as lightly as haste allowed. Mother Justicia spoke again, this time aloud. "Sister Catriona, you said that the new recruit, Sister Rayne, showed great potential during the testing, but her change was very slow. Has she fully *turned* now? We should extract a new bracelet from the stone for her."

Politeness demanded that Catriona reply in kind. The echoes that never accompanied her *directed voice* seemed confusingly unnatural. "Not yet, Mother. It's taking longer than usual."

"Never mind, it'll happen. It always does," Mother Justicia said.

Catriona had helped Mother Justicia shuffle the lodestone into position against the wall of this circular chamber when they had snapped across from the Temple of the Wraith. It hulked to one side, its blocky shape glistening with seething magical energy that made it uncomfortable to look at for more than a few moments. She'd never seen one of the *shifting* bracelets formed, and stood too entranced to look away from the process while too revulsed by the lodestone's corrupt geometry to look closely. Mother Justicia both caressed and directed the stone with a bony hand, tapping here and tracing looping script there. She coaxed a curling slice from the lodestone's surface, which coiled itself into a rolling shape that clattered to the stone floor before spiraling to a stop on the carpet. The bracelet, teased from stone, looked metallic, but stone and circlet shared an obvious bond. Catriona knew that the bond would allow a practiced bracelet wearer to return to this stone when needed. Distance proved no hindrance, as the newly arrived sisters from Wraithwatch proved.

Mother Justicia called after Catriona as the girl wound down the minaret's stairs. "Don't show her how to use it until she turns."

* * *

Pacing in the tower, visions of flames sprang forth in Mother Justicia's memory. She knew the only way to save humankind from its stunted, basest instincts was to disarm it. Magic was too great a power for careless, unwise hands. If even one more parent, sister, or child had to flee the cold flames of magic, it would be one too many. She turned her mind's eye away from the night when she returned to her village to find it smoldering

126

around its only two survivors.

It pained her to use young women in her mission to drain the magic away, but they were the only ones into whom she could pour her powers. For reasons known only to the inscrutable gods, if they even existed, she had become the vessel and sharer of the power to make magic disappear. The cost was terrible. Eyes and ears burnt away from her disciples, just like the heat had marred her face as she ran to the wailing boy amidst the ruins of the burning village. They received gifts in return for the memory loss and the scarring, her girls. Blinding speed and agility, second sight and hearing, their directed voice, their ability to leech magic from others. But no power would repay their sacrifice if the mission failed. They must snuff out the magic that humans would misuse forever if the temptation was not removed. Mother Justicia would use the lodestone and the eleven-pointed star to funnel the powers she'd doled out back to herself, leaving it to one quick slash of her knife across her throat to quell the world's magic forever, once they'd drained everyone else.

Would they regain their sight, their ears, their faces, if she pulled the magic from them? She could not—would not—ever know. That worried her hardly at all, although retrieving the eleven-pointed star amplifier from Mossmarch was a crucial task. What bothered her now was the magic of animals, although she found it dubious that the creatures she'd seen had *natural* abilities. Were the powers of humans leaking, being purposely sent into the animals at Temple Pang, or was this something the missing sisters of Temple Pang accomplished? Had they managed this somehow? Or perhaps those fat, bald men that popped into both temples caused it. Would the Mothers of Midnight need to accelerate their mission to prevent further tainting of the animal kingdom? And why had her spy not warned her in advance of the strange assaults on both temples? Questions abounded, and decisions loomed.

CHAPTER 17 - FADING SEA

The Same Day

"But have you any experience as a shiphand?" Roland asked Minimus. Dust from the caravan's progress into Wraithsport clung to his unwashed curls.

Jing Jing nodded, his head bouncing in comical fervor. Minimus managed less enthusiasm, a shrug of musclebound shoulders only, preferring to stick closer to the truth. "Well, I survived a shipwreck. Does that count?"

Roland rolled his head from side to side in an internal debate. One of the caravan guards, among the many who'd warmed to Minimus after he'd rolled away the boulders that blocked the mountain pass, clapped him heartily on the back. "That's the best kind of experience possible for a sailor. At least ye can swim, boy. That's a better start than I'd have."

Sometimes being honest and open was a bane. Minimus wondered what his friend Dando would say in this situation. Probably nothing. "Uh, yeah, swimming is good. I can whip up dinner for twenty, given proper ingredients and implements, if that helps."

Roland laughed. "Well, you're nothing if not persistent, Sang of Seven Rocks. Let me have a word at the docks with my old friend Missing-Arms Sven. He can make use of your strength even more than I do, and most pirates fear him, so he's an excellent master to sail with. But I'm asking him only *after* that last wagon is unloaded."

Roland thought to himself that he'd seen no one smile so wide as they bent under the weight of a heavy wrestle-vine arch.

* * *

Minimus contemplated what it felt like to be a sandwich, a butter knife, or a cart wheel. He figured he understood their sadness as he watched Roland and Missing-Arms Sven gesture in his direction and barter. Sven counted out eleven goat molars into Roland's waiting purse. After more haggling that Minimus found more animated than strictly necessary and a shouted request across the dockyard to "Lift that barrel, there, boy," a few more teeth changed hands. Everyone left with a smiling face. Not least Minimus, who was now the lowest-ranking crewman on the *Sea Camel*.

Minimus, of all people, should have known better than to guess at someone's appearance based on their name. Missing-Arms Sven possessed two more arms than the boy had imagined. Perhaps his name should have been Suspicion-Eyed Sven, Gangly Armed Sven, or Charcoal-Face-Painted Sven. The man bristled with weaponry; sheathed daggers lay strapped like accusations to his forearms and thighs, a pair of long-handled axes slung across his back, and the gentle curve of a Hammarskaldian dueling sword swung from his left hip. Black tracings framed his eyes and ran from below them across his cheeks as if he'd cried a river of coal, completing his intense presence.

Later, during the voyage up the Wraithwatch coast, Minimus learned that the name came from Sven's boyhood tendency to make off with unattended weapons. Visitors to his parents' house would often complain about their missing arms. This was a man who Jing Jing could admire.

Sven called across the foreshore, "Boy! What are you calling yourself again? Sang? Start loading those barrels. The *Sea Camel* lies moored over there. And there are no bunks left. If you find anything that could double as bedding, snatch it. Settle yourself in the hold."

Minimus hoisted the nearest barrel overhead, sensing the surreptitious and possibly jealous glances of the toiling stevedores. Jing Jing tailed him as they trotted past Roland and Sven. Minimus nodded a silent thank you to Roland. "Bedding for me *and my monkey*, right, Captain?" he asked Sven, not daring to look him in the face.

"Why not?" Sven replied. "Monkeys bring good luck."

Jing Jing scurried ahead, needlessly warning the other dockworkers to give Minimus space. As he hustled the first barrel up the gangway, the boy said quietly to Jing Jing, "Good luck? Good luck to your crew with holding onto their valuables, that's what I'd say."

Minimus still held the metallic band snatched from the wrist of the captured Mother of Midnight, and although the monkey had left the caravan carrying only his precious jar of eyeballs, several bits of jewelry and eight goat's teeth of dubious provenance lay hidden in the briny liquid. He'd fished them out and shown them to Minimus once they were out of sight of the caravan. The boy knew not from whence or whom Jing Jing had stolen this treasure, but there was no good way to return the items, much less explain how he'd come to possess them in the first place. This small cache of treasure meant that Jing Jing sported a new and rather well-embroidered jacket from a children's clothier, and they set off to sea with a bulging hamper and two sets of middling-quality cutlery. They would dine royally, even if confined to a bilge-ridden nest.

Rubbing tired arms, Minimus stood beside the monkey on deck as they waited to cast off. "Check out Seymour," the boy said, leaning down to look at Jing Jing's jar. "They must be moving that captured girl somewhere—the eyes are changing focus."

* * *

The passage to Yinti in the queendom of Golden Shores involved a meander north along the Wraithwatch coast to Hornport before setting out across the Fading Sea. Although not the most direct line to Yinti, this route allowed the ship to call in at ports large and small along the coast. The prevailing winds between Hornport and Yinti would be at their back, avoiding the endless tacking involved in a diagonal crossing from southern Wraithwatch.

The days followed a common pattern. Minimus had few duties while at sea, so he stuck mostly to the hold, awaiting intermittent contact with Rayne when she could snatch a few quiet moments alone to exercise her newfound communication powers. When he and Jing Jing took fresh air on deck, he could see why other seafarers feared Sven. The man spent little time giving orders or piloting his ship, instead surging to and fro across the decks, whirling his axes or throwing daggers at human-shaped wooden targets. Whether through fear or masterful organization and discipline, the ship's crew ran itself.

With no safe place to moor, the ship breezed past the wrestle-vine beach. Minimus watched his former fellow farmers stand up on the sand bar and stretch their backs as they followed the passing ship's progress. He knew that would be the most entertaining part of their day, unless one accidentally stood shore-side of a wrestle vine and had to hack his way out of its greedy grasp.

At each port, Minimus needed to spring into action. A supervisor would identify the goods leaving ship as they approached, and the boy's job was to stage them on deck near the gangway for efficient offloading. As soon as stevedores lashed the ship to the dock, he would manhandle the goods ashore. Master Thorn would have referred to this as *boyhandling* instead of manhandling. Materials awaiting shipment were piled high on the docks, and Minimus then hauled them aboard, piling them as directed into the cargo hold following an inscrutable system that factored in the cargo's destination and the ship's overall balance.

Sven would spend his time ashore concluding negotiations for the incoming and outpouring cargo, occasionally gripping the hilt of a dagger or an axe handle if there were differences of opinion. This resolved any ambiguity with unsurprising speed. The ship's cooks fussed around the port town, restocking their larders. Sailors flooded the docks, chatting idly with the local dockworkers or less idly with girls, women, and other colorful characters that arrived at the seafront to follow the action entailed by a new ship's arrival. Eventually, with every necessary interaction completed, Sven would shout, and any crew still ashore would sprint back to the ship. Minimus was always aboard by this point, and he and Jing Jing would lean at the rail where Sven told them to stand, waiting to set sail once again.

Sven would make a last pass among the onlookers, making some covert deal and separating interested people from the crowd. He would herd them to one end of the dock or another—into a position where they could wave to the ship as it left the harbor. Then he'd sprint up the gangway, and the dock workers would release the last rope tethering the ship to the dock. He told Minimus that it was tradition for the newest crew member to wave farewell to each port, so the boy would stand as handsomely as his over-bulky form and uncut hair would allow, giving the knot of chattering people slow waves. A few would wave in return, but most simply pointed his way. Occasionally, someone would call out before being shushed by their mates. A few times, he thought they called him by name, but Minimus realized this dreaming would only make him more lonely. Nobody in Wraithwatch ever recognized him as the hero of the five trials. He figured the waving was a Wraithwatchian tradition, because they'd not done anything similar on *Boundless*. Boy and monkey would wave until the townsfolk were too small to distinguish as individuals, then retire to their nest among the barrels below deck.

CHAPTER 18 - VEN

The Same Day

Former queen Jada cursed herself for pacing, annoyed that the jumped-up little Red Bean princess could crawl under her skin so easily. She'd show those upstarts who truly deserved to rule Outer Pang.

Her muttering paused as a messenger knocked at the door of her quarters, waiting only a moment before entering. Did he not know to never disturb a queen without her explicit approval? Apparently, the Vennese treated their honored guests with less formality than was proper.

"News, my lady."

Familiar in his all-white emissary robes, Jada forgot about the slight of his unceremonious entry. This was the messenger she and Queen Veronica had dispatched as soon as news of the magic-blasted ship had arrived.

"What word do you bring? Do they agree?"

The messenger responded with the odd Vennese nod, glancing down and to the right, signaling agreement. "I spoke directly to the sect's leader, a Mother Justicia. We'll need additional negotiation to iron out the finer wrinkles, but she's completely on board with the proposal."

A smile broke across Jada's cruel lips. "Excellent work. Tell me more about this Mother Justicia."

* * *

There was an odd friction, Princess Tasha thought, between luxurious hospitality and constant alertness to impending catastrophe. She and her Golden Shoresian escorts had spent the better part of a week in a wing of the Vennese palace that proved difficult to find fault with. The beds were comfortable, the royal chefs' creations enjoyable, and the court's array of entertainers were at their disposal. And yet, Tasha felt nervous about venturing out, even with her ferocious guardswomen. She did not feel a hostage, yet determination pressed upon her to stay in Ven. Veronica had advised Tasha to remain until safe passage across the Fading Sea could be guaranteed. The magical attack at Temple Pang was unsettling, and Tasha still sought a lever to pull, hoping for a way to reopen the diplomatic discussion she'd botched upon arrival.

Jada had appeared twice at dinner, ignoring Tasha and excusing herself early from Queen Veronica's side. But on these occasions, Jada's silver hair fell in less austere waves, and her eyes showed perhaps a hint of sympathy toward Tasha's tension.

"We have good news, Princess," Jada began at the second dinner. "After contacting the leader of this new order that has taken control of Temple Pang, we stand on favorable ground for negotiation of a peace accord. The three of us can set off tomorrow for discussions to seal the deal. Will you stand with us?"

Tasha viewed Jada's friendlier tone as a trap and took a moment before responding.

"We'll sail two ships across the sea. You can take one from Ven, Queen Veronica with me. We have much to discuss, and if she sails with us, I'm sure we'll all know where we stand by the time we make land."

Jada deferred with a quick glance at her cousin. Queen Veronica nodded with the slightest movement of her head. "I'd be delighted to travel aboard your ship, Lady Tasha. I will be sure my complement of guards does not outnumber your own." She waved to an attendant. "Have the *Fair Winds* readied for Queen Jada. And prepare the small queen's guard—we sail aboard the *Sun Seeker* tomorrow morning."

Princess Tasha waved to the messenger. "And tell my crew to prepare for my arrival down there. Have provisions laid on. We'll set sail at dawn."

Veronica covered her mouth as she laughed. "Dawn? By the lords of the air, no. We'll depart after breakfast."

CHAPTER 19 - MOSSMARCH

Two Days Later

The dark-cloaked figures moved with the same preternatural speed Virgil Longspeaker had witnessed during their earlier incursion. This time, they ignored the girls scattering into every available alleyway, leaving the market. They were intent on Sala Doon alone. As the Mothers sped into the square and crossed toward Sala, Mirko, Dando, and Virgil, the birds attracted to Sala's eleven-pointed star amulet had whipped into action. They rose from the cobblestones at Sala's feet and arrowed across the courtyard. In glowing waves, the birds dove in swooping passes toward each of the five hooded figures, finding no purchase with their beaks but making the intruders pause, duck, and weave to avoid their impact.

With his normal lightning-fast survival instincts, Sala grabbed the horn of a nearby goat, which rose at speed. Mirko grabbed a hoof, and in a moment, the two men were atop the sloping thatched roof of the Crossed Swords. Dando froze for a moment, but stood from the men's usual outdoor table to defend himself before the Mothers zigged and zagged their way through the cloud of birds.

Virgil heard the swish of flying daggers. He raised his lute like a two-handed sword but then had another idea. He needed time to process it. Sala had thrown four or five knives in a blur, and with a series of thuds, one of the approaching Mothers found herself pinned to the wall of the blacksmith's forge. Despite her contorted dodging, two of Sala's blades pierced her cloak, one through the hood and the other at the hemline. As she ripped herself free, leaving the torn-away hood dangling from the wall, she broke stride and stalled, looking in disbelief at her forearm. A still-quivering blade stuck out from it, blood beginning to drip on her left shoe. The scarring over her eyes crinkled in panic, and for once, Dando and Virgil heard a sound come from a Mother of Midnight's mouth. The scream of pain echoed from the walls, unlike the direct voice that Dando alone had heard during their previous appearance.

The injured girl turned toward her companion, who had bounded from table to roof. Readying to make the leap to the sloping thatch where Sala and Mirko stood back to back, a second girl twitched her head. The wounded Mother of Midnight twirled her uninjured arm, spinning a metallic bracelet, and popped out of existence. Virgil knew from Rayne's stories this meant she'd returned to Temple Pang.

Four Mothers remained. Three had reached the rooftop above Virgil and Dando, navigating through the dense cloud of darting birds toward Sala and Mirko. The fourth halted just beyond striking distance from Virgil, looking up at her companions. A veil kept her scarred features from view, but her lips moved silently. She pulled back her right sleeve, and an indigo ring of magical energy sizzled into existence around her drawn-back elbow. From Rayne's descriptions, Dando realized this must be Sister Catriona.

In Sala's mind, a commanding and harsh girl's voice intruded. "We can smell it. We know you have it. Surrender the star, or we will rip and blast you apart to get it."

Even though he could not hear the Mother of Midnight communicate directly, Mirko knew Sala well enough to understand that surrender was never on the cards. In his mind, Sala knew that whenever blasting, ripping, flogging, or keelhauling were threatened, the punishment would never disappear after a surrender. He may as well go out fighting.

As the nearest Mother's grasping hand snatched at the chain around Sala's neck, the knife-thrower thrust his hips forward and back-flipped to the roof's ridged peak. Although not nearly as fast as his attacker, he was fast enough. Her hand glanced off the chain holding the eleven-pointed star without securing the prize.

With the outrageous level of chaos in the Mossmarch market square, no one would have dreamed that Virgil Longspeaker would raise his lute and strum the first few chords of the Ballad of the Mothers of Midnight. Even he doubted it was a good idea, and he had a long history of thinking bad ideas sounded appealing. But he trusted Rayne, and something she'd said made him decide to open his mouth and belt out the first verse.

The first few strains of Virgil's song drifted from below. Sala wobbled then hurled himself feet-first down the sloping roof. His slide along the thatch cast an outraged shower of chaff in all directions. Mirko flung himself out of the way of another marauding Mother, using the neighboring stall's suspended cloth roof as a makeshift trampoline to break his fall.

The first line of the ballad could use revision, Virgil thought. Maybe it shouldn't be "Black cloaks fluttered across cobbles cold". He could use 'wove' instead of 'fluttered'. That aligned better with the clothing reference to 'cloaks'.

He continued with the rest of the first verse. Just like Rayne promised, it worked. Well, it worked a little.

The remaining Mother on the courtyard floor winced, covering one burnt-away ear. The whirling coil of magic she'd launched spun wide of its mark. It whizzed past Sala's flailing arm, raging as it spat toward the palace wall. It struck a glancing blow, masonry falling as a crenelation toppled. The magic looped away into the sky.

One of the Mothers atop the roof, disoriented by the singing, slipped and fell backward. The one that had nearly snatched the chain from Sala's neck dropped to one knee on the roof, and the last staggered as Sala slid past her.

In a rare fit of courage, Apostle Dando used the only weapon he had to hand. A long, black urchin quill piqued the fabric at the thigh of the Mother who'd loosed her magical blast. Its magic hadn't worked to rejuvenate his truth-telling powers, but it made for a serviceable weapon. She recoiled a step.

Sala spun into a forward roll as he reached the roof's edge. Although it let him land in a graceful dismount on the cobbles below, it proved a tactical error. The chain with the eleven-pointed star rose from his neck as he spun, remaining suspended in midair long enough for the fair-skinned hand of his pursuer on the rooftop to snatch it away. She pocketed it in a blur.

Sala rolled to a stop, feeling for his missing chain. The falling Mother bounced in a painful-looking back bend, collapsing the table she landed on before crouching and shirking off the impact. The other two Mothers of Midnight leapt from the roof, speeding past Mirko's rise in an awkward bounce from the trader's tent. Virgil had barely begun the second verse when the four stunned and staggering Mothers retreated. Their prize obtained, they flourished their bracelets to wink away from Mossmarch.

* * *

Assuring his friends that the Mothers of Midnight must make their way using conventional means to Mossmarch, and that the magical bracelets only provided rapid transport back to Temple Pang, Virgil offered to buy the first round after the attack at the Crossed Swords. By the time he returned to the outdoor tables, Dando had righted and realigned them in their usual haphazard pattern. He plonked down four spilling mugs of gorgonflower ale as Mirko held court. Two goats hovered behind him and the ever-present twittering of birds had reconvened on every free table edge and neighboring tree branch. Mirko would need extra lung power to speak over the animal noises.

He held a device in his hands, showing its workings to Sala and Dando. "It's ingenious, I tell you. Master Thorn's gift to me comes from a place of devious inspiration. These straps hold it to my arm, like so."

Mirko strapped the device to his right forearm, pulling his baggy pickpocket's sleeve up way past his elbow.

"It's spring loaded, so this extending piece stays concealed in my sleeve when you push it up against the catch, just here." Mirko pushed against the springs until, with a snick, an extensible arm settled into place, held by a ridged catch. "And then, if I bend my wrist way back, it pushes this trigger arm here, and the snatcher springs out, then coils back. And these little claws open and close. They're gentle, too. Here, Dando, hold out this apple."

Dando opened his palm and placed the apple atop it, stem up. Mirko ruffled his sleeve again to conceal the device. Raising his hand above Dando's outstretched palm, but remaining a dagger's length away, he snapped his other hand's fingers.

This brazen distraction fooled none of his companions. They'd seen him in action too many times to be duped by such a simple trick, and their eyes remained glued to his other sleeve. Even so, all they saw was him flexing back his wrist and a blur as the apple disappeared up his sleeve.

"Well, that's impressive," Virgil said. "But I'm still unclear how *you* ended up with the eleven-pointed star."

A lopsided smile cracked Mirko's lips. "I was bouncing up from the stall next door's springy roof fabric as that ornery hussy jumped down from the Crossed Swords' roof. And as anyone familiar with the Leatherfoot legend knows, if I'm around, you'd better keep your valuables clutched in your hands, not jingling in your pockets, or they might disappear. Tactical mistake on her part. I couldn't quite reach her as we crossed paths, but the extra reach of Master Thorn's snatcher gave me just enough opportunity. And Mirko Leatherfoot never wastes an opportunity."

Wiping ale froth from his lips, Virgil clapped Dando on the back. "And how about you, lad? That land urchin quill your guild sent didn't help return you to your truthsaying ways, but you managed to jab one of the Mothers of Midnight. Only you and Sala can claim that feat, and it took Sala about nine thrown blades to accomplish the deed."

Dando phrased his answer as a question but accidentally followed it up with a lie. "Well, didn't I tell you I did special training in Interviki hand fighting as part of my order's training? I was the grand champion and even wrestled the Lion of Og on three occasions."

Dando examined the long, fine-pointed quill. It had a few threads from the girl's legging snagged at the tip. He was settling into his inability to tell the truth now, and tinged every statement with a shade of sarcasm. "I wasn't scared in the slightest this time. And like Rayne promised, those girls *loved* your singing."

Virgil strummed an intentionally mis-fingered chord. "As they should, my friend. As they should."

CHAPTER 20 - TEMPLE OF THE WRAITH

Six Days Later

Even as their horses trotted into the forest surrounding Pearl Wash and reached the first inklings of rising terrain, Master Thorn felt the inspiritive bond the Backwards Man had mentioned. It was as if an invisible cord entered the back of his neck and gently tugged at his innards, tempting them to return to the market square and Lazarus Thorn's puppetry. He felt like one of his own marionettes, jerked on an invisible thread.

Skain Two-Hearts had regathered his fighting force and rode with his squire on one side and Master Thorn and Maxima Li on the other. "So let me get this straight. You two have been apart for three fivespans. You're both from Outer Pang, and you accidentally spotted each other in the market square of Pearl Wash, a continent and ocean away?"

Master Thorn nodded, caressing Maxima's musclebound arm as she directed the horse they shared. "Even further than that. Wait until you hear what we figured out from chatting with the Backwards Man! Maxima and I are not even from the same *world*. She is from a village in Outer Pang in your world, but detonating mountain rams blasted Ezra and I through from our familiar Wraithwatch to yours. That's why neither of us could understand why we saw the temple full of shaven-headed monks—before the blast—when you expected the coven of the Mothers of Midnight. Maybe they shifted through to our world as we entered yours?"

Skain nodded, lips wrinkling as he processed the idea. Ezra chimed in from behind them. "Apparently, this world is the *obverse* of ours. Perhaps the other way around. Or both. And there are big differences. Like magic. On our side, only animals have magical powers. Every land animal and bird has a special power. And here, it's humans. Although I guess not all humans."

Master Thorn pointed above the looming mountain peaks to the still-spinning ring of wraithlight above the temple. It remained bright enough to see during the day and flickered with exquisite beauty each evening. "Apparently, we can use the balloon to fly through that ring and return to our familiar side."

Skain nodded, more vehemently this time. "This makes a kind of sense. But does this mean we won't see the Mothers of Midnight here again? No Mother Justicia? No disciples? They won't be able to pass across the ring. Unless, of course, you donate them your flying contraption if you make it across. Maybe our magic is safe, thanks to those exploding goats. We can redouble our efforts on Temple Pang, assuming the Mothers there did not get sucked across, too."

Ezra expounded on several theories he'd been pondering since their meeting with the Backwards Man. Skain took interest, but Master Thorn pressed a cheek into the fabric of Maxima's shirt. After a time, he pulled himself higher in the saddle so he could speak quietly into Maxima's ear, his beard arrowing over her shoulder. "Now I understand all the things you described that made little sense at the time. People with magic. Your village. And you must have thought I talked a load of cobblers half the time, too. I can't wait for you to see Minimus again. We'll start searching as soon as we cross."

Maxima's voice came in a rumble, as she kept to low tones so only Master Thorn could hear. "You'll find, my love, that *most* people think you talk a stream of old toot, not just me. But yes, I figured out we were from two worlds once I accidentally returned here. Situations, customs, and especially the magic. It made more sense looking back than when I lived on your side."

Master Thorn murmured again. "I still can't figure out how you moved between the two faces. When you left us, you just thinned out and disappeared, like the down from a puff-flower blowing off in a high wind."

"Well, I was raging both times. I thought my village had disappeared around me when I had started growing into my strength and a group of snarky and cruel boys wrestled me to the dirt behind the tannery. Next thing I knew, they were gone, and so was the entire village. And you'll remember how mad I got the last day we spent together. I'm so sorry about that. I was tired, hungry, and hot. Especially tired. A terrible combination. Something snapped."

Master Thorn ran soothing fingers through Maxima's short, dark hair. "Yeah. I could have forged a family set of cutlery on the fire of your rage. Maybe you have secret magic that moves you from your side of the world to mine, but only when you're angry enough? But you're back now. Let's focus on staying together. And finding Minimus."

* * *

As the air grew colder and the snaking mountain road's switchbacks slowed their horses' pace, Ezra questioned Skain about his name. "I'm guessing they don't call you two-hearts because you really have two. What's the story?"

Skain's squire laughed, but Skain himself answered. "I'm surprised nobody else has told you. Here, let me show you."

He unlaced the front of his chainmail shirt and pulled back the fabric of his doublet to reveal a puckered horizontal scar across the top of his left pectoral. "I was stabbed many years ago. The blade went clear through me and poked out my back. It must have missed slicing through anything vital, but even so, it was a year before proper movement returned to my left arm and shoulder. Everyone joked I must have two hearts to survive that."

Ezra's eyes widened. The scar was wide and gnarled enough that it made imagining surviving the wound difficult. "During a raid on the Mothers of Midnight? Is revenge another reason for you to keep on with your campaign?"

Skain shook his head. "Hardly. I got involved in a street fight in Pearl Wash. A clutch of brigands passing through town harassed a disfigured woman in the street, and I intervened. I'd thought a few words would discourage them, but as it turned out, my chest bore the brunt of the interference instead. In a way, it worked, though. Seeing my wound, the men scuttled off out of town without bothering the poor woman any further. She helped me as I lay there bleeding."

Master Thorn leant from his saddle to look more closely at the long-healed scar. "Looks like they didn't sharpen their blade properly. See the scar's ragged edges? If one of my knives ran you through, this would be a nice clean line. And who stitched you up? They didn't even bother to align the top and bottom of your tattoo!"

The tattoo tugged at Ezra's memory strings. He'd seen that stylized eagle flapping off with a fish somewhere else. The figurehead of the *Boundless*, maybe? He filed it partway down the list of things that would probably occur to him overnight.

∗ ∗ ∗

The Temple of the Wraith appeared largely as they'd left it. Its gate lay on the ground, exactly where it had flown from its hinges under Skain's magical blast. A balloon's basket sat near the base of the curtain wall's interior side where Skain's men had left it. The purple fabric of its envelope lay folded into a precise square alongside, trailing lines arching limply to the basket's lip. Armed with the thick needle and heavy fishing line he'd brought from Pearl Wash, Ezra would need to unfold the cloth to locate and sew shut the rip that preceded the crash.

No residents roamed the place; no wisps of smoke rose

from the cookhouse. Neither monks nor Mothers of Midnight had returned, although with the revelation of their transportation to the obverse world, neither Master Thorn nor Ezra had expected the Mothers to return without powerful magical intervention. Maxima helped the two men spread the balloon envelope, equally keen to prepare for a return to the other world.

Ezra dared not look at either of them as he sewed his way down the ragged tear. "What about this bond between you and Lazarus Thorn that the Backwards Man told us to avoid? Isn't that going to anchor you here, in the obverse, if we attempt to fly through yonder ring? And even you, Maxima—this is your world. Do you think whatever magic—or science—circles overhead will let you through?"

Master Thorn released the two handfuls of fabric he'd been aligning and tutted. "Longshanks, stop being such an optimizer."

Ezra raised his goggles to regard Master Thorn. "I like to think I make things more efficient, but what does that have to do with my question?"

"Not *that* kind of optimizer. An opti-miser. The kind that is miserly with optimism! The Backwards Man said three people would fly through the wraithlight in a balloon. Now there's three of us, and I see no reason not to believe him."

Ezra knocked on his conch helmet for good luck. "I hope so, I really do. But there's optimism and then there's believing second-hand gossip passed along from the future to a weird turnip farmer who never leaves his fields."

Master Thorn rubbed the back of his neck before realigning the fabric so Ezra could continue stitching. He still felt the tingle of the invisible inspiritive bond with Lazarus Thorn. It mingled with an icy river of dread. "Let's get this mended and then pray to the wind lemurs for a well-directed breeze."

* * *

Skain sent two of his men to help Master Thorn prepare

dinner. He had arrayed the cooking implements in a line along the slate tabletop next to the hearth and had selected a basketful of potatoes, an array of dried herbs, and a wheel of hard cheese from the larder. Distracted from his contemplation of an inferior kitchen knife by the men's arrival, Master Thorn pointed the nicked blade at a chunk of unknown material that one of Skain's men unwrapped.

"What in the name of the dolphin's shrine is *that* thing?"

The man looked puzzled. "What, this? It's salted pork. Brought it from town. We can dice it and sprinkle it on top of whatever you're making."

"What's pork? Looks like the core of a giant pink mushroom," Master Thorn said.

The man held the open paper on his palm and offered it to Master Thorn to sniff. "You know, pork. From the pig farm just outside town."

Master Thorn contemplated the idea of a pig farm. In Inner Pang, pigs roamed free. The rage boars were best avoided, lest you find yourself at the end of a curved tusk. But ironskin pigs were cute in their own way, their magically armored hide making them impervious to even sabreclaw attacks and therefore unafraid of humans. "So, it *is* part of a mushroom? They use the pigs to root them out?"

"Nah, mate," the man replied. "This *is* the pig. It's pig meat with salt added to preserve it."

Master Thorn aborted his plan to sniff the unidentified item and took a step back. "But their magic. Doesn't it … oh, never mind. I forgot, no magic. So, you imprison pigs, then kill and *eat* them?" Waggish minstrels in Inner Pang told stories of barbaric hill people—who doubtless hadn't even *heard* of cutlery—dissecting carrion as if it was fish and eating it. But that behavior was inhuman. Only animals should eat one another. "Ew! Place it well aside. You barbarians can scarf some at dinner when I'm not looking. And keep that knife away from the proper food!"

* * *

It always seemed unlikely to Master Thorn that Ezra's conch shell helmet would protect him from any kind of mishap. Especially a balloon crash. They'd cheated death by surviving one such incident already, and it defied belief they could manage another. But if nothing else, it was the traditional balloon pilot uniform, goggles and helmet. A tradition established by the only such pilot in the familiar or the obverse worlds.

When a light breeze shifted late in the morning, Ezra was eager to set off, reporting that the wind was as mercurial as Master Thorn's route planning when he traveled aboard the cutlery merchant's cart. He didn't even listen to Master Thorn describe how he'd meticulously planned the route according to season, national feasting days, and the ebb and flow of dining customs. Instead, he asked for a couple of Skain's men to steady the basket and discovered that *all* the men had swarmed the courtyard so they could see the launch. Even the trial inflation just after dawn had drawn almost everyone.

Although she was eminently capable of clambering into the wicker basket herself, Master Thorn held out a hand for Maxima Li. After bounding into the basket, she maintained her grip on his hand and lifted Master Thorn up, legs swinging wildly. She giggled as she hoisted him into the basket.

Ezra snapped his goggles down, which made his instructions emerge with a more nasal intonation than usual. He gestured vaguely to Skain and his men. "Okay, lads, I think we're ready. The envelope sewing job has proven sturdy, and the parachute valve at the top worked perfectly this morning. If we're not ready now, we'll never be, so cast off the ropes if you'll please."

Maxima clapped her hands in glee as the balloon rose from the courtyard in slow majesty. "It's working!"

Ezra spared a moment from his fussing over the furnace and turned to her. "Madam, did you ever doubt me?"

Master Thorn chimed in. "He's made up an entire language to bamboozle you into believing everything he says, my dear.

Calls it *science*. But to be fair, he's nearly always right."

Ezra muttered to himself as he opened the grill atop the furnace a fraction. "I hope *you* are right, my friend, about the inspiritive bond, and about Maxima. And I hope this wraithlight wheel takes us back home and doesn't shred us into oblivion. More hope here than science, I fear."

Skain waved, and his men cheered as the balloon cleared the wall and drifted toward the spinning, glowing mass overhead. The breeze was faint but blew in their favor. All three felt that they were heading in the perfect direction.

Then, the balloon angled off course. As they rose higher, it drifted away from the wraithlight. "No, no, no!" Ezra called. "A cross draft."

Master Thorn peeked over the rim of the basket. His view of the ground below confirmed his fear. The balloon was indeed drifting in the wrong direction. "Cross draft? I don't feel any breeze."

Ezra knocked his helmet with a clenched fist. "Well, you wouldn't, would you? The balloon moves at the same speed as the wind, so you can't detect it."

Maxima didn't care for looking down, and her hold on Master Thorn's arm made his flesh bulge above and below her clenched hand. "Well, let us go back down. We can try again later when the breeze is right."

The balloon reached the correct height but was drifting further from the wraithlight. "It's no use," Ezra cried. "Look where we are—there's no place to land now. It's all mountain slope below. We'll have to wait until we're out of the mountains and set down on the flat somewhere. Maybe we can hire a farmer to cart the balloon back up to the temple."

Master Thorn felt as deflated as the balloon after their earlier incident. His voice came out in a monotone. "But that'll take days or weeks. We'll never find Minimuuuuuus—"

He never completed the sentence because the balloon shot toward the spinning wraithlight with unexpected speed. The basket swung beneath the purple fabric envelope so the whole contraption flew at an angle, purple fabric leading the charge.

The three passengers latched onto the basket's rim as if it was a prized possession being tugged at by thieves. They would never agree on who screamed the loudest, but there was definite shrieking.

Within a few moments, the balloon passed through the wheel of wraithlight, disappearing as it went. The inner disc of the phenomenon was a ghostlike silver, and the balloon crossed its plane, leaving ripples behind as if it had sunk into a pool of mercury. As the basket trailed behind, now at a sharp angle to the ground, all three stared across its lower lip at the craggy mountainside far below. The speed at which the wraithlight sucked the balloon through kept the trio pinned to the floor, legs straining against the forces at play.

Ezra was now lower than Master Thorn and Maxima, who had their backs against the highest part of the basket. The whole of the balloon had passed beyond the wraithlight, still tugging its dangling lines and basket along at speed. Through his terror, Ezra viewed this as an encouraging result. If the ring had destroyed the balloon, the sac would have collapsed, the lines would have gone slack, and the basket's full weight would have sent them crashing to the mountainside below.

A moment later, Ezra was through the silvery membrane, ears popping and begoggled eyes adjusting to the sunnier day and the now visible balloon angling overhead. The silver plane of the barrier between his world and the obverse bisected the balloon basket and obscured the section containing Maxima and Master Thorn. Maxima's flexing arm appeared on Ezra's side first, and then the basket caught on something, ropes above groaning under the pull of the balloon. The rest of her inched through in a series of jerks. Her head and other arm popped through the membrane with a last rush like a birthing calf. She turned her face toward the not-yet-visible corner of the basket. The part where Master Thorn stalled under the irresistible pull of his inspiritive bond to the obverse.

Unseen by his two companions, he felt the basket jerk to a stop as the hand that held Maxima's tore from her grasp. That hand flew to the back of his neck, where it felt like a fishing hook attempted to tease his spine from his body. He caught odd glimpses from backstage at a puppet theater in Pearl Wash, where Lazarus Thorn paused mid-show, unable to speak or maneuver his marionettes. Then, he felt himself losing substance. His other hand no longer gripped the basket's rim, instead sliding *through* the wicker. His body followed and oozed its way backwards, obeying the pull of the invisible bond.

As his body retreated and became less substantial, the basket stuttered through the silver barrier until it disappeared from the obverse forever, its dangling tow rope slithering after it.

What now? he thought. He knew this question's answer. He would never reunite with Minimus Mu, and he had lost Maxima. Again! Neither were forgivable, and the long drop below his resolidifying body would prove a fitting punishment.

This was not part of any plan Master Thorn would devise. Or even follow. Lazarus could put on the world's greatest ever puppet show, and it would be less significant than a speck of dust on Minimus Mu's wrinkled tunic. The greatest musicians could sing along beside the stage, and they would sound less appealing than a choking bog goose compared to a single breath expelled by Maxima Li. Bond or no bond, Master Thorn knew where he belonged, and he paid his blistering hands little attention as he grabbed the rope whizzing past his chest.

The balloon was righting itself when Master Thorn left the wreath of wraithlight with a distinct pop. Maxima's wail morphed into a quizzical note, and she fought back her vertigo enough to lean over the side of the basket to see what had snapped the tow rope taut.

Without even a word, she hauled on the rope, pulling Master Thorn up. With a final clasp of his wrist, she hoisted him on board, hugging him so tightly that he had to slap raw hands against her arms as a sign to ease up, the air knocked from his lungs.

The prevailing winds swept the balloon up over the mountains that divided Wraithwatch from Astella and out to sea, ushering them north and then west toward the first possible landing spot, the Queendom of Golden Shores.

CHAPTER 21 - GOLDEN SHORES

The Same Day

Compared with the modest exchange of goods at each town as the *Sea Camel* wove its way through the islands that dotted the Wraithwatch coast, the loading of the ship in Hornport was a mountain of labor. On the second day of the Fading Sea crossing, Minimus didn't want to rouse his aching muscles enough to swing himself from his hammock. But Jing Jing's monkey ears had heard something above decks, and he wouldn't stop screeching and tugging at the boy's tunic until Minimus followed him.

Squinting into the pallid sunshine, Minimus's eyes could do nothing less than pop open. High overhead, the familiar purple fabric of Ezra's balloon sped westward, the crackle of its hot-air furnace just audible.

Captain Missing-Arms Sven raised a charcoal-lined eyebrow at the antics of boy and monkey, who hollered and waved their arms overhead at the balloon. Some of his other men waved at the spectacle, but Sven took particular interest in Minimus's reaction.

"They won't hear you," he growled. "Not that high up, with that furnace blaring in their ears. These salty scoundrels haven't seen a balloon before, but I'd wager you two have, eh?"

Minimus's shoulders slumped, realizing that Sven was right. Ezra would never hear them, and nor would Master Thorn if he was still aboard. And they'd look like ants swarming over a discarded sea biscuit from that height.

"Yeah, I've seen it before. I thought I might—maybe, you know—find my—a person I recognize on board."

"Ah, my boy," Sven began. This wounded Minimus, forcing memories of Master Thorn calling him the same. He knew Sven meant nothing by it, but sometimes it took only a word or two to change his mood. "I think you'll find people you recognize—or maybe ones who recognize you—when we hit the Golden Shores. Closer to home for you, eh?"

Minimus looked at his sandals. "I figured I'd find people who recognized me here, too. But that Ee Clot at the wrestle vine farm sure didn't, and wouldn't believe a word I said."

Sven laughed. "That old coot? He'd have a hard time recognizing his own nose. Have you seen his eyes?"

Minimus gave a begrudging chuckle. "Heh. Yeah. But you'd think that would give him two independent chances to recognize me. So, how long before we reach Yinti? Maybe the balloon will put down there."

* * *

It took another two days of fair-weather sailing before the *Sea Camel's* crow's nest called out the first sighting of the domes and spires of the Golden Shores' capital. It took a further day to unload. Minimus considered bolting into the distance as soon as he set foot on land but felt the tug of responsibility to pay back Sven.

After the exchange of crates, parcels, barrels, and bundles was completed, Minimus sought Missing-Arms Sven.

"Look. I know you paid Roland for me, and there's nobody here for you to sell me on to, but I need to leave. Set out for home. I hope you'll understand."

Sven fingered the curls of his coarse beard just above the

beard ring. "More than you know, boy. I get it. A worker like you is hard to find. I'm sure there'll be grumbling when we next unload. Let me have cook make you up a travel hamper. Unless you find that balloon friend of yours, it's a hard road back to Inner Pang. Or the Red Bean Queendom. Or wherever you're bound."

Wasn't it obvious that Minimus was not a native Red Beaner, seeing as he was four times their size? Still, he felt an unexpected twinge—not of regret for abandoning his post as chief hod carrier, but for leaving behind such an unexpectedly generous man.

* * *

As he walked through the narrow, crowded streets of Yinti, trailed by Jing Jing, Minimus ignored the subtle pointing fingers and whispered comments as he passed. Two months ago, pride would have puffed up his chest, believing that every onlooker knew him as the champion of the five trials and savior of the Red Bean Queendom. But now he'd reverted to his natural state, aware that nobody was in awe of his accomplishments, only shocked that a boy could be so strong. Calloused, he turned his back on the rabble that saw him only as an over-muscled freak once he'd understood their dehumanizing interest.

Aboard ship, he'd daydreamed that he would saunter up to the palace, and Queen Angstaad would welcome him to her country and send a guard of honor to accompany him on his quest to reunite with Master Thorn. But after recent experiences, he knew that approaching the guardhouse and claiming he was Minimus Mu—*the* Minimus Mu—would be futile. Anyone strong-looking could claim that. How would the guards identify him if they'd not been at the trials in person? Heck, Minimus would barely believe himself if he was in their armored shoes. It would be a long road indeed as he headed west on foot. But he'd make it. He had Jing Jing's optimism to spur him on and a burning desire to find Master Thorn. If he could reach Evermere, Queen Violet and her citizens would know him and offer help.

"Well, Jing Jing, we have enough food to last us for a couple of weeks, but I'm going to disappoint you. It's ship's rations. Maybe we can top it up with fruits and nuts from the market. How about a nice loaf of warm bread, too?"

The monkey jumped up and down at his side in excitement, making Minimus wonder, not for the first time, whether he could understand human speech.

The market was a wonder of smells and sounds, a splendor after the monotonous creaks and bilge reek of their sea voyage. Soon, boy and monkey's bellies were warm with fresh food and tea. They headed through the far side of the market toward the road that would take them north then west, through Inchin, Inner Pang, and then to the Red Bean Queendom.

If Jing Jing could identify Minimus's voice, the boy wondered, could he pick out a particular horse's whinny? Because he swore he heard Mr. Apples somewhere close at hand, the horse that he and Rayne had ridden to retrieve Princess Tasha's tiara. Could the horse Queen Violet had gifted him after the trials, last seen swimming away from the sunken *Boundless*, be here in the Yinti market?

His first glimpse of the white-fringed left ear and the distinctive Red Bean style of braiding the crest mane convinced him in an instant that Mr. Apples had survived the shipwreck and somehow made it to a horse-trading stall in Golden Shores. The pirates that sank the *Boundless* must have hauled aboard the madly paddling horse, just as Minimus had hoped.

Multiple bundles of injustice fueled the rage that coursed through Minimus's veins. He knew not why the pirates had attacked the *Boundless*, nor did he care. But as a result, he'd nearly drowned, the cutlerer's cart he called home had sunk to the depths, and he'd lost Master Thorn, the man who'd raised him from a baby when nobody else would. Reuniting with Mr. Apples was a natural first step in righting that list of calamities.

Jing Jing took slinking steps to the side of the stall where a group of bearded, sun-lashed men offered two horses and an array of goods for sale. He slipped behind the draped canvas of the next stall's side divider, lifting its hem to peek at proceedings. Minimus took the direct route. He strode to the rail where Mr. Apples stood tethered and untied his reins. The horse nickered a welcome and stamped a front hoof in excitement.

"This is my horse, and I'll be taking it."

One of the men tending the stall grabbed Minimus's forearm, attempting to stay his untying progress. "We found this horse at sea, lad. Bounty rules make him our horse, not some grubby child's. If ye likes the looks of this classy steed, ye can cough up the goat's teeth."

Minimus looked at the man's grip. Although the two were of similar height, and despite the wiry strength of a seafarer, his hand could only half encircle Minimus's forearm. As he flexed his muscles, Minimus raised his gaze to the man's eyes. With a slight raising of eyebrows on both faces, it became clear that each understood who would emerge victorious in a wrestling match. It was also clear that Minimus's rage and honor meant he would not offer to pay.

There was a slight waver in his voice as the pirate held Minimus's gaze. "Uh, Graven, I may need a hand escorting this urchin away."

Although unusual, street fighters from every queendom would agree that being hoisted overhead and tossed into a deep metal tub teeming with live crabs signifies that a fight is over. In the Yinti market square, however, this was only the beginning of the fight that Minimus Mu found himself ensnared within. Fortunately, it was Minimus doing the hoisting and not the dancing around trying to remove three dozen clamping crabs, but even so, this was just the opening salvo—an instant later, three burly pirates advanced on him, and he heard the disheartening jangle of running footfalls echoing behind him. He figured the sound was not people rushing to his aid. At best, they would be onlookers, but more likely, additional lackeys from the pirate ship.

Minimus had taken part in many defenses of Master

Thorn's cart before, and each had its own flavor of chaos. This one was no different.

One of the men who sprang from the rear of the pirates' operation stumbled and tripped on his descending trousers. Jing Jing shrieked with almost human laughter as he whirled the fallen man's belt in his motion-blurred hand, lashing a second man's cheek in the process and leaving a welt. That man recoiled and paused for a moment, then charged.

But Minimus was otherwise engaged. His shoulder barge knocked the wind from the third pirate's lungs and he collapsed, wheezing, butt-first into an open barrel of pickles. The man became wedged with feet and arms flailing, unable to grip anything for leverage. Minimus rolled beneath a table, continuing under a curtain into the neighboring kitchenware stall.

Popping to his feet, he noticed a few things about his new environment. The proprietor froze in surprise, bent over a ceramic mug, a metal tea strainer lowered halfway. With minimal appraisal, the boy noted that the man's wares were of inferior quality. Probably crap imported from the island queendom of Del Carta. This was fortunate, because Minimus otherwise would have felt guilty at flipping the next charging pirate over his shoulder into a shelf laden with plates and cups.

Dancing around the still immobile stallholder and through the shattered stoneware, Minimus grabbed the wooden handle of the kettle suspended over the stall's small fire pit. Master Thorn would never have contemplated brewing a cup of tea with water not yet at a full rolling boil, but the flung kettle and its spraying water were searing enough to halt one of the new pirates flooding into the stall. Scalded, he screamed as he turned away from his newly arriving squad, batting at his burnt neck and drenched tunic.

Despite his quick reactions and devious combat techniques, the odds soon overwhelmed Minimus. No matter how strong the boy or quick his monkey, facing seven pirates—or was it eight?—was never going to end well. Minimus heard Mr. Apples whinnying encouragement beyond the curtain, but he'd need more than horsey reassurance to wriggle free from the grip of the four pirates that piled atop him and outweighed him two to one.

A stern voice rang with a harsh edge from somewhere beyond the jumbled pile of bodies roughing up Minimus Mu. "Lads. LADS! I suggest you let go of that boy if you fancy keeping your organs within reach."

Minimus felt necks crane to see the threat's source.

It carried on. "Not now. RIGHT now!"

The men pinning Minimus made no move to release him. Another voice questioned the command, from further away.

"Ah. Missing-Arms Sven. We should have sunk the *Sea Camel* when we had the chance."

Ugh, more pirate reinforcements, Minimus thought, hearing the new voice. The sounds of multiple weapons being unsheathed sunk through the pile of unwashed humans to reach his ears.

Sven replied, and the amount of scorn in his voice stung even Minimus. "Had the chance? Your leaky tubful of inbreds would have to catch us first. That ragtag pile of warped boards and not enough nails can barely sail itself across a pond. And you may notice, I have a weapon here for each of you and several to spare. They're asking to be used in sweeter voices than you'll ever hear from me—or your own regretful mothers—so I'd suggest you clear off before you're too disfigured to be seen above decks."

There was no spoken reply to Sven's last command, but the growls of rage followed by ominous thuds and strangled screams let Minimus's imagination paint a picture. Soon, the mass of men pressing him flat lightened, their cutlasses slipping free as they rose. The last proved keen to keep Minimus pinned to the floor, but that was never going to work. It was child's play for Minimus to hurl him off. Jing Jing held up the curtain like a curtseying courtier, and Minimus crawled beneath it to emerge beside Mr. Apples.

Four pirates lay in a groaning jumble, each bleeding or missing important parts. Sven held a short-handled axe in each hand and whirled toward the remaining men who shrunk deeper within the cowering kitchen merchant's tent. Instead of advancing on them, he severed the tent's support poles in an efficient spin, collapsing the weighty fabric atop the men.

Weighing the alternatives, they opted not to struggle their way out, knowing that Sven's bristling arsenal awaited them.

Sven wiped his axe blades on the collapsed tent and let one dangle from each hand. "Saw you with that horse at the trials, boy. Best be off before anyone else takes exception to you reclaiming him."

* * *

By the time man, boy, horse, and monkey had reached the northern gates of Yinti, Sven had explained that he'd recognized Minimus on sight in Wraithsport, even if nobody else seemed to. He'd more than recouped his outlay of goat's teeth as they shimmied up the coast, charging the local townspeople a nominal fee to see the famous Minimus Mu and his faithful monkey Jing Jing wave from his ship's rail as it left each harbor.

"You could ask Queen Angstaad for help, lad. I saw her with you at the trials of the All-Seeing Eye," he said.

Minimus forced a smile. Others always thought life came easily to famous people, but reality constantly proved otherwise. He shrugged. "This isn't a queendom-saving mission. Now that I have my horse back, it'll be easier to find Master Thorn. If I can locate the balloon or make it to Red Bean, we'll be okay."

Minimus mounted and Jing Jing sprang up behind him. Sven cut a rugged figure against the low sun, nodding farewell. "May the wind fill your sails, boy. Or whatever she should fill if you're on horseback."

* * *

When the road north forked, Minimus Mu nudged Mr. Apples left, abandoning the coastal route to Tempa in the queendom of Inchin and instead veering toward Inner Pang. The three travelers, familiar with the barren desert terrain that lay ahead, took pleasure in the scenic countryside of Golden Shores. Orchards and fields of colorful crops gave way reluctantly to low forested hills that persuaded the flat, straight path of the road to develop a personality. Mr. Apples overtook an occasional trade caravan, bringing grains and fruits to Inner Pang, or merchants laden with spices and metalwork, headed in the other direction.

Ambling along in the slanting afternoon sun on an empty stretch of road that wound around a rocky outcrop, Minimus failed to identify the signs of danger. Mr. Apples opened his nostrils full bore and snuffled in as much air as he could. Then his ears rose and angled forward before he flattened them. An experienced horseman would have noticed these signals right away, but Minimus was accustomed to being the one to haul Master Thorn's cart. The novelty of riding his own mount had not yet evaporated. He jinked the reins and urged Mr. Apples through the hairpin turn around a pile of rocks.

As the horse reluctantly turned, the sounds ahead became audible even to human ears. Minimus at first pictured the bass thrum of a river coursing through a rocky gorge, but when the cries of terrified people mixed in, he realized the deep animal roar wasn't rushing water.

And then they were upon him. Two donkeys pulled a covered wagon, its driver struggling to rein them in as they tried to break from their harnesses. Behind the wagon, a trio of pikemen leveled their long weapons at a pair of raging bonfires—moving bonfires, roaring with animal malice as they advanced.

Fire bears!

Occasionally, when Master Thorn's cutlery cart had stopped at an Inner Pangan market, a customer might regale the younger Minimus Mu with yarns of a fire bear encounter. A few of those retelling the stories bore burns that added credence to their tales of woe. The moral of every story was the same: fire bears were best encountered in fables, not reality.

Gobs of flame arched through the air from the bear-shaped infernos' swinging arms, making the pikemen duck and dodge. One man's weapon was already alight, its shaft turning to ash under the cloying flames. The other two realized although they could menace the bears, getting their weapons too close to the intense heat of the bears' fur would render them, too, useless.

Even a complex Master Thorn plan would include the obvious option: turn and flee back the way they had come. Minimus froze for a moment, watching as the donkeys bucked away from the flames, approaching his position. Uncertain whether—or even how—to assist the beleaguered wagon party, he eventually hauled the reins and chose discretion. Better to retreat and consider how to fend off the bears than to block the road like a lump of lead. Jing Jing pulled at the scraggly clump of hair that now dangled to Minimus's shoulders, and as the horse turned, the boy saw what had piqued the monkey's excitement.

Blocking the path behind them was another bear, its shaggy brown fur only now igniting. With the jumble of boulders hugging the hillside to their left and a steep drop-off to their right, there was no escape route. The bears had chosen the perfect ambush spot.

Jing Jing would probably be the only one to survive the encounter; it would prove little challenge for him to hop up the rocks or scrabble down the slope. But Minimus, his horse, and the travelers now behind him had no room to maneuver. If untethered, the more sure-footed donkeys might skitter down the scree of the slope, but that escape route looked like certain leg-breaking territory for a horse. And who would pause their screams of terror to free the donkeys from their harnesses at this point? Maybe the donkeys could use their deafening magical voices to chase off the bears, but Minimus had his doubts.

The boy leapt from the saddle, his landing creating a cloud of dust. If Mr. Apples could escape, Minimus would not stand in his way. He felt Jing Jing at his side, a clenched hand gripping the fabric of his trousers. They watched in a combination of wonder and terror as the new bear transformed from furry animal to a blazing figure of fire. The flames started at the bear's shoulders, creeping down across its torso before expanding rapidly along its fore and hind legs. The creature's head was the last part of it to ignite. It leant back and roared, sparks bouncing from the rocks and rolling down the hill like alarmed lightningbeetles.

Mr. Apples pressed himself up against the boulder at the road's fringe, not daring to bolt down the ravine. The bear stomped toward them, raising its paws to accentuate its height. If nothing else, Minimus figured he could stand between the flame bear and his animal companions. Perhaps the thing would be content with turning only him into a flame-roasted dinner. Dropping his gaze from the attacking flame bear for a second, he grabbed Jing Jing by the collar of his woolen jacket and gave him a heave up into the uneven rock face, ushering his friend to find a safer space. Then he turned and stood his ground as the bear took one thudding step, then two. He turned his head away from the raging heat, closing the nearer eye.

The inferno cooled for a moment as a cascade of rocks tumbled and caused the bear to leap back. With an anguished sound that Minimus had heard once before, the panicked donkeys had used their own defensive magic. In this case, it was misdirected. Their braying sent a visible cone of sound upward as they craned their necks, straining against the harnesses. One cone tinged the afternoon sky with an eerie blue while the other struck the rocks on the hillside above. The powerful sound dislodged several. They fell streaming across the roadway between Minimus and the flame bear.

But that proved the limit of their defense. As the donkeys reared on their hind legs in panic, the magical raging sound, which they should have directed at the bears, flew harmlessly into the air above.

The bear advanced on Minimus again, this time with renewed ferocity. Above the din of bear growls and crackling thunderous flame, fresh sounds reached Minimus's ears. A whirling noise and then something akin to the steam of a freshly forged sword being plunged into a blacksmith's basin.

The bear bent into a vicious down swipe that would either burn or knock Minimus's head from his shoulders. But then it paused as something struck its chest. Hot water droplets spattered Minimus's face, and the flames flickered and died across the bear's torso. A second water bomb landed, glancing off the bear's shoulder. Its head and limbs followed suit; their fire fizzled out, too.

A helmeted head peeked down at Minimus from atop the wall of boulders, piercing blue eyes inspecting him. The figure swept an arm holding a drooping sling in a sign of riddance as their voice called, "G'wan, bear, get out of here!"

Doused and damp-looking, the bear gave the newcomer an accusing stare, then slunk off on all fours up the rock face. Minimus felt safe to stop squinting against the heat and turned. He saw the same thing further along the road: two drenched bears scrambled away from the path in the direction indicated by four more Golden Shores guardswomen. It was hard to know if fire bears got embarrassed, but the hunched shoulders and furtive backward glances gave Minimus that impression.

The warrior closest to Minimus climbed hand-over-hand from her perch, arriving on the road with the clank and jingle of light armor. She raised an eyebrow so it became obscured beneath her silver-tinted helmet. "Did 'ya lose your water packs? It's not safe through these hills without proper defense."

Minimus must have left his mouth ajar, because the woman added, "We use the air bladders from bearded lungfish. Fill 'em, tie 'em off, and sling them." She whirled her empty sling as a demonstration. "The bears are actually quite cute once you extinguish them, don't you think?"

"Uh, nobody told me—" Minimus began, before he was cut off by the shout of a familiar voice behind him.

"Minimus? Is that you? By the smoke of the Underworld, what are you doing here?"

Finally, someone recognized him. And not just any old

someone. The woman pushing past the wagon and removing her winged helmet had a familiar tracing of blue tattoo surrounding her right eye, and her shaven hairline looked sharp enough to cut through leather. This was Queen Angstaad of Golden Shores, who had fiercely defended Minimus at the trials.

Minimus took a knee, and Jing Jing, swinging down from above, copied him. "Uh, hello, your elegancy."

Queen Angstaad reached them. "Don't be silly, Mu. I should be the one kneeling to you. Get up. You, too, monkey."

Minimus rose, and Queen Angstaad gripped his forearm in both hands, a typical greeting among the fighting forces of the Golden Shores. Callouses landscaped her hands from years of swordplay, and she held on for a long moment, smiling. "You're as foolish as these first-time traders, I see. What are you doing roaming these hills without extra precautions?"

Minimus still felt it was not his place to talk to a queen, let alone one who had just saved his hide from becoming bear dinner. "Uh, sorry. I'm trying to catch up with Master Thorn and Ezra. They're in his balloon. And something terrible is happening in Mossmarch, and to Rayne. I need to rescue her."

Angstaad's lips flattened. "I saw the balloon overhead yesterday, drifting west. And tell me why *you* need to save Rayne and Mossmarch. Didn't you know you're only the solitary hero once in your life, Minimus? Shouldn't that be *we* need to save Rayne?"

By the time she'd sent the merchant wagon on its way with a supply of bearded lungfish water bombs, and a fine dinner of herbed octopus roasted over a campfire, Minimus had filled in Queen Angstaad about the Mothers of Midnight, Rayne's capture, and how he'd lost Master Thorn and Ezra. He didn't know why he had thought he should attempt this mission on his own, but he was glad to have the Golden Shoresians now at his side.

Queen Angstaad shoved a plate his way. "Minimus, your superpower isn't your strength. It's your bravery in the face of an unfair threat. You need to use that to encourage other people—then you can bring the strength of ten, a hundred, or a thousand Minimus Mus."

CHAPTER 22 - TEMPLE PANG

Four Days Earlier

Catriona felt Mother Justicia's disappointed rage before her master spoke a single word. The girl knew the magic infusing her had marred her own face, but when the older woman tore back her cowl, Catriona felt her confidence and self-doubt about her own appearance shrink to a nugget that sank to the depths of her gut. Crinkled waves of burnt skin covered most of Mother Justicia's face and trailed down her neck, spreading in ribbed terraces across her chest. Sparse patches of coarse hair marked the few spots on her scalp the searing had missed.

Unlike everyone else she'd befriended within the sisterhood, Catriona seemed to be the lone girl to take comfort from Mother Justicia's presence, along with the standard doses of fear and insignificance. It was something about the smell of Justicia's chambers, or maybe the way she moved, or her aura of confidence. Catriona found notes of reassurance in her leader's ways.

Justicia used her spoken voice, a hoarse accusation that contorted the thin contours of her scorched lips. "With all your powers, you return empty-handed and with a knife in Sister Anthea's arm! I don't even want an explanation. But hear me now, Catriona, we need that eleven-pointed star back. It's key to our full powers."

Trying not to make her answer sound like an excuse, Catriona felt she owed Mother Justicia a summary. "The man who has it, he's a knife-thrower with skills unlike any I've ever seen. He's bristling with blades. And we had the star. I don't even know how it disappeared again. But we will get him next time, this knife-wielder."

Catriona felt Mother Justicia's ire transform into curiosity. Mother Justicia continued, this time using her magical voice. "*Bristling* with blades, you say? So, a man covered in knives has our magical artifact?"

Catriona nodded. "Until we find him, yes."

Mother Justicia ushered her away with a wave of her hand and shaded her face once again beneath her hood. "Do as I told you. To Sister Rayne."

As Catriona's feet padded away and down the stairs, Mother Justicia shook her head at her own blindness. Not her burnt-away eyes, but her failure to consider a story told to her years before by the Backwards Man. Had the artifact she needed to rid everyone of their magic hung from her neck this whole time? Could it be as simple as combining the eleven-pointed star and the lodestone?

She would take Catriona to Mossmarch and retrieve the cursed thing herself. But first, she had visitors to welcome.

* * *

Rayne had become alert to any sign of movement in her wing of Temple Pang. Although she could dismiss her secret conversations as a lonely girl talking to herself, she thought it best that no one overheard her speak to Minimus, Virgil, and Dando. Sometimes, she could communicate without speaking aloud, but she couldn't always restrain the urge to vocalize. She cut short the chat that flowed through a puppet theater in Golden Shores at the first echo of approaching footfalls.

"Mother Justicia said we must repeat the ceremony," Catriona called. The bar securing the door rasped free, and hinges creaked as she pushed it open.

In the courtyard, wan sunlight failed to push through presiding gray clouds. The rockeaters were nowhere in sight, and Rayne worried about their chances of survival with their magic drained away. A goat scuffed at the flagstones with an aggrieved hoof, no longer able to hover.

Catriona pushed Rayne's shoulders downward until the girl's knees banged to the floor, then took a crouching position behind her. Rayne felt strands of unkempt, dangling hair tickle her ear tips as Catriona snaked an arm around her and urged the jagged coral amulet into her hand. The previous cuts had nearly healed, but Rayne braced for them to reopen, for the icy toxins of magic to writhe through her veins once again. This time, instead of wrapping her fingers around Rayne's head, Catriona clasped a muscular arm around her waist while her other hand crunched Rayne's palm against the cruel edges of the coral.

"We close the gate and open the eyes," Catriona muttered.

The amulet's slicing rim brought stings of pain, but this time no magic coursed through Rayne's system. After a moment, Catriona growled in disgust and pushed Rayne away, standing as the girl sprawled.

"What was *that?*" Catriona spat. "Trying to pull a trick on me, are you, little scumbag? I thought you said you had no previous magic?"

Her face a map of confusion and restrained fury, Rayne spun onto her back, her palms bracing against the flagstone floor. Blood trickled from the palm, cut by the amulet. "Why? What happened?"

Catriona rubbed her thigh. The healing puncture continued to itch where that fop in Mossmarch had pricked her. Maybe it was infected. Her only instinct was to snatch the girl and drag her before Mother Justicia for evaluation, to see why the coral had failed to turn her twice. She would never normally bother replying to such a little wretch, helpless before her, but for reasons she couldn't understand, she felt compelled to answer.

"Not only didn't the coral's magic take effect, I *saw something.* You made me see it! That damnable drinking house in

Mossmarch. Two men flying high above the land. A fat boy with awful hair. How'd you do that?"

She rubbed her thigh again before moving her palm to another annoying itch. It felt like a plant had taken root at the base of her neck and sprouted tendrils from between her shoulder blades.

Rayne did not answer. She just sat on the courtyard floor with narrowed eyes. Catriona hauled Rayne upright by the collar, and she noticed the smaller girl, too, rubbed frantically at her own neck.

* * *

Again, Mother Justicia moved with blinding speed, flitting across the tower's floor and snatching Rayne's wrists into her bony hands. Up close, Rayne noticed that the scarring of the other sisters was nothing compared to the older woman's disfigurement. Crinkled, poreless undulations covered one cheek and half her neck, the mutilation extending across a prominent collarbone to disappear beneath her robe. She'd been caught in a fire, this one, Rayne thought.

As quickly as she'd snatched them up, Mother Justicia flung Rayne's wrists away.

"Nothing there, Cat," she said. "Just *my* magic, still working its way along. Slowly, for some reason. Nothing of her own. Leave her in her room. She'll make the change soon."

Rayne found Catriona oddly talkative between prods from her rod. Statements burst from Catriona, the inner voice almost reluctant, murmuring to Rayne.

"I can't remember anything, not before Temple of the Wraith. I know I had my own magic before. You've seen it. And I know my name was Sun—Mother Justicia called me that one time. Catriona Sun. Said I'm from Astella, like her. But that's all. Not like you. You remember *everything*."

Catriona shoved Rayne's shoulder, pushing her into the chamber she'd come to loathe. But before she could slam the door, Rayne blocked the opening. She rubbed at the lingering tingle at the back of her neck.

"I'm a Sun, too," she said. "Rayne Sun. And I don't remember my parents, either. But I saw something, too, in the courtyard. It felt like he was your father, the man I saw on horseback. Handsome. Same shaped face as you. He looked right at me."

Catriona shoved Rayne again, harder this time, slamming the door and sliding the locking bar into place.

CHAPTER 23 - INNER PANG

Two Days Later

Master Thorn circled the balloon basket's tight confines under Maxima's watchful eye, his pacing asking a wordless question which Ezra Longshanks answered.

"It's the wind. Or lack thereof. I can't control it, and it's not as if we have a tame wind lemur here to tease us along."

An exasperated breath escaped Master Thorn's clenched lips. "This science of yours. Even a plodding horse could outpace it today. I just want to reach Evermere. Get Queen Violet to organize a search party for Minimus. You heard what the Backwards Man said. He's here somewhere, I can feel it."

Ezra dared not say that he'd heard no such thing from the Finder or Berentz; that this was Master Thorn reading too much meaning into too few words.

"Fine," Ezra said instead, turning the crank that doused the flames of the burner.

Master Thorn's eyebrows raised in alarm, a few majestic hairs rising above the level of his scalp. "Wait, no! Don't let the balloon plummet. One crash was plenty enough for me. I'm sorry I questioned your science." He clutched Ezra's arm. "Come on! I don't know how to work this thing. I swear on the gilded fork of Kung-Ra, I apologize. Save us!"

Ezra regarded Master Thorn, eyes smiling where his lips did not. "We will not crash, my fellow fool. I'm putting us down gently near this bean field. We'll pack up the balloon and go on horseback to Evermere."

Master Thorn released his grip. "Oh, I see. Good plan. Sorry about that Kung-Ra swearing. And is that soup I smell from the farm below?"

Maxima enveloped the slender man in a hug from behind. "You're such a worrier, Thorny. And that's definitely soup."

* * *

Master Thorn and Maxima helped the bean farmer's wife in the kitchen while Ezra negotiated with the farmer's son, a boy in his late teens with a smooth face marked with scattered freckles. Maxima chopped vegetables for the next meal, her knife blade a blur, pausing occasionally to stir the pot-bellied kettle of soup with a long-handled ladle. Master Thorn's contribution was evaluating every kitchen implement, taking approximate measurements of spoons, colanders, and tongs against his outstretched forearm. The worn butter churn attracted particular attention.

Ezra stuck his head past the kitchen door frame. "It's settled. Drazen will cart the balloon up to my storehouse in the City of Jade, and he says we can take two of his horses to Evermere. I've worked with him before, during my many visits to Inner Pang, so he knows I'll repay him heartily on my next visit. Two of us will have to ride double, and maybe … um …"

Maxima continued to stir the soup as she laughed. "It's okay, old man. You can say it. I should ride alone while you two share a horse?"

Ezra forced a cough. "Well, one of them is a draught horse, and his magic seems strong. He should be able to carry you. But I don't want your wisp of a man to be the pebble that starts the landslide, if you know what I mean."

Her laugh was surprisingly high-pitched. "Fine, fine. You

can cuddle him during the day, and I'll take over at night," she said.

After a fine lunch of bean soup, the trio and their two borrowed horses trotted north with a hamper full of provisions that the farmer's wife forced into their hands. They traveled through vegetable fields toward the City of Jade and the Red Bean Queendom beyond it.

Ezra nudged Master Thorn, who insisted on sitting in front to take the reins. "Hey. Tell Maxima that story about the burning of Vinetally that the Backwards Man told us."

CHAPTER 24 - VINETALLY, ASTELLA

Seventeen Years Earlier

When Berentz, the Backwards Man, was eight years old, he set out with his father in their turnip cart, heading to the fishing village of Vinetally, nestled on the southern shore of the Pearl Lake. Cresting the last hill before the slope into town, a horrific sight confronted the pair.

Berentz watched his father's face twist as the ruined tableau came into view. With his full lifetime of experience soaked into his mind, he made for a precocious child. The boy knew what lay in store for them from his backwards journey through time, but had long since given up foretelling events to his father, who chafed and sometimes raged at the inevitability of it all. Taking in the destruction, his father glared at Berentz and shook the cart's reins. The mule broke into a trot toward the smoldering remains of the town.

Several stubborn patches of flame burnt wood, metal, and flesh alike, in smokeless blue fury. This was no natural fire but the obvious result of powerful magic. Nothing higher than waist height remained. Where before there was a hodge podge of thatched dwellings, workshops, fishing boats, and storehouses, now there were unobstructed views of the lake beyond.

"The boy's aunt. She's going to run from just over there,

through the cornfield," Berentz told his father, pointing. "There's nothing you can do to help the only two survivors, standing there on the bank of the former village pond. Wait a few minutes for the lad to calm down, then ride forward, carefully. I need to tell them the future."

With every building, fence, dock, and tree razed, the teenaged boy who stood astride the stone block and leaned against the still-standing statue of an eagle snatching up a wriggling fish became the only magnet that could draw an onlooker's attention. The remaining soundless flames could not muffle the shrill cries of the swaddled newborn girl held in his arms, the boy's anguished and strangled outpouring of grief, or the frantic calls from the woman emerging from the cornfield. The scene was rife with destruction and despair. Fiery violence had reduced a village of a hundred hardworking Astellans to a trio of stricken survivors.

Berentz's father raised the reins to urge the mule back into motion, but Berentz held his arm, staying him until the time was right. "Not yet, father. He's still too angry, too dangerous."

"But he needs help, son. Forget the risk. We should go now," the man said.

"No. He needs his aunt first. Let her reach him. The infant is fine. Perfectly healthy, despite her mother dying as she took her first breath. That's what fuels the boy's anguish." Berentz waved an arm at the ruined village. "All this, it's his doing—the boy. His powerful magic. His anger at the loss of his love, the burden of his baby girl."

The woman ran from the margins of the cornfield, skirts hiked up, calling to the boy as she passed into the area of destruction. "My dear, my love. What's happened? Who did this?"

The unscathed boy stepped atop the rectangular stone but turned away from the calling woman, unwilling to meet her worried gaze. Regret, shame, and self-condemnation twisted his face. Shifting the mewling baby into the cradle of one arm, he thrust a palm in her direction. "Stay away from me! You can't save me! Can't control me!"

Still, the woman ran. "My poor child! Let me make it better. Auntie Justicia will make everything better."

Tears ran down the boy's cheeks, spattering the baby. Palm still held like a shield, a wobbly, rippling circle of magical energy snaked up the length of his arm. It sped up as it proceeded from shoulder to hand and shot across the desolation. When the spinning, crackling circlet struck the woman, it spun her and knocked her to her knees. The conflicting signals she radiated as she leapt back to her feet and ran limping to the boy and baby already haunted Berentz. He'd seen it before. The woman's jacket smoldered away to embers of flaming rag. Much of her hair fell away, the remnants blackened and curled from the magical fire. The fire spared a patch on the side of her face that had turned from the attack, but both eyes, an ear, and her lips danced with limning flames that only snuffed out when she reached the boy. Yet amid all this hideous injury and clear agony, she would not stop, could not stop, and did not stop until she enveloped the boy in a loving, sheltering hug.

"I tried, Auntie. I tried and couldn't save her," the boy repeated as the three anguished figures united. "And then I got so angry. So angry I did something. I didn't know my power, but look …"

* * *

Berentz's father's authoritative voice and action persuaded the trio aboard his farmer's cart. The woman had collapsed from the pain of her injuries and the infant's father's head hung in blank resignation. After the young man had settled the baby into a comfortable-looking nook among the turnips and had draped Justicia's burnt areas with blankets soaked in lake water, Berentz made his father retrieve the rectangular stone where the woman had run to her nephew. He knew Justicia needed it as part of her journey and that it would ultimately heal her— on the inside, at least.

Berentz's father wondered why his son had collected a jarful of leeches and insisted on bringing them along on the trip, but he'd stopped questioning the boy's motives five or six years earlier. Still, he was curious to watch Berentz release the leeches to rove about the stone they'd recovered, and amazed when they glowed with an inner light. Berentz called them *medical leeches*, and he allowed them to slither back and forth under the soaked blankets, roving the unconscious woman's burns. Although the young man barely looked in his direction, with eyes only for his newborn daughter, Berentz explained they glowed with absorbed magical powers that would work on Justicia, urging her skin along a quick path from rawness to scar tissue while easing her pain and stabilizing her vital signs. The boy and his daughter appeared unaffected by the fire, but Berentz explained that a palmful of leeches would nourish and soothe the newborn, whose missing mother could not provide succor. The boy kept the baby girl close, speechless, and eyed the leeches suspiciously, showing nothing but his back to the travelers as the cart bounced along the rutted road to Pearl Wash.

On the agonizing and mostly conversation-free journey, Berentz told Justicia what she needed to hear. The story she would tell him years later, when she sought him out on his farm. The Backwards Man, a seer cloaked in an eight-year-old's body, doled out his wisdom in nuggets, unsure whether Justicia of Vinetally would believe him or even understand. On some level, he believed he must have said the right things, based on his future encounter with the scarred woman. She answered in murmurs and grunts as the leeches worked their magic.

"I can see a few things in your future," he had reassured her. "It's my special power, although you may not believe it. Yet."

Beneath the glow of wriggling leeches, Justicia did not reply.

"The stone," Berentz said later that afternoon. "The one from Vinetally where your nephew stood. It's infused with the combined magic of everyone from the village, as well as a significant amount of the boy's own power. You will tell me, many years from now, how you used it to create an entire order of disciples."

Justicia only groaned in response.

The next day, when Justicia looked less drained and asked for water, Berentz described her future's most important details.

"You will learn to tease magic from the stone. When I meet the future you, part of your story is how you conjured an amulet—an eleven-pointed star—from the chunk of rock, that holds its own special powers. But most important of all, you will tell me it was the prediction about the man covered in daggers that brought you to a final resolution. This dagger-covered man will cross your path, bringing a powerful talisman, and combining it with the stone becomes your turning point. It's that conjunction that brings your whole life's work, your mission, to a close. Watch for this man, Justicia."

CHAPTER 25 - SEA OF SORROWS

Three Days After the Balloon Landing

Mother Justicia had always used carrier pigeons to return messages to the Temple of the Wraith. It was a primary method used by her spies to warn of impending raids. But she was not familiar with the message jays that cooed from their straw-filled roost in Temple Pang. The messenger from Ven had recognized them immediately, and suggested taking one with him to allow a swift reply. The woman had gripped his hand briefly, detecting no trace of magic, before agreeing.

When the message jay returned, it did not seek its coop, instead flapping into the tower room where Mother Justicia ruminated over the lodestone. She looked for a message tied to either wrinkled orange ankle, but seeing none, returned to her thoughts. When a woman's voice interrupted her solitude, she searched the room until she realized the bird was speaking in perfect human tones.

The message jay repeated the speech twice, then flapped away, leaving a tingle of magic itching at Mother Justicia's palms. She now knew the pact was good. Temple Pang would have added protection and a supply of magic-wielding citizens to drain. Finally! A nation that aligned with her mission to remove the temptations of magic from every human. Despite the confusion of the past while, this news settled her nerves.

With the cadre at Temple Pang falling into a comfortable pattern, maybe she could turn her attention to either reclaiming the Temple of the Wraith or locating the missing disciples from Temple Pang. Tracking down the amulet was a priority that needed attention, but not an emergency; she'd sail to Mossmarch after she'd dealt with the current visitors.

Mother Justicia sent her voice to several sisters in the temple below, describing the reception for the Vennese ships that protocol demanded.

* * *

A surprising level of bustle energized the docks of Port Rise, in Ven, as the *Sun Seeker* and *Fair Winds* left port. Princess Tasha, from the landlocked Red Bean Queendom was no expert, but even to her casual eye, it looked like more than the usual fishing boats had set sail. Well-outfitted three-masted sloops teemed with armed men and women who moved with a precision the crab trawler crews lacked.

"Last chance to restock the granaries around the north coast of Ven before winter. The fleet will return here and hunker down through the cold storms ahead," Queen Veronica assured her.

The queen and princess set sail together, with Jada pacing them in the Vennese ship. Each woman traveled with her own complement of guards. They left under sunny skies, but clouds rolled in early on the first day of their passage.

The crossing dipped the boat through troughs of frothy waves, lining the decks with rime, and left Princess Tasha queasy despite her comfortable quarters. The Golden Shores guardswomen were either unaffected by seasickness or stood too proud and disciplined to show any of the signs. Perhaps one or two looked a lighter shade of pale than usual, but Tasha would never embarrass them by asking.

After three days tacking northeast, Queen Veronica leaned at the rail as the *Sun Seeker* inched under half-furled sails, admiring the harbor beneath the regal gaze of Temple Pang.

The sun threatened but failed to fully break the conspiring clouds. A pair of Vennese guards flanked the queen, and Tasha sported four of her own guardswomen as she joined Veronica.

Tasha turned to the much taller figure, locking eyes. "I'm glad, aboard ship, our chats were unhurried. When we first met, your mood had me worried. Call me absurd, but I'll hold you to your word that you'll not use your sloops and corsairs to interfere in Mossmarch affairs. I will petition the council to allow you to state your position: satisfaction for everyone at the end of the Outer Pang transition."

Veronica gave a slight nod, her hair dancing in the breeze. "Darling, I promise you, I'm returning to Ven right after these negotiations. You'll not see me directing a fleet of ships anywhere but home. Look, there's a greeting party waiting for us on the dock!"

As welcoming parties went, these figures waited more still and more sinister than Princess Tasha thought proper. The reception wore dark cloaks with deep hoods, fabric drooping to their noses. At the nearest cleats, a pair of hooded figures fastened the *Sun Seeker*'s flung hawsers, securing the ship. Another dozen awaited the lowering of the gangplank, motionless and indecipherable.

One figure pulled back a loose sleeve as a glowing ring of magical power spun into life at their elbow. Although the voice that reached Tasha came from everywhere at once, an accompanying feeling identified the cloaked woman limned in the glow at her elbow as its unmistakable source.

"Tasha of Evermere? Alight and surrender yourself!"

The princess glanced at her guardswomen, uncertain of how they would react. But they showed no hint of responding. Could they not hear the voice?

The woman on the dock spoke again. "You, from the Golden Shores—bring Lady Tasha here. You can all surrender together."

This brought an immediate reaction. The four warriors accompanying Tasha drew their short swords even before the last syllables of the unechoing voice dropped. The rest of the guards sprang into battle crouches on deck, advancing to form a protective circle around Tasha. A moment later, Queen Veronica's men, too, drew their weapons and ushered her away from the bristling circle of Golden Shores metal, backing her into the V of the ship's prow.

The gangplank thudded to the dock's weathered surface amid a moment of tense silence.

Tasha motioned for the two guardswomen between her and the dock to move aside. She spoke to the hooded woman whose forearm bristled with crackling energy. "We'd understood, beneath your hood, you'd asked us to this place to work face to face at a way to find common ground—not for you to push us around." She turned to Queen Veronica. "My good lady queen, now that we've seen this terrible reception, it's my suggestion that diplomacy's failed, and we should now set sail."

Tasha expected Veronica to be equally shocked by their hosts' threat, but the queen smiled before answering. "From my position, the diplomacy is working to perfection. We'll set sail presently, but not with you. You should disembark, little girl, before somebody gets hurt."

Tasha's face flushed while her stomach grew cold. Her discussions aboard ship had seemed too cordial to be true, given Queen Veronica's kinship to the displaced Jada. She summoned up what bravery she could, hoping her quaking was less obvious than it felt, and spat back a reply.

"I should have my guardswomen cut you down where you stand, but I don't want that to occur by my hand. *You* can depart and return home with Jada; we'll address the fallout of your treachery later."

She motioned to the gangplank, ushering Veronica away, but the queen budged not an inch. Three more guardsmen rushed to reinforce her position at the front of the ship.

The disembodied voice spoke next, and everyone heard it this time. "Tasha. Down here. Now! Last warning."

Arms wide and palms facing the Golden Shores fighters who swiveled their heads, alert for an attack from any direction, Tasha made no move to comply. On the dock, the woman gave an exasperated tilt of her hood. Princess Tasha imagined eyes rolling skyward beneath the veiled hood—how could she know no eyes graced the scarred face below? With an almost casual roll of the shoulders, the woman extended her arm, and the ring of chattering flame rolled up its length, speeding as it rose. Her arm pointed above and to the right of Tasha's guardswomen, and a moment later, the roiling circle shot past the throng. The fire's coldness left a faint frost on the cheeks of those it passed. It struck no one, but flashed over the deck and into the distance, severing a few lines and taking a semi-circular bite from the foresail's lowest span.

With Queen Veronica's even colder laugh ringing in her ears, and a fresh circlet of magic forming around the dockside woman's elbow, Tasha knew there was no way to fight against this overwhelming threat.

All rhyming failed her. "Do you want us to drop our swords?"

This time, the woman on the dock opened her lips to answer. Her voice was quieter and more girlish than her non-spoken words had sounded. "Whatever. We're not frightened of swords. Come down with no more trouble, and you'll remain unharmed."

Descending, surrounded by her taller companions, Tasha didn't even bother to acknowledge Queen Veronica's taunt. "I'll keep your ship waiting with me in Port Rise. And I'm sticking to my promise. It'll be *Queen Jada* that leads my fleet to Mossmarch, not me."

CHAPTER 26 - INNER PANG

Three Days Later

"See those birds circling? I think we've found the strange phenomenon that coaxed me into the hills," Queen Angstaad said, shielding her eyes from the morning sun and pointing ahead.

Minimus scratched his head. "I know you said there were reports of animals massing and their magic flaring in the reaches of Golden Shores, but don't birds *always* circle in flocks?"

Angstaad gave him an icy stare. "You *dare* to contradict a queen?" She waited for a look of panic to cross the boy's face before bursting into laughter. "I'm joking, Minimus! Brighten up!"

It took a moment for the blood to return to his extremities and for the visions of his amputated head bouncing down the palace steps to subside, but then Minimus, too, laughed.

Queen Angstaad continued. "You're right, of course. But see the variety of birds in that churning cloud? Each species normally flocks only with its own. And that's what the rumors described—we've heard reports of bears, boars, rams, and several types of birds wandering around together, as if under the spell of a silent call. It all sounded very unlikely, but let's hurry ahead and see what's attracting these squawkers."

After a few minutes of riding, more animals came into view.

A family of sabreclaws trotted alongside two fire bears, a variety of birds darting between and over them. The flight paths centered on a lone boulder, and a number of birds rested their wings atop the house-sized chunk of granite. Neither sabreclaws nor fire bears normally encouraged closer inspection by humans, and despite the calm progress of these beasts and the casual looks they gave the horses, Angstaad motioned to her guardswomen to ready their fire-extinguishing weapons and swung her horse in a wide approach to the boulder. She clearly wanted to keep her distance from the dangerous predators.

As the riders' arc revealed the shady side of the boulder, Minimus could not restrain himself, and called to the wizened man resting at its base, "Sir! You, there! You'd better scramble—that rock seems to be attracting a pack of bears and sabreclaws. Quick, now!"

Queen Angstaad and her troops took off at a canter. It appeared the man would need help in the next few moments. He looked dozy, as if he'd been asleep. He rubbed his bald head and stroked a hairy, horned calf that lay beside him. Minimus thought if those words of warning hit his own ears, he'd jump right out of his clothes to get away. Jing Jing cheered in his high-pitched monkey language as Minimus tugged at the reins and urged Mr. Apples into a fast trot. He was unsure what he could do to help the very capable queen's guardswomen, but he felt obligated to move himself toward the possible fray.

Mr. Apples pranced to a stop a few paces back from where Queen Angstaad and her women bristled with swords and water bombs at the ready. The three fire bears ambled on all fours, shoulder to shoulder with the four juvenile sabreclaws, not yet erupting into flame despite the nearby and threatening-looking warriors.

The man at the boulder's base finally rose, still unalarmed. His bald head was half in shadow and half glinting in the sun. Minimus was close enough to notice the gray discs marring the man's eyes—long-established cataracts. That explained why he gripped the neck hair of the small shaggy brown cow that shimmied itself upright alongside him; the beast seemed his companion and guide. The knee-height creature's long horns marked it as a fully grown cow, not a calf, as Minimus had first thought.

The sightless gaze fell somewhere between Queen Angstaad's warriors and the vistas across the dry plains of Inner Pang. "I think they're only curious, not dangerous," he said.

Queen Angstaad remained unconvinced. "In my experience, both bears and sabreclaws go from curious to deadly at a moment's notice. How about we escort you away from here, old man?"

The man's laugh was like the rustle of dry plains grass. "They aren't the first of their families to visit me, and I can almost guarantee you they won't be the last. I follow a call, and always enjoy traveling companions who hear it, too. They'll not bother me—or you, even—while I wander, will they, Petunia?"

He ruffled the floppy brow of matted hair that threatened to obscure his miniature cow's eyes. The creature shivered its shoulders and snorted in reply.

"He seems able to calm these birds, bears, and sabreclaws, Angstaad. I mean, your elegancy," Minimus said. "Maybe we could go closer."

He rummaged in the saddlebag at Mr. Apples' flank. "Would you like one of these spiceflower buns I packed in Yinti, sir?" Minimus dismounted and approached the odd pair.

"Be careful, Minimus," the queen said. "We'll have our swords and water at the ready, just in case."

The man perked up at Minimus's words. "Are you Minimus Mu, perchance?" he asked.

"Indeed. Have you heard of my success at the trials of the All-Seeing Eye?"

The old man pursed his lips. "No, my boy. I know nothing of those trials. But I think I've met you before. Do you recognize this?" From an inner pocket in his traveler's cloak, he pulled out a two-tined fork with a shaft longer than his forearm. Minimus recognized it at once, and a tear ran down his cheek.

"That's—that's a two-tined eel roasting fork. Nobody makes them like Master Thorn," the boy said. "Looks like the grip could use a rebinding."

"I knew it!" the man replied. "It's my favorite utensil ever. I bought it from Master Thorn while your mother held you to one side of the cart. I can hear her voice now. In those days, I could still see shadows, so to me, you were a blurry, baby-sized glob of drooling happiness."

As a foundling, Minimus knew the man must have mistaken a woman holding him near the stall for his mother. It was a coincidence to run into a man that recognized him from a chance encounter three fivespans ago, but Master Thorn's artistry often had a lasting impact.

"Was he extraordinarily strong as a baby, too?" Queen Angstaad asked.

The man pondered this question. "I couldn't really say, what with him looking just a blur. But he had strong lungs, I'll give you that. I still hear a trace of that hollering in his voice now." He held out a hand lined like a map. "My name is Nikolai, and this is my guide, Petunia. She of the shaggy coat and mossy horns. Where would I be without her? And sit, sit, I'll brew us some hexroot tea."

Queen Angstaad and her swordswomen looked dubious about tea-brewing with several dangerous animals in the immediate vicinity, but the bears and sabreclaws sank to the dusty earth and looked drowsy. It was as if they, too, awaited hot drinks.

The man sparked a small fire and maneuvered his kettle into place with well-practiced rummages in his gigantic pack. Apologizing for his shortage of cups—and water—he prevailed upon Queen Angstaad to unpack her troop's tea set as they chatted.

Angstaad explained she wandered the borders of Golden Shores and Inner Pang, investigating reports of congregating magical animals.

"There's always a rotating menagerie following me, it

seems," he replied. "When I was younger, I figured I was just lucky to have such companions, but now I think they're hoping for a change from wandering fool into carrion. Nothing attracts a following more than promises of a fresh meal."

When asked where he was heading, Nikolai replied, "You'd be best off asking Petunia where she's heading. I've always trusted her instincts, and she hasn't led me astray yet. But recently, I've dreamed of a city of tiny dwellers and a lofty temple. Snuggling up with Petunia normally gives me hints about where she's taking me."

"The Red Bean Queendom!" Minimus exclaimed. "That's gotta be your next stop. We're on our way there, too. You should come with us. There's room up here on Mr. Apples for you, if you think Petunia can keep up."

The man smiled, looking vaguely in Minimus's direction, and stroked his tiny cow's mane. "She's not over fast, my girl, but she can trot all day. What do you think, Petunia?"

* * *

Their mistrust of the sabreclaws and fire bears diminished with each passing hour. Two of Angstaad's swordswomen kept an uneasy eye on them the first night, but when Minimus rose at first light, he saw the big cats, the bears, and the shaggy little cow curled up together like a patchwork quilt of mixed texture furs.

The bears sidled off as their mounted party left the hills, and they lost the sabreclaws somewhere around the change of landscape between Inner Pang's dry plains and the green pastures flanking the south shore of the Jade River. Minimus knew the river would lead them to the city of Evermere with its buildings split into two scales: one size supporting the foreigners who helped work the port, and the other scaled to the Red Bean Queendom's thigh-height natives. Each remembrance of the queendom took the boy's thoughts to its fairest daughter, Rayne, imprisoned in Temple Pang, waiting for her captors' poison to take hold. Chance had once thrown him and Rayne together, and ties to their wildly different masters had pried them apart. In another world or another age, they could have avoided separation, but both thrived on their tenuous link. He relished their few snatches of conversation around the puppet theater, made possible only by Rayne's transformation. She had described the scarring that would cover her eyes and ears, and Minimus had seen it firsthand on the Mothers of Midnight during the wagon train's ambush. Rayne was so beautiful, and although the boy found it hard to imagine her without eyes, he decided she could be nothing but radiant.

Two bands of dust-encrusted mercenaries, bristling with weaponry, overtook them as they rode, their own progress slowed by Petunia's pace. Although both groups met Angstaad's inquiries with mostly 'none of your business' comments, she pieced together that they were headed to Mossmarch under promises of payment by former queen, Jada.

Arriving midmorning at Inner Pang's capital, the City of Jade, they paused only to restock their provisions. Its buildings' colorful paintwork suggested a vibrant culture which made every attempt to cast off the stark and often boring terrain of Inner Pang.

"I see several tattoos peeking from beneath your tunic," Minimus said to Nikolai as they rode onwards. "Daggers pointing up your neck and poking from under your sleeves, there."

"They often call me Nikolai Nineteen Points," he said. "There are nineteen tattoos, and each one a blade. Nineteen regrets from my youth, you might say. But it's a good nickname, I guess."

He rolled up a sleeve to show off the full scale of one inked-in illustration. Its contours were less crisp on wrinkled skin than they would have been on his younger self, but the detailed shading and artistry were unmistakable.

"Were you in an army?" Angstaad asked.

"By the Hammer of Az, no, my lady. I lack the courage for that nonsense, begging your pardon. Even before I lost my sight, I followed my nose, finding odd jobs here and there."

"Then why cover yourself in weapons?"

"It started as a reminder. In the streets of Hjelmstrath, in Hammarskald, where I was born, I saw a reiver nudging his horse through town, eyes aflame with the misplaced dream of spoils our town had never possessed. He cut down a raggedy child in the street. Her only crime was begging from an outsider who looked rich enough to spare some food or a trinket. The memory is vivid: the blood and the way her tiny frame lay untouched in the street for three days until a farmer carted away her remains for fertilizer. It returned to me each time I gazed at my forearm. And although I cannot see today, if I touch that arm, I return to that day. My eyes still see the past better than the present. And because I added a new blade for each atrocity, I can also see the future. Humans are vicious creatures, accustomed to using horror to fuel their greed. I stopped at nineteen because if I'd continued, there wouldn't be an uncovered spot on this worn carcass. That's why I spend my life with Petunia, here. She's a beacon of gentleness and love. Every animal loves her, and who wouldn't? We could all take a lesson or four from her."

Minimus had seen the casual cruelty that Nikolai bristled against, but it was Angstaad who summed up his feelings. "Well said, Nikolai Nineteen Points. Well said. I carry a sword, but only from necessity and experience. I'd happily relinquish it if everyone drank Petunia's tea."

* * *

Minimus had long grown accustomed to the curious stares as he moved from dusty town to riverside market, so it was not the woman's open-mouthed gape he found unusual; it was her size and unhidden musculature that gave him pause.

Amid the assault of sounds and smells dockside as the crew of misfits rode the Jade River's bank, two signals niggled at Minimus Mu's senses.

The first was the strong-looking woman who stared at him,

loitering outside the filthy-curtained entrance to a low timber-framed warehouse. With her outlandish frame, surely she of all people would understand the constant unwanted attention, and could afford Minimus the courtesy of concealing her interest. But there she stood, squinting at him, an unreadable expression wrinkling her broad features as she stared.

The second was something nameless. A string of familiarity tugged at the periphery of Minimus's senses like Jing Jing pulled excitedly at his tunic. Minimus brushed the monkey away, tried to ignore the gaping woman, and cleared his mind of distractions to decipher the subtle signal. When it thrust its way to the forefront of his attention, Minimus pulled Mr. Apples's reins, forcing the horses behind him to stop, too. It was a voice, drifting from behind the warehouse's curtained door. A voice with a sharp edge of criticism, undertones of snark, and coated with a syrupy layer of helpfulness. An unmistakable voice. A voice which Minimus had longed to hear, from the wrestle vine beach, across the Fading Sea, and into the foothills of Golden Shores.

"You're sitting on a treasure trove, I tell you," Master Thorn said to an unseen trader. "With but a few days of refabricating these knives and forks, I could double their worth. You could sell them from here to Oceanplat without so much as raising an eyebrow."

Minimus and Jing Jing hit the dusty ground at the same time, the monkey racing ahead toward the warehouse doorway. The woman who'd been staring at Minimus reached out as the boy approached the curtain, still rippling from Jing Jing's passage through its bottom hem—not to stop him but with some other inscrutable gesture. Minimus brushed past her, taking in her full stature as he flung himself past the fabric into the warehouse.

The full impact of their prolonged separation hit both Master Thorn and Minimus Mu as their eyes met. In well-timed good fortune, the boy swept up the older man in a bear hug just as Master Thorn's knees buckled with relief. Tears ran down to drip from the point of the snowy string of beard as

Master Thorn said, "My boy! Put me down so I can get a good look at you. Have you been getting enough food? Eating off proper plates?"

Minimus experienced a new feeling. He realized it was the feeling of being together *again*. All his memories, until recently, included Master Thorn's presence. The longest they'd been apart was the few days when he and Rayne had ridden across Inner Pang to retrieve Princess Tasha's tiara, but then, a reunion of boy and master was a given. When the balloon slipped from Minimus's grasp and drifted away from the sinking ship, a reunion felt unlikely, then impossible.

Jing Jing wrapped his thieving arms around Master Thorn's left leg as the man wiped away more joyous tears and prodded Minimus's thighs and belly. "Have you grown? You look even stronger."

Leaning to one side, Master Thorn looked at the doorway. Turning his head, Minimus saw the woman from outside filling it. Queen Angstaad's eyebrow rose in an unspoken question on the fraction of her face visible between the broad woman's elbow and waist.

"Thorny?" the woman said.

"Yes, yes," Master Thorn replied, then turned to the boy. "Minimus, I finally found her again. This is your mother, Maxima Li."

CHAPTER 27 - MOSSMARCH

The Next Day

Apostle Dando was full of questions. They were his new favorite part of communication, since a question is never a truth or a lie. While his compulsions ensnared and constricted every statement like a Del Cartan drop serpent, questions rolled from his tongue, free as birds. This one, he whispered, though, so only Virgil could hear.

"Do we *really* want to get involved with this? I mean, tailing after Minimus in the trials was one thing, but now we're actively interfering in a dispute between queendoms."

Virgil looked at him with furrowed brows. "Of *course* we're getting involved. First, you heard Rayne. They've captured Princess Tasha, too, and thrown her into a cell at the temple. That's wrong, no matter how you look at it. And second, we already agreed to help Sala and Mirko. If we turn our backs on them now, we might as well run mewling into the Pang Wastes. That's not who we are."

Dando knew the time for decisions was not only upon him but past, and that he'd already made them. Vennese sails and banners were visible in the wide mouth of the Moss River, heading upstream toward the port where truthsayer and balladeer shaded themselves by leaning against the rough wall of a dockside storehouse. The Mossmarch walls rose across the river, ivy-clad and imposing.

As the first of the sixteen ships tied off at the furthest upstream of the riverside berths, the pair wandered over to meet the disembarking troops. Given the lack of defenders, the invaders could have waltzed up the river road singing sea shanties, shimmied across the wide bridge, and skipped unopposed into Mossmarch if they'd wanted. It seemed odd for an unarmed guildsman and a wandering minstrel to be the only representatives of Outer Pang meeting an influx of foreign troops. But as the curious few onlookers knew, without their interim ruler, Princess Tasha, making decisions, everyone in Mossmarch either remained loyal to Jada but too timid to admit it, or was ambivalent and would not confront the Vennese without a whip at their backs. Doubtless, the various factions among the city's armed complement peeked from the city walls or skulked among its alleys, awaiting a sign of emerging authority for or against their former queen. At least the guards at the gate showed token resistance—the sounds of clanking chains echoed across the river as they lowered the portcullis.

It would be poor form to belt out "The Ballad of Minimus Mu" to those sympathetic to the former queen, so Virgil opted for "Wrecks beneath the Sea of Sorrows" as a greeting for the casual invaders, some of whom looked decidedly green from the rough passage.

As officers ushered each complement of troops into dockside ranks, Virgil approached those barking orders and introduced himself, holding out his cap as if expecting a donation. "Virgil Longspeaker, official chronicler of the trials of the All-Seeing Eye, at your service, good sir. And I have here Apostle Dando of the Truthsayer's Guild, who brings a message."

With their reputations preceding them, this was the perfect stage for deception. Apostle Dando adopted his most earnest expression and delivered his fabricated message.

"Your troops are meant to assemble a few hundredlengths further downstream. That patch of forest in the distance, just there? That's where. Royal orders, apparently."

The commander of the troops from the first ship scowled and looked Dando up and down. He certainly fit the part of a truthsayer, based on his outfit, and his smiling face betrayed no hint of nervousness. But still, why would *he* be relaying orders?

"Seems far to march and rather exposed. I'll just wait here for direct orders, I think," the man grunted, shifting from foot to foot as if he still swayed aboard ship.

Dando leaned in, urging the man to treat his next statement as a more private message that maybe his troops should not overhear. "You know they've captured the Red Bean princess in Temple Pang, don't you?"

Dando stared the man in the eyes, forcing a reply. "Aye, so I've heard," he growled.

Dando cocked an eyebrow. "The messenger who came to me—do you think he'd tell a random ne'er-do-well in Mossmarch that news? He knew to trust me to deliver the orders and knew *you* would trust *me*. I'm a truthsayer, magically bound to repeat nothing but the truth."

The apostle could almost hear the gears of logic spinning within the sailor's rugged head. Eventually, the commander pulled back from Dando and pointed his troops upstream, away from the city walls. "Look alive, you laggards! We make for yon patch of forest."

With troops on the move, it was simplicity itself to deceive the columns of soldiers from the next seven ships to follow their compatriots. Virgil received no donations in his proffered hat, but it surprised him how well their deception progressed. This could buy time before the city filled with Vennese fighters. And it took the troops' roving eyes away from Sala and Mirko's upcoming scheme.

But then, a familiar blonde figure strode down the gangplank of the ninth ship. Jada wore a newly fashioned tiara, its black metal points adorned with pigeon-blood-red rubies from the Sinistera Hills in western Ven.

* * *

Sala Doon crouched in his position just upstream from the furthest inland set of cleats, where the lead ship had tightened its hawsers. He longed for action, stretching his limbs and cracking his knuckles while he waited for enough ships to moor and disgorge their troops before he enacted his plan. He was no sailor, but he cursed the ship navigators' caution as they furled most sails and crept to the quayside against the outbound river currents. He re-stretched while Dando and Virgil worked their charms and the arriving troops marched away toward the woods at the river mouth. Mirko would signal him soon.

Sala wore a straw-colored cloak, intended as camouflage against the thatched warehouse roofs that ran the length of the docks, his current skulking zone. His cloak shadowed his left arm, and its arsenal of extra-weighty throwing knives bristling along the studded leatherfish sleeve. The suggested plan was to tackle the five ships nearest the Mossmarch bridge, but Mirko had talked him up to six. His friend loitered in his calf-length jacket further along the nose-to-tail line of corsairs and sloops, where he feigned disinterest as he leaned against a barrel, picking at a fingernail with a stubby dagger. He held it overhead to catch the sun for a moment before pointing it at Sala's position, the agreed upon signal to coordinate their next actions.

The two renegades had yet to resolve their long-running discussion about whose thievery technique was the most noble. Sala insisted that his victims, while no less aggrieved at their losses than Mirko's, carried on afterward in a better frame of mind. He maintained his victims were offered a choice—to either experience the pointy end of a few thrown daggers, or redirect their bounty his way. The choice was theirs to make and, he thought, they must seldom regret it.

But Mirko's way, Sala argued—all that sneaking and snatching—left his unwitting contributors angry at themselves. Couldn't they have secured that window better? Paid more attention to the precious goods at their market stall? If only they'd taken their wife's advice and trained a guard dog! Not only did Mirko take their wares, but he left them in self-accusing agony.

The discussion was endless because Mirko took a less philosophical approach to justify himself. As a boy, with his mother lost to plague and father lost to indifference, he'd hovered around a camp of ruffians who'd needed to scramble for every hard-earned crust and goat's tooth. He'd survived by squeezing through the holes they could not, reaching spindly arms between bars to unlock gates, scaling walls, or jumping from roof to roof. He practiced his remarkable sleight of hand for hours each day until he could lift a goat's tooth from a fastened purse with little more than a brush of his fingers. His method of thievery was based on what he was trained to do; what he was *born* to do. If he took Sala's highwayman approach, threatening travelers with a blade, someone would end up accidentally skewered, and Mirko wasn't sure if it would be his victims or himself. He figured if sticking with what you knew was the only choice, it was also the *right* choice.

At that moment, with this plan, there was no disagreement whatsoever. Each would use his own specialist skills in perfect harmony. Mirko hoisted the wicker cage, waking the romp of baby otters piled in a furry jumble within. He spoke to them with good cheer as he slung the strap attached to the top of their cage over a shoulder and headed to the river side of the dock. "Okay, kids! Today, you get to come to work with Daddy."

Mirko's philosophy of sneaking around mostly involved looking like you belonged, like you were a normal part of the scene. Sure, he would skulk or merge into the shadows when circumstances required, but he generally preferred inconspicuousness to concealment. Pack slung over his shoulder, he sauntered, whistling, toward the target ship. Its troops misdirected by Virgil and Dando, the ship was nearly unmanned, with only a few of its crew chatting riverside. Mirko scanned for watching eyes, timing his approach to the mooring for least likely observation.

With a last glance, he pulled off his boots, strapping them to the back of his belt, and then balanced on the hawser for a moment before sprinting up its taut and sharply angled length. He wasn't named Leatherfoot because of lineage. Mirko had earned the nickname through his skills at balancing barefoot on any material. He'd been known to traipse across ropes much thinner than the hawser and occasionally at steeper angles. At the point where the line strained through its hawsehole, Mirko climbed over the ship's railing, landing with grace on the deck. He checked whether his feat had attracted any attention and felt a strange pang of disappointment that nobody shouted or pointed. He thought he could pick out Sala Doon's concealed outline atop the warehouse roof near the lead ship. Hopefully, his friend had seen his skillful ascent and could compliment him on it later.

Shoulders pulled back, he crossed the deck as if on an official errand and descended a ladder to the hold. Hearing no movement below decks, Mirko took a waxed paper packet from an inside pocket of his long jacket and scattered fresh fish tiddlers on the floor. The otters could smell it—their weight shifted in the cage at his back as they swarmed, searching for the source of the scent. He lowered the cage and eased the clasp on its door open. It needed his quickest reflexes to allow only four of the eight baby otters out, but he squeezed the door shut again without pinching any paws or tails. The four set upon the shiny silver fish, squeaking in joy.

Mirko dropped a Long Jin thunderclap ball to the floor and cracked its tough paper coating with the heel of a still-bare foot. It would take a minute or two for the air to penetrate to the munition's powdery core. He muttered a quick, "Sorry, little guys," to the otters as he bounded back up the steps. Intent on their dinner, they ignored him.

As he passed each of the three coils of mooring line spaced along the dock-facing side of the ship, he shook a few rope leeches from a metal tinder box. They lit up in a magical orange radiance as they reacted to the thick rope. No self-respecting rogue, liable to find himself bound hand and foot in a weak moment of misjudgment, should venture out without a secret cache of rope leeches!

He considered the leap from the rear deck of the seventh ship in line to the bowsprit of the eighth, but even with a run-up, he adjudged it too far. But anyway, the plan was to use the slender rope and grappling hook coiled at his belt, so Mirko obliged. With a deft flick, the small hook crossed the distance between the ships, hooking its own rope as it spiraled around the bowsprit. Mirko swung in a deep arc between the ships, releasing one hand to grab the rail as he rose, tethered cage bouncing against his back. He left the rope and hook behind, swinging his legs over the rail. Again, luck was on his side, and the eighth ship also lay deserted. Although sailors always professed to be more at home on the sea than on land, they sure broke for shore when it appeared!

Mirko repeated the process on this ship: otter dinner, Long Jin thunderclap ball, rope leeches. He reckoned the thunderclap ball on the other ship would erupt soon, so he hastened down the gangplank. A crewman ascending as Mirko strode down looked him up and down, clearly puzzled.

Mirko smiled and nodded to the sailor with a cheery, "All done, mate," intended to confound his confusion.

They passed midway along the gangway. Mirko veered right at the bottom, heading for a gap between two warehouses, and dropped the now-empty cage to the pavement. He passed close behind Virgil and Apostle Dando, who were about to talk to a storm-faced woman that any Outer Pangan would recognize. Mirko tipped his hat to her, offering a, "Good day, your excellency," before continuing into the shadows between the buildings ahead.

* * *

In the pastures beyond Mossmarch, Sala Doon had practiced with his heavy throwing knives on various thicknesses and tensions of rope. Sharpened viciously, he found, with a full throw, he could slice apart even the thickest cords of woven hemp. A small smile cracked his normally serious demeanor; he'd sliced ropes thicker and with more slack than the Vennese crewmen used to secure their ships here in Port Moss.

As always, Mirko's balancing skills impressed him. Once Mirko had boarded his first target ship with no alarms raised, Sala knew it was time for him to act. He stood and sought firm footing on the sedge and reed thatching that capped the dockside warehouse. He needed a solid base to brace himself for the full power needed for these throws.

The first of Sala's heavy blades snuck free from its loop on his left arm bracer. He took aim at the lead ship's middle mooring line, stretched back, and let the dagger fly. It spun end over end in a flattened arc toward the ship. Clean cut! A severed line slapped the ship's side, its other section losing tension and wilting to dangle over the edge of the reinforced river bank.

The second throw was just as accurate. And the third. Freed from its mooring, the ship's upstream-pointing prow swung into the Moss River's calm but relentless current. The gangway scraped along the dock before the gap between hull and bank became too great, and the wooden slab splashed into the water. Sala crouched into a low run, rising again to repeat the throws on the second ship in line. After his knives separated it, too, from its moorings, the first raised voices below threw panic into the air. A muffled explosion further along the line of ships punctuated the alarm.

Mirko had confided in Sala that he originally thought *well boring otters* were named because they were extremely uninteresting. But they were not boring at all. People harnessed their magical powers to bore wells without the usual back-breaking labor. Although comfortable on land, otters naturally took to water to make their homes, to protect themselves when threatened, and to hunt for prey. Well boring otters possessed magical powers that helped them flee to water whenever frightened. A pulse of magical energy would open a channel to the nearest water, removing enough material in an instant to allow the otter and its whole family to flee down the tunnel to a place of comfort and safety. Enterprising folk took advantage of this ability, placing an otter or two on a patch of land where they needed a well shaft sunk, and then scaring the creatures. Bam! An instant tunnel formed beneath the otters to the closest water, usually a wellspring below ground. All hail the well boring otters!

As Mirko's first Long Jin thunderclap ball detonated with a resounding bang, the otters aboard that ship panicked and opened four wide-bore holes as escape routes into the river beneath. The thunderclap was noisy but not dangerous, so the otters would swim away unscathed. Not so the ship. It listed at once, taking on water so quickly that it strained at its restraints only a moment later. With the rope leeches weakening the mooring lines, the ship would tip into the currents and ground itself in the shallow river delta within minutes.

More shouting rose from below, the calls expressing a mix of confusion, surprise, and despair that was music to Sala's ears. He untethered the third ship with four skillful throws. One didn't fully sever the line, but a second shot took care of the frayed section. As he leapt from one rooftop to the next to ready his knives for the fourth ship, the clutch of Vennese troops disembarking from Jada's ship spotted him. The twang of bowstrings foreshadowed inbound arrows. Sala ducked and rose, releasing his next three blades as arrows pierced the surrounding thatching.

Much like a craftsman will find a way to build something using his favorite tool, a military unit will fall upon its preferred weapons. The Vennese had a reputation for combat with fire, and sure enough, the next volley included flaming arrows, their shafts lined with flammable grease. Sala Doon liked neither the number nor the qualities of the swarm of incoming projectiles, so he leapt higher on the roofline and vaulted his legs over the peak, seeking safety on the building's far side.

Jada liked the choice of weapons even less. Sala heard her outraged yell above the rest of the panicked voices. "You imbeciles! Those are *my* dock houses you're setting ablaze. By the rivers and lakes, stop with the fire!"

Hearing the first crackle of burning thatch from over the roof's peak, Sala decided his work had come to a premature end. He'd let four of the six ships on his target list loose into the tugging river's currents. Escape was critical to the plan, so he slid down the backside of the roof, somersaulted to the ground below, and turned to vanish into the woods behind the dock houses.

But then a thought struck him. He could make the most of his best throws without direct line of sight. They were calculations based on knowledge of his target, wind speed, distance, blade weight, and air temperature. He could see the mooring line of the fifth ship through the narrow alleyway between warehouses. He calculated.

Sala pictured the fifth ship, remembering exactly how far apart the lines had been lashed to the dockside cleats. He checked the height of the building between him and the dock, getting a feel for the arc he'd need to clear it. A light wind from the west. He closed his eyes to ignore the flames sneaking over the roofline and let three of the heavy blades fly. Hearing Jada admonishing the Vennese troops, he improvised and flighted a fourth dagger.

Virgil told Sala later that only two of his first three arching blades struck their targets. They severed two lines, but he overthrew the third dagger, left quivering where it lodged into the ship's rail. But the tactic was still a success. The fifth boat swung into the current, its remaining mooring line straining as the other drifting ships bumped and jumbled mid-river. Eventually, the hawser snapped, freeing the loosened ships to meander downstream toward the scuppered, half-submerged victims of Mirko's sabotage.

Opening his eyes, Sala Doon reconsidered his fourth spinning knife. He wasn't a killer—his livelihood was based mostly on threats and thievery—so he was unsure why he'd launched a blade toward Jada. If he killed her, maybe the invasion threat would dissipate, but chaos might break loose instead. Either way, Sala would have to run. Inner Pang might not be far enough, and he considered what life might be like in

Droz. And then a second thought struck him like a physical blow: in his mental image of Jada's position, he'd set aside everyone else scurrying around the dock. As he reviewed the scene in his mind's eye, he realized that two figures likely stood between the warehouses and Jada. This was the first time in his life he regretted releasing a thrown blade. He clamped his eyes shut and imagined he could feel the last knife's weight in his palm. But imagining did not make it so; the knot in his stomach pushed his eyes open, telling him he'd crossed the line from highwayman to assassin.

He'd taken the last known position of every person into account—they were mere obstacles to avoid—but if he'd mis-thrown, even by a fraction of a degree, his blade might strike either Dando or Virgil. He'd last seen the two of them speaking with Jada.

Sala could not vanish into the trees without knowing where the fourth throw landed. He turned and squeezed through the narrow space between the warehouses, heading back to the fray and the unknown landing spot of his fateful dagger.

"Not you two morons again!" Jada spat at Virgil and Dando as she stomped across the quayside. "Out of my way before my patience frays enough to make you both a head shorter."

Dando dared reply. "Ahh, your elegancy. I see you have mistaken me. It was my twin brother, Dando, that served at the trials. My name is Apostle ... Fernando. We graduated from the guild together. We thought it best to bring you the news with all haste."

Virgil nodded with too much enthusiasm for even his own liking. "Oh yeah—the news!"

Dando half-expected an elbow, but avoided any need for Virgil to prompt him and continued with no uncomfortable silence. "Presumably, your everlasting excellency, you've heard about Golden Shores. But the intelligence whispers now mention that Inchin, Meer, and even Red Bean have sent troops to confront any threat of insurrection. They must be but mere days away. Hours, even! It was smart of your troops to muster along the coast, away from the city where who knows which way allegiances lean?"

He raised his eyebrows in an effort to stifle an inner laugh at how easily deception surged to his lips. From a corner of his eye, he caught Mirko's departure from the ship toward the warehouses behind the quayside. The trickster paused and spoke to the former queen, once again avoiding suspicion through brazen action.

"Too true, Apostle!" Virgil added, continuing their performance. "The reinforcements may be just beyond sight. But you and I had better make haste and begone from these open spaces. We wouldn't want those foreigners to hear our loose lips prattling around Queen Jada's ears, now, would we?"

Jada's eyes narrowed, and a sneered reply formed on her black-painted lips. But before she could express her disdain, surprise, or whatever other acidic emotion stirred within her, with a whoosh of air in Virgil's ear and a heavy thunk, a weighted blade passed between the two men to strike home in the narrow space between Jada's booted feet.

In an instant, her guardsmen swarmed to form a protective cordon around her. Normally one to take umbrage at being shoved aside, in this case, Virgil was glad of the interrupted conversation. With a sharp tug at Dando's voluminous sleeve, the balladeer turned and headed for the Moss Bridge.

"That scoundrel!" he muttered, running a hand through his shoulder-length hair. "Sala's bloody dagger throw only went and sliced off half my locks on this side. I'll be the laughingstock of the bard community!"

CHAPTER 28 - TEMPLE PANG

The Same Day

The coal rayvn witch, Alianthe, had barely slept. Her witchsenses had kept her on high alert all night, as the building feeling of the past several years grew until it consumed her mind. She could read the blurry portents and knew that the moment drew near when Mother Justicia would attempt to remove magic from every animal. She possessed few ways to help the humans with the power to intervene.

Early revelations made her bring Rayne and Minimus Mu together, as Alianthe could feel their roles were key. She'd long known the two must work together to counter the threat. She was working on the girl's escape. But a stronger compulsion filled her now. She detected something unexpected, something her visions and witchsenses hadn't noticed earlier. It was as if there was a *second* Rayne that needed her attention. In a flash of wisdom, she saw a snatch of the future, a time when cruelty must be blunted if her magic, and all magic, was to survive. Her four furry legs yearned to push her into flight, and her glossy black wing feathers rustled in the gusty breeze from the Sea of Sorrows as she reached out to locate a suitable conspirator. She knew what to do.

* * *

Alianthe arrived first at the unbarred window of Sister Catriona's chambers. Her coal rayvn features ruffled upon landing, making the eyeless disciple of the Mothers of Midnight turn her scarred face to the sunlight. A moment later, Alianthe's accomplice, a silver-striped fragrance glider, scratched to a stop beside her. Fragrance gliders could not fly like a bird, but the webbed membrane that stretched between their front and back legs allowed the squirrel-like creatures to glide considerable distances, normally from tree to tree. This one drifted on a warm breeze from the tall birch tree near this side of the temple to Catriona's window ledge.

In a series of gestures and subvocalized chirps, Alianthe gave last-minute instructions to the fragrance glider before fluttering away. To Catriona, the pair's communication would have been indecipherable. Alianthe knew of the human's magical sight and hearing. It was this wild and unexpected magic, somehow borne by humans into the world, that threatened all animals. She barely dared hope that the cuddly creature could blunt the girl's impact.

Catriona, despite her magical might, shrunk back as the fragrance glider drifted from the windowsill to the bed beside her. The creature was hardly threatening, not much bigger than her handspan, and its soft dark fur lay decorated with pleasant silver stripes. From an arm's length away, the little animal looked Catriona in the face and chattered in a high-pitched voice before inching closer.

Catriona caught a whiff of baking bread and pine forest. She wouldn't know until she asked Rayne later that fragrance gliders could release any scent. With no magical animals in the obverse, she couldn't appreciate how rare it was for a fragrance glider to bond with a human. In those extraordinary instances, tales told of a symbiosis brimming with happy remembrances, which the creature could elicit in a human by sensing their deepest memories and teasing them to the foreground with near-forgotten smells.

Sister Catriona's initial hesitation melted when she reached out and stroked the furry tuft between the fragrance glider's tiny pointed ears. She was charmed by its silky softness and the way the creature leaned into her affectionate stroke. It crept closer still, and before she knew it, the thing's gliders furled as it snuggled against her leg. A pleasant odor of horsehair reminded Catriona that she'd been thinking about Rayne's vision. A man on horseback. She closed her eyes and chipped at the locked-away memory, finding the extra scents of Mother Justicia's soap and the layered ozone of magical fire sneaking in uninvited.

The purring glider gave Catriona a warm feeling of companionship that her shared bond with the other sisters or even Mother Justicia failed to provide. She hoped the small furry bundle would stay at her side. So did the witch, Alianthe.

CHAPTER 29 - RED BEAN QUEENDOM

Three Days Later

Every fantastic Master Thorn story was laced with embellishment but built on a mountain of truth. Minimus Mu wished he could believe this one was complete fiction. His own mother had abandoned him as a toddler by slipping into another realm? He could see a resemblance; his strength could definitely place Maxima and him in the same family. Was there something about the eyes, too? The fineness and lawlessness of their dark tufty hair? He didn't want to look at her or think about the similarity between her and the sketches in Master Thorn's notebook. Questions ran too deep, the likely answers too painful.

The boy tried to focus on the joy of reuniting with Master Thorn, the thing he'd yearned for since their separation at sea. Wiry beard scratching Minimus's chest, the man hugged him as close as he could, limited by Minimus's girth. While other orphans' masters could be harsh, Master Thorn took such care in raising him, his crusty shell protecting a well of tenderness beneath. It was almost as if—

"Wait!" Minimus began. "If this person is really my mother, are you ...?"

Master Thorn nodded, slowly at first, then violently. He took one of Minimus's huge hands in both of his own. Master

Thorn opened his mouth to speak three times before words emerged, and even then, they were fragmented, laden with more emotion than sense. "I couldn't … I just thought … there was so much to explain. But look, I saved you the last runcible spork from the cart."

There was *way* too much to explain, Minimus thought. An engraved item of cutlery wouldn't help. The father he'd dreamed of had been with him his entire life, cloaked in deception. His mother *had* abandoned him, yet made an impossible return. The boy pushed Master Thorn and the proffered spork away, turned his back, and stomped out of the warehouse, leaving silence in his wake. He took four long strides, six, then halted. A tear of frustration carved a jagged line across his cheek as he shook his head.

The hand gripping his shoulder from behind was too small to be Maxima's and too insistent to be Master Thorn's. He knew whose it must be, and to shirk off a queen's touch would be a breach of etiquette too serious to reconcile. Master Thorn had trained that reflex into him. He turned.

"I heard it all, back there," Queen Angstaad said. "Listen. Master Thorn is not as courageous as you—maybe nobody is. Imagine how hard it would have been for him to explain to you, as a child, how your mother abandoned you. How he'd failed to prevent it. How his failure left you a half-orphan. Sure, it's wildly unfair, but I imagine he wanted you to feel like a character in one of his fabulous tales, or a felt-covered marionette from his puppet shows. He couldn't make you an errant prince, but he sure as the seven bells of Phan Tong could make you a courageous orphan who plies the world's finest cutlery routes. Give it time, and the story of the orphaned boy can change into the tale of the child whose parents always came for him, even across impossibly separated worlds."

Minimus sniffled, rubbing his runny nose on his tunic's sleeve. He needed Jing Jing, and the monkey appeared, tugging at his leggings as if summoned by magical communication. It was only natural to scoop the monkey up and run calloused fingers through his back fur as Jing Jing's lanky arms encircled the boy's neck.

"Please tell me you're just Jing Jing," Minimus said. "You're not a rhinoceros disguised as a monkey, are you?"

Jing Jing said nothing, and that was enough.

* * *

Minimus and Jing Jing rode several paces ahead of everyone else as their party crept along the banks of the Jade River, and the next day he refused to look back as their horses clopped through the forest to intersect with the Moss River. He knew that his questions and accusations would most likely roll from his tongue in hurtful spurts. He wasn't even sure what questions to ask. It was only as Nikolai Nineteen Points negotiated passage aboard a moored barge for himself and his little cow that Minimus broke his silence.

"Your destination is Mossmarch?" he asked the old man.

"I'm headed wherever Petunia takes me," he said with a laugh. "She knows best. But we're not going to Mossmarch. Not exactly. Somewhere beyond the river mouth, I think. The feeling for our destination will grow within me as we get closer, I expect. It always does. My girl always gets to where she needs to go, somehow. And I may have lost my vision, but I get glimpses of where we're going through her."

* * *

Asking at the palace gates to see the queen was never something Minimus Mu or Master Thorn would consider, even after saving the queendom. But when the queen is your peer, hesitation fled, and Queen Angstaad didn't even ask. She simply pushed the crossed pikes of the two door guards aside and informed them of her intentions as she entered the full-sized reception hall from which smaller doors led to the Red-Bean-scale chambers beyond.

"I need to speak to Queen Violet. Do send a footman at once," she said.

The guards struggled visibly between their instincts to protect the palace and their awe at the power and directness of the Golden Shores' warrior queen. Angstaad ran a calloused hand through her closely cropped blonde hair and sent a penetrating look in the direction of the footman, who the guards had not yet instructed. The man stood frozen to the spot, a tense sweat threatening to darken his impeccable purple suit jacket. He would not have reached Angstaad's waist, and the weight of her gaze soon forced him into a stuttering heel turn.

"I-I'll-I'll fetch her, your elegancy," he spluttered before hurtling through one of the small lacquered doors.

Master Thorn cast an objective eye over the party. Their sweat-encrusted, dusty traveling garments screamed affront to the spotless palace reception floors, and he had no gift to offer the Red Bean Queendom's ruler, if she did indeed appear. He wished he could shrink into the wallpaper, but when his gaze fell upon Minimus, his tension eased. The boy had saved the queendom from being absorbed into Outer Pang in clothes no better than these, so surely the queen could forgive an edge of scruffiness. And Angstaad and her swordswomen looked, if anything, more road-hardened than Jing Jing or Maxima.

Stillness prevailed, the only sounds the shuffling of the two guards' feet and the clack of their pikes as they tried in vain to position them in a way that would be unthreatening to Angstaad's fighters while still keeping an appearance of guarding the entryway. It was a long few minutes before the small door flew open, and Queen Violet burst into the reception chamber. Even in her alarm, her words rhymed with flawless ease, as was the way of Red Bean royalty.

"Queen Angstaad, you're a feast for my eyes, a cooling breeze under sunny skies. And Minimus, who we all love best, with Master Thorn and another guest?"

Minimus bent, allowing Queen Violet to kiss him—twice on each cheek!—and take his larger hand in both of her tiny ones. "Umm, yes. Queen Violet of the Red Bean Queendom, your elegancy, this is … uhh … Maxima Li. She's from the

Outer Pang coast, sort of. And you know Jing Jing, of course."

Violet's gaze bounced between Minimus and Maxima, but discretion prevented her from any prodding. "I owe this monkey gratitude, too. He helped our queendom, just like you."

She didn't need to bend too much to smile eye-to-eye with Jing Jing. "And even though we love you so, I'll check your pockets before you go."

Minimus chuckled for what felt like the first time in a year, adding to Master Thorn's mortification.

* * *

Over dinner at the specially crafted table and elevated chairs that allowed Red Beaners to dine at a polite height with taller guests, Queen Violet's husband, Alfred of Evermere, chatted with easy charm. He regaled them with tales of his embarrassing *faux pas* during official state visits, the endless series of misadventures that befell Princess Tasha and Rayne as they grew up, and his close encounter with a rampaging Vondabeast. Minimus smiled, nodded, savored every mention of Rayne, and tried to avoid looking at Maxima, who the butlers had seated opposite him, to Queen Violet's left. Although he examined each item of cutlery and tableware with squinting precision, Master Thorn held back any design or fabrication criticisms. Still, Minimus noticed he avoided the clumsy-looking bean fork in favor of the six-tined bristleskewer.

As the footmen served the first dessert course, Queen Angstaad turned the conversation to practical matters. By the time they'd finished their plates of dainty eiderquince and jewelberries, they had run through Tasha and Rayne's plight. In response, messengers had been summoned and dispatched to mobilize swordswomen from the Golden Shores and a bargeload of the renowned Red Bean archers. Queen Violet also sent a call to the royal library to have her scholars find the correct legal actions to oppose any machinations from Jada or her cousin.

The Mothers of Midnight did not seem to Minimus like a peril best confronted with armies or laws, but who was he? Nothing but a confused non-orphan who bounced around dusty plains dragging a cutlerer's cart and accidentally saved a tiny queendom from ruin.

When the sliced cake arrived, his glance fell on Maxima's plate, even if he deigned to look no higher. He noticed that she'd used her fork on the eiderquince and was left with only a spoon. Without meeting her eyes, he slid his own fork across the table to her. At the rate his cake would fly down, he could easily reuse his spoon.

CHAPTER 30 - SEA OF SORROWS

Two Days Later

"Not much of a sailor, myself, but we should go with you," Sala said. A worried expression crossed his face as he imagined Virgil and Dando sailing the choppy strait to reach Temple Pang. He and Mirko sat with their backs to the wall in the shadiest corner inside the Crossed Swords. Their normal outdoor table lay too exposed, with the threat of Vennese troops just over the river and no opposing forces arriving.

"Nae nonsense, mate," Virgil replied. "You two are the only reason Mossmarch is not overrun already, owing to the shipwrecks clogging the river and the nervousness following that disaster. The Outer Pang forces don't know who to follow, and the Vennese remain camped across the river by the forest. You need to stay here and work your chaos. Besides, Dando and I are too lovable to get into any real jeopardy with those Mothers of Midnight types. We'll scoot across, work our charms, spring Rayne and Princess Tasha loose, and be back before supper tomorrow. Or, at worst, in time for two swift rounds before last orders here at the Swords."

Mirko swished his head in a gesture somewhere between agreement and resignation. "How will you get a boat?" he asked.

Dando clapped him on the shoulder. "Well, brother, that's where you can help us. Know anyone willing to lend one to a pair of well-regarded gentlemen?”

"Aye, I know plenty of folk like that. But I'll ask again, where are *you two* going to find a boat? Joke! Joke! Let me think.”

Mirko cast a sidelong glance at Sala and raised an eyebrow. "Dare we?" he asked.

Sala rolled his eyes. "You're not thinking of …? Really? Not Foul Phrased Phinneus! Mirko, you rogue!”

* * *

Phinneus Farage was well known by the river folk and all who worked the docks at Port Moss, and was of particular interest to scholars at the Outer Pang University who studied how profanity filtered into everyday use. Phinneus was known to have introduced more than seventeen commonly used swear words, among them two of the most creatively vile. It turned out he also had expertise in locating marine equipment that had gone missing from its various rightful owners, and seemed to Sala and Mirko a likely source of a small boat to borrow for nothing more than calling in favors.

Foul Phrased Phinneus clenched an unlit pipe between surprisingly intact rows of yellowing teeth, its downward-pointing bowl a distraction that Dando struggled to ignore as Sala introduced them. The man's face was shaped somewhat like the western cape of Long Jin, if you imagined it with a jungle of oddly colored hair to its north and an archipelago of salt and pepper beard along the south coast.

"Ye're a ███████ truthsayer? I'll be a ███ ██████ if I do any business with you, you ██████-lipped ██████ ██████.”

This sounded like a poor start, even though Dando had never previously heard a couple of the terms Phinneus spat out. "Actually, I'm *not* a truthsayer. Just borrowed my cousin's robes to avoid being interfered with. A truthsayer could never deny he *is* one, am I right?”

Phinneus scratched his chin through the wisps of his beard

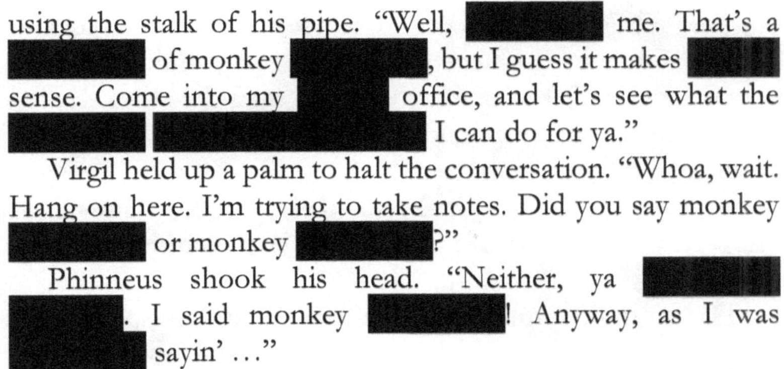

using the stalk of his pipe. "Well, ███████ me. That's a ███████ of monkey ███████, but I guess it makes ████ sense. Come into my ███████ office, and let's see what the ███████ ███████ I can do for ya."

Virgil held up a palm to halt the conversation. "Whoa, wait. Hang on here. I'm trying to take notes. Did you say monkey ███████ or monkey ███████?"

Phinneus shook his head. "Neither, ya ███████ ███████. I said monkey ███████! Anyway, as I was sayin' …"

It took coaxing, but after a few more misunderstandings and with every visitor considering rinsing their ears after departing, they secured a boat. Technically, Phinneus didn't own the boat, but he claimed as long as it was back within two days, everything would be ███████ glorious.

* * *

The sailing skiff was exactly where Foul Phrased Phinneus had described. Virgil and Dando untied it and pushed themselves through the reeds and away from the shore where the Moss River met the Sea of Sorrows, just downstream from Mossmarch.

There was an unspoken and probably missing element to the plan to sail across the strait to Temple Pang. "Uh, now what?" Virgil asked. "Do you want to pull those ropes, Dando, and see what happens? I'll grab this, um, steering thing?"

"Are all musicians this clueless? In the Truthsayer's Guild, they'd *never* teach everyone to sail. They consider it a worthless skill. Now, could you look like you know what you're doing and thread this jib line around the winch and through that cleat, so we can get the breeze in our sails?"

Virgil adopted a whiny tone. "Ooh, in *my* order we learn this. In *my* order, we learn that. We truthsayers are better than everyone! But can you write a song, my friend? No! So, you can stick your jib and your cleat up your arse while I steer us to the temple."

The skiff's sails puffed and flapped into action, rocking Virgil back onto the bench, nearly dumping him astern. He wrenched the tiller to one extreme and then the other, making the boom crash from side to side. After a few wobbly moments, the skiff stabilized.

"Oh, now I get it," Virgil said. "If I push this thingy right, the boat goes left. And if I pull it to the left, we turn right. Easy peasy."

Dando took some slack from a sail, and they sped up the coastline, Temple Pang looming offshore in a light mist. "Huh. Maybe there should be a song about that: 'The Ballad of not Sinking,' perhaps?"

* * *

Mother Justicia paced the round tower chamber, touching the lodestone on each pass. Abandoning the Temple of the Wraith had been a wrench, but instead of Temple Pang offering serenity, her unease grew with each passing day. She normally sensed the magic of people nearby, and the flickering of each of her proteges in the temple gave her a grounding, a sense of reassurance. But two oddities needled her continually.

One was the *lack* of magic. None of the monks she'd expelled possessed any trace of magical powers. And when she'd ventured to Mossmarch, she detected nothing there either, even in the dense pack of the market square. In Astella or Wraithwatch, every fifth person would display some sort of power. Could the missing sisters of Temple Pang have been so successful in draining the magic from the western continent when she herself had barely scratched the surface in the east?

The second was the *presence* of magic. Specks and wisps of power pervaded the island of Temple Pang, with every land and air creature seemingly infused with magic. She'd not once felt an animal stir with powers until she arrived here, and now she detected it everywhere. The Backwards Man had once used the lodestone to enchant a bowl of wriggling leeches with magical power, and she understood how the stone's powerful concentrated magic might accomplish that, but here it was everywhere. Birds, vermin, those bloody goats floating in every courtyard, and the critters chewing through solid rock. How could everything look so similar but feel so different? It was like someone had whisked away her familiar, comfortable sandals and replaced them with footwear that oozed and pinched at every step.

Once again, she wondered—had her followers here in the west completed her mission, not simply eradicating magic from humans but transferring it into animals? Maybe the missing technique was within her grasp, as yet unnoticed. A trip to Mossmarch to sniff out the eleven-pointed star had become critical. She'd wrought it from the lodestone itself, and the prophecy of the dagger-covered man holding the key to her mission suggested she, too, could do what her local disciples seemed to have accomplished, if only she had the amulet back in her hands.

Her mind rippled with thoughts of how easy it was to siphon away the magic of the local animals. Should she finish the job and remove every trace of magic from the area, or would it prove harmless to allow the animals' magical powers to endure? She knew in her bones that humans could not be trusted with such power, but could animals? Was it okay for them to use it instinctively, without the plans and malice of her own kind?

An internal twinge snapped her from her musings. The transition that infused her girls with their powers gave them but a shadow of her own magic, accumulated over years of exposure to the lodestone. Some could detect other human magic over short distances, and the best could even drain away others' powers without needing physical contact, but none had the range of their leader. Mother Justicia sensed the flicker of a new magician arriving on the island. It intruded with an odd resonance, this magic, but it was a welcome feeling after so long. She hurried to the east-facing window, unable to resist the tug of the interloper's faint power.

Two men bickered in hushed tones far below, both

dragging a line attached to a small boat as they hauled it ashore. She sensed buried magic in the less-colorful of the pair. It was time to exercise her abilities and remove this man's magic before he could make mischief on the island.

* * *

"Ugh. It's on firm ground. We don't need to move it the extra handspan so you can tie it off to that tree," Virgil complained.

Dando had discovered that there was no such thing as a lying question. He'd also figured out that if you let a lie trail off halfway, the deception could linger in the unspoken part. He tried it on Virgil. "Uh, haven't you heard of tides? Or waves? If we don't tie it off…"

"By the black dog of Og, couldn't your order have trained you to be wrong? At least occasionally? Okay, heave one more time. In one … two … *three.*"

At first, Apostle Dando thought he'd strained a muscle with the last tug on the rope, but it felt different from any other sprain he'd experienced. This one jabbed viciously, like a giant hair being plucked, a hair rooted in his very core. And it tugged him toward the tower of Temple Pang, looming above. He turned sharply and looked up, rubbing his lower ribs.

"I just felt something weird," he called to Virgil. He paused, mouth agape at the fact that he'd said something truthful for the first time since the encounter with the Mothers of Midnight in Mossmarch.

"With your ingrained weirdness, I'm not surprised," Virgil replied. He seemed not to notice that Dando had spoken a truth.

Dando continued, testing his newfound change. "Your name is Virgil Longspeaker. And I am a truthsayer!"

Virgil froze. "Wait. Did you just say—? It wore off?"

Dando's smile widened, threatening to eclipse his entire face. His nods grew ever larger. Not only could he communicate properly again, but he could resume his duties as a truthsayer. His new constraint to utter the truth was oddly freeing.

In the tower above, Mother Justicia experienced a moment of confusion. She'd tried to take the man's magic but had somehow only flipped it around. She closed her eyes and examined him more deeply. Her relief at finally finding a magical human disappeared as she realized what her more detailed probe had discovered. He wasn't a magical human after all; his powers were due to an infection of sorts. An animal's magic had penetrated and sat *beside* where a human's powers would normally originate. She knew she could remove it but needed to be closer to work such an intricate extraction.

Mother Justicia leapt from the tower window.

CHAPTER 31 - MOSSMARCH

The Same Day

Sala Doon and Mirko Leatherfoot knew better than to show their faces outside the shadows, rat-run alleys, and less reputable alehouses of Mossmarch after their riverside exploits. The mood in town was difficult to decipher. Sure, many had grumbled and bristled at the interim rulership of Princess Tasha, but the same people had previously complained about Queen Jada. Even the murmured tavern conversations among Jada's guardsmen swung both ways. Some saw opportunity in the change, while others yearned for the stability from before Jada stirred up tensions. The Vennese troops, at first, remained across the river, wondering when the rumored approaching forces from the east might appear. They spent long afternoons resharpening swords and suggesting unworkable ways to recover their logjam of ships.

It wasn't long before ragtag bands of mercenaries arrived at the oft-closed city gates, looking for someone, anyone, who might make good on the promised sword-for-hire payout. They raised tension on the streets, with the citizens of Outer Pang still trying to go about their normal business, but increasingly nervous to set out market stalls, open the doors to taverns, or cart their crops without armed protection. A few scuffles broke out, but outright fighting remained unjustified until the various forces established proper battle lines.

After a few days, Jada could bob with the rising tide of rumor, suspicion, and whispers no longer. With no attackers on the horizon, a covered wagon, pulled by two fine stallions, crept across the humpy bridge and through the imposing gates into Mossmarch, accompanied by a tight press of pikemen and sword bearers. Satin ties held back the curtains on the wagon's windows, and from the shadowed alley leading from the Crossed Swords to the root sellers' cellars in the maze behind, Sala and Mirko watched Jada's profile as she gauged her reception. A few cheers revealed her most fervent supporters, but the dominant sound was background chatter as onlookers spoke to each other behind cupped hands or in hushed whispers.

"I don't think anyone will oppose her with Tasha imprisoned at Temple Pang," Sala said to his friend.

"Not the warmest reception, I'll admit, but I think I'd agree. It'll be a waltz back to the palace, and she'll be curled up in her tower with that crazy tiger in no time. She'll have a face like thunder, though, when she notices we've been dipping into her jewelry boxes."

Sala rolled his eyes at the array of birds gripping the eaves and gestured at the five gravity-defying cats that paced the alley walls as if they were tabletops. They all stared at Sala with saucer-like gazes. "I've had enough of my menagerie of followers. We don't know what to do with it, and nobody will buy it. It's time to put the star back."

Mirko turned to peer at Sala's face. "Why don't you just discard it somewhere? Make it someone else's problem?"

The knife-thrower replied with a hint of mirth riding beneath his words. "Whoa! Are you feeling okay? Mirko Leatherfoot persuading me not to break into a building? It's hardly an inconvenience. We just need a coil of rope. Oh, and a truthsayer. And a super-powered hovering goat, tiger repellent, and a timetable of the guards' rotations."

Mirko nodded, as if considering how easy such a job would be. "Some disguises, a massive pillow stuffed with everbounce leaves, and a tame abomination bird wouldn't go amiss, either. I'm in! When do we start?"

CHAPTER 32 - TEMPLE PANG

The Same Day

As the sound of flapping robes attracted Virgil and Apostle Dando's eyes to the tower window above them, they confronted a startling vision. Mother Justicia flew, plummeting arms-out and feet-first toward their spot on the shore. The reestablished truthsayer thought he heard Virgil emit a high-pitched shriek at the sight, before he realized it was his own voice. He couldn't be sure Virgil hadn't joined in.

She slowed as she fell, crackles of magical energy limning her palms. Her face appeared lit from behind, her scarring on full display. She hovered for a moment, her feet a handspan above the mossy rocks, before settling. The glow diminished, leaving sparking traces on Mother Justicia's fingertips.

With only a rustle of robes and a blur, Mother Justicia was at Dando's side and snatched up his wrist. This time, he was certain it wasn't Virgil that whimpered. She clung to his hand for a mere moment before stepping away, at a normal human pace this time.

"Ow!" Dando cried, brows knitting. He rubbed his chest. Had the woman grabbed him and tugged with her uncanny speed? No, it felt like something deeper that she'd manipulated. Like the sensation he'd experienced as they hauled the boat, but rougher, more jarring.

He tested his truth-telling. "Uh, Virgil, you and I accompanied Minimus into the caves of the All-Seeing Eye."

Truth. Virgil looked at him side-wise, unwilling to let the interloping Mother Justicia out of his sight.

Maybe nothing had happened. Dando tried a lie. "Afterwards, Minimus told me he liked me better. That your songs were long and boring."

That was a definite lie and made the minstrel forget about the imposing magician confronting them. He glared at Dando.

"He said that? When?"

Dando burst out laughing and hugged his companion. "I can lie, Virgil! Or tell the truth. I feel like a regular person again."

Virgil maintained his scowl for a moment, but a smile tugged at the corners of his lips. "Yeah. A normal person trained in sailing, languages, diplomatic protocol, and all-around smugness. Very normal. Exceptionally normal. As normal as—"

Mother Justicia cleared her throat with obvious intention. Who were these bumbling fools? They cut short their embrace and looked at her once again. She pointed a finger with a slight arthritic bend at the apostle. "Where'd you get your magic?"

Dando furrowed his brows. "You mean my truthsaying? My order pricks us with a blue land urchin quill. Their magic has the side effect of making one unable to lie."

This made a sliver of sense to Mother Justicia. It was why her initial draining attempt had failed, and why the power within Apostle Dando felt like it was *beside* his core, not surging within it. Animal magic, again. Somehow, the world had become infested with it. Maybe something that originated on the western continent, because she'd seen no signs of it in Wraithwatch.

Virgil, his peril now returned to focus, remembered the way he'd fended off the Mothers of Midnight in Mossmarch. He raised his lute and fingered a standard opening chord. Maybe his music could incapacitate the witch, and Dando could subdue her somehow. It wouldn't have surprised him if witch-roping was a core training element of the Truthsayers' Guild.

But before he could strum the strings, they popped free of the lute, twanging and severed. Mother Justicia had blurred for a moment, moving too quickly for Virgil to process, and now stood in her original position, clutching a newly palmed dagger. It looked familiar to Virgil, and sure enough, when he checked his belt sheath, his blade was missing.

"We'll have none of that here, boy," she said. She cast the dagger over her shoulder, where it spun into a clump of bushes. "Normally, I'd tell you to piss off in your boat from whence you came, but I'm taking it. If you can refrain from breaking into song, you look harmless enough that the sisters might give you some bread behind the kitchens, but suit yourself. I care not."

Mother Justicia turned her back on the two new arrivals and used her interior voice to call to Sister Catriona. It was high time they recovered the eleven-pointed star and finished their mission.

* * *

Dando and Virgil perched on a slab of flat rock near the tower's base, watching Catriona and Mother Justicia push their boat through the reed bed before hopping in. The apostle was concerned about the boat—they'd promised Foul Phrased Phinneus that they'd return it to the place they'd taken it.

He shouted down to them, using the most pleasant voice he could muster. How well could they even hear with their ears burnt away? "Hey, gracious ladies! When you cross, could you maybe leave the boat near the—?"

The eyeless glance that Mother Justicia sent in his direction was so full of scorn he dared not complete his request.

"Uh, never mind," he said. "Have a safe crossing."

Virgil clapped his friend on the back. "You know Phinneus will call us ███████ or monkey ███████, right?"

There was a nervous edge to Dando's laugh. "Yeah. Or ███████ ███████."

Virgil set down his de-stringed lute and gave it a longing glance as he stood. "I wish Rayne could contact us here, but she said she could only see us at the Crossed Swords. We don't have a boat, but we can still do a spot of rescuing—right, my friend? Or, at the very least, ask for a loaf of bread."

CHAPTER 33 - RED BEAN QUEENDOM

The Previous Day

A soapy, hot bath can relax anyone, yet the freshly scrubbed Minimus Mu paced the stable yard while he waited for the stragglers to appear. Every minute they spent here was a minute he was not dedicating to Rayne's rescue.

Maxima, already mounted, worked her shoulders up and down, punctuating the stretches with sighs of exasperation. Eventually, she edged closer to Mr. Apples and directed her complaints at Minimus. "Thorny's got some apparently important business in the kitchens, but I'm pretty sure he's only offering guidance on organizing their knife collection, which they'll ignore the moment he leaves."

Minimus returned her gaze, noticing her eyes were a shade darker than his own. "Yeah. Once he got into a heated discussion at the back door of a fine dining restaurant in Traders' Rest where the proprietor insisted on stocking the cutlery drawers alphabetically. Master Thorn scoffed, saying it was moronic to organize by anything other than implement length."

Side by side, they regarded Queen Angstaad, who fastened several weapons and two stuffed saddle bags to her horse, checking each strap and buckle three times. Without turning,

Maxima rustled inside her own saddle bag and plucked out two hand-sized bundles wrapped in red tartan cloth.

"You look hungry," she said to Minimus. "Might as well start on elevenses while we wait."

The wrap passed from hand to hand and the pair munched while waiting for Master Thorn. When nothing but crumbs remained, the arguing voices of Ezra and Master Thorn preceded their arrival. Something about whether moonlight was silver or white. Ezra remained on foot as Master Thorn mounted, and Jing Jing grabbed sandal, knee, then saddle to swing up in front of Minimus. He pulled a tiny silver candlestick holder from the roomy inner pocket of his fancy jacket, showing it to Minimus with a solemn but somehow satisfied expression before returning it with a flourish.

"I'm headed back to the City of Jade and my balloon, lad," Ezra said, clapping Minimus on the thigh. "Maybe I can see something helpful from the air at Temple Pang. All I need now is fair winds and to avoid exploding golden rams."

Queen Angstaad was not one for long goodbyes, and the speed at which she cantered from the stable yard left no room for further dallying. The swordswomen she'd summoned massed somewhere behind them, but ahead lay a hard ride along the Moss River and a confrontation with the Mothers of Midnight, former queen Jada, and likely trouble with Ven.

CHAPTER 34 - MOSSMARCH

The Next Day

Animals often provided more than their physical and magical powers to aid humans. The companionship of Mr. Apples to Minimus, the bond between the boy and Jing Jing, even the fluttering expectation of the birds surrounding the hobbled old man and his breadcrumbs as they rested at the bench beside the flowing River Moss, all were examples of the harmony between human and beast. But gabbling hounds strained this relationship.

Gabbling hounds were pack animals by nature, but when separated from their packs, they often latched onto human companions, following them around relentlessly with territorial pride. This behavior alone never imposed much, and the dogs proved loyal, warm companions. But their magical power often caused anguish. A gabbling hound could read the thoughts of its human companion, and felt compelled to vocalize them in human speech. This meant a running commentary of their internal musings accompanied any person befriended by one. There would no longer be such a thing as privacy, and the resulting embarrassment, jeers, and interest in one's personal thoughts often drove those afflicted with a gabbling hound to seek the solitude of remote places. Some would even go to extreme lengths to rid themselves of their over-attached four-legged friends, but it's hard to deceive when magic lays your inner thoughts bare. Abandoning or killing a gabbling hound was of little use. Its magic would signal other hounds near and far telling them to form a pack and follow the human, resulting in multiple disciples commenting on innermost thoughts and dreams.

To the witch Alianthe, the gabbling hound she found sniffing around the cobbled fringes of Mossmarch's market square was nothing more than another animal friend. A useful one, for she passed no judgment on its magical powers. She rather used them to her advantage. And ultimately to the hound's advantage, too, if it could play a part in preserving the world's magic from the threat of Mother Justicia and her order.

And so, the voice of a dog interrupted the joyous reunion between Minimus Mu, Master Thorn, and the roguish disruptors of Jada's fleet, Sala Doon and Mirko Leatherfoot. The knee-height black short-haired hound, ears pointing skyward, nosed at the boy's leg, leaving a damp splodge. Its voice could have passed for a slow-speaking farmer with the deep bass tones of a barrel-chested man, not a smallish dog. "Uhh, Minimus? Minimus Mu?"

All five humans broke off their excited conversation mid-sentence and looked down at the interloper.

"My friend, she's foreseen something. Um. Something important. She, uh, needs your help."

The hound paused here and let out a tiny howl but broke it off and continued. Minimus scratched behind the dog's ears as it spoke.

"You met that, uh, what's it called? A *skarsenkýr*?"

Here the hound looked up at the eaves of the adjacent cobbler's hut where a row of twittering birds flanked a single large coal rayvn before continuing. "Um, sorry. A *small cow*? Friends with a blind tattooed man?"

The hound paused again, waiting for confirming nods.

"Well, uh, whatever happens, you need to stop her from getting to Temple Pang. If the witch at the temple sacrifices the little cow on her magical stone, well, uhm——" The hound howled again, longer this time. "It'll be bad. Uh, real bad. It will take away our magic. Every animal. In every land. End of everything. My friend says she cannot have animals stop the little cow. Because she makes every animal friendly, in the end. Must be humans that stop her from getting to the temple."

It felt weird to start up a conversation with a stray market dog, made even odder by the uncertainty that a gabbling hound could even understand a stranger, but Minimus thought none of these things and continued patting the dog as he questioned it. "Nikolai and Petunia left us a while back. On a river barge. How would we even find them?"

The hound craned his neck once again. Smaller birds ceased their chatter and hopped closer to the coal rayvn, packing in as tightly as their shapes would allow.

After a short pause, the dog continued in its laconic tones. "Um, my friend says she can help you with that. Follow the birds, and they'll follow the little cow. Uh, like this."

As if in response, the row of smaller birds launched as one, looping around the market square three times before arrowing off to the west. They returned a moment later and settled once more beside the coal rayvn.

"And, ahh, she says not to take that star with you. The witch can smell it and she'll know you're coming." The hound turned its attention to Sala Doon, who nodded.

"Was planning on ditching this thing anyway," he said, smiling at the idea that he was talking to a dog reading someone else's thoughts. "And we were already planning on a visit to Temple Pang to free our friend. But tell me, my slobbering pal, why should we take orders from a talking dog?"

Again, the hound paused, barking twice and considering another howl. "My friend says she's working on something else. Um, something that will help you. Would you like to see your little friends returned? From the temple?"

Minimus felt his heart race at the suggestion. "She can bring Rayne here? And Princess Tasha?"

"Uh, watch the west. The west. My friend will bring them to you the way she first brought them to your side."

This made little sense. Minimus Mu and Master Thorn had first met the Red Bean Princess and her handmaiden after a passing drift goose had inadvertently carried them across Inner Pang in a hollowed-out gourd. Who could convince a drift goose to do *anything*, let alone snatch two Red Beaners from their prison?

The gabbling hound lost interest in the group and sloped off, following an unknown scent in a zig zag across the square. Minimus Mu looked up and to the west, scanning the horizon.

CHAPTER 35 - TEMPLE PANG

The Same Day

Alianthe fluttered from the square, opening her witchsenses, searching for a drift goose. They were rare and mostly solitary birds, their vast wingspans carrying them on thermals across every sea and queendom. With a stroke of luck, she sensed a mating pair nearby, warming themselves and scouting potential egg-laying sites in the ashes of the collapsed roof of a dockside warehouse, burnt in the recent chaos.

It took persuading, but after an unspoken negotiation, the drift geese took to the air with a long run up, leaving the warehouse through the charred hole in its thatched roof. Alianthe drafted in their wake, relieved to avoid the full strain of the onshore breeze from the Sea of Sorrows.

* * *

Princess Tasha was nowhere near finished cursing her own naivete. How could she have trusted Jada and her cousin? No matter what Rayne said, Tasha feared her mother's reaction to this diplomatic and decision-making failure. But local matters pulled her from dwelling on her remorse.

"It doesn't seem to work very well, this conversion to

becoming one of them," Rayne said, brushing a knot from Tasha's otherwise flawless auburn waves.

"But look at their faces," Tasha said. "Their eyes. And ears! My courtly graces would never permit such disgraces. You said their memories fail when the change takes hold. We must escape, so let's be bold."

"I don't think we can manage that by ourselves," the handmaiden replied, finding the return to subservience jarring, even though Tasha was also her childhood friend and always treated her fairly. "I can send messages out to the places I recall most vividly. Dando and Virgil set out from the Crossed Swords already, and now Minimus and Master Thorn journey this way, too. We should wait it out. Get this first conversion ceremony out of the way. They'll be here soon."

A tear crept down Tasha's stress-creased face. "But what if they erred when, for you, they prepared? When they work me today, I convert right away? Or if for you it takes longer, because you're just stronger than I—if my face scars, I shall die!"

Rayne figured the idea of being weaker than her own handmaiden was a more frightening thought than any facial scarring. Tasha was raised to be a queen, taught to be strong and decisive, while her father had plucked Rayne from a rayvn-infested orphanage to be nothing more than a companion. But she also knew that Tasha was no pushover. She had charm backed by resolve, and selecting her to be interim ruler of Outer Pang was no accident.

"My lady, the conversion won't work on you, just as it failed on me. Twice!"

The sound of a key in the locked door signaled Catriona's arrival to escort Tasha to the courtyard for the ceremony with the coral amulet. Rayne had intentionally left out the part about the way the stone would cut Tasha's hand during the ceremony. The princess cared little for blood, but she'd tolerate it in the heat of the moment. Catriona's bitter voice rang inside both their heads. "Come!" was all she said.

Rayne hugged Tasha close, willing her to be brave. As they

separated and Tasha headed to the door where Catriona waited with key in hand, the voice continued, "Both of you. I want you to watch this time, Miss Sun. You can endure the change together."

Despite being locked in her room most of the time, Rayne had learned a partial layout of the temple. She could have led the party to the courtyard without much dithering. Soon, there was sunshine on their faces. Catriona motioned with her rod to a corner, and Rayne moved away from Tasha, following the implied instruction. She noticed it was the coziest, sunniest corner, and that Catriona had used only a harsh pointing motion, not a prod. She felt another tug at the base of her neck, as if an invisible plant took root.

Catriona looked away as she spoke to Tasha, her magical vision allowing her to see the whole courtyard regardless of which way she faced. While she had been curt and violent with Rayne during the first conversion attempt, Catriona proved oddly frank as she directed Tasha.

"When you squeeze, it doesn't really hurt much, especially if you look away from the blood. We try to scare girls into telling us if they have pre-existing magical abilities, but it doesn't affect the conversion. We like to know ahead of time. Lords below, why am I telling you that? Anyway, squeeze, concentrate on the amulet's warmth, and you'll be like us in a day or two. Fast. You'll see and hear *everything*. You'll be much more powerful, understand why we need to drown out magic, and why people can't be trusted to use it."

As Catriona dangled the coral amulet before Tasha, Rayne saw the silver-streaked face of a fragrance glider peek from the shadows of her cowl. After the princess took hold of the amulet, Rayne noticed how Catriona slid her free hand to the glider's chin, stroking it. The scents of lavender and fresh mist from a cool lake suddenly infused the courtyard.

Catriona's head jerked with tiny movements like her sightless eyes searched the courtyard for a hidden trinket. The hand that stroked the fragrance glider moved to caress one side of her face, moving gingerly down her neck and across her exposed collar bone, as if gauging the sensitivity of an old wound.

"She's his aunt?" she said to herself, using her spoken voice. "My father's aunt?"

The lavender morphed into a burnt smell—not acrid, but the purifying scent of a field cleared of scrub. A shadow flickered across the sun for a moment, but Catriona failed to notice it, lost in reverie as she stroked her collarbone.

Whether instinct made Rayne spring to Tasha's side to protect her, or whether she had an inkling a rescue mission was underway, she would never know. But by the time the drift goose slowed his descent with a powerful flap of wings whose tips nearly touched opposite walls, the two Red Bean women stood shoulder to shoulder, the coral amulet discarded at Tasha's feet.

In an instant, the oversized bird's gentle talons pinched the folds of the pair's clothing, and they were aloft, the stones of the courtyard retreating below. Catriona's astonished lips formed a perfect O beneath her cowled upper face.

The drift goose had a firm hold on Princess Tasha, but before Rayne was more than her own height above the floor, she felt a wrench, tugging at the back of her neck. It tore her from the bird's talon to land in a bruised heap on the sun-warmed stones below. The goose flapped again and turned as it cleared the courtyard wall, one claw still clutching its dangling prize.

Catriona was stunned only for a moment. Her free hand curled into an uncomfortable-looking rictus, and she tapped her rod on the stones. Although she saw nothing, Rayne felt it. The draining of magical power. Catriona soaked up the drift goose's magic and the broad-winged bird flapped twice as hard, careening wildly as its magic-assisted lift failed.

When Catriona raced up the steps to the parapet that flanked the courtyard, Rayne followed, unbidden and ignoring the scrapes from her recent tumble. The drift goose crashed to the ground at the fringe of the temple grounds, clods of bracken marking its awkward landing. The princess stood after a moment, caressing the stricken goose's neck and sending anxious glances back at the temple. A second goose circled near the shore beyond, and a few moments later, it coasted through and snatched up Tasha, heading seaward. The first goose ran along the ground, making three abortive attempts to take to the air before collapsing in an exhausted heap.

Catriona let out a barely audible yelp, and the repellent scents of decay and burnt flesh wafted from the fragrance glider. She rubbed the back of her neck, turned, and beckoned Rayne to follow.

"Back to your room, girl. She's calling me to go. And I'm in trouble now, for this. But for once, I'm unafraid. Unafraid of her." Catriona didn't understand why she'd told this whelp of a girl her feelings. The words had slipped out before she could prevent them.

CHAPTER 36 - MOSSMARCH

The Same Day

Summoned to her leader's side, Catriona remained silent as they sailed the strait on the Sea of Sorrows to Outer Pang's shore. It was only as the two hooded women sloshed ashore that Catriona spoke, using her interior voice. "I allowed her to escape. The princess."

Mother Justicia pushed the small boat she'd taken from Dando and Virgil out to sea. They had their bracelets and could return to the lodestone in an instant whenever they desired.

"I know. I saw," she said, with no inflection to hint at malice, disappointment, or forgiveness.

Of course she saw, Catriona thought. Mother Justicia's magical powers were much stronger than her own, and directing her attention to the conversion ceremony seemed only natural.

"Sorry, Mother. I'll make sure that other tiny one converts properly when we return. Let's try the coral amulet again."

They trudged toward Mossmarch, its walls just visible over a patch of trees skirted by the path they followed. After a few minutes, Catriona breathing hard to keep up with Justicia's magically assisted pace, the older woman answered.

"It doesn't matter," she said. "Once we get this star, I know what to do. I wrought it myself from the lodestone's magic, and the prophecy told to me many years ago by the Backwards Man makes sense now. I'll get the thing from the man of daggers and recombine it with the stone. That will complete my mission, draining all the world's magic."

Catriona dared not stroke the fragrance glider that snuggled deep within her hood, afraid to betray its position and even more afraid that she'd betray its extended kin with the threat of Mother Justicia's magical apocalypse.

"Why didn't you do this sooner?" she asked.

With a deep sigh, Justicia used her scarred lips to talk aloud. "I never knew until now. The stone absorbed deep magic back then. I didn't know I had the means this whole time. But the prophecy must be true. In my future, I apparently tell the Backwards Man about this person bristling with daggers, that he possessed an artifact, and how it brought my mission to an end. He carried that message back through time and told me when he was but a boy and you were a newborn. He wasn't *predicting* the future, he'd *already seen* it. I told it to him. Myself. Let's get the unnatural thing and finish our jobs. I'm weary of everything, and nobody in Mossmarch can stop us."

* * *

It's common knowledge that fluttering flags will petrify a hovering goat. This is why every onion farmer's field is ringed with flagpoles and why root cellars normally have a small flag or two dangling over the doorway. Otherwise, the onion-loving goats would swarm like locusts, feasting on their favorite food, farmers unwilling to shoo them away lest they become cursed by the goats' bad luck powers. A few optimistic peasants left onions on their doorsteps, hoping to attract elderly goats that might die of natural causes, leaving behind their valuable teeth. A full head of goat's teeth could mean the difference between a comfortable year and growling bellies. This rarely worked, though; goatherds retrieved most goat bodies. Their extendible poles and nets snagged not only their own perished goats, but wild goat bodies that drifted on the wind.

Sala Doon's plan was less complicated this time. It would be far easier to return the eleven-pointed star to Jada's tower than it was to filch it. There would be no reflecting tiger, no tussles with the guards, and no strenuous tower scaling. All he needed was a stick and an onion.

Master Thorn nodded at the elements of the plan, seeming to approve of their simplicity and odd cleverness. He opened his mouth twice to add suggestions, but Maxima's raised palm silenced him each time. Minimus smiled to himself. Maxima must be well-practiced in quelling Master Thorn's enthusiasm for ill-planned action. He should take notes.

As the sun lowered, Mirko pointed out the hole in Sala's plan, and that he'd need that pillow stuffed with everbounce leaves. He hustled off holding a length of fine rope and a grappling hook, and returned just as the sun sank below the level of the city walls with a finely embroidered and nearly weightless blue cushion the size of a dining table.

"I still can't believe they leave the second-story windows of the senior guardsmen's residences unbarred," he said. "I'll have to have words with Princess Tasha about her security when she returns. Anyway, here's the cushion. Minimus and I can move it to the right spot when the time comes."

The low undulating clouds glowed purple and indigo with the sun's last rays as Sala set off from the food stand where Mirko, Minimus, Master Thorn, and Maxima sprawled around a rickety outdoor table. He loped as inconspicuously as possible across the grassy patch toward Jada's tower, hoping that any onlookers would be used to the cloud of birds and menagerie of small mammals summoned by the power of the eleven-pointed star flitting through the city. A goat he'd befriended hovered at waist height, snuffling tirelessly at the folds of his satchel.

Arriving at the base of the tower, Sala scanned the area for unfriendly eyes, received a surreptitious thumbs up from Minimus, and enacted his plan. He fished out the star-shaped artifact and wound its chain around his left hand. In that same hand, he grabbed his pointed stick and, with a swift move, opened his satchel and skewered a large onion. The goat immediately reoriented itself, eyes bulging at the sight of such a large, well-formed treat. Sala had measured the stick for just this purpose and held the onion at full arm's length above him, grabbing the goat's hind leg as it floated upward, lunging for the onion.

With the goat's levitating abilities enhanced by the star pendant, it pulled Sala in a smooth spiral, subtle shifts of the onion stick guiding it toward the dimly lit window. When he was three-quarters of the way up, the goat, yearning for its tantalizingly close snack, let out a loud bleat that echoed through the maze of buildings below. The staccato beats of the drawn-out bleat began a series of chaotic events that no plan could have accommodated.

Jada's head poked through the high window's casement, her blonde hair catching glints of moonlight. At a food stand below, four figures edged forward on their chairs. Jing Jing pointed a spindly arm from beneath a table, uttering a single monkey chirp. Their gazes lingered on the tall window for only a moment before movement diverted their attention elsewhere. From the shadows of a narrow alley across the grass and gravel clearing, a short figure emerged, calling in a clear and familiar rhyming voice.

"Minimus Mu? Is that truly you? There's no time to waste. We've got work to do."

Princess Tasha broke into a jog across the open ground, unaware that Jada watched from above.

Minimus must have looked shocked and puzzled, so Tasha updated him as she hurried. "Once again, I'm on the loose, borne here by a rogue drift goose! We must stop Temple Pang, Ven, and Jada, protect Outer Pang from its three invaders."

Ahh, a drift goose. Minimus remembered the day he'd met Rayne—and Tasha—as if it was yesterday, as they emerged from a hollowed gourd that had flown from the Red Bean Queendom to the border between Inner and Outer Pang, carried on the broad wings of a drift goose. Whoever spoke through the gabbling dog had made good on their promise. Rayne must be somewhere close behind the princess.

The four companions rose from their chairs, Minimus and Maxima dwarfing Mirko and Master Thorn. They waved her across. The princess reached them and stopped, panting. She anticipated Minimus Mu's next question.

"The goose could not rescue Rayne, Mu. She dropped from its claw as we flew. But I have a plan to free her, too. You'll see her soon, I promise you."

Minimus looked away, unable to meet the princess's gaze. He knew it wasn't her fault, but that didn't prevent him from blaming her for appearing here instead of Rayne. Jing Jing tugged at his sandal, holding up Seymour, the jar of fanglimb eyeballs, and tapping on the glass. If he had bothered to look, Minimus would have seen every eyeball pointing directly across the clearing, but in his glumness, he shooed the monkey away.

When Mirko gestured to Tasha and pointed to Jada's position just above the hovering Sala Doon, he noticed something odd. Jada was no longer watching Tasha's approach. She didn't seem bothered by how close Sala was getting to her window. She was looking further across the clearing, which grew brighter, lit by something other than sputtering torchlight. He had a bad feeling about her attention, and turned his head slowly in the direction of her gaze, half-dreading what he'd see.

Catriona and Mother Justicia stood at the far side of the clearing, a whirling blue-black blaze of magic encircling the younger woman's elbow, making the gray gravel appear purple beneath their feet. Justicia's voice sneered inside everyone's head.

"I can smell it. Taste it. See, sister? It's that blade-encrusted fool there who holds our belonging." A hand thrust from beneath her robe, pointing upward to pick out Sala Doon.

She continued, shaking a finger to indicate a higher position on the tower. "And you, snake? I haven't heard a thing from you since our agreement."

Jada raised her chin, defiant. "Don't paint me with that brush! I said I'd deliver all the people with magic in my former queendom. I should say, my *current* queendom. But there are none. You made a deal for a resource we do not possess, so more fool you. The laws of the land are on my side here, Justicia."

In a blur, Mother Justicia advanced to the middle of the clearing, Catriona trailing her a moment later. The whirling ring of power around her elbow crackled with the desire to be released.

Justicia shook her head slowly. "I do not make deals under any laws. My deals are based on principle, not wording. You have failed me, you black-hearted weasel. But no matter. I'll take what's mine and everything will soon be over."

Jada thought it odd to be called a weasel, as if it was an insult. Weasels were among the most useful animals, their magic enabling them to find lost items with ease. But the tone of the comment sounded both insulting and more than a little intimidating. Although she resisted the urge, Jada could not help but shrink a step back into the tower. She'd seen glimpses of the power these women controlled and would prefer it aimed at the miscreant hovering nearby.

Now at Minimus's side, Princess Tasha bristled at this intrusion into the heart of Outer Pang. She was still officially in charge of the queendom and called out with the burning flame of righteousness in her voice. Her words rang across the clearing with more volume than should have been possible from one with such a slight frame.

"Stop there, ladies! Don't you dare! This queendom fair, as you can see, if not to Jada, belongs to me. Armies muster close at hand and if you don't vacate our land, you'll feel our arrows and sword-strikes land. Last chance, vacate, before it's too late, lest your ugly heads adorn our gates."

Catriona's ring blazed brighter, and Justicia turned to the princess, an exhaled laugh escaping her scarred lips. She didn't even bother to reply. In the dim light, it was impossible to track Justicia as she sprinted across the clearing. Showers of dispersing gravel and flying clumps of earth marked the wake of her footfalls. Mirko and Minimus had barely moved toward the tower. Only the cloud of birds accompanying Sala reacted quickly enough.

The area at the base of the tower burst into incandescent illumination as the birds swooped, each blazing a different color as they darted and wove across Mother Justicia's path. Halting her dizzying run, Justicia's form appeared amid the swirl of streaking, squawking birds defending Sala and his magical amplifier. She dodged with uncanny speed and precision, avoiding all contact with the winged attackers.

Minimus outpaced Mirko despite the everbounce cushion wedged beneath one arm. He was closing the gap when Justicia raised both hands, forearms straining as her fingers knotted. The blaze of lights winked to nothing, and the birds scattered. The goat gave a puzzled bleat, framed in the light of Jada's window, and plummeted.

Sala released the falling goat's leg as Justicia closed the remaining distance to the tower and sprang onto its wall, her momentum allowing her to scale it at speed. It was as if she pulled a plough, her feet scattering lichens with each step and her body angling upward as she powered toward Jada's window.

Sala's outstretched arm caught the window frame and he jerked to a stop, crashing against the tower wall as he dangled.

"Take it," he called to Jada, as he flicked the eleven-pointed star in an arc toward the open window.

Jada's cupped hands closed to receive the flung prize, but in vain; Justicia's run had taken her all the way up the wall, and she snatched the artifact as she passed the window opening. The leader of the Mothers of Midnight fluttered to the ground in a whirlwind of hems and sleeves.

Jada's angry voice flew from the window where Sala swung, scrambling to solidify his grip by adding a second hand. "My tiger! What have you done to my tiger, you witch?"

The everbounce cushion had been Mirko's solution to the loss of goat hovering power. It would prevent a bone-breaking return to earth for the knife-thrower. But he could not have expected a plummeting goat, fully affected by gravity after being drained of its magic. Minimus dove, taking a mouthful of grass for his efforts, and propelled the cushion toward the tower wall. With a rewarding sound like a spring being vibrated, the speeding goat caught a corner of the skidding cushion and bounced to the turf with little more than a lung-busting exhalation as it landed on its side. It sprang to its hooves and gave a trial bleat.

Justicia used her inner voice and spoke to Catriona alone. "I felt it, that thing cowering in your hood. You need to get rid of it before I exterminate it for you."

She dangled the eleven-pointed star before her apprentice and almost smiled. "He sure was bristling with daggers, just like the Backwards Man promised. Now this is mine again. Ours. Now, blow that tower! She deserves nothing less, the two-faced traitor."

The clearing lit up once again as Catriona flicked the ring of magical energy from her forearm like a discarded apple core. Chunks of masonry crashed to the ground from the gaping hole midway up the tower as cracks in the remaining wall appeared and snaked to ground level.

The tower tilted even as Catriona and Mother Justicia twirled their bracelets and returned to Temple Pang.

CHAPTER 37 - TEMPLE PANG

The Same Day

After scissoring over the low wall to the vegetable garden and tiptoeing around a precisely ordered spiral of carrot stems, Apostle Dando raised a fist to knock on the weatherbeaten wooden door to the kitchens of Temple Pang. Virgil grabbed his wrist, delaying the knock for a moment.

"Just tell them the truth, eh? I know you don't have to do the whole truth thing anymore, but just say we've accidentally lost our boat and are wondering if they can help us. That's basically true."

"Yeah, yeah, Virgil, I'll use my judgment. I won't tell them everything, obviously. Like that we're here to spring loose their prisoners or that it was their terrifying leader that commandeered our boat. But I'll mention the part about wanting help. And probably slip in a suggestion that a cup of tea and a nice plate of pastries would really hit the spot."

Virgil released his wrist, and Dando poised to knock again, but turned for a final comment to his friend. "And absolutely no singing, right? I won't even mention you're a talented musician."

"A poet. Just say I'm a poet. Maybe an epic recounting of the Trebuchet of Far Inchaway would cheer them up. Am I right?"

Before knuckles met with wood, a voice echoed through

their heads.

"It's not locked. Come on in, you idiots."

Four sisters of the Mothers of Midnight tended the well-equipped kitchen, which opened into a dining hall with long wooden trestle tables and faded tapestries of an impossible to discern religious nature.

Virgil shrank back a step into the garden, but Dando stepped inside. "Wait, is that Kinterlandti peach stew I smell? One of my order's brothers prepared enormous cauldrons of the stuff while I was in training!"

It was the first time either had seen a smile pass across the face of a Mother of Midnight, but the girl stirring a ladle in a deep iron pot couldn't conceal a twitch at her lips' corners. It was answer enough for Dando.

"Sister Alice is from Kinterlandt," the soundless voice said.

Dando took a few more steps until he could peer inside the pot. "Wow! Looks spectacular. What else are you making? Maybe I can help—I was apprentice to the head chef of the Truthsayers' Guild for six months and picked up a few mouthwatering recipes along the way."

Virgil rolled his eyes so hard they could almost have bounced their way to the other side of the kitchen and clinked down the wide drain hole. But he quickly recovered as he pondered how the kitchen team knew they were outside. He didn't know which one was speaking, so he scanned all four partially hidden faces. His head swiveled in jerks, marking the position of each of the four young women. One flitted in the uncanny Mothers of Midnight style to slide the bar across the door they'd just entered, and she snaked a locking pin into place. Her nonchalant lean on the door frame did nothing to hide the fact that he and Dando weren't leaving.

"Hang on a minute. Did you hear what my friend and I discussed outside?" Virgil asked.

He had a pretty good idea which one of the Mothers of Midnight responded. The girl with the hint of a smile's lips crept higher. "You mean the part where you were planning to free our prisoners? Or your comments about Mother Justicia's charming nature? No! We couldn't possibly have heard that."

"And you're just letting us walk into the temple like this? Shouldn't you be tying us up and heaving us off the tower?" Virgil asked.

The smiling girl laughed out loud. "You two buffoons are hardly a threat. Any one of us could dismantle you while sleepwalking. Plus, if we tied you up, you'd be unable to take over dinner prep, would you? I'm Sister Alice, and this, I believe, is your ladle."

After seeing the Mothers of Midnight in action in Mossmarch, Virgil knew she was right. They couldn't run and they sure couldn't fight.

"Okay, then. Where are the aprons? I don't want to get slop on my kilt while taking orders from mister super chef over there."

CHAPTER 38 - MOSSMARCH

The Same Day

Moonlight flooded into Jada's chambers as a fragment of wall facing the clearing sloughed away. Jada squeezed herself against the wall furthest from the damage, gripping the fur at the neck of her pet tiger, who pressed quivering beside her. Sala Doon steadied his grip on the windowsill, glancing down to assess the damage.

Mirko's voice rang out, the first time Sala had heard panic creep into its usual resonance. "I'm repositioning the everbounce cushion. Just hang on for another few moments."

A jagged crack opened between the tower and the rest of Jada's palace, running from midway up its height to the ground. Master Thorn pointed. "If that crack widens, the whole tower's coming down!"

Without conferring, Minimus found himself shoulder to shoulder with Maxima. They drove their full strength into the tower, legs skidding to find purchase on the packed earth at the base, hoping to avert disaster. At first, they felt the stone blocks grinding toward them, but their combined strength halted the subtle movement, maybe even reversed it a fraction.

Through gritted teeth, Maxima grunted, "Link arms. Spread wider."

Their heads nearly level, Maxima snaked a bulging bicep

under Minimus's straining forearm and clapped her hand onto his shoulder. They inched apart, their combined wingspans now bracing a wider swathe of the fragile tower. With their straining upper chests compressed against the wall, each pressed a cheekbone to the cold stone, and the pair found themselves locked in eye contact for the first time.

Minimus regretted not taking any of the earlier opportunities to talk to his mother. "It's going to fall and crush us, you know," he said, grunting through a clenched jaw. "We can't hold it up forever."

Maxima grunted as she shifted her feet into position for better leverage. "Of course we can. I will not let you die. Not ever. And you're the son of Maxima Li and Master Thorn. You can't give up. You're relentless."

The tower did not share Maxima's enthusiasm. In her chambers above, Jada hauled on the tiger's scruff, attempting to coax it through the door into the main body of the building. The tiger had almost overcome its obvious fear when the tower shifted, leaving a gap between the doorway and the corridor beyond, exposing them to the onlookers below. The crack leading down widened, and one of Sala Doon's hands lost grip. His legs swung precariously.

As Jada urged the tiger to leap the gap, Mirko called, "Sala, I'm shifting the cushion. You can let go now. Trust me, I'll make sure you land safely."

If Mirko could have seen Sala's face in the dim moonlight, he would have noticed screwed-shut eyes and a hasty prayer to the bird gods of Droz, which probably didn't exist but it couldn't hurt to try pleading with them one last time. Sala let go and dropped from the tilting tower.

Princess Tasha's voice rose above the grinding stones and worried murmurings of Master Thorn. "Jada, don't wait for the tiger. Show him how. You can leap that gap if you go now."

Not one to take advice, Jada shrugged off Tasha's suggestion. "He's too scared! I need him to go first or he won't follow."

She slid on the tilting floor before gaining enough traction to ram her shoulder into the tiger's haunches. After a moment of resistance, stripes rippled alive and the tiger leapt the gap, skidding on sparking claws in the hall outside Jada's chambers.

Maybe it was the tiger's mighty heave, or maybe it was the natural progression of the tower's collapse, but either way, the gap widened, and the crack split wider. Jada slid away from the door as her floor tilted further. A shower of crumbling mortar rained on Minimus and Maxima's shoulders as they shouted under redoubled efforts to stabilize the falling tower.

At the tower's base, Mirko's placement of the everbounce leaf cushion was just good enough. Sala landed on one corner at speed, the high fall accelerating him enough that even Master Thorn doubted there was a plan that could save him. The impact knocked his breath from his lungs, but the everbounce leaves proved up to the task. Sala careened up and slightly away from the cushion in a low arc, tucking into a tidy roll and landing in a deep squat beside the mat.

Above, the tower broke fully free, masonry shooting out at all angles. Jada slid across the tilted floor with her feet and one hand on a speeding rug, attempting to balance herself in a useless gesture that would still leave her unprepared for the fatal fall to come. Her limbs left the floor, and she was in free fall, descending in a slow cartwheel.

Sala Doon had practiced his entire life to make spectacular knife throws. He could take advantage of high winds to bend a throw around a building's corner and hit a falling apple with regularity, so he figured he had a chance to shove the everbounce cushion across the grass to Jada's landing spot. But tremors shook his arms after having the wind knocked from him, he'd never thrown a cushion of this size before, and who knew how quickly it would slow down with the inestimable friction of the grass, gravel, and chunks of fallen tower. His mind sped through intuitive calculations as he tracked Jada's trajectory and visualized where she would land—a spot just below the branches of the tree where he and Mirko had escaped to during their theft from the tower.

Of the many variables, Sala figured the only one he could

remove from the equation was the friction slowing the cushion as it skidded along the ground. He grabbed its corner and rotated in a full circle to give it enough momentum. It launched through the air, spinning as it went on a course planned to intercept Jada's fall.

Even as he released it, he knew he'd miscalculated. The cushion flew better than expected. It would land a good few arm-lengths beyond Jada's landing spot. He couldn't even curse at his failure, his lungs filling in rasping gulps.

Sala sank to his knees and watched the cushion fly away. Master Thorn and Tasha, unrhyming, bellowed for Minimus and Maxima to run from the falling tower. Jing Jing bent forward and covered his eyes, unwilling to watch.

In a way, if Sala's throw had been accurate, it still would have meant the end of Jada of Mossmarch. The collapsing tower's broken husk fell at an angle, almost reaching the tree he'd used as a guidepost for Jada's landing, and its heavy pointed bronze finial stabbed deep into the earth in the exact spot where the cushion should have landed.

But as the spinning everbounce cushion sped beneath Jada's upside down figure, she snagged an edge with her outstretched hand. It carried her a little off course, and she wrestled it mostly beneath her as she landed.

Minimus and Maxima scuttled away from the collapsing tower, with the boy hunched forward in a sprint and Maxima looking over her shoulder as she followed, batting away chunks that threatened to hit her boy. They dove to the grass, a massive mess of plaster dust and scraped limbs, gasping. The collapsed tower thudded to the earth just beyond their outstretched feet. Master Thorn leapt atop the heap of exhausted muscles, as did Jing Jing. Both wept with joy.

Beside the finial that stuck from the soil like a titanic arrowhead, Jada both screamed and laughed as her tiger watched with doleful eyes from the rent-open corridor high above. "I think that hag made me break my leg," she said amidst sobbing laughs. Her lower left leg lay at an unnatural angle. Bone and blood glistened in the moonlight.

CHAPTER 39 - TEMPLE PANG

The Same Day

Catriona rematerialized at the lodestone a few moments before Mother Justicia, startling the three sisters who were sweeping and tidying the round chamber. Her bracelet still swung in small circles from her upthrust wrist. She quieted its motion with her other hand.

Mother Justicia had barely appeared before she motioned to the three girls. "Out, out! Get to the kitchen for a tea break."

Catriona ushered them through the metal-bound door and made to close it behind herself, but Mother Justicia spoke again. "Not you, girl. You stay. I want you to see this."

Catriona closed the door, letting the latch slide into its groove with a quiet click. "As you wish, Mother."

"I *do* wish you wouldn't call me that. But never mind. I've been chasing this moment—*we've* been chasing it—for over fifteen years. Needlessly, it seems."

Since arriving at Temple Pang, Catriona had felt increasingly emboldened when it came to Mother Justicia. She felt both closer and more independent from the inscrutable woman, a formless tug of familiarity draining away her fear, insecurity, and anxiety. For the first time, she omitted calling her order's leader *Mother*. It felt freeing. Maybe next, she would call her *Auntie*.

"Tell me again about this prophecy, Justicia," Catriona said.

Mother Justicia stepped closer and took Catriona's braceleted hand in both of her own. They, too, were scarred, but the rippled skin still held a softness and warmth that Catriona had not expected. "You were only just born, crying for your mother in your father's arms, when I was told. A memory of the future, really, not a prediction. That I'd meet a man bristling with daggers and take something to combine with the lodestone to drain magic once and for all. That it would complete my mission. Until that scoundrel knife-thrower stole my star, I had no idea the solution was right under my chin the whole time. But now, I can finish it. We can return to a normal life. One without fear of destructive magic."

Catriona felt a deluge of thoughts rush through her. Would the ceremony Mother Justicia was about to perform flatten animal magic in this part of the world? Like her friend, Rayne, kept repeating, this would doom them, taking away their natural abilities. But was Rayne truly her friend? She'd done nothing to earn the girl's respect or trust. And what about her own magic? Would she miss her ability to rain down destruction, to feel superior to everyone else? Would she even be able to see and hear still?

But one thought overruled them all. Mother Justicia knew her father? Was it the man that Rayne had seen last time they touched?

"You knew them? My father? And my mother?" she asked, freeing her hand from Mother Justicia's gentle grasp.

Catriona felt the older woman's close inspection. "That's not the point, girl. We're almost finished. No more villages razed by magical wildfire. No more tragedy borne from uncontrolled, rage-driven magic. We can finally be at peace. Come, I want you beside me when we settle this."

Justicia took Catriona's hand once again and led her to the lodestone. She withdrew the eleven-pointed star from an inner pocket and placed it in the center of the lodestone's rough upper surface. The two items shared their color but stood apart in their reflectivity; the stone's dull hue was a fitting background to the glints of torchlight that picked out the star's finely cut angles. The lodestone remained hard to look at, its shape seeming to change in a continuum of tiny quivers, urging the gaze to turn away. Catriona forced herself to lock her magical sight on the gruesome object, wondering if it would be the last thing she'd ever see.

Mother Justicia hovered a palm over the star. "I suppose I'll focus on the goal. Summoning all magic back into the stone. That must surely work, but I wish the Backwards Man told me exactly what to do. Exactly what my future self must have described to him." Leaning in, she locked her elbow and pushed the star down onto the lodestone's surface.

At first, nothing happened. Catriona felt Justicia redouble her focus. After a moment, the lodestone paused its normal shuddering, and the woman's palm pushed downward. When she lifted her hand, the eleven-pointed star was gone, its outline etched into the stone. Magic surged, maybe for the last time, Catriona thought.

Catriona experienced a boom too loud and too low to hear. Their clothes rippled, and a tremor crept through the bones of Temple Pang. A brief sensation tugged at her, as if she stood upon the rim of a gigantic drain and was almost pulled down by the last spiral of downflowing water.

Mother Justicia gasped, then wept, thinking she'd finally accomplished her life's mission. But Catriona could still see. And hear. She summoned a spark at her elbow, then quenched it. The smell of her father's hair and the smoke of a campfire infused her senses as she stroked the fragrance glider that crept from the folds of her hood onto her shoulder.

Her hand paused at its furry neck as a vision flared through her. A man riding the waves. His skin flashed with knife tattoos. He approached the Sea of Sorrows even now. The real prophecy would arrive soon, and Catriona knew she would face a choice.

CHAPTER 40 - MOSSMARCH

The Next Day

Princess Tasha had warned them to leave town because fighting might break out. The Vennese forces marshaled around the river port, and mercenaries from the south loitered near the city gates, trading barbs with the diffident and heavily armed Golden Shoreswomen camped to the east. Smaller groups—both in numbers and in height—of archers from the Red Bean Queendom had been swelling the ranks of Queen Angstaad's forces in recent days. None of them knew what lay in store, so they remained in a state of uneasy alertness.

But Minimus Mu, Master Thorn, and Maxima Li cared little about impending battles. They knew only how to stay together, with Master Thorn spinning plans to free Rayne that veered from fanciful to dangerous. Sala Doon and Mirko Leatherfoot thrived on peril and chaos, so they paced and plotted in animated tones.

By mid-morning the day after Jada's tower fell, word spread through Mossmarch about the Council of Queens to be held that afternoon. Princess Tasha, the interim ruler of Outer Pang, had called for it. The event followed laws laid out in the articles of *The Binding of the Queendoms* and formed the basis of time-honored attempts to resolve inter-queendom conflict.

Patchy sunlight caught the colorful attire of several figures.

They stood at the top of the wide marble steps that swept to the graceful colonnade arching across the palace's gleaming façade. The bleached leather strips of Queen Angstaad's battle kilt and her gleaming breastplate shone in stark contrast to the young woman who stood, dwarfed but regal, beside her. Princess Tasha wore a formal robe of deep purple. Next to Angstaad stood Queen Veronica of Ven, her blonde hair fluttering about her jawline in a breeze too light to disturb Angstaad's close crop. On formal occasions like the Council of Queens, tiara-wearing was traditional, but all three stood with their heads uncovered. Angstaad had not returned to Yinti since encountering Minimus, Princess Tasha felt it inappropriate as an interim ruler, and Veronica was never one to bow to any tradition not of her own invention.

Mossmarchers packed the open area before the steps, the crush expanding to fill the streets and alleyways beyond. Jing Jing perched on Minimus's shoulder, mirroring Master Thorn, whose oblique view of proceedings took a leap in quality when Maxima hoisted him over her head, legs dangling down her broad chest.

As is often the case with ceremonial proceedings, the speakers used a thunderbird to project their voices. The tiny bird, with a magically amplified voice, would mimic and repeat each of the women's statements, fluttering between them as needed.

"Outer Pangans," Princess Tasha began, pausing while the crowd settled. "We come to you in a time of confusion. Peril drifts in the air. Let's have no delusion. Your happiness is threatened by fire and sword, yet I bring us here for an accord to continue in peace while we focus on the attacks by the Mothers of Midnight, which we must make cease."

Angstaad raised her chin in agreement with Tasha's sentiment. The thunderbird settled on Queen Veronica's outstretched finger. Some in the crowd may have picked out a hint of mockery in her intonation, but most focused on her words.

"Come, come, my little friend. Surely, it's not peace we

want; it's justice. I'd propose we bring out Queen Jada and let the people of Outer Pang decide the way forward." She opened her arms to the crowd, a ray of sunlight picking her out as if the clouds moved under her command. "Am I right, Mossmarch?"

There was cheering from the throng, but probably less than she'd hoped for or expected. Most in the crowd feared to commit to either Princess Tasha or the former queen. Taking sides between rulers had often proved disastrous in the past. Nevertheless, Queen Veronica smiled faintly at the response.

A footman opened one palace door, twice as tall as any man, and held it for a slow-moving pair. Unlike the others, Jada wore her tiara, its black metal points a harsh contrast to her white-blonde cascade of hair. Her face bore a pinched expression, the pain of her broken leg apparent with each jink in her stride. She could have commanded bearers to carry her out on a litter, but this made more of a spectacle of her entrance, one hand gripping a cane to take the weight off her dangling leg and the other hand clutching the jeweled collar around her enormous tiger's neck.

Queen Angstaad reached reflexively for a sword she was not allowed to carry at this council before stepping between Tasha and the slow advance of Jada.

"You cannot come to council armed with that thing! Someone get this reflecting tiger out of here before I call my swordswomen in to handle it."

Queen Veronica's face morphed from calm civility to a jawline tense with restrained aggression. She stepped forward, coming nose-to-nose with Angstaad. "Your swordswomen—and *you*—will never leave the city alive if that happens. You're outnumbered three to one."

Angstaad pushed Veronica so hard she stumbled backwards and fell to the marble floor. A gasp rippled across the crowd. She awkwardly returned to her feet while the thunderbird fluttered to Jada.

"People of Mossmarch," Jada began. "You know I am your rightful queen. The pathway to peace is to restore me to power.

With our army and Ven's fleet—"

Here, some wag in the crowd shouted out, "Ven's *underwater* fleet!" Mirko and Sala laughed at Minimus's shoulder, but glanced around nervously.

Jada continued, "With our army and Ven's fleet, the other queendoms wouldn't dare challenge us. And also, my jumped-up friend Angstaad, Antonio here is no longer a reflecting tiger. He's just a tiger. You heard what that crone Mother Justicia did to him."

The situation devolved from there, the thunderbird flitting from one shouting woman to another. Princess Tasha called for upholding the law, leaving her in charge of Outer Pang until the prescribed term was up. Angstaad and Veronica continued to escalate their threats, while Jada looked tiredly for support, gesturing to the Mossmarchers filling the square.

Minimus Mu could take the arguing no longer. While others in the throng's crush had little hope of moving anywhere, Minimus swam through the crowd like water. Angry responses to his pushing faded as people noticed his bulk. With the royal argument still in full flight, Minimus loped up the palace steps two at a time, pausing halfway to address the women atop them. Princess Tasha felt a wave of relief flow through her as she saw the friendly face and nudged the thunderbird in his direction.

With a monkey on one shoulder and a tiny bird on the other, Minimus's voice rang out and silenced everyone. "We all want the same thing," he said. It was a simple statement, but a puzzling one, considering the blazing arguments of a moment before.

"Who in the seven ovens of Yarl are *you*?" someone in the crowd bellowed.

Minimus spun to face the crowd. He remembered Queen Angstaad's encouragement, that he could use his hard-won fame from the trials of the All-Seeing Eye and his ability to relate to hard-working commoners to accomplish the unthinkable.

"I am Minimus Mu, champion of the Red Bean Queendom

and cutlery maker's apprentice."

The same voice called out again. "I heard Minimus Mu has a pet anteater. Why do you have a monkey? And doesn't he have green hair?"

Another voice chimed in, "Let's see him lift a giant rock!"

Murmuring began across the assembly, threatening to rise into a din even a thunderbird couldn't speak over. But then a familiar shrill voice cut across them as a woman in a flour-spattered apron berated the crowd. Her two burly sons lifted her above head-level so her grating voice and chastising gaze could pick out any dissenters. It was Mistress Masha, proprietor of the celebrated Mossmarch institution, Masha's Pie Shop.

"Shut it, you lot! That means you, Ponty, you clot-headed maggot. That there is Minimus Mu, as I live and breathe. Such a nice, polite boy. He's eaten more of my pies in the last week than any ten of you gluttons combined, and I heard his story right from the lips of that truthteller Danko, or whatever his name is. And that off-tune crooner youse all seem to rate, Longspeaker. He sang me the whole ballad of the boy. He lifted a boulder even Pierro could barely manage. And where's that fool, Lord Vendark? He's been pricked with the truth-telling quill. He'll vouch for the boy."

Lord Vendark was a frequent and widely mocked crier of the daily news in the market square, forced into this demeaning duty after his dastardly behavior at the trials of the All-Seeing Eye and compelled to tell the truth by land urchin magic.

"He's over here," came a call from the crowd's edge.

A few Mossmarchers shuffled aside, revealing Vendark's sheepish grin from his position at the mouth of a side alley. With signs of obvious reluctance, he pointed at Minimus, his drooping mustache twitching in a tic as he nodded, confirming the boy's identity.

Minimus spoke again, his magnified voice addressing the quieting crowd. He pointed a thumb over his shoulder. "That lot, they're princesses and queens, so maybe they're not looking for the things you and I want to see. Masha is right. I'd be happy to sit at the Crossed Swords with a pie in each hand and a bowl of dates for Jing Jing here. I'd love to travel from town to town with Master Thorn, spreading our cutlery to people like you who can appreciate the simple things in life.

"Does it matter who's queen? Well, a little. You need someone who's fair, who will protect you, but mostly who will leave you alone to live your lives. Fighting between queendoms will bring nothing but trouble to you, to Ven, to Inner Pang, Red Bean, and Golden Shores. And for what? To decide which one of the four women behind me sits in the palace? Come on!

"But you know what *really* matters? Who's going to halt the Mothers of Midnight? Who will stop them from snatching your daughters, your sisters? Who's gonna prevent them from knocking down every building in Mossmarch? Who can protect our animals from their vile magic-draining powers? I miss my friend Rayne, kidnapped by that Mother Justicia. I miss her terribly, and I don't care who's queen of Outer Pang. Don't look up there—look across the Sea of Sorrows and figure out how to wash this black stain from our queendoms."

Minimus paused for breath, realizing he had nothing more to say. The crowd remained silent, in tune with his words and awaiting more: a call to action.

"Do we want more pies and less fighting? Are you with me, good people of Mossmarch?" he called.

"Of course we do!" screamed Mistress Masha, setting off an avalanche of cheering.

Oddly, considering the venom toward everyone she typically displayed, Jada was the one who quelled the cheering with plain speaking and heartfelt words. "I won't stand for any more animals to have their magic, their very essences, torn from them, like my poor Antonio," she thundered. "Ven and Outer Pang will send our armies and our fleets to Temple Pang, and stop this outrage forever."

She glanced at Queen Veronica. As they locked eyes, it was clear they hadn't discussed this beforehand, but Veronica's curt nod was enough to show their continued alliance. Since her uncrowning, it was no longer Jada's place to command her armies or ships. Realizing this, Jada considered her next words. Before she could decide, Princess Tasha motioned for the thunderbird. Her softening expression made Jada believe things would work themselves out. As Jada twiddled her fingers, the thunderbird fluttered to Tasha.

"Outer Pangans, it seems you'll find Jada has not just herself in mind. As you can see, she joins with me against our common enemy across the western sea. This is just the turn that makes her earn another opportunity. Can you see it in your hearts for her, not me, to rule again over your fine country?"

A smattering of applause built to chants of, "Jada! Jada!" By the looks of the enthusiasm across the crowd, Minimus's appeal had worked. The people had no stomach for armed clashes in the streets, but found unity in their desire to banish the Mothers of Midnight.

Queen Angstaad gave a palms-down signal to quiet the crowd so Tasha could speak again. Crossing the top step, the princess reached only to Antonio's hackles, and she ran her hand along the tiger's furry flank before turning to Jada, who matched her serious expression. "The royal transition, I'd like to suspend. Send the armies out, under your control, my friend."

The words sounded friendly, but Minimus watched the two women exchange gazes. Something about the narrowing of four eyes hinted at a deeper jousting match that the friendly speaking tone concealed. Should Outer Pangans once again call Jada queen? Tasha had left Jada's status vague. Intentionally vague, he figured. There would be another round of confrontation between the two when the chance arose.

Queen Angstaad bounded down the steps to Minimus's side and raised his arm in a signal of victory for the commoners. Knowing he was one of them, the throng surged up the steps, eager to meet, touch, and praise the champion of both the trials and the unseen people. A few tried to lift him above the crowd, and while Minimus appreciated the attempt, they underestimated the strength required for such an act. In the end, they settled for allowing him to walk amongst them.

The boy received promises of almost more pies than he could imagine.

CHAPTER 41 - OUTER PANG COAST

The Next Day

Shadows dripped across Mossmarch as the dawn sun clawed its way up the sky just high enough to peek over the walls. The clatter of troops shuffling about reached the ears of six weary-looking figures. They tore off bits of bread and dipped the chunks into an overflowing ceramic pot of bloodberry jam at their slanted table outside the Crossed Swords.

"I thought I'd seen the last of my noisy bird audience after losing the cursed star pendant," Sala Doon said to his companions.

Minimus clapped Sala on the shoulder with a meaty palm. "These aren't *your* birds any longer. They're *our* birds. The quicker you pull your boots onto those manky-looking feet, the sooner we'll be off, and the earlier our ears will get a rest from this twittering."

Sala complained to no one in particular, but tugged at his first boot. "Couldn't we get a few squads of these swordsmen to chase and capture him?"

Master Thorn replied, "Have you seen how slowly they're organizing? No slight against Princess Tasha, Jada, or Queen Angstaad, but getting the Outer Pangans, Vennese, and Golden Shoreswomen aligned takes a lot of negotiation power. You got them off to the races, Minimus, but they're having trouble locating the finish line. If we wait for them, Sala, you'd have enough time to enjoy my most epic puppet show ever before we even set one foot in front of the other. Queen Angstaad loaned us these horses, so let's make use of them. I've already packed two full picnics."

With their shadows still stretching ahead of them like spindly caricatures, five riders and one excitable monkey left the gates of Mossmarch behind, heading west toward the Sea of Sorrows, following the ever-morphing cloud of swooping bird guides.

$$* * *$$

The tide battled the outflowing Moss River at the port town of Mossmouth. A waist-height, long-haired cow led a blind man down the broad and bowing gangway from a river barge that had squeezed past the foundered Vennese ships to reach the sea. She maneuvered him through the press of dock workers and piles of cargo destined for seafaring craft. A few stray cats zig-zagged in their wake, sensing Petunia's welcoming influence, but dropped away as the pair ambled toward the edge of town, heading for the more rugged path along the sea coast.

"Oh, you want to go even further, do you girl?" Nikolai Nineteen Points murmured to his companion and guide. "Across the strait? Really?"

Nikolai never worried about where Petunia led him. Sometimes she was happy to stay in a remote town in the rural outlands of a queendom, and other times she succumbed to wanderlust, traipsing across landscapes Nikolai would never see, or braving dangers others might shy away from. But things always worked out. Where a shortage of charitable people made a blind man's life difficult, a menagerie of friendly animals would pitch in.

Nikolai felt the fresh sea breezes on his cheek and the sharp tang of salt-infused air in his nose when the airborne arrow of Mossmarch birds passed overhead, circled around, and then descended to pay their respects to Petunia. Animal visitors were commonplace, so there was nothing to alert Nikolai to the fact that the birds led a set of wanderers intent on preventing Petunia and him from going any further.

Just beyond Mossmouth, Nikolai heard approaching hoofbeats and nudged Petunia aside so the riders could pass. He held on to a whorl of reddish shag at the little cow's neck. With his ear for voices, he recognized Minimus Mu's call at once.

"Nikolai, good to meet you again!" the boy said, slowing Mr. Apples to a crawl as he trotted up beside the man and his hairy companion. "We heard you were heading this way to Temple Pang."

Nikolai turned his head toward Minimus, but ended up pointing his face at a stubby tree to the boy's left. "Greetings, Minimus. Is that monkey with you still? I loved hearing him talk to himself. Delightful background chatter!"

"Ha! He's just in front of me here, chewing a date. It's sometimes the only way to get a break from his pestering. So, how are you planning on crossing the strait?"

Five horses halted, a couple bending to chew the long grass of the verge. Everyone else was happy to let Minimus do the talking, unworried about stopping an old, blind man. The hard part had been locating him, but their guide birds made the job easy enough.

"Planning? I don't go in for planning any more, lad. I leave that up to my four-hoofed friend here. She's far better at it than I could ever manage. But it's funny that you knew Temple Pang as my destination. I didn't know that myself until just now, as Petunia nudged me off that barge. Can you feel her intentions, too? I thought it was only me."

Minimus looked to Master Thorn for guidance, but an impatient flick with the back of his hand urged him to continue the conversation. "Uh, no. Well, I don't think so, anyway. Someone else told us. To be fair, it was a dog, if you can believe it. Said we should convince you not to go."

Petunia shouldered Nikolai back onto the track, and they started walking. It was as if she had heard what Minimus said and bristled at taking orders. Minimus nudged Mr. Apples to keep pace.

"Huh," Nikolai said. "I never thought that dogs were wise. But anyway, I'll be hard to convince if Petunia heads over the water. I can't very well wander off without her. And she follows her own counsel. Always gets to wherever she points her horns, one way or another. My memory is so bad! Did I already tell you about that time we crossed a river in Long Jin by walking across the backs of dolphins?"

Minimus considered his own encounter with helpful dolphins, so he felt Nikolai could well be telling the truth, regardless of how outlandish this sounded. And he'd seen Petunia's effects—or were they Nikolai's effects?—on wild and dangerous animals.

"No, I don't think you told me that tale," Minimus said. "But listen, Nikolai, there's strange magic about. The message given through the dog sounded trustworthy, and the fate of animal magic is tied to your visit to the temple, apparently. The head witch wants to use Petunia somehow to produce a weapon against magic. I know it all sounds weird, but how about you take a detour with us back to Mossmarch? Delay your visit until after Princess Tasha, Queen Angstaad, and Jada remove the witches that have taken control. I'm sure we could organize a few days of feasting if you'd stay with us for a short while. You could continue to Temple Pang after that."

Although Nikolai claimed to have no control over his pet cow, he didn't seem to mind trying. He stroked her unruly back hair and spoke to her in low soothing tones. "How about it, Petunia? A warm bed and a spot of feasting could soothe a few aches in our bones and bellies, no?"

Man and tiny cow stood silent for a few moments, both gazing toward where the swells of the Sea of Sorrows rose to lick the upper lip of the low cliff that separated the roadway from a sheer drop off. Droplets of spume swirled in the eddies of the cool sea breeze.

"She'd like a warm and cozy reception, too, it seems," Nikolai said, turning. Tension drained from Minimus's shoulders that he hadn't known was there. He realized confrontation with a friendly face was harder than raging against an angry opponent.

"But now that we're at the seaside, she wants a quick taste of the waters first before we go. That seems like it will satisfy her. Go on, Petunia."

Nikolai twirled the curly hair at her neck around a hand, and the cow edged to where the waves, mostly spent, sent ripples across the slanting hard granite ledge between the road and the sea.

"Mind the edge, Nikolai," Minimus called. "Can I hold your hand, just in case?"

Nikolai shook his head. "No, no lad, Petunia is my eyes. She'd never let me put a foot wrong."

Petunia stopped just short of the cliff's edge, approaching during the lull while another wave built up the energy to rise to her level. Nikolai clung to her, seeming to enjoy the spray and breeze that rippled his tunic.

Master Thorn edged his horse forward so it stood haunch-to-haunch with Mr. Apples. "Why would the wee cow want to drink *salt* water?"

The question prompted an acidic churning in the pit of Minimus's stomach. It felt wrong. There was no way for Nikolai to escape them, dependent on a cow that could never outrun their horses and armed with nothing but his nineteen dagger tattoos. But now was not the time to take chances, so Minimus dismounted and approached the old man.

"Here, sir, let me hold your ha—"

Minimus took a step back from the brink, stunned by the appearance of an eyeball almost as big as him, belonging to a colossus rising on the incoming wave that lapped at the clifftop.

Nikolai and Petunia had already stepped over the cliff's edge as Mirko shouted, "Slab whale! Get back, Minimus!"

Named for their broad table-like backs, slab whales had been known to capsize even the largest ships as they rose from the depths for air. This one had somehow felt the need to surface right at the sea cliff where Petunia waited. For a moment, the cow and man rose above the level of the land, unsteady but still standing on the slab whale's back, with the massive creature only half submerged in the cresting wave.

Everyone but Maxima sat frozen on their horses as Minimus stepped toward the now-sinking whale, the roughened hide sliding along his fingertips. The flat area where Nikolai and Petunia balanced would soon be level with the clifftop once again. The boy bent at the knees, timing his jump with the retreating wave and whale.

As he sprang, a powerful hand grabbed his collar and toppled him backwards. With a whoosh of departing breath, Minimus landed on his back, the damp from the wave-slicked rock cold against his bare triceps. For the first time, Minimus Mu found himself scolded by his mother. He both hated and loved it.

"Boy, what were you thinking? Only an idiot would jump onto a slab whale's back if he can't swim. Didn't that shipwreck teach you *anything*?"

There was a pause. The dominant sounds interfering with the silence came in the form of Minimus recovering from having the wind knocked from his lungs, Maxima's angry, nasal breathing, and the retreating wave that allowed the slab whale to sink below the cliff edge. Maxima broke the silence, pointing to a steeply sloping fork of the coastal path.

"And anyway, that cove down there is where my home village would be, in the proper version of this forsaken world. No houses down there, but I see a ship anchored. We can still make chase."

CHAPTER 42 - ASTELLA

Twelve Years Previous

It took five years from the razing of Vinetally for Aunt Justicia to become Mother Justicia. The wet nurse that kept her infant great-niece alive would become her first recruit at the abandoned Temple of the Wraith. Once Mother Justicia had pushed magical powers from the lodestone into the young woman, she would travel to create an outpost at Temple Pang.

Justicia's nephew had been called Silvain of Vinetally, but he needed a new name to wash away the memories of the destruction he'd caused. He arrived in Pearl Wash, daughterless, as Skain. He still possessed the ability to summon destructive fire, like his daughter, and would use that power to become a leader—a warrior.

When Justicia's plan to steal away every human's destructive magic needed new recruits to her army, Skain took up the cause of fighting against her. He was a proficient fighter but somehow never successful in defeating the new threats the Mothers of Midnight posed to the girls and magic-bearers of Pearl Wash. He led many forays against the Temple of the Wraith, but all ended in the same result: his companions drained of their magical powers and the Mothers only gaining in strength and reputation. The Mothers raided an ever-expanding territory, reaching the coasts of Wraithwatch, the lake towns of Lakkenfell, and throughout Inner and Outer

Pang in the west.

Catriona was twelve when Skain made a clandestine visit to the Temple of the Wraith, warning his aunt of the plans for an upcoming raid. He could hardly tear his eyes away from his transforming daughter, but he dared not reveal himself.

"I call myself Skain Two-Hearts, now," he said to Justicia. "I tell others some old toot about my stab wound, but really it's because I lost one heart in Vinetally and I leave the other here, with you and Cat."

Tears rolled down Justicia's unscarred cheek, and she turned away, her determination to rid the world of its magic redoubled.

CHAPTER 43 - SEA OF SORROWS

The Present

Master Thorn may have been correct when he criticized the time to rally and organize an army and navy, but he sorely underestimated the drive of the four royals. Even as he rode with his oddly matched companions through Mossmouth, a small strike force assembled at Mossmarch's river port.

A company of Queen Angstaad's finest swordswomen, shoulders pulled back proudly in their shining breastplates, boarded two warships under the direction of Vennese sailors. Squads of the Red Bean Queendom's archers were already aboard, taking positions at the rails for the brief crossing to Temple Pang. Animal handlers from Jada's guard moved crated animals aboard each of the ships.

Two queens, a newly empowered former queen, and a princess watched proceedings. When almost everything looked in position, Queen Angstaad turned to her companions, her blue facial tattoos standing out against her pale skin. "It will not be easy, besting the Mothers of Midnight," she said. "But thanks to your ideas, Jada, I think we have every chance of returning, successful, by morning. Look for me here."

Jada looked less exhausted than the previous day. She'd arranged her ghost-white hair in its normal artfully wild splay, and the dark metal of her tiara topped eyes and lips framed with immaculate black liner. She looked like herself once again, if one ignored the loosely draped bandages beneath which medical leeches worked on repairing her fractured leg.

"You aren't sailing off with half my menagerie without taking me," she said to Angstaad. "They're animals under my care. It was my idea to use them, and I'll sink into the Sea of Sorrows with them if need be. You take the ship on the right. I'll command the other."

Queen Angstaad's eyebrow may have arched a fraction, but not enough to cause any kind of international incident. She turned on a heel and jogged to her allotted warship. Before following her example, Jada leant close to Princess Tasha.

"If I don't come back, you should rule again. I want Outer Pang in steady hands for what might follow, and between you and my cousin, I'm sure you can defend our people. In a few ways, you'd be a better queen than I."

As Jada limped off, leaning on Antonio, Tasha thought she should express her thanks. The unexpected concession and confession from Jada, who she'd once thought of as a heartless, selfish tyrant, somehow made her stumble for words. She wanted to remind Jada that just because the transition had changed, there was still a power vacuum. She wanted to say *You missed the details of what I said, and made yourself queen inside your head. For what you tried against Red Bean, I'll never truly make you queen.* Instead, words fell from her lips that left a sour remnant on her tongue. "I will, Jada, I will. But you'll come back to me once you're finished at Temple Pang."

Dammit, Tasha thought to herself. *I could have said 'finished across the sea'.*

* * *

The winds blew with little gusto from behind the island of Temple Pang. The two warships tacked multiple times on approach toward the temple docks. Queen Angstaad's swordswomen had heard about the warning shot fired from the temple when the Mothers of Midnight had captured Princess Tasha, and they chafed to reach shore, where they could go to work. The Red Beaners, too, longed for land, but realized they'd be called into action before the swordswomen. Only the two queens and the Vennese sailors radiated calm.

The sun was low in the sky when Temple Pang's outline sharpened and the two warships approached its harbor. Aboard her ship, Jada comforted both herself and Antonio with calming strokes as her animal handlers uncrated their cargo. She signaled to the sister ship for them to do the same.

The flamingos of her menagerie ruffled their pink wings as they emerged from the crates, blinking at the setting sun and shifting from leg to leg. Jada knew there was a chance they would fly off, possibly bristling against a sea voyage and yearning for a return to the safe ponds and curated shrimp farms behind her toppled residence tower. But flamingos avoided flying across open water like the Sea of Sorrows, so she hoped even the narrow strait between Outer Pang and Temple Pang would keep them aboard ship.

A few of them looked landward, as if they might attempt to flee to the island, but after a bout of nervous hopping, the flamingos found comforting spots on deck and settled into their one-legged balancing act. The birds on the other ship arrayed themselves around Queen Angstaad, as if she was an honorary flamingo herself. "Figures," Jada muttered to herself. "She always fancied herself queen of the birds."

* * *

As the ships neared bowshot range, dark-hooded figures flowed with superhuman speed across the dock. Two women stood in silhouette with the setting sun behind them, high on the upper wall that flanked the temple's conical tower.

Catriona turned to Mother Justicia. "How many ships do you count? Sixteen? Twenty? I'm not sure I can recharge quickly enough to sink them all."

Her mistress's voice still quivered with disappointment and rage at the unsuccessful merging of the star and the lodestone. "I feel powerful magic at sea, but from elsewhere. Not the ships, although there's strange magic there, too. Anyway, do your best. There are enough sisters on the dock now to repel anyone you can't finish."

Mother Justicia turned away from Catriona. "I'll find this other source of magic. You deal with this side."

Alone again, Catriona's mind worked at the conundrum. Was her mission to steal magic away? Or was it to protect everyone from its wild destructive power? She stood with the sun warming her back, preparing to use her powers against her fellow humans.

The fragrance glider at her shoulder sent the sickly smell of decaying flesh along with a hint of drying cut grass and her father's hair. Trying to ignore it, Catriona built up a spark and then a ring of fire around her right elbow and howled into the sky.

CHAPTER 44 - TEMPLE PANG

The Same Day

"I'm not so sure about this plan," Mirko Leatherfoot mumbled. "I'm used to *sinking* ships, not stealing them." He had to repeat himself louder so his companions on the rowboat could hear him over Maxima's powerful oar strokes and the shouting from the shore.

For Master Thorn, this comment ran like water off an eel's back. Most of his plans had more naysayers than supporters. "It's really quite simple, Mirko," he said. "Although the ship's owners there on shore don't like it much, we have their only rowboat. We'll row to the ship, sail across, rescue Rayne, and make our way back by reversing the steps. I'm sure once the ship's owners hear about our mission, they'll forgive us."

Mirko shook his head. "It's not whether the plan will upset anyone that I'm worried about. Have you ever known me to look for forgiveness? Heck, I stole from your market stall last year and walked away laughing. It's the sailing part. Minimus can't swim, and neither can Sala. I can only stay afloat for a couple of minutes, tops. We don't have Apostle Dando—who somehow knows how to do everything—to pilot the ship, and the last time you were on the seas, it didn't turn out so well. Even if we survive this crossing, we must figure out a way past a temple full of crabby and outrageously quick zealots, find Rayne's room, spring her loose, and escape with our heads still attached. Plus our side mission to stop a blind man and tiny shaggy cow on a slab whale's back. Your plan is light on details about all that."

Minimus knew that the *details* of a Master Thorn plan came not during the planning phase, but in the *doing* phase. He looked at the crew arrayed in the crowded rowboat. With Jing Jing's cunning, Sala's exquisite accuracy, Mirko's crafty acrobatics, Master Thorn's ever-present good luck, and Maxima's strength, he was surrounded by a team more capable at the *doing* parts than any he could assemble in his imagination. Sure, they lacked wisdom, but once they freed Rayne, she could add that to the mix.

Maxima avoided more questions about details by giving a simple answer. "I don't just row boats. I sail them, fix them, and build them. In my world, I lived just behind those shouting men. If you gave me wood, pitch, line, and sailcloth, I could sail you within the week, dry as firewood, across this strait with my eyes closed and one hand tied behind my back."

Mirko laughed, revealing his chalky teeth. "Maxima, what idiot would try to tie a hand behind your back? He'd end up with two black eyes and an arm torn off, I'd wager."

The words didn't sound like a typical compliment, but Maxima smiled. She rowed in silence until they slid beside the rope ladder dribbling down the side of a single-masted cutter. Jing Jing shot up the ladder in an instant, as did Mirko, eager to put distance between himself and the Sea of Sorrows' dark waters. Sala held the ladder for Master Thorn and Minimus, scrambling up himself as Maxima shipped oars and tied off the rowboat so it would follow behind the bigger ship.

She inhaled deeply to appreciate the strong fishy smell of the craft, and declared it in need of proper repairs but fully serviceable. Maxima barked orders and soon the sails were up. She even allowed Mirko to take the long-handled tiller and steer for Temple Pang.

As they crossed the strait, aiming for the beaches on the opposite side of the island from Temple Pang's docks, Master Thorn peered through the spyglass he'd found settled into a holster beside the tiller.

"I see the whale!" he called out. "Well, I see a man and a little cow that look like they're floating on a platform. They're headed toward the port. Looks difficult to balance atop the slab whale's back, so they're moving slower than our ship. We'll probably reach shore around the time the whale can sidle up to the deep-water dock. And there are a bunch of Vennese warships about to crowd the harbor, too!"

* * *

Minimus knew Mirko was fully into the spirit of the Master Thorn plan when he suggested the details for entering Temple Pang. They'd moored behind the island and Maxima had rowed them to shore with powerful, efficient strokes. Salty water dripped from their boots and sandals, but drenched them no higher than calf level. Jing Jing, on a wading Minimus's shoulders, and Master Thorn, in Maxima's cradling arms, remained completely dry. A locked wrought-iron gate opened onto a low-walled garden. After an acrobatic tumble over the wall, Mirko checked the door to the temple under which wafted delicious cooking smells. Also barred.

Needing to find a stealthy entry point, Mirko traced his proposed route with his finger. He would pop to the top of a root shed at the back of the vegetable patch, jump to an overhanging tree branch and scamper along it. From there, it was a considerable leap to a courtyard wall which he considered only a minor risk, a shimmy up a drainpipe to the slate roof of the kitchens and in through an open window to the chambers on the top story. Rayne had described as much of the internal layout of the temple as she could remember, but her location was still vague in everyone's minds.

"And what should *we* do? Don't forget we need to free Rayne but also intercept Nikolai Nineteen Points," Minimus said.

"Just wait here, and get the rowboat ready," Mirko said. "How many rooms can there be? I'll grab them both."

"But Rayne's room is normally locked. Don't you need Maxima and me to rip the door off or something?"

Mirko fished in his pocket and brandished a ring with a jangling set of thin metal shims. Lock picks.

"That's a terrible plan," Master Thorn said. "In a good plan, *everybody* does something."

With a flourish, he produced a dried date, and handed it to Jing Jing. As the monkey's hands rotated the fruit in a nibbling frenzy faster than the eye could track, Master Thorn scratched him under the chin. Despite much evidence to the contrary, Minimus still failed to believe that Jing Jing could understand human language, but Master Thorn addressed him as if he were a child.

"Now, Jing Jing, see that kitchen door there? When you get inside with Mirko, find your way to the kitchen—I know that won't be hard for you and your rumbling tummy. Unbar the door and then unlock the gate to the little yard behind it so the rest of us can get in. Then we'll follow the plan. Some of us can rescue Rayne while the others whisk Nikolai and Petunia away from Mother Justicia."

Maxima pointed at the low wall surrounding the space behind the kitchen door. "Look how low the wall is. No need for Jing Jing to unlock the gate—we can scramble over it."

Master Thorn furrowed his brows and screwed up his lips. "Since when did any proper plan involve me scrambling over a wall? Let the monkey do his work, eh, my love?"

Before he scuttled after Mirko, Jing Jing tugged at Minimus's cloak and mimed holding something cylindrical between his long-fingered hands. It took Minimus a moment to remember he'd stashed one of the monkey's favorite items in an inside pocket. He rummaged, finding the jar of fanglimb eyeballs cushioned between two gentlepea sandwiches. It clinked against the bangle the monkey had stolen from the Mother of Midnight.

Minimus scratched between twitching monkey ears and handed over the jar. "Oh yeah! Seymour! It's like your good luck charm, isn't it?"

Jing Jing's natural agility made Mirko's remarkable balance and lithe leap from the bowing branch to the narrow wall's top look like child's play, but soon two pairs of legs slithered into the upper-story window. Minimus thrilled in anticipation of Rayne's half-forgotten face peeking around a corner as they reunited. But his daydream was interrupted when a crackling ring of flame lit the sky on the temple's opposite side. A familiar ring of destruction flew at an unseen target in the Sea of Sorrows.

CHAPTER 45 - TEMPLE PANG

The Same Day

Sister Alice, perched on the countertop watching Dando direct Virgil Longspeaker through the process of rolling out dough, was as surprised as the two men to see a monkey swing in through the narrow opening of the inner courtyard's window and skate to a stop on the slate floor of the kitchen. Her other three sisters had been called to the docks in response to a disturbance, so jitters tugged at her. Something unusual was afoot. The monkey wore an embroidered jacket and clutched a jar beneath one lanky arm. The eyeballs in the jar—she'd seen them before. And they'd seen her before. Each one glared at her again.

"Hey! You?" she shouted. "How'd you get here from Wraithwatch? Where's that wristband you took from Sister Mariana?"

Sister Alice slid from countertop to floor before Virgil even said, "Jing Jing? What the—?" Her first step was quick but the next few were a blur. In a moment, she closed the gap to the monkey.

But Jing Jing matched her speed with his own speed *and* agility. His feet and hands burnt with blue energy as his magic kicked in. He sprang to a tabletop in a flash, and before Dando had fully turned from the soup caldron, the monkey was clattering his way along a rail of suspended pots and pans, hugging the ceiling. With one hand still cradling the jar of eyeballs, he made his escape from the speeding Sister Alice in a series of jerky swings, his free hand and tail propelling him. Dando noticed that, during one moment of free flight, Jing Jing snatched a dried apricot from a hanging hamper and pocketed it in his jacket before sliding along the rail with the same magic-infused hand.

As Sister Alice lengthened her stride and sprang from floor to counter in a lunge calculated to intercept the scurrying Jing Jing, Dando and Virgil heard her voice inside their heads call for help. She'd intended the message for her sisters, but it was directionless and panicked, unlike most of the disciples' silent communication.

Her intercept path was true, but Jing Jing rarely traveled in a straight line. He veered from the pot rail, his tail clinging for a moment to a cupboard handle. From that position, his bowing legs pushed him into a slide beneath a baker's table, jar held high in both hands, the eyeballs still tracking Sister Alice. He screamed monkey chatter the entire length of the slide before popping atop the locking bar of the exterior door where Dando and Virgil had entered the kitchen. He banged on the door with a foot three times before springing away as Sister Alice slammed into the wood where he'd loitered a moment before. The locking pin arched away from Jing Jing's furry hand and the bar clunked to the floor at Alice's feet.

Virgil turned from the cutting board, apron wafting flour in puffs around him. Was there someone out there? Had Jing Jing just intentionally unlocked the door?

The monkey dangled from a rafter, one finger lodged in a knot hole of the beam high above the kitchen floor. Unable to reach him, Sister Alice sped on unperturbed. She hoisted an earthenware mixing bowl and flung it at Jing Jing. As the bowl sped upward, another door—one of the pair to the temple's interior—flew open, and two Mothers of Midnight shot into the room. The sounds of more footsteps echoed in the hallway's distance beyond. The eyeballs in Jing Jing's jar tracked each new entrant.

* * *

Outdoors, four figures huddled with their backs pushed against the exterior side of the garden wall. Minimus turned to the others and said, "Did you hear that? Sounded like three knocks and a thud against the kitchen door. Jing Jing's signal?"

Master Thorn's ridiculous tufted right eyebrow rose until it met the wisps of gray hair above his crinkled forehead. "Slight change of plan," he said. "I *will* scramble over the low wall instead of waiting for the monkey to unlock the gate."

Maxima and Sala Doon were already in action, rushing over the drystone barrier. The knife-thrower avoided a myriad of vegetable shoots as he sprinted to the kitchen door and flung it open to a sight that both surprised and discouraged him.

Seeing Apostle Dando and Virgil Longspeaker preparing dinner would have brought a laugh to his lips had it not been for the three raging Mothers of Midnight in the dining hall. From experience, he wouldn't hit any of them with even the most accurate of throws, but he knew one thing for sure: he'd rather face three of them than five.

As a bowl was thrown toward Jing Jing by Sister Alice, Sala released two daggers. They flew not at the women who had burst into the hall, but at the door that had rebounded on its hinges after their urgent entry. The first blade flew in a flattened arc and struck pommel-first, hurrying its closing motion. A second dagger arrived a fraction of a second later, delayed by its higher arc. Its point lodged into the crack between door and frame, just above the latch that had snicked into place when the first blade urged the door shut.

Above his head, Jing Jing didn't bother dodging the thrown bowl. Sister Alice's accuracy wasn't even in the same queendom as Sala's, and the bowl smashed to shards more than an arm's length from the dangling monkey.

"Take his magic!" one of the new arrivals shouted to Sister Alice, pointing at the monkey. "We close the gate and open the eyes!"

"I've tried!" Sister Alice shouted, an exasperated edge infusing her reply. "I think it's those accursed eyeballs stopping me. Same as in Wraithwatch."

Sala assessed his opponents as Maxima burst through the exterior doorway, her arms brushing both sides of the frame. Behind the two recent arrivals, the door latch jiggled weakly against the wedged knife. Fast, but not so strong, Sala thought, if they couldn't knock the door from its hinges or dislodge his blade.

Minimus barreled through behind his mother, and Sala was almost surprised to hear his own voice calling to them. "Go through that other door. Find Rayne or Nikolai. I'll hold off these three."

The first part made sense, but he didn't believe the last part of his own command himself. How could he take on one Mother of Midnight, let alone three? Dando and Virgil would be useless, and he'd urged away two of the strongest people in all the queendoms.

By the time Master Thorn's face appeared in the doorway, Maxima and Minimus had moved further into the dining hall, but the two hooded newcomers had flitted to the kitchen area and snatched up long-bladed kitchen knives. Jing Jing plopped to a dining table on Sala's right, offering solidarity if not much in the way of combat skills. Sala saw the fanglimb eyeballs jerk to his left, preceding—by an instant—Sister Alice's advance around the end of the kitchen island. All three of the sisters moved their heads in swift turns, continually tracking the seven interlopers as potential threats.

Sala thought of the ways he'd avoided bullies and scraped his way through childhood as a street urchin. He'd always been a good knife-thrower, but that alone didn't bring food or prevent a gang of stronger, older boys from throwing him to the street and grinding his face in the mud. No, he had to exploit their weaknesses, not rely only on his strengths. Playing on their fear by pointing behind them to an imagined palace guard, or a jab with a pointy ring to just the right spot behind the knee might be the difference between broken ribs and a narrow escape.

He knew the Mothers of Midnight were not physically strong. It would be easy to overpower one, if not for their speed and agility. He could use Jing Jing's jar of eyeballs to give him a moment's advance notice of their movements. But neither of these things made for a full plan of attack. If Mirko was here, he'd keep out of sight and sneak up behind them, using misdirection as Sala had seen during many previous swindles.

That was the missing piece! Sala had a plan.

In the meantime, Maxima had already taken Sala's command to heart. Gripping the corner of one of the dozen trestle tables laid out in even lines, Maxima shoved it toward the knife-jammed doorway and the end of the kitchen island where the two knife-wielding sisters prepared for their attack. This bought Sala more time. When Maxima Li shoved a table, it *flew*.

There was nothing quite like two hundred pounds of table cartwheeling toward a person to make them reconsider their life choices, and the two sisters had to rely on not just their speed but a bit of luck to keep them from ending up as a jumble of broken bones against the ovens. One dove past an incredulous Dando's feet and the other shot into a cupboard full of pots and slammed the door shut behind her. The thick wood of its structure absorbed the flying table's impact.

Minimus joined in the havoc, heaving tables of his own in every direction as he and Maxima cleared a diagonal path through the dining area to the exit. They'd just lumbered through the doorway and slammed it behind them when Sala caught the eyeballs moving in that direction, too. The sister who'd slid across the kitchen floor was up and leaping between the tops of each stable-looking table remnant to give chase. She'd be through the door and onto Minimus and Maxima in mere moments, her knife carving them up.

An aged rope held a thick wooden plank upright that could hinge down to bar the door. Sala threw two more daggers that found their marks with precision. One severed the rope and the plank swung down into the receptacle at the doors far side. The second knife sank into the door frame just above the bar, preventing anyone from lifting it. The sister struggled with the embedded dagger momentarily before turning to point her knife at Sala.

Sister Alice grabbed a rolling pin and the cupboard door burst open. All three Mothers of Midnight turned to face Sala, their chief threat. He was the centerpiece of a triangle of terrifying menace, head twisting to keep tabs on all three opponents.

Master Thorn edged his way to Virgil's side, and although the sisters kept tabs on him with their swiveling heads, their focus was solely on Sala and Jing Jing as the only genuine threats.

"I'll need more ammo!" Sala called. "Almost out of daggers."

He threw three more, one at each of the sisters, buying time as they contorted themselves to avoid being struck. At first, he thought Jing Jing had abandoned him, but as the monkey vaulted away, he placed the jar on the kitchen island directly in front of Sala. This meant he needn't look away from his attackers to see the pickled fanglimb eyeballs' movements, and they might warn him about the path of the one behind him. Master Thorn pulled open a drawer, and with blinding agility, the monkey plucked item after item and threw them in a rainbow over his back directly toward Sala.

Many of the items Jing Jing threw clattered to the floor at Sala's feet, but he moved as quickly as his reflexes would allow, plucking spinning cutlery from the air and throwing it at the sisters to keep them occupied. Spoons, table knives, even a saltshaker. He knew his actual plan of attack could work when he saw their eyes tracing the projectiles that might strike them, but ignoring the ones he intentionally threw wide. They were like predators with forward-facing eyes tracking their next meal, not like prey whose eyes roved for threats from all sides. But still, the unfathomable speed of the three Mothers of

Midnight would outmatch his plan. He'd need luck and a little help.

That luck came in the form of a well-placed Master Thorn elbow. The elbow nudged Virgil just below the ribs. "Ballad!" he hissed to the minstrel.

The prompt ended Virgil's shocked paralysis at the outbreak of mayhem around him. He surprised even himself by extemporizing a new verse in the Ballad of Minimus Mu, belting it out in his powerful baritone.

This was enough to halt the knife-wielding sister behind Sala for a moment before she leapt toward him from atop a half-overturned dining table. A sour grimace crossed her lips before she sprang, the song somehow grating against her magical hearing. It was enough. Sala gripped the handle of a heavy cleaver that Jing Jing had added to the cascade of items emptying from the cutlery drawer. With a glance at the eyeballs to confirm where the leap would take his attacker and a lightning assessment of the ceiling height, he spun and let fly.

As the sister flew toward him, her knife slashed in a murderous overhead attack. Above, the spinning cleaver severed the rope holding a suspended iron ring of torches that lit the dining hall. The falling ring met the downward path of the stabbing knife, knocking it from the sister's hand before the blow could fall. And still, the heavy iron ring descended, crashing neatly around the flying girl's form and pinning her arms to her sides before crashing to the floor.

Didn't bother tracking the cleaver throw, did you, girl? Sala thought. One bully down, two to go.

As he plucked a heavy marble pestle from the shower of implements Jing Jing cast over his shoulder, he saw Master Thorn snatch an item from the monkey's hand. "Don't give him *that*, it's a DeCantell serving spoon. Unbelievably valuable!"

Virgil continued to sing, and the second knife-wielding sister staggered upright in front of the open cupboard where the music had stunned her for a moment. The pestle throw was well wide of her head, and she didn't even bother to dodge as she hefted the knife and coiled to spring at Sala. But behind her, Sala's true target collapsed. The pestle knocked the conical arrangement of burning hardwood that heated the upper oven asunder. Two blazing logs toppled onto the hem of the girl's cloak, igniting its dry fibers. She abandoned her jump, rolling on the floor to douse the flames. Dando dropped his ladle and tackled her. Still singing, Virgil joined him.

Sister Alice was already in full motion. Sala knew that a rolling pin strike with her speed behind it would crack his skull and he'd barely turned to meet the onslaught, let alone grabbed a flying cheese grater to defend himself. His human speed had proved no match for the magic of all three Mothers of Midnight. Oh well, two out of three was not a terrible attempt. Maybe Master Thorn or Jing Jing would find a way to subdue her after his sacrifice.

He was correct. Human speed couldn't match magical speed. He only had time to notice that the cutlery drawer lay empty and a lemon zester flew past his nose, the last of the cascade of mismatched items. But monkey speed? At the Crossed Swords and other fine debating institutions across Outer Pang, heated discussions would fail to resolve whether monkeys could outpace a Mother of Midnight in full flight. "Maybe Jing Jing had a wee head start," Dando might say. "How would you know? You were floundering on the floor with one of the sisters," Virgil might counter.

Regardless of who was actually faster, the outcome of the fight in the kitchen hall of Temple Pang was clear. After three footfalls of enchanted monkey paws up Sister Alice's back, Jing Jing knocked the rolling pin from her hand just before it struck Sala Doon's undefended cheekbone. Yes, he suffered a vicious slap that left a palm-shaped welt on his cheek, but he was only stunned, not killed.

When Sala recovered his senses, Sister Alice lay unconscious atop him. Master Thorn leant over her, breathing hard and examining the bent handle of a silver serving spoon-turned-truncheon. He accused his own hand of treason. "Sheesh. The DeCantell! What a disaster."

Apostle Dando pinned the second sister to the floor with a foot on the fallen torch-holder ring, extinguishing the flames one by one, and Virgil sat atop the still slightly smoking cloak of the third sister, her cheek pressed into the tiles under his weight. He stopped singing and a worried expression crossed his face. "Uh, Master Thorn, can you check on my croissants? I think they're done."

CHAPTER 46 - SEA OF SORROWS

The Same Day

Herd animals used their numbers as a defense against predators, hoping that the sheer size of their community would discourage attacks. This worked up to a point, but the hungriest and most fearless of attackers would still stalk the flanks of the largest herds.

Flamingos used magic to work against the boldest enemies. Sure, there was strength in numbers, but what if their flocks looked even larger, swelled by magical images? In this way flamingos rendered most attacks fruitless. Each flamingo could project several copies of itself while changing their local surroundings to lend an air of continuity with the environment. Not only did this make their flocks appear much larger, but it also meant an interloper springing at the graceful curve of a pink neck would more than likely grasp at an insubstantial copy, leaving the actual birds a chance to escape.

When Catriona let loose a spiraling ring of pure magical destruction, it didn't burn a hole through the wooden deck of a Vennese ship. It crashed through the image of one, roiling the sea behind it instead. That ship's image shimmered a moment before reforming, false flamingos standing proudly at its rails.

Catriona stared at her open palm and forearm for a

moment, wondering if her powers had faded. Her destructive magic had never before failed to puncture and punish its target. The ship's shimmer suggested a form of illusion she'd never seen.

Just beyond the ships, in the open sea, the spurt of water from the blowhole of a flat-backed whale shot skyward. She could feel its magic just as she felt magic emanating from each ship. Maybe the creature had somehow created the illusory fleet? She shook out her shoulder and summoned another spark to test the mirage once more.

Jada laughed as she leaned against Antonio's striped haunches. It was a scathing chuckle, practiced to demean anyone she targeted. Although Catriona could not hear them, Jada aimed a few words directly at her and Justicia.

"Every peon in Mossmarch has seen my birds and knows their powers, and these magic-wielding *girls* are so easily fooled? We're coming for you, Justicia!"

After the first blast sizzled harmlessly to the salty waters, Queen Angstaad scanned the waves to either side of her. Maybe it was the flamingos reacting to the threat, but it looked like there were thirty warships advancing on Temple Pang's harbor now, not twenty.

A second ring of magical fire frothed the sea to Queen Angstaad's immediate left, passing through another of the mirage flamingo ships. She flinched as a wave of steam crested across their bow, but it passed in a moment. It took a short while for the girl at the tower to rebuild her power, so it was a game of chance whether she could strike Angstaad or Jada's ships before they reached the docks. The odds were in their favor, but the armored queen still muttered a prayer to the lords of the deep to spare her a downward journey before she'd accomplished her mission.

The warships surged to within bowshot range of the cloaked Mothers of Midnight on the docks, and Queen Angstaad looked across four mirage ships to where Jada raised her arm, preparing to let it fall as a signal to the Red Bean archers to loose arrows.

Would the flamingos mimic bowshots? Angstaad was uncertain, but her combat instincts tingled and her voice rang across to Jada's ships, warning her not to give the order. If arrows rained down from only two of the ships, their opponents would identify and blast them from the water before they reached the docks. Jada looked puzzled, but she motioned for the archers to stand down. She had an instinct for cunning, but accepted the Golden Shores queen was the expert in matters of combat.

High above, Catriona watched her third attack fizzle into the sea. Determining that the ever-expanding fleet proved nothing more than a distraction, she turned on her heel and re-entered the tower, keen to discover whether Mother Justicia had located the approaching source of powerful magic. The faint magic from the ships must be just the magical projection of this other unknown entity, possibly the whale, and designed to distract them. As she turned, the fragrance glider nestled across the back of her neck. Catriona smelled mint and the creature's fur as it purred.

* * *

Queen Angstaad and her clutch of swordswomen plucked repulser lizards from the crate that Jada's animal handlers had opened on deck. The scaly, multi-hued creatures were long enough to cover most of the forearm bracers where the women settled them, their long-toed claws scratching the skin beneath as they took hold. Occasional heavy-lidded blinks interrupted the gazes between lizards and swordswomen as the Golden Shores forces clustered near the gangway, preparing for the warship to grind against the dock. There were not enough lizards to go around, so Angstaad arrayed her warriors, placing those with the lizards at the leading edge the phalanx. She took a position in the center of the second row.

Her ship and Jada's juddered two adjacent piers at almost the same time. The Red Bean archers leaned against the upright spindles of the ship's railings, arrows nocked.

"Let fly!" Jada called to them as Vennese sailors flung the gangways to the dock.

Arrows sped toward the throng of cloaked figures swarming the dock below. A few sliced through fluttering cloaks, but the Mothers of Midnight bent and shimmied with their uncanny speed, ducking and dodging around the projectiles with effortless grace.

Still, Angstaad thought, they're distracted enough to cover our approach. Her band of swordswomen shouted a battle cry in unison as they thundered down the angled gangway, blades reflecting the red hues of sunset.

CHAPTER 47 - TEMPLE PANG

The Same Day

Turning away from the ships below, Catriona froze. Rayne spoke to her for the first time using her interior voice. But it came to Catriona not through her magically enhanced ears, but from somewhere else. It almost felt as if Rayne stood *behind* her. Without thinking, she shifted the fragrance glider aside and rubbed the back of her neck.

"Really?" Rayne's voice chided. "Your mission is to remove magic because of the horrible things people do with it, and now you'd blow ships full of people out of the water? I'm seeing through your eyes, sister. Do you notice any of these people using magic? And your grand plan is to take away animal magic too, leaving them defenseless? People will probably start eating them!"

Catriona stood stock still, taking a moment to figure out how to respond through this new channel. In a way, she felt relief. The communication signaled that Rayne was finally transforming. Or maybe not. This was something different, not the normal interior voice used by her sisterhood. It was like she had a third ear that heard only Rayne. No background noise. Neither sounds from her immediate surroundings nor with the echoing she had become accustomed to as she ranged her magical hearing to nearby places. The tiny girl was an anomaly.

"We close the gate and open the eyes, Sister Rayne. We take magic from man, not beast," she said.

Rayne sounded angry. "Open your own eyes, girl. We were both there in the courtyard when you showed me how to drain magic from animals. And I saw what you did to Jada's tiger, through your senses, as if I was there. Mother Justicia is the one opening the gate, and she's going to let loose all manner of trouble."

Catriona understood her order's powers, but their vision never extended more than a handful of paces. "You saw that? In Mossmarch? How?"

Rayne had neither the patience nor the time to explain her own augmented senses. "It doesn't matter, Cat. Open your own eyes before it's too late. What does your little furry friend tell you?"

For a moment, Sister Catriona felt the urge to run to Rayne's room and flee the temple with her, leaving the rest of her order to conduct their mission. The smells of spring meadows and ripe avocado wafted from beneath her cowl. But then, Mother Justicia's interior voice boomed through her skull and blotted out all feeling and reason.

"Come to me, Sister. I'm inside the front gate with a very interesting man. Covered in daggers, just as promised."

CHAPTER 48 - TEMPLE PANG

The Same Day

Queen Angstaad was accustomed to her warriors, with their years of physical training and mastery of swordplay, making quick work of less disciplined opponents. But the Mothers of Midnight were no ordinary opponents, and her senses were on high alert as the phalanx pushed forward.

"Protect the width of the dock!" she shouted, hoping the swordswomen on the neighboring jetty could hear her, too. "We can't let them get behind us!"

She knew from Jada's descriptions that the black-cloaked figures were not physically strong. They possessed neither the toughened hands and feet nor the hardened musculature of her sisters. But their speed trivialized other shortcomings. Already, a dozen robes flapped as their owners zig-zagged along the dock, daggers and short knives at the ready. The Mothers of Midnight flashed in, one by one, blades blurry with motion in the sunset's glow.

The intuitive reactions of her swordsmen parried half of the strikes, but Angstaad knew the other blows would have carved up exposed arms or legs, maybe necks or gaps between armor plates. Only the repulser lizards saved them from decimation after the first wave of attacks.

Perhaps the lizards blinked more frequently, but their magic protecting them from physical harm made them fearless. The rapid dagger strikes ended with points turned to one side or another, and a few blades clattered to the floor, wrenched from twisted wrists.

The Red Bean archers switched strategy, their yeoman selecting a specific target to receive concentrated fire. After a few salvos, one of the Mothers of Midnight staggered back, unable to dodge every arrow in the prickly thicket descending on her. She limped off behind her compatriots, a steel-tipped arrow jutting from her thigh.

Angstaad's phalanx had a minor success, too, charging along the dock quickly enough to knock two retreating sisters against each other. One fell into the inky waters and floundered toward shore.

But overall, impasse prevailed. With their darting attacks brushed aside by the repulser lizards and wary of the concentrated arrow fire, the Mothers of Midnight withdrew to the junctions of the quayside and the thrust of the piers. Angstaad knew her enemies could communicate without words, and had expected the uncanny silence that surrounded her opponents. No hint of their tactics would blow on the breeze to her ears. She urged her swordswomen forward. Maybe they could push the scar-faced sisters beyond the gates, where her forces could encircle the temple and somehow seize Mother Justicia. Against an enemy this capable, outnumbered but not nearly overmatched, a feeble strategy like this was the best she could hope for.

Ten paces ahead, one of the cloaked women pushed to the front, fingers curling in practiced patterns and wrists circling in tight spirals. The pair flanking her sped forward, snatching a pair of lizards from the swordswomen's forearms.

That shouldn't have been possible. Nobody, regardless of their speed, should be able to work around a repulser lizard's magic. The woman who stepped forward every few moments, head bowed in concentration—she must be thwarting the lizards' magic.

As the sister stepped forward again, flanked again by two dagger-armed figures, Queen Angstaad called to the archers, pointing her sword. "Focus on the middle one. Break her focus!"

Clusters of arrows arched from the ship's rail, the yeoman sprinting on his short legs to the opposite side to relay the strategy to the other ship. The blitz made each target dodge and weave. The forays to snatch lizards continued, but only erratically and at much longer intervals.

Soon, Angstaad slid into the front row as the number of lizard-armed swordswomen thinned. She nicked the forearm of the marauding Mother of Midnight who stole her own lizard away. But losing her magical protector left her crouching deeper and moving the point of her sword in jerky movements that would have caused her childhood dueling trainer to throw up her hands in exasperation.

At her left, a sword rang against the dock's planks, dropped as a blurry figure left a gash down a pale-skinned forearm. Angstaad pushed her injured swordswomen back, a replacement from the second row slotting seamlessly into her place.

Jada's voice, wavering, rose above the twang of bowstrings and occasional clash of sword against dagger. "They've shut off the lizards' magic. What do we do now?"

Angstaad regretted the pride and folly that had blinded her into thinking her best warriors, combined with the Red Bean archers, could overwhelm the Mothers of Midnight. If they retreated to the ship, they'd be picked off one by one. If they stayed on the dock, likewise. There was only one direction to go with any chance of success.

"Whirl those swords as fast as you can spin them, my sisters!" she called, her voice echoing from the temple walls and quayside storage huts.

"Push them back! Push them to the temple! Charge on three! Two! One!"

At least they could go down like proper Golden Shores heroes, racing at full pelt into the thick of their enemies. Arrows thrummed from over their shoulders as the two phalanxes of swordswomen whirled and leapt toward their slender and lightly armed but magic-powered opponents.

CHAPTER 49 - TEMPLE PANG

The Same Day

Catriona strode through the inner courtyard archway, her enhanced vision noting the portcullis and the main temple gates overlooking the harbor on the opposite wall. The intricate ironwork of the lowering portcullis blocked the path, but through the open gates beyond, she noticed the bulk of her sisterhood engaging with Queen Angstaad's swordswomen on the docks below.

Lips pressed together in a tense line at the sight, she communicated with Mother Justicia using her inner voice. "Shall I go down, Mother, and finish the invaders?"

Mother Justicia beckoned Catriona, to where she stood in close conversation with a wizened man who stroked the shaggy rust-colored fur of a miniature horned cow. "Don't bother," she said. "The newcomers are no match for your sisters. We've an important guest here. Guests, actually."

So used was Catriona to her order's eyelessness that she barely registered the way Nikolai Nineteen Points pointed his face not at Mother Justicia, but somewhere over her shoulder. Much more interesting were the tattoos on his forearms, creeping up his neck, and jutting from beneath his ragged pant hems. Daggers! Had Mother Justicia's news from the future been correct but too vague, making them waste time on that roguish knife-thrower? Was this the man who had flashed across her mind in the momentary vision? Catriona felt simmering but powerful magic in the courtyard. Something new worked its enchantment here. She probed the man before her, his blankness nudging her into a realization. The signals wove through and around the cow.

Mother Justicia's voice was unusually pleasant; it was rare to welcome guests to one of their temples. "This gentleman is Master Nineteen Points, Catriona. He told me an amazing tale, that his companion here, Petunia, summoned a slab whale to transport them across the strait. That she dragged him across the continent just so she could see our magical stone. Remarkable, isn't it?"

As the man turned his face in Catriona's general direction, she could see the cataract-beset eyes and understood why he clung to Petunia's hair. "Nice to meet you, Catriona. We have indeed traveled far, but the journey is often as pleasant as the arrival. We had many enjoyable and harmless adventures along the way," he said.

But inside her head, at the same time, Mother Justicia elaborated. "It wasn't the eleven-pointed star that I needed to end magic. The artifact isn't even an object. Can you feel the power in this animal? If I unite her with the lodestone, as she desires, I'll have the power I finally need. *We* will have the power. It's nearly over, my girl!"

Mother Justicia bent to Petunia's level. "May I pet her?" she asked Nikolai.

Nikolai did not answer immediately, but Mother Justicia hadn't expected nor cared about the answer. With a burst of speed, she knocked Nikolai's hand loose from where it held the cow's long strands of hair. Even as Nikolai recoiled from the slap, Mother Justicia encircled an arm beneath Petunia's front legs, scooped her to waist height in a show of wiry strength, and sped away from the startled man toward the inner tower.

She called to Catriona to follow as her speed-blurred form darted across the courtyard and scaled the outside of the ivy-coated tower, using momentum, the textured face of the tower, and one-handed tugs at the anchored vines to run up the vertical surface to the flat roof above.

"Come, girl! Leave the man behind. We don't want him sabotaging our ultimate efforts," she called to Catriona as she trotted from view, heading through the window of her chamber atop the tower.

Catriona was unsure why Mother Justicia did not use her bracelet if she wanted to get to the lodestone—perhaps she worried that Petunia's magic might affect the trip somehow. But there was no reason to expend her own energy scuttling up the wall like some sort of witch. With a twirl of her upraised wrist, she activated her bracelet, sparing a half-apology to Nikolai Nineteen Points as she evaporated.

"I'm sure your little cow will be okay. I'll bring her back down, after …"

But after *what?* she wondered. It seemed likely the after would be far different from the *before*.

* * *

On the level between the courtyard and the tower, Mirko Leatherfoot found himself uninterrupted and unobserved. The Mothers of Midnight had left the locked doors of the former monks' quarters unguarded, drawn to confront the ships in the harbor.

The first three barred windows he crept up to revealed empty rooms, but the fourth held six women. Two crowded at the tall window opposite the door, reporting on the ruckus at the harbor to their companions. By the looks of their cropped white-blonde hair, Mirko figured they were Golden Shoresians.

He called to them from the hallway, the second "Hey!" loud enough to make the nearest one turn. Her lean arms looked to Mirko like she could scale a rope to the top of a ship's mast as easily as others could walk the deck. "Where's Rayne held?" he asked, still keeping his voice low.

The woman tapped her cellmates and beckoned them to the

door. All six squeezed between the bunks and crowded around the square framing Mirko's face. "Two doors down," one said. "They were holding Princess Tasha there, too, but we saw her escape on a drift goose."

"Thanks," Mirko said, and turned from the window, fishing his lock picks from a pocket.

The woman called after him, louder than Mirko liked. "Wait! Release us, too. We're from Queen Angstaad's guard. We can help you get Rayne to the docks."

Mirko whirled and held a finger to his lips to silence her. He whispered through the door. "I'll let you out, but we've brought a boat ashore behind the kitchens. Help me get her there, not to the docks."

The lock proved rudimental and fell victim to Mirko's dexterity with the picks after a few moments of rattling. There were four more guardswomen in the next room, and all ten grabbed items from their rooms as makeshift weapons. A quill, a book, a broken table leg—all looked serviceable to Mirko's eyes, judging by the way the women held them, ready to strike.

Rayne must have heard the whispering and rattling in the hall, because her eyes latched onto Mirko's face as soon as it appeared in the doorway of her makeshift prison. "Let's get you out of here," he whispered. "I've got a certain Minimus Mu and Master Thorn downstairs, who are eager to see you."

With six of Queen Angstaad's guard ahead and four behind, Rayne hurried the party along the hallway, deeper into the temple. "We'll take the spiral tower stairs down to the dining hall. I've been that way before, and we can sneak out through the kitchen," Rayne urged.

Where their hall met the stairs winding both upward and down, everything devolved into chaos. Following the patter of quick footsteps on the roof above them, an outraged voice shrieked into the tower above. Mother Justicia. "What are *you* doing here?" she shouted aloud.

And from the hallway joining the tower stairs from the opposite wing came the slapping gallop of sandaled feet. Three scarred faces, hoods down, approached at speed. Whether the

Mothers of Midnight had spotted the party of Golden Shores guardswomen or they responded to Mother Justicia's call, Mirko would never know, but events moved quickly, and he lost hold of Rayne's hand as the rearguard split them to join in the expected fray.

Mirko slid to the third step down the spiral staircase before regaining his balance as the warriors pushed past to confront the knife-wielding Mothers of Midnight. Their surge shunted Rayne upward, toward the commotion in the tower. A phalanx of Angstaad's guardswomen blocked the junction, heaving themselves into every open space with their ragtag weapons. This blocked any possible way for Mirko to barge through and retrieve Rayne. He bounded down the steps, three at a time.

* * *

As Catriona materialized a few paces from the lodestone, an unexpected scene confronted her. Expecting to see only Mother Justicia and the magical cow, two other familiar faces somehow jarred her into momentary stasis. Were those the two powerhouses that had tried to hold up Jada's tower after she'd blasted it? Friends of the dagger thrower they'd mistakenly sought? It was hard to forget physiques like that, and the oversized boy flexed and flushed as he staggered under the lodestone's weight, halfway to the far window.

It was odd, Catriona thought, the way he struggled with the stone. Yes, it was heavy, but she and Mother Justicia had moved it from across the tower without much effort, and neither of them was particularly strong. Yet here was this boy, lifting the lodestone, every muscle bulging in a deadlift. But the stone didn't dangle straight down. It tugged his arms at an angle, as if it repelled itself away from the open window he'd made his goal. And the stone looked angry. Normally, its shape was hard to look at, but in the boy's grasp, it liquified at the edges, almost enveloping one of his hands as it strained against his efforts.

"Put that *down*! NOW!" Mother Justicia raged, dropping

Petunia to the rug.

Minimus Mu replied through gritted teeth, taking another two shuffling steps toward the window. "I can't. Can't let you do this. Not with Petunia. I'll sink this cursed stone into the sea before you can ruin the world. We know what you're trying to do, but couldn't stop Nikolai from bringing Petunia here."

Catriona knew the boy would never get past her and Mother Justicia. She couldn't just blast him without risking the stone or the tower's structure, but it would be child's play to speed past him and prevent him from reaching the window. Even a few nudges, with the strain his flexing muscles sang out, would make him drop the writhing thing. But the woman with him didn't seem to understand the powers she faced. She planted her feet wide, positioning her broad-shouldered frame between Mother Justicia and the boy. Her nostrils flared and her fists clenched and unclenched to prepare for whatever she thought might happen next.

As Rayne's face peeked past the doorway at the top of the stairs, Catriona flushed with both disappointment and relief that the girl had not yet transformed. Rayne burst into the room and was able to blurt out, "Minimus! I knew you'd rescue me!" She took four of her shortened strides before three blood-splattered Mothers of Midnight coursed through the doorway behind her, reddened knives whirling.

CHAPTER 50 - TEMPLE PANG

The Same Day

Fleeing the percussive combat at the junction above him, Mirko Leatherfoot sped to the base of the spiral stairs to see if he could find help. Sala Doon, the only one who'd proven capable of fending off the Mothers of Midnight, must be down here somewhere. But he found no knife-thrower, no impossibly powerful mother and son, not even a crafty thieving monkey. Only a blind man, feeling his way along a silent hall, framed in the fading light of the courtyard behind him.

"Nikolai! Where's your wee cow?"

The man's cataract-filled eyes turned to the sound of Mirko's voice. "I recognize you. Inner Pangan? Friend of Minimus, yes? The lady of the temple took my Petunia. Left me to fend for myself, which is never a good thing, as you can see. But I think it's okay. Seemed like Petunia wanted to go with her, inspect this stone thingy." Nikolai Nineteen Points looked somehow frail without Petunia, his shoulders slumped and his arm extending a tattooed hand, seeking a guide. "Help an old man up the stairs, would you, son? She's up there somewhere."

Mirko looked behind him, twice, hoping a figure might emerge from the direction of the dining hall and kitchen. But without an interruption to use as an excuse, the master of deception, whose calloused hands sometimes hid a tender heart, reached to take Nikolai's extended hand.

"There's a pitched battle halfway up," Mirko said, "Angstaad's guardswomen are trying to fend off a trio of the Mothers of Midnight. That's a fight we want to stay out of."

Nikolai shook his bald head. "Don't worry about that. Petunia never lets me get hurt amid any fighting. She'll protect us."

Mirko doubted the old man's assurances. Even if Petunia might somehow protect Nikolai from the women, he doubted the protection would extend far enough or to someone like him. But the grunts and shouts of the struggle above had gone oddly silent, save for the patter of quick feet and an arhythmic thudding on the stairs above. Mirko tugged Nikolai forward and, against his best instincts, led the man upward.

The approaching thunks revealed themselves as a decapitated blonde head bouncing down the spiral stairs. Mirko watched it for only a moment before tearing his eyes from the catastrophe at the landing.

He half-closed one eye and tried to look up and beyond the landing. "By the great hairy beard of the Sea Prince, I wish I was blind like you just now, Nikolai. I'll never unsee this. No danger here, but come up on this side. It's a bit … umm … slippery over there. And take a big step here, there's some … stuff. Lift your hand off the wall for a couple of paces, too. It'll stay cleaner that way."

* * *

At Mother Justicia's knee, Petunia's powerful magic felt like a blazing inquiry. Under her touch, she could tell the animal was as powerful as any source of magic she'd previously encountered. It radiated even more energy than the lodestone, which pulsed with the combined magic of every townsperson in Vinetally and reverberated with echoes of the blast that had killed them. The cow was interested in the lodestone, drawn to its power, and deep within herself, Mother Justicia knew she could play the role of catalyst. Combining these two sources of intense magic could draw every other iota of magic from the world. Never again would there be a tragedy like Vinetally.

Did the cow's intuition somehow grasp this link? Did she see the same opportunity to bring two magical powerhouses together, to let the Mothers of Midnight accomplish their mission? Justicia figured she did.

Mother Justicia felt life's commitment was finally over. The future relayed to her by the Backwards Man, the blazing magic of the cow that had crossed continents to seek her out, her great-niece by her side. It all fit. Nobody could stop her and Catriona from uniting the power of this animal with the lodestone. The boy and woman before her were insects to shoo away. The tiny girl had not yet turned and had only a glimmer of the Mothers' magic. Mother Justicia sent her voice to every sister. "Disengage, my family. We're done here. Return to the temple and I will free us all."

To the three blood-splattered disciples in the room, Mother Justicia indicated the lodestone with an outstretched finger. "Make him drop it. Now!"

Maxima Li waved back a finger of her own, a warning. She shrugged, bracing for an attack. But strength is no match for blinding speed. In an instant, two of the eyeless sisters appeared behind her. Minimus hauled the lodestone a step closer to the window but then abruptly dropped it, narrowly avoiding a crushed toe in the process. The shaft of a narrow-bladed knife emerged from his forearm after a lightning quick attack.

Finally at his side, Rayne clung to Minimus's leg as he stared at the metal piercing his arm with an uncomprehending look on his face. The sister that had inflicted the wound had moved on to help her accomplice slide the lodestone back toward Mother Justicia and Catriona.

"Look what you've done to him!" cried Rayne, a pair of tears falling to Minimus's thigh. A glare cast in Catriona's direction stung, but Catriona remained immobile at her mistress's side. Rayne saw two cowering fragrance glider eyes glowing softly beneath Catriona's hood.

Mirko hauled Nikolai into the circular chamber just in time to witness the impasse and, despite his inexperience, felt a rush of magical power and knew its source at once: Maxima.

Catriona felt the flare of magic burst alive, too. It came from nothing, like a fanglimb tentacle bursting from calm dark waters and lit every fiber of the woman who slid the dagger from her son's arm and clenched the wound shut in a powerful, single-handed grip.

Rage. Pure rage flashed from the eyes of Maxima Li toward Mother Justicia, as if they were windows on a furnace of unimaginable heat. Every muscle in her massive frame sprang taut, shoulders massing to meet the cabled tendons in her neck, free hand curling into an expansive fist. Tendrils of flame roamed her outline. "Nobody!" Maxima spat through gritted teeth, relinquishing Minimus's injured arm to his own staunching grip. She took a step toward Catriona and Mother Justicia. Everyone in the room froze, the power palpable.

"Nobody …" Another step. "Touches …" Step. "My *boy*!"

Catriona looked to Mother Justicia, who stood unbudging, now only a step from Maxima. Her hand curled into the form Catriona knew she preferred when sapping magic from another. As sometimes happened during the taking of particularly powerful magic, a trace of rippling orange current passed between Mother Justicia's coiled fingers and Maxima's puffed out chest.

Master Thorn may have been able to stifle Maxima's explosive rage, but he was two levels below, in the kitchens. Perhaps his calming hand might have stemmed the surge of power within her. Maybe a whispered reminder of his love could have persuaded her to retreat with her son. But he wasn't there. Instead, Maxima screamed at Mother Justicia, "You're coming with *me*, now!"

Catriona saw the flow of the channeled frisson between Maxima Li and Mother Justicia reverse direction. The flames licking Maxima crackled and rose as she drew magic from the leader of the Mothers of Midnight in an unexpected turnabout. Petunia backed behind Justicia and cowered at the lip of the window.

Dread rose from deep within Catriona's heart. One of her sisters moved to protect Mother Justicia, breaking the stream. Catriona felt every hair on her body spring erect as the sensation of mounting destruction coursed through her. It was the same feeling as when she sparked her own chaotic fire but magnified. It was different, too. For the first time, she expected a blast not of her own making.

"Uh oh," she said in a flat tone. She shouldered Mother Justicia backwards through the window. The two of them fell to the flat roof, joined by Petunia, who leapt with them.

Rage whirled in the chamber, surging toward the window as the crimson sun behind Petunia and the Mothers of Midnight was interrupted by a shadowy terror.

CHAPTER 51 - TEMPLE PANG

The Same Day

Angstaad noticed that the Mothers of Midnight had little training in knife play. Although her complement of swordswomen grew smaller with every few running paces, they'd been stopped by injuries, not by killing strikes. A dagger through a forearm here, a slashed calf there. If she possessed even half the speed of these cloaked women, she'd rampage through the lot of them by herself.

Still, their swords whirled, presenting a dangerous barrier to keep forays against their phalanx at a minimum. Their numbers cut in half by the trail of injured women left in their wake, the Golden Shores formations met and merged as they forced the Mothers of Midnight back toward the gates to Temple Pang.

Jada shouted encouragement alongside an occasional tiger roar from her pet, and arrows continued to clatter among the retreating throng of their opponents. With another twenty paces to go, only a quarter of the swordswomen remained unscathed. A few dragged themselves along in the phalanx's wake, but a quick glance showed Angstaad the stragglers had more courage than ability to fight.

With only Angstaad and seven of her countrywomen remaining at the vanguard, shoulders aching, the Mothers of Midnight froze, as if listening. A moment later, Angstaad heard a sound, too. A familiar sound: the rush of hot air into a flying contraption.

Ezra Longshanks burst into view, the shadow from the purple fabric of his balloon rushing across the landscape. He flew low to the ground, borne on a stiff breeze from the west. His head flitted, searching for a landing spot. Crazy curls of unkempt hair bounced beneath his conch shell and goggles as he fiddled with an anchor dangling from the balloon's basket.

A few Mothers of Midnight angled their heads in the direction of the balloon, but as a group, they flitted into the courtyard of Temple Pang, the gates and portcullis slamming as they left the quayside roadway.

Angstaad urged her remaining swordswomen to the closed gates while she sprinted to a small clearing above the harbor, outside the walls. Ezra's anchor carved a furrow in the earth, and he dangled precariously on the basket's edge, thrown to one side by the sudden halt. She worried he'd topple from the flying device, although it hovered so low to the ground he might yet survive the drop.

With a wriggle, his feet returned to the basket's floor. Only his conch shell helmet fell from the balloon, cracking on the rocky patch below. "Huh. That landing was a tad urgent, eh, your elegancy?" he said.

Angstaad craned her neck as the sun's last rays faded. "Agreed, master scientist. You chose a good time to map the island. Seems to have scared off our adversary. Now, we just have to figure out how to invade the temple and capture Mother Justicia. Any suggestions?"

It felt like a victory, of sorts, but Ezra, Queen Angstaad, and Jada had no way of knowing that the retreat was Mother Justicia calling off her disciples, not due to anything they'd accomplished.

CHAPTER 52 - INNER PANG

Fourteen Years Earlier

The first time Master Thorn witnessed a blast that tore open a rift between his world and the obverse, he couldn't understand what had happened.

It had started with a simple gripe. "There's no place to fish in this godsforsaken dust bowl," Maxima complained.

Master Thorn knew this, but there were too few customers to limit his cutlery cart to a coastal route. The hardscrabble hamlets deep in Inner Pang were glad of any passing merchant, and if the three of them wanted to eat, they needed to keep moving to the ignored places neglected by other traders. He nodded and muttered an agreement.

But maybe not enough of an agreement. Maxima continued, her tone and ire rising, "And there's no shade on this bumpy wheeled cart. I'm hungry, too."

Master Thorn lay a hand on Maxima's forearm that looked even smaller than normal compared to her tensed muscles. "We'll reach Seven Rocks soon, my love, and then it's a quick journey to Mossmarch. We'll see the Sea of Sorrows before you know it."

Maxima shrugged away the touch meant to offer comfort. "Don't you start thinking a few *my loves* will solve this," she grumbled.

Maxima's simmering would likely have diminished across the next few bends in the bumpy cart track had the shrill cry of a hungry baby not interrupted the solitude. Minimus bounced in a makeshift woven cradle among the elaborate cutlery drawers of the cart, a ravenous four-month-old. His tufts of dark hair foreshadowed an unkempt mop to come, and at least seven chins rolled into a chubby neck and shockingly tubby torso. His legs wobbled as they kicked, his cries escalating.

"And you!" Maxima shouted, not turning to face her son. "You've taken your father's crankiness and tripled it with your unhalting tantrums!"

Maxima leapt from the cart, thudding to the baked earth of the Inner Pang plains, dust erupting around both sandalled feet. She swept an arm to encompass a frightened-looking Master Thorn and crying Minimus Mu.

"I'm *done* with you two."

Tears of frustration splashed to the floor but failed to penetrate the sunbaked earth. Maxima bent, hands to knees, breathing deeply as she wept.

Master Thorn saw the telltale flames of uncontrolled fury flicker across Maxima's shoulder blades, leaping without burning her tunic. He'd seen them before, when the rabble in a market had tried to take advantage of Master Thorn or when she'd left a trio of staff-wielding brigands cast to the side of the road in a jumble of broken limbs. But never sizzling like this.

The fires blazed behind her eyes as she shot upright, extended her back, raised fists to the dull sky, and raged.

"I want to go *home!*"

The fire that burst from her that time washed across Master Thorn like a wall of warm water. Minimus stopped crying and never complained again. Although the fire harmed neither man nor boy, it sent one wheel of the cart rolling away at high speed and melted most of the cutlery within the cart's panoply of storage nooks.

Maxima disappeared. Master Thorn thought he saw the air rip for a moment, the heat haze giving way to a foggy morning.

Maxima folded at the waist as something yanked her through the rift before it closed with a sound like a wet trout hitting a fishmonger's fileting table.

* * *

In the tower of Temple Pang, Maxima Li knew that her strength could not protect her son from the sinister speed of the Mothers of Midnight. She had already failed the boy when he was a defenseless infant and had figured she could repay those missing years by staying at his side now that they had been reunited.

Already stabbed, and at the mercy of five of the sisterhood's cloaked and heartless order, there was no reason to think they'd let Minimus live if he tried again to come between Mother Justicia, Petunia, and the cursed stone. And if nothing else, Maxima knew Minimus would persevere with that task until he had nothing left to give. There was a reason he'd succeeded at the trials of the All-Seeing Eye.

If Maxima couldn't protect him here and now, she knew how to drag the threats into the other world, her own world. She'd done it before, and she could do it again.

Jaw clenched and unable to utter a proper farewell to her son, she released the fires of rage, channeling them through the window at the scrambling trio on the rooftop beyond.

With a sound like ripping fabric, a vertical tear shredded the air between Maxima and Minimus. Magical fire swirled behind her, circling the room to form a blast that shot a gout of flames into the cool night air, spewing arms of enticement toward the cowering figures of Catriona and Mother Justicia where they crouched with Petunia.

The flames washed over Minimus, Mirko, and Nikolai Nineteen Points like a warm bath. But it had an immediate effect on Maxima. She slid between the margins of the slit between Temple Pang and the obverse. The whooshing pull dragged her feet out of sight, while her hands clung to either side of the flapping rip. The three sisters remaining in the chamber followed. Their feet scrabbled, failing to find traction on the floor of the tower. One by one, the flames licked and tugged at them until they shot past Maxima into their own world. The lodestone inched and scraped its way toward the fissure, shaking with resistance, yearning for Mother Justicia.

Rayne, too, experienced the wrench. For her, it felt as if she had one of Virgil's lute strings attached to the back of her neck, and someone plucked a scale on it, each note tugging harder, trying to pull her to the rift. She slid on her heels, hands failing in their clutch at Minimus's knee as she skidded backward toward the opening held wide by Maxima. A channel opened between her mind and Catriona's; she could feel the other girl's panic as she too juddered across the rooftop toward the windows and the rip between worlds beyond. They were being drawn to the obverse like two prisoners chained together, a savage guardsman yanking on their bond.

Just as she thought she would speed away from Minimus and fly through the opening, a powerful hand gripped her forearm. Minimus's other arm seeped blood where he'd released his wound, but Rayne knew he would never let her go again.

The blast of fire that sought Mother Justicia met with an unexpected resistance. Just as the spurt of reddish fury reached her position on the rooftop outside the tower chamber, the shadow that had obscured the setting sun folded itself around Petunia. Not only Petunia, but also Catriona and Mother Justicia, who clutched the window's edges as the rip in reality drew them too toward the obverse. The six wings of an abomination bird wrapped around the trio as the cavernous beak ducked beneath the feathers and the steely talons scattered tiles beneath its thunderous landing.

The booming caw of the angered bird reverberated across the island and the flames licked and broke against its impervious barrier of glossy black feathers. If Minimus hadn't seen Petunia tame fire bears, stroll side by side with sabreclaws, and ride atop a slab whale, he would have written off cow, girl, and woman as bird food. But he somehow knew that Petunia had tamed the aggression of an abomination bird in a scheme to protect herself from the threatening flames of Maxima Li.

With the same fierce speed with which the fires had erupted, they retraced their paths, returning to Maxima as she lost her grip on the fold's edges and the rip slammed shut. A single abomination bird eye peeked from beneath its front wings before the thing deemed the environment safe again, and it opened the other two sets to reveal the unscathed cargo within.

Maxima Li had returned to the obverse, taking three sisters of the Mothers of Midnight with her, but she had failed to drag Mother Justicia or Catriona with her. Rayne froze where the margin had snapped shut, mouth agape, peering as if she could still see a fragment of the rent torn in their world's fabric.

Minimus met Rayne's gaze and knew she was calm, free from the power that had threatened to drag her with Maxima into the obverse. Why would she feel the tug when the flames seemed to only affect locals of the other world? The question distracted Minimus for only a moment, before he seized the chance to continue his mission.

Releasing Rayne's arm, Minimus grabbed the lodestone. The thing pulsed, recovering from the flames of Maxima's wrath, and had scraped across the floor of the tower to ooze at Rayne's side. He lifted it now with less effort, and he made quicker progress toward the far window.

CHAPTER 53 - TEMPLE PANG

The Present

Mother Justicia grabbed Catriona's hand as the protective wings of the abomination bird unfurled before them. "Did you see your sisters fly through that hole?" she asked.

"I felt the tug, too, Mother. The same as when magic washed over us at the Temple of the Wraith. I kind of *wanted* it to take me."

Mother Justicia paused. "Odd. I felt—"

Her head snapped toward the window and the movement inside the tower chamber. "That boy! So persistent! Stop him before he embarrasses himself, Catriona."

With a glance at the savage beak of the abomination bird to confirm it wouldn't snap at her, Catriona's robe fluttered behind her as she vaulted the windowsill and intercepted Minimus as he heaved the lodestone toward the far window. She was too late to pull back one of his straining arms, but she passed the stone as it flew, slapping it three times along the top edge, guiding it downward. For a moment she worried that the stone might crack, but it struck the window's lower lintel and crashed to the floor, still in one wavering piece.

Minimus bent to raise the stone once more, but Catriona placed a hand atop his, saying, "Leave it, boy! *She* will be far more savage."

Minimus looked over his shoulder at the other window, where Mother Justicia was lifting Petunia through the frame. The abomination bird shoved its beak through the opening, too, its beady eyes pools of darkness, but seeming more curious than bent on destruction. He considered whether he could push Catriona away and chuck the stone out before Mother Justicia reached him. Just as he was about to begin his heave, he witnessed a visceral reminder of his opponents' speed as they confronted a new threat.

From the staircase, Sala Doon sprung forward, a blade in each hand. Master Thorn's snowy beard peeked around the corner from behind the knife-thrower with Jing Jing sweeping aside the thin dangling beard to look for Minimus. As Sala surveyed the room, he snatched both hands back, as if a lightning porcupine's quill had pricked him. His knives were gone. Had Mother Justicia really run *along the wall* before snatching them away? The woman slapped the blades together, making a tink-tink sound before asking in an amused voice, "Looking for these, my friend?"

Minimus knew an undistracted Mother Justicia could knock the stone from his hands before he'd even raised it knee high. He stood and stepped away from the stone and Catriona, rubbing his arm. Its injury had faded after the wave of Maxima's fire washed over them.

Master Thorn's wide eyes found Minimus. "Where's Maxi, my boy? I heard it. That noise. Again."

Seeing his father opened Minimus's heart to the sacrifice he'd witnessed only a few moments earlier.

"She's gone. To the obverse. Home."

His knees buckled and Minimus sank to the floor. Master Thorn rushed to him. Rayne tried to step towards the collapsed boy, too, but found her hand was stuck. She couldn't even *see* her hand. Her arm faded to nothing just beyond the elbow. She could wriggle her fingers, but her hand must have gone through the rift just before it snapped shut.

As if fired from a slingshot, Catriona appeared at Rayne's side. "I can feel it. Your hand," Catriona said as she rubbed her own. "You can't pull it out?"

Rayne yanked twice, hard, but her arm remained embedded in the invisible seam. She felt waves of panic well through her as she struggled. Catriona reached inside her hood and lifted out the fragrance glider. "Here, take Twinky. She'll calm you down while I figure out what to do."

The wide-eyed little creature looked back at Catriona for encouragement before settling around Rayne's shoulders. The smells of lavender and dewy leaves wafted. Rayne wasn't sure she felt any calmer, but at least her rapid breathing hadn't escalated. Still sniffling and shedding errant tears, Minimus crawled to her side, Master Thorn in tow. Rayne felt her heart rate slow. She still couldn't free her hand, but with Minimus's arm encircling her waist, Twinky wrapped around her shoulders, Jing Jing stroking her thigh, and Master Thorn murmuring encouragements to them both, she felt as close to home as she had in weeks.

Sala Doon and Mirko stood poised for unformulated action, and Nikolai Nineteen Points shuffled across the room, arms feeling for obstacles, until Petunia met him a step away from Mother Justicia.

"Really?" he said, looking down as he stroked Petunia's dangling beard. "She wants to do that? How ridiculous!" He turned and addressed Mother Justicia, orienting on her voice. "My companion here tells me you have a plan to use her in some way to steal away the magic of animals. Is that right?" he asked.

Mother Justicia shook her head. "Not animals, no. People. I need to disarm the weapon that we cannot trust *people* to use. I've witnessed too much harm, too much haste, too much anger, and I'll not countenance its use when I have the power to banish it forever. I can feel it—if Petunia and I work together, we can make the world a peaceful place."

"But people don't have magic," Nikolai replied. "Only animals like my Petunia."

Mother Justicia's voice hardened, rising as it took an edge. "What are you talking about? Catriona here inherited the ability to blast boats out of the water and topple towers. I have enough magic to power a whole temple full of disciples, an echo of my nephew's desperate magic. The tiny one there, she's got a power I don't even understand. And did you not see that woman? She tried to blast us beyond the veil. No magic? We open the eyes and close the gate!"

Despite the chastising tone, Nikolai produced a genuine laugh. "See her? No. You may notice I see nothing. But I can listen, which is more valuable. So, listen while I tell you some stories Petunia wants you to hear."

Justicia inhaled deeply and her neck muscles drew taut beneath scarred skin as she prepared to ignore Nikolai's request and continue with her life's mission. At her side, Petunia turned her gaze behind the woman and a scaly claw of the abomination bird extended and curled around Justicia. It did not close tight around her frame, but the intent was clear. Justicia decided she had time to hear the man's story after all.

"My little cow and I walked from the harbor at Stonk, in Del Carta, as pirates set the quayside alight. I could feel the heat and hear the screams. A wagon train brimming with captured children passed us as it crept through a freezing mountain pass in Hammarskald, bound for a slaver's ship on the east coast, no doubt. I even heard rumors that girls are being torn from their mother's grasp in the markets at Mossmarch.

"If the travels with my little friend have taught me anything, it's that whatever you perceive filters through your experience, your humanity, sight or no sight. You don't need to see through only your own eyes. Petunia and I both know that. You can expand your view of the world, by paying attention, by listening to the music, by marveling at the fine lines of sculptures created by talented artists. Or listen to nature, the greatest artist of all.

"And in all my travels, except for your own actions, none of these atrocities raged from people using magic. They sprang from dark hearts and corrupted emotions. I cannot see *for* you, but consider taking another look. Maybe the magic you rail against, the ill-considered use of power, could be aspirational, not purely destructive. Can you listen to the glory of the choir, or perhaps even conduct them, instead of stilling their errant tongues?"

Despite the abomination bird's talon, it surprised Catriona that Mother Justicia had not cut off Nikolai mid-speech, and doubly surprised her that she didn't stick her acid tongue into the silence that followed. Dare she add her own feelings?

Her voice cracked at first, faint, before trying a second time, louder. "You've seen the animals here, *Auntie*. We cannot take their powers. Look at my Twinky. And Sister Rayne tells me this isn't even our world, that we belong in another place. Through the open crack. If you really want to drain magic, let's go back there and do it."

"Hush, my girl," Mother Justicia said. "I know I'm going to do this. I told the Backwards Man with my own lips."

In a blur, she wriggled loose from the abomination bird's grasp, snatched Petunia once more, and halted at the lodestone. It pulsed with dark light as the cow's hooves touched its surface.

CHAPTER 54 - TEMPLE PANG

The Same Day

Ever since that urchin quill had jabbed her, outside the tavern in Mossmarch, Catriona had felt compelled to tell the truth. It pained her most when Mother Justicia asked a direct question, because she knew she gave the answer her mistress least wanted to hear.

Her aunt's voice rang in her head, harsh. "You still believe in our mission, don't you?"

Catriona swallowed hard, her lips moving even as she willed them to be still. The truth burst out. "I agree with Nikolai, Auntie. We should leave magic alone. Let the marvelous animals live their lives. Let people be people, with everything that entails. But let's work on making ourselves, all of ourselves, better."

Mother Justicia spluttered. "Then keep your magic, girl. See how it treats you."

Jamming a palm to the lodestone between Petunia's legs, Mother Justicia poured her power into the stone. The eleven-pointed star, submerged deep within, pulsed, sending waves of green-tinged power over every surface of the stone.

"I release you, my girls!" she shouted.

On the docks below, Catriona's sisters fell to their knees and wept, their memories returning even as their magic-assisted vision and hearing failed. The long-forgotten faces of families and friends flooded back to replace the supreme speed and agility that now abandoned them. Her magical command excluded Catriona, whose face drained of color as the power thrummed throughout the temple.

Mother Justicia's legs strained as she pushed the lodestone toward Rayne, the cow jostling atop. Catriona stepped between her great aunt and Rayne, but Mother Justicia shooed her away with words. "I won't hurt her or your precious little fuzzball. I just need her to help me through to the other side. Open your eyes and help me open the gate."

Even Minimus and Master Thorn gave way, knowing there was little they could do to stop Justicia. Sala and Mirko stood helpless. Only Nikolai moved toward the lodestone, feeling once more for Petunia.

"Help me squeeze it open, little girl," Mother Justicia said, sliding the lodestone into position and slithering her own wrinkled hand along the forearm that disappeared into the unseen rift to the obverse. The older woman's fingers pushed against an invisible barrier as they reached the point where Rayne's hand should have been. She closed her eyes and hummed for a moment before pushing again. Her hand disappeared, too.

Rotating her arm to face the opposite direction from Rayne's, she strained. Blue rivers of energy poured down her arm, lighting her veins from within. "Push, girl, push!"

Catriona could see both their hands rematerializing as the veil between worlds retracted a second time. A slender hole appeared in the gap between Rayne's hand and the back of Mother Justicia's. With a heave, the rift opened again, tearing to human height. The three scar-faced sisters that had disappeared earlier lay battered and unconscious in a splay at the end of a featureless tunnel. Justicia heard objections from somewhere out of sight. More Mothers of Midnight at the far end! She realized now that the Temple Pang beyond the rift was the one from her own memory, different than the one populated by meek monks. The reply to her disciples' shouts, escaping from the obverse, came in the form of a familiar voice uttering curses that would make Foul Phrased Phinneus blush.

Master Thorn and Minimus perked up at the sound. They called in unison, sending conflicting messages.

"Run, Maxi! She's coming through!" called Master Thorn.

All Minimus could utter was, "Come back, Mum."

If Maxima Li could hear their calls on the other side, they would never know. But there was little time for her to react to the shouts. With a sucking sound and the smell of burning hair, the lodestone, cow, and three humans shot through the crack and disappeared into the obverse. Rayne thumped onto the floor, freed.

CHAPTER 55 - BETWEEN WORLDS

The Same Day

It felt like a hallway, although it had no walls, ceiling, or floor—only distant views into the tower of Temple Pang at either end. Their feet—and hooves—struck something that must have been a floor, but all was white beyond the tears in the world's fabric.

Catriona struggled behind the others, caught at the division between the hallway and the room and its occupants they'd left behind. With straining effort, her shoulders entered the tunnel, and one hand rubbed at the back of her neck as Mother Justicia urged her onward with an impatient gesture. As if mired in a sucking swamp, Catriona pulled one foot and then the other into the tunnel. Once she had cleared the barrier between worlds, she shrugged and strode forward, moving freely.

Mother Justicia pushed the lodestone along the undefinable floor, leading the others. Petunia followed, reunited with Nikolai Nineteen Points and his loving clutch of her neck shag. Catriona trudged at the rear, glancing back at Rayne and Twinky, still visible in the distance. She rubbed her neck and its vicious itch.

"Your mistress is wavering, you know," Nikolai called to Catriona. "It's not over. And as I tell everyone, Petunia goes exactly where she's needed. It doesn't seem to me like she needs to help someone take magic away."

Mother Justicia was indeed deep in thought, her mind freed of recent events as she strained to shuttle the lodestone back to *her* Temple Pang. Once they reached the other end, she'd use Petunia to enact the ritual and drain magic from the people of her world. There would be no animals left as collateral damage, no grousing from Catriona on that front. That's what she'd told the Backwards Man, right? That she had finally sucked away everyone's magic?

Or had she? All the Backwards Man had told her, all those years ago, was that she would complete her mission. But he did not specify that she would remove magic from the world. That omission matched the size of Justicia's new doubt. How could Berentz not mention such a momentous change? And wouldn't she have removed his magic, too, halting his backwards progress through time? Maybe her mission would end because she discovered eradicating magic from humans would be like ripping out their tongues. Wagging tongues were often troublesome, but always essential. Perhaps the old man was right.

"Of course, I'm right," Nikolai Nineteen Points said, smiling back at Catriona and winking a sightless eye.

But the girl paid him no attention. A sound behind them like a sheet being jerked from a clothesline accompanied the sight of Rayne, yanked into the tunnel by the inspiritive bond to her obverse sister, Catriona.

CHAPTER 56 - ASTELLA

The Same Day

Skain Two-Hearts stumbled and lurched to one side as he attempted to mount his horse. The gates and stalls of the Pearl Wash market square seemed to whirl for a moment before settling into their familiar, level pattern. A chamber of his heart he'd kept sealed for so long had been prized open, not by an intruder but by the reawakening of someone he'd held within. He fell to one knee as his horse stamped impatiently.

Skain realized his impatience and knotted stomach over the past few weeks was not the presence of duty and inactivity weighing him down. It was an absence. He'd been able to feel that his daughter was protected, under the care of his aunt for all these years, but that feeling had been yanked away. And here amidst the traders of Pearl Wash, he felt Catriona come a step closer, filling that void. He wanted to go to her, to beg forgiveness for losing her mother, for destroying her home village, for pushing her away in his pain and keeping her away despite visiting the Temple of the Wraith as spy and conspirator with the Mothers of Midnight so many times. He'd thought the shared mission with his aunt was pure and for the betterment of all, but the only feelings rending his two hearts were ones of regret and longing for his abandoned daughter.

What would he even tell her, if he could see her now? That he'd always planned to reunite with her after the Mothers' mission succeeded? That he was too dangerous to be around, with his wild and furious magic? But she possessed it too, Justicia had told him. She could control it—steely where he was weak. She'd know his words formed a web of lies supporting a meager nugget of truth, just as he did.

His squire found Skain with his face pressed to the muddy cobblestones, talking to himself. "Just come home, Cat. Come home, and I'll tell you everything. I can't make it right, but I'll stop it from killing us both," he cried. He felt his daughter moving closer.

CHAPTER 57 - TEMPLE PANG

The Same Day

As suddenly as she'd plopped to the floor, Rayne flew through the air and slipped into the rift between worlds in its final moments. Her fingertips were the last visible sign of her departure, straining to keep hold of the world she shared with Minimus Mu before slipping away.

"I saw it! The bond!" Master Thorn shouted. "When the same thing almost snapped me back to Lazarus Thorn in the obverse, I only felt its invisible tug. But did you see that shimmer? The clutch of gossamer threads between them? Rayne must be bound to Catriona."

Minimus Mu howled at the second loss, anguish pressing against the open wound of losing his mother a second time. He flailed at thin air, finding no purchase on the rift that had winked out of existence. No magic remained in his world to reopen it.

Jing Jing tugged at the boy's sandal strap, excited. The monkey jumped up and down, screeching and pointing at his own wrist.

Maybe that could work, Minimus thought. There was still magic in the room, after all: Jing Jing's magically powered hands.

"Go on then," he urged. "If you can reopen it with your hands, you'd better do it quick."

Jing Jing shook his head in violent motions. He pointed to his wrist again, raised his arm, and spun it in tight circles overhead. Only then did Minimus understand the monkey's suggestion.

"Oh, you genius!" he said, fumbling in his pocket for the metal bracelet the monkey had stolen from the Mothers of Midnight. He slipped it onto his wrist and twirled it around, like he'd seen Catriona do outside Jada's tower.

* * *

Catriona tried to comfort Rayne, who'd snapped to her side. They could both see the hint of the threads that bound them, sizzling in the uncanny light of the tunnel. Catriona felt Rayne's intimate presence, almost like a curator of her deepest thoughts, and in return, she felt Rayne's panic and burning desire to return to Minimus. Rayne ran back toward her world, arms pumping, but it retreated further with every step she took. "I don't think we can return that way. But I'll look out for you. See you settled in Pearl Wash or at the Temple of the Wraith. Despite our differences, you are my sister, Rayne."

Catriona tried to brace her arms against the sides of the dreamy corridor, hoping to hold Rayne in the tunnel long enough for her panic to fade and make the transition easier. But she lacked the power to do much; even standing still, she felt her palms glide toward the far end. The two girls slid inexorably in Mother Justicia's wake toward the obverse Temple Pang.

A powerful but momentary wind gusted past the girls toward Justicia's end of the tunnel. Catriona's cowl blew back, and it almost dislodged the fragrance glider from beneath Rayne's fluttering red hair. With a pop, Minimus rematerialized atop the lodestone, halting Mother Justicia's push just as she was about to move the artifact across the threshold of the dreamlike passage to the tower room of her world's Temple Pang. He still swirled the bracelet in tight circles around his thick wrist, as if he needed to keep it moving or risk fluttering back to his end of the corridor.

Minimus ignored Justicia's surprise, vaulting over her and pushing between Nikolai and Petunia with Catriona and Rayne in his sights. Rayne persisted in her vain sprint against the passage, only a step beyond Catriona. Minimus found progress difficult, too, but he willed his powerful legs to edge him past Catriona. With another few forced strides, he closed to Rayne and cradled an arm around her waist. They pushed together but soon slid toward the obverse once again.

"Leave me, Minimus, I can't go back," Rayne cried. "I'm attached to Catriona. That inspiritive bond Master Thorn told me about through the puppet theater? To Lazarus Thorn, on his balloon trip; there's one between Catriona and me. Leave me and push yourself back home."

Legs still straining against the uncooperative tunnel floor, Minimus spared a glance over his shoulder. He'd left Rayne behind once before, when they'd followed their masters after the salvation of the Red Bean Queendom. He wasn't going to repeat his mistake. "Catriona, cut this strand and free Rayne. You can't pull her into your world. I let us separate once before, and I'll never do that again."

Catriona shook her head. "I've tried. I can't break the bond. Even though we can see it now, it just springs away if I try to grab it. And I don't dare use my magic against it. Who knows what would happen?" she shouted back. The obverse tugged at all three of them. Catriona struggled to interpret her emotions. Duty had called her to follow Mother Justicia, but perhaps her trust was misplaced. She had a father somewhere at the far end of the tunnel who she'd never met, but a father that had shackled her, eyeless and earless, to his aunt, Justicia. And in that world, she had a purpose, but a purpose that Mother Justicia would dissolve once she hauled the lodestone and Petunia through the fast-approaching portal. At the tunnel's other end lay a world with fabulous animals like her Twinky. She had no family there, but Rayne had treated her honestly and seemed like she would make a steadfast friend if Catriona left the Mothers of Midnight behind. Her magic might accomplish some good in that world, too, while in the old world she'd used it only for destruction. She had but moments to decide.

Mother Justicia lifted the lodestone over an invisible step and plunked it to the floor beside a hovering sister of Temple Pang. The obverse's attraction doubled and everyone in the tunnel slipped closer to its far end.

Minimus spun Rayne to face him. "If we can't go back because of the bond, I'll go with you to the other side. I love you, Rayne, and we won't be parted again."

Mother Justicia stepped into the obverse through the rip, followed a moment later by Petunia and Nikolai. Minimus still strained against the forces that tugged at his sandals, his clothes, and his every move, hoping one last push might sever the bond and allow them to return home. He drew even with Catriona and felt his heel tingle as it slipped from the tunnel into the obverse. The fragrance glider released a cloud of panicked scent—hovering goat fur, abomination bird feathers, and the earthy scent of rock-eater debris.

The tingling in Minimus's heel stopped, and he took a step back down the tunnel. Catriona moved ahead of him, and movement became easier. Soon, the three of them were running toward the other end, where Master Thorn's wrinkled brow looked for signs of the rift.

"It's getting easier, now that I know we should *both* go to your end," Catriona said. "Better hurry; the tunnel's getting shorter!"

Minimus needed no further coaxing, but the obverse end of the tunnel tugged at the bracelet. He cast it behind him, where it spun toward the lodestone like a magnet, and he felt the tugging diminish. He pushed harder and faster than any pursuer could match. His cradling arm scooped up Rayne and they caught up to the speeding Catriona just as the tunnel's two ends met in a thunderclap. He hunched his shoulders as the three of them burst back into the tower in his own world, protecting the two girls as he rolled to a stop.

A wave of nearly-visible magical energy rushed outward

from the slammed shut rift between worlds. It brought with it the bitter tang of Mother Justicia's resentment, tinged with Petunia's optimism and bristling with the unbridled power of the banished lodestone. It rippled hair without any rush of air, tickled the chamber's periphery with sparkling colors, and washed through the back window, settling somewhere in the carrot garden beyond.

Almost everyone in the room laughed in relief, except for Master Thorn who wiped tears from his eyes. Some fell for his loss, and others for his returned son.

As Minimus rolled onto his back, Rayne hugged his neck, her feet reaching only to his waist. "I'll be the first to say *I love you*, in this world."

"Yeah," called Sala Doon. "But everyone in this world loves Minimus Mu."

CHAPTER 58 - ASTELLA

Five Months After Temple Pang

Berentz laughed aloud as a goat drifted on a light breeze past his window, punctuating the quiet atmosphere of the turnip farm with confused bleating.

"It's that day already, is it? Come on in, Justicia," he said, tugging the sticking door open to a summer day where insects drifted on the breeze and the crops opened their arms to mother sun.

Justicia was at the door, her dark cloak replaced with a hoodless red tunic. Her scarred face was no surprise to Berentz, who had last seen it when he was a boy. Skain Two-Hearts tethered a trio of horses at the drinking trough that Berentz kept filled so he could enjoy occasional glimpses of the region's wildlife. Meandering along the pathways between rows of turnips, a knee-high shaggy cow led a weather- and time-beaten man.

Berentz smiled at Justicia's arrival. "Even though I know it's coming, the first time—or is it the last?—that I see my goat Marigold hovering above the garden, I can't help but laugh. She's so confused after a lifetime stuck to the ground."

"That's Petunia the cow at work, I'm afraid," Justicia replied. "Seems she had her own mission the whole time. She's easing magic into the animals of our world. Mostly small stuff, like the goats, glow-in-the-dark butterflies, that sort of thing. I noticed a badger riding some kind of invisible animal last week. Maybe a dog or a pig, judging by its height. Nikolai claims he has no idea what Petunia does, but I suspect he's not telling us everything. Fortunately, I haven't seen an abomination bird here yet. They have these monstrous six-winged birds on the other side."

Berentz nodded. "Hmm. That's how it starts. There are so many interesting animal developments to come. You'll be amazed, and maybe afraid, too. Anyway, I know you have something to tell me, and I notice your nephew there, like many others, wants to stay as far from me as possible."

"Yeah, don't mind Skain. He's cautious to avoid you. Not just for your insights about the future, but for your role in the past. When he last saw you, he'd just destroyed Vinetally, a time he'd rather forget about, even if it's not possible."

A distracted look came over Berentz's face, and flashes of that terrible day flew unbidden from her own memories.

"He's sacrificed the only thing that he salvaged from that day. Twice, really—his daughter, we named her Catriona eventually, almost came back with me here, to this side. But at the last minute something pulled her back. At least, that's what I tell Skain. In truth, I think she forced her way back. I hope it's better for her there, among her sisters. Too much pain in this world."

The Backwards Man took Justicia's hand, sensing the scar tissue along its outer edge. "I've heard that if you take Skain up to the Temple of the Wraith, Catriona will learn to speak with him. She has someone who will teach her to communicate over the greatest of separations. Only to deeply familiar places, mind you. Take him there. It may be a week, or a few months, but Catriona will finally speak to her father, as her father. He'll feel it's worth the wait, however long it takes.

"And what about your mission?" Berentz asked. "I know you will choose your words carefully."

Justicia nodded. "Very carefully. But now that I have lived

through everything that happens, I know what to tell you, without telling my past self things I was unready to hear.

"After Vinetally, I knew humans could not be trusted with the savage magical powers that Skain unleashed in his anguish. That we should remove this weapon for good, using the power concentrated in the lodestone from the village square. And that my mission—" Here, Justicia paused, and took a long look at Nikolai chatting to Petunia in the long grass beside the turnip field before returning her gaze to Berentz. "My mission. I needed something to nudge me into a position to accomplish it. I met a man covered in daggers. He has something I need to complete that mission. That's really everything you—or my earlier self—need to know."

That seemed the correct amount to tell the Backwards Man. Should she also tell him about her new sisterhood? How they traveled as emissaries, training the daughters of the queendoms to use their magic in productive ways, not in anger or vengeance? Probably not. And thinking across the last two decades, yes, she'd done much to regret, with many people hurt or lost because of her misguided quest. But for the first time since she'd caught sight of the smoldering remains of her village, she felt something long forgotten stir inside her. Berentz's off-hand comment about the animal magic yet to come gave her hope. Something new blossomed inside her, fertilized by the ashes of despair.

Not wanting to reveal more, lest her story, retold, poison her past, Justicia turned from the doorway, but then spun back. "And thank you, Berentz. I never thanked you or your father after Vinetally, but it made a world of difference—may have even made a different world."

Berentz smiled. "Or two, perhaps. It was, and will be, nothing at all. Nothing you wouldn't have done if our positions were reversed. Sometimes, I think this is why I was granted this odd power—only to tell you your own story and set you on the correct, if painful, path. I will not see you again, Justicia, although I will cross paths with Nikolai and his serenely powerful little cow several more times. She needs a bit of guidance, and it comes to her from my limited knowledge of the future, through him. Oh, and I've left a sack of this year's particularly fine crop of turnips for you at the gate. Have your nephew grab them on the way out."

CHAPTER 59 - MOSSMARCH

Five Months After Temple Pang

Apostle Dando brought a round of frothy ales to two of his favorite customers, joining them at the still-rickety table outside the Crossed Swords. Virgil Longspeaker, his co-owner, sat with them, picking at his lute.

"Don't start, mate," Virgil said to the settling Dando. "These two don't want to hear about the cost of getting the roof re-thatched. It's all part of the fun of the fair, running a tavern, if I'm not wrong."

Dando sighed, gesturing to Sala Doon and Mirko Leatherfoot. "If I'm going to complain to anyone, it should be these two. It's that cavorting on the rooftop fighting off the Mothers of Midnight that ruined the thatch in the first place!"

Virgil strummed a chord between each section of his reply. "But look on the bright side. Now that the monks have returned to Temple Pang to help the blind and partially deaf former Mothers of Midnight run the animal sanctuary out there, our beer exports have gone through the roof. Not literally, although I daresay they could. But both the monks and the young women seem to enjoy a quality barleymalt. And did you know it's seething with fragrance gliders over there, now? It's like nearly every former Mother has her own perfumery."

Dando cut off his friend. "They probably drink our ales in such quantities because, on my last visit to the temple, I stressed the all-natural ingredients. Water from the coldest well in the Meer foothills. Amber barley from Hammarskald. Golden hops shipped in from Del Carta."

Mirko clapped Dando on the back, a rumbling laugh tumbling from deep inside his belly. "That's my boy! They still think you're a truthteller, don't they?"

Dando smiled in return. "Well, I may have forgotten to mention that their lovely former order drained me of my truth-telling magic. But they're obsessed with our ale now. Virgil's baked specialties, too. We trade them for vegetables from their extensive gardens; they're doing a brisk trade now that their carrots are growing like weeds. We're considering opening a second branch of the Crossed Swords at the temple's quayside. Lovely views across the Sea of Sorrows, and with blind barmaids, even Foul Phrased Phinneus might get served, if he can keep his lips pressed together for more than a minute."

Sala Doon nodded approval. "Hey, and speaking of the Truthsayer's Guild, you heard Catriona is on her way back to Mossmarch already, right? We need her for a bit of business. Mirko and I—and a certain benefactor—have something lined up."

Dando nodded. "Eleven new truthsayers arrived two days ago, and they said Catriona was on track to be certified within the week. Also, Rayne has a secret way of communicating with her. She told me Cat is already on the road. She'll return to Mossmarch in no time."

Virgil raised an eyebrow in Dando's direction. "What? She's only been there a few months! How is she supposed to follow in your footsteps and learn to be a sailor, master chef, archer, snake charmer, and champion flame bear tamer in that short a time?"

"You forgot to mention savior of the nineteen queendoms, my friend, and mildly entertaining business partner," Dando said. "Anyway, yeah. She must be a quick learner. Or maybe she threatened Sifu Pan with being blasted out of existence by her magic unless he graduated her early."

Mirko latched onto Dando's earlier comment. "*Eleven*

truthsayers? Why would we need so many in Mossmarch?"

"Obviously, because it takes eleven of them to replace one of me," Dando said.

Virgil slapped at his lute. "Hilarious. It'll probably take fifteen of them to clear up the order's reputation after the whoppers you've been letting loose recently. But haven't you two heard about Princess Tasha's new endeavor, when the dust settled from her kerfuffle with Jada? After she pointed out a few choice rules from the *Binding of the Queendoms* and clarified that she'd only left Jada in command of the army, not restored her to the throne, Queen Angstaad had to step in and separate them. Eventually they settled on letting Jada continue as marshal of the military, and Queen Veronica of Ven will take up the transition for the next few years. But after these repeated arguments, Princess Tasha decided to travel the lands to set up these things she's calling *embassies*, one in each queendom. They'll hold representatives from each of the other eighteen queendoms, so that silly cross-queendom spats don't escalate into full-blown conflicts. They'll meet regularly, observed by note-taking truthsayers, sipping fine tea and snacking on delicacies from across the world. All served on Master Thorn dinnerware and accompanied by the finest spoons imaginable, if I were to hazard a guess. I hope it works—we've seen enough international mishaps to last us three lifetimes."

Sala threw up his hands, high enough to expose the handles of the daggers strapped to his tunic-covered forearms. "So *that's* what Rayne was talking about. She said Tasha was taking her away on a multi-country trip until Minimus stepped in. They both wanted a simpler life, preferring the cutlerer's cart to the royal retinue. Minimus saying he wouldn't part from Rayne again was enough for Princess Tasha to send them along with her blessings."

Sala threw a pebble to shoo away a nosy coal rayvn perched on the tavern's precious roof. He could have hit a hummingbird at thirty paces but aimed a fraction left. In a way, his time with his own menagerie of animal followers had mellowed him. The bird seemed satisfied that it had accomplished whatever inscrutable mission brought it to their table, Sala thought. It flapped away with languid wingbeats.

Virgil plucked a few more notes from his strings. "And did you hear they've invited me to be the official balladeer for the ascension trials in Golden Shores? Queen Angstaad realized she enjoyed queening less than cavorting across the lands and seas looking for trouble, so she's handing over the reins to the queendom. Did you know they don't pass the tiara down to their daughters, there? The wisest and best of the graduating swordswomen's academy class becomes queen. How clever is that?"

"Nice one!" Sala said. "We're headed there, too. Probably scoop Catriona along the way, if we're lucky. Want to ride with us?"

* * *

Master Thorn worked the forges of Mossmarch night after night, with Minimus at his side. There were long silences, a few accusations from boy to man, and much soul searching on Master Thorn's part. He remained unsure of how he could withhold the story of Maxima Li from Minimus when he had recited so many other trivial tales. He knew it began as a way to protect the child's tender heart, but the secret had grown over time into a thorny barrier.

"I'm a foolish old man and do not deserve forgiveness, Minimus," he said one evening, a dropped tear turning to steam as he leaned over a freshly forged runcible spork.

The boy, too, wiped at his cheek with a grubby sleeve. "I'm glad I had a little time with her. It answered many questions I'd never asked."

Passing Mossmarchers would have been forgiven if they mistook the silhouette of the boy for a man, and the slender frame of Master Thorn for a wiry teen. A colossal arm draped across Master Thorn's shoulder as Minimus leaned in and hugged him to a burly shoulder. "And maybe you don't deserve forgiveness, but you most definitely deserve my love. I'll tell you right away if I ever forgive you."

Their new cart—although Minimus wondered how it was possible—seemed to contain even more drawers and secret compartments than their old cart, each one stuffed with pristine wares. It required a pair of draught horses to urge it into motion, and Princess Tasha had selected two handsome beasts for the task. Mr. Apples could wander alongside, freed of heavy duties.

As Master Thorn worked on his fabulous fabrications, he considered Ezra Longshanks's proposition. That man and his science! Master Thorn was happy to remain oldfangled, if there was such a thing. Ezra wanted to pilot his balloon back through the portal above the Temple of the Wraith, if it remained, and explore the obverse further. Map it. In the end, Master Thorn let the balloonist drift away on his own. Maxima was over there somewhere, but he'd lost her twice and couldn't subject Minimus to a quest that would most likely end in failure. Every plan he concocted to reunite with Maxima lacked an acceptable degree of certainty. He was the boy's only family, and the boy was his only love left in this world. Instead of drifting off on a crazy mission, he and Minimus had written a book's worth of pages to Maxima Li since she banished herself to the obverse at Temple Pang, and Ezra promised to deliver the sheaf of papers on the off chance he could find her.

One of the notions Master Thorn noodled into his letters was an idea for Maxima's return. If she could blast herself out of this world into the obverse, maybe she could blow her way back here, too. Open a rip like the shimmerings over the Temple of the Wraith. He wasn't sure how this would work, but bent Ezra's ear about the possibilities his science might offer. There was a whole page scrawled with reminders of his past behavior that he knew would aggravate her. He hoped she could focus on that and return to him, with Ezra's help. That would be a Master Thorn kind of love story, he thought, using his faults to lure her back. And if she returned, she'd be one of only four known magical humans in this world. The missing

Sister Mariana, whose bracelet Jing Jing had stolen during the caravan attack in Wraithwatch, was still out there somewhere. Catriona, of course. Rayne. And maybe Minimus, too? Was Maxima's strength part of her magic? Had it passed down to the boy?

With the cart loaded, the horses fed and ready, and enough pies, salt cod, and apples to last them until—well, lunch time if Minimus had his way—the boy nudged Master Thorn's elbow. "I heard you pledged to Ezra, back in Astella, that you'd pedal my runcible sporks across all nineteen queendoms to honor me," Minimus said to his father. "I think Mum would want that life of adventure for us, don't you? Which queendom will we start with?"

Master Thorn raised an eyebrow to a peak sharper than most of the salmon knives in the queendom of Droz. His eyes flitted between his giant son and the beautiful knee-height girl beside him. "Let's let Rayne decide, eh, my son? Apologies, Jing Jing, but she's the wisest member of our traveling business empire now."

Last Words

Thank you for reading *Master Thorn and the Mothers of Midnight*. If you enjoyed the story, leaving an online review is a good way to let other readers know how to follow in your footsteps.

Sala Doon, Mirko Leatherfoot, Catriona Sun, and Angstaad of Golden Shores will return in *Sala Doon and the Demon Carrot*.

Who wouldn't want fantastical magical plants? Roguish knife-wielder Sala Doon finds out the hard way that special powers are best left to the animal life of the Nineteen Queendoms as he struggles to complete a mission that seemed difficult enough without an interfering carrot. Alongside his friend Mirko Leatherfoot and accompanied by a surprising team of companions, a rescue attempt unravels and secrets abound. Can the fate of a corrupted Queendom be decided by the bonds of friendship and a few underhanded deals?

Join my mailing list and find more at pattisontelford.com

Pattison Telford lives in Toronto, Canada, surrounded by non-magical people, animals, and the occasional evil vegetable that nevertheless possess certain charms.

9 781778 124082